BEFORE I DISAPPEAR

BEFORE I

DISAPPEAR

DANIELLE STINSON

Feiwel and Friends

New York

A FEIWEL AND FRIENDS BOOK
An imprint of Macmillan Publishing Group, LLC
120 Broadway, New York, NY 10271

Our books may be purchased in bulk for promotional, educational, or business use.
Please contact your local bookseller or the Macmillan Corporate and
Premium Sales Department at (800) 221-7945 ext. 5442 or by email at
MacmillanSpecialMarkets@macmillan.com.

Library of Congress Control Number: 2018955251
ISBN 978-1-250-30319-6 (hardcover) / ISBN 978-1-250-30320-2 (ebook)

Book design by Katie Klimowicz
Feiwel and Friends logo designed by Filomena Tuosto
First edition, 2019

1 3 5 7 9 10 8 6 4 2
fiercereads.com

For Mom and Dad.

You taught me most of what I know about love.

"*Can you hear the music, Rosie?*"

It was just a question. Six little words that would change everything. Only I didn't know it then.

Midnight had come and gone. I'd just gotten home from another double shift at the restaurant. I rinsed my face in the kitchen sink and braced my weight against the countertop.

"*Can you hear the music, Rosie?*" Your voice threaded through the dark.

"*What?*" I wiped the grime from my eyes and found you in the shadows.

"*The music. Can you hear it?*"

All I heard was the passing of the freight train that crossed the tracks behind the trailer park. That and the laboring whirl of the space heater from the little room I shared with Mom.

The way you were looking at me, your face strained. I wanted to take that strain for you. I wanted you to tell me what had caused it, so I could fight it for you. But how can you fight something you can't even hear?

"*Where's it coming from?*" If I could find this music, maybe I could make it stop. Maybe I could pull you a little closer to where I was instead of where it was you were always drifting to.

"*From the dark,*" you answered without hesitation. "*It's always there, but now it's getting louder. It shouldn't be this loud.*"

My gaze wandered out the window, across the darkened lot. Empty except for the metal carcasses of a few rusted-out cars.

When I looked back, your shoulders were bending under some invisible weight. My heart gave a tug in my chest. The way it always did when

I felt like I was failing you. Which was a lot of the time. "There's nothing out there, Charlie."

"Not there." *You got up and walked across the room, wearing one of my old T-shirts. It hit you at the knees. You reached for the map tacked up over the fold-out table. It was wrinkled and water stained, scattered with red dots from North Carolina all the way to this middle-of-nowhere town in Nevada. Gently, you smoothed the paper and stared not at it but through it, at something only you could see. Your finger raced across the tangled knots of border lines and interstates until it stopped.*

"Here."

I leaned over your shoulder. "Fort Glory, Oregon?"

Your violet eyes cleared as you raised them to mine. You nodded.

My pulse jumped at the look on your face. You spent most of your time halfway suspended between here and somewhere else. But there was nothing dreamy or distant about your expression now. You were looking right at me like the entire world was no bigger than that beat-up map between us.

"We'll have to hand in our notice. Sign you out of school. Maybe in a few weeks we can—"

You shook your head. "Now, Rosie."

You'd never asked to move. Not once in all the countless times we'd done it. Not even when things got hard. And now you wanted to cut and run?

I took a breath and forced the words past the lump in my throat. "What happened? Whatever it is, you can tell me, Charlie."

"Nothing happened. Not . . . yet." *Your forehead scrunched the way it sometimes did when you were looking for words. Like the ones you needed didn't come in any language I could speak. Half the time, whatever you really meant to say got lost in translation.* "It's important. This is important, Rosie."

You looked at me with Mom's eyes. The kind of eyes that made me want to move heaven and earth just to make them light up. I'd known it from the first moment I saw you lying in a bassinet at the foot of our parents' bed. From the first time I'd held you in my arms. There was something inside of you. A light I could feel without seeing. It made me want to do whatever you asked. Only you never asked for anything.

Not until that night. Not until that question.

The clock struck one over my shoulder. My next shift started in a few hours. My back ached, and my head was starting to pound, but I just nodded like whatever you'd said made sense to me. One thing was perfectly obvious.

We couldn't stay here.

Mom was getting antsy, and too many people were starting to notice us. Last week, you'd come home with scraped knees and a cut under your eye. The day before that, I'd caught a bunch of kids following you home. They scattered when they saw me, but sooner or later they were going to come around when I wasn't here.

These things never got better. They only ever got worse.

It was time to leave. I looked down at the map.

Fort Glory, Oregon.

It was as good a place as any.

My eyes caught on the name again. A glimmer of recognition flashed through me. A feeling almost like déjà vu. I'd read that name somewhere. I stood up a little straighter when it came to me.

I waited for you to go back to bed, and then I slipped into the room I shared with Mom. Quietly, I lifted the edge of one of my maps and unpinned the small folder hidden behind it. It held a few pages I'd printed out at the public library when we lived in Colorado, two moves ago. The only secret I'd ever kept from either of you. Something that belonged only to me.

I stared down at the papers. A complete list of all the Hands for

3

Hearths affiliates nationwide. I scanned the list, and there it was on the second page.

Fort Glory/Maple, Oregon.

You said we had to go there. That it was important. Maybe you were right. This was a sign as much as any green billboard hanging over a highway.

Mom didn't say anything when I told her we'd be leaving in the morning. We'd gotten our paychecks earlier that day so there was no reason to drag things out. If I'm being honest, I would've given anything for her to fight me on this. On anything. But Mom didn't fight. She just nodded and rolled over. The decision fell to me. Like everything always did.

"Can you hear the music, Rosie?" you'd asked.

I closed my eyes and joined Mom on the bed. I could still picture the Hands for Hearths brochure in my head. The smiling faces of those people as they stood in front of their brand-new homes. Homes they built with their own two hands.

No, I didn't hear the music, Charlie. I didn't hear anything but the sound of Mom's breathing and the thudding of my own heart. But I could feel it, stirring inside of me. An ache in that part of me I tried hard to ignore.

I couldn't hear the music, but maybe I could see it. A line of notes stretching far into the distance. A road that led toward something I'd been chasing down for as long as I could remember.

Secret dream hidden behind the walls of my heart.

Secret wish you somehow heard and gave to me.

ONE

The woman is one of them.

Her clothes are my first clue. The predawn crowd at the Dusty Rose diner is made up of fishermen and loggers—men who like their coffee black and their boots broken-in. The woman's sweater and slacks have that department-store sheen. But it's more than what she's wearing. It's the way every eye in the room cuts to her and then away. A sudden lull in conversation that screams a warning in my ear.

Stranger.

I wipe down the counter and keep tabs on the woman hovering by the entrance. When we first moved into town, most people assumed Mom, Charlie, and I were part of the small group of invaders that has descended on Fort Glory over the past month. An army of tabloid journalists carrying notepads and handheld recorders. UFO chasers, criminologists, and environmentalists. Even a few government types. They've been flocking here these past few weeks, drawn by the strange reports. It wouldn't be a problem if their general nosing around wasn't also keeping the tourists away. Let's just say, the locals aren't too thrilled.

By now, most of the residents have accepted that my family has nothing to do with these "invaders." All the same, they haven't rolled out any red carpets. In a way, I'm grateful. As long as the people here are preoccupied with the outsiders and the rumors that brought them here, they're too busy to wonder about us.

The woman makes a beeline for the corkboard wall. It's littered with announcements in colorful scraps of paper. She rips down a bright pink pamphlet and studies it with narrowed eyes.

After a quick glance at the clock, I duck under the counter to gather my things. My first shift started at four thirty this morning, and the next one isn't till tonight. Charlie and I start school today, but that isn't what has my stomach tied up in knots. I can't stop thinking about the Hands for Hearths application hidden in my backpack. Twelve pieces of paper that could change our lives forever.

And Mom has no idea.

When I stand, the woman is waiting for me on the other side of the counter. She's got sharp features and an even sharper gaze. *Cop.*

I push the unsettling thought away. Her clothes are too nice, and she doesn't have that world-weary look that comes with the job. Must be another reporter. Like the other strangers flocking to Fort Glory, she's here for something that has nothing to do with me.

"Coffee," she orders, taking a seat by the big window overlooking the Oregon woods. Despite offering the best view in the house, that section of the diner is mostly deserted. There's a reason for that. He is sitting at table nine.

The young man glances up from his breakfast when the reporter slides into the booth two rows up. He studies the woman, and I study him while I dig in my bag for my keys. He's older than I am. Around nineteen. A faded Mariners cap is pulled down low over his forehead, emphasizing a strong nose and jaw. Even with a dusting of scars and light stubble, he has the kind of face most seventeen-year-old girls would cut out of a magazine and plaster on their bedroom walls. I'd be lying if I said I didn't notice. Still, it isn't the way he looks that interests me.

It's the way other people look *at* him.

It goes like this. Every day, the boy at table nine comes in just before sunrise. As soon as he sits down, there's a noticeable shift as the men in the nearby booths give him their backs. They don't say a word as they freeze him out, and for his part, the kid ignores their existence. That alone would make him interesting, but there's something else, too.

The pink pamphlet. The one the reporter grabbed from the wall.

The first time I saw it, the boy from table nine was tacking it to the board by the front door. Frankie, my boss, tore it down before I could check it out. Some variation of this scene has played out every morning since I started working here. That was five days ago—long enough to make me wonder what's on that pamphlet to make the boy at table nine so wildly unpopular.

I'm shrugging into my coat when a hairy hand drops onto my arm. "The woman at table seven," Frankie wheezes. "Find out what she wants."

"I've got to go. Gloria—"

"Has the biggest mouth in six counties." Frankie jerks his chin toward the waiting woman. "We don't need any more headlines dragging the name of this town through the mud. Take her order and send her on her way. Call it a favor."

The sun is already starting to rise over the parking lot, but I owe Frankie. He didn't have to hire us without a scrap of paperwork when we rolled into town last week. Then again,

Mom tends to have that effect on people. Or more specifically, on men.

The reporter wastes no time getting down to business when I place a steaming cup in front of her. She slides a crisp bill across the table. Ten dollars. That's a week's worth of frozen dinners. A new pair of shoes for Charlie. I need the money, but not as much as I need this job.

"Can I get you something else?" I ignore the bribe.

"Do you live in Fort Glory . . ." She scans my name tag. *"Rose?"*

"My family moved here a week ago." We don't have a TV and the truck radio has been busted forever, so I had no idea what kind of a media storm we were walking into when Charlie pointed to the dot on the map that marked this quaint Oregon town. By the time I figured it out, it was already too late. One look at the town nestled between a sea of Douglas firs and an ocean of waves, and I'd fallen hard.

"These are floating all over Fort Glory." The woman holds up the neon pamphlet. "Someone is going through a great deal of trouble to imply a connection between the problems in town and the work they're doing with the DARC." She puts the pamphlet on the table, and I get my first good look at it. The headline could've been ripped right off the front page of the *National Enquirer.*

DEEP ATOMIC RESEARCH COLLIDER KNOCKING ON THE GATES OF HELL. ANIMALS RUN FOR COVER AS DARC UNLEASHES ANCIENT EVIL.

I had no idea what a collider was until we moved here. Honestly, I'm still vague on the details. Something about smashing atoms together. Whatever it does, the DARC is the biggest machine in the world. Or so claims the giant billboard corrupting the scenery on the way into town. That billboard is just the beginning. The DARC is incorporated into the name of every business establishment within a ten-mile radius. There's an information center dedicated to it right next to city hall, and every gift shop is stacked with T-shirts and other overpriced merchandise proudly proclaiming: *The DARC: The Ninth Wonder of the World*, or *Particle Physics: The Final Frontier!*

To say that the DARC is a big deal to these people doesn't come close to covering it. It's their one claim to fame. The attraction that brings in the big tourist dollars and the reason they *matter* to the outside world. And this reporter is here to mess with it.

"Do you know where these are coming from?" she asks, jerking me out of my thoughts.

My eyes dart to the boy staring down at his eggs. His faded jeans and ball cap don't give off the crazy vibe. Unapproachable, maybe. Rough around the edges, definitely. But not crazy. His shoulders tense while he waits for me to call him out. It's his lucky day, because that's not my style.

"No idea. Sorry."

The woman adds a ten to the bill already on the table. "You sure about that?"

Her nasal voice carries in the diner. Utensils stop clinking. Sentences trail off into nothing. Frankie runs a filthy rag over the clean counter while he pretends not to listen. Like everyone else, he wants these strangers gone.

The lingering silence makes the moment feel like a test. The boy at table nine has no fans here, and neither will I if I cover for him. It's stupid, but a small part of me can't help admiring him for showing up here day after day in spite of everything. That takes guts, and it makes me think he's here for more than the strong coffee. He's here to prove a point.

"Someone has to know." The woman shrugs. "Small town like this, people talk."

Her words leave a sour taste in my mouth. The kind of "talk" she's referring to is one of the reasons Charlie and I have switched schools as often as other kids switch pairs of shoes. It's impossible not to notice Mom, and Charlie...Charlie is Charlie.

"That pamphlet has been there for weeks," I lie. "No idea where it came from."

The boy looks up quickly. I don't meet his eyes.

"Shame." The woman puts the money back into her purse. "I'm doing research for the *Oregon Chronicle*. In addition to the drastic spike in crime, there have been reports of other strange happenings. Disappearances. General unrest. Have you noticed anything odd? Anything out of place?"

"Other than you?" I don't mean it to be funny. Or rude. It just comes out that way.

Frankie covers a laugh with a cough. A few of the men nod their heads. I thought they'd blackball me for helping the boy at table nine, but I read the situation wrong.

The boy might be a problem, but he's *their* problem.

They'll handle him their way.

Their grudging approval is worth the glare she levels at me.

"Thank you for your time." She moves toward the group of loggers sitting at the counter. As one, they turn like a wall of flannel, shutting her down.

A small smile creeps across my face. Say what you want about small towns, but the people look after their own.

The woman's mouth hardens. It's a lost cause and she knows it. With one last scowl, she walks out of the diner.

The door has barely closed behind her when the squeaks of chairs and stools fill the air. A chorus of banging starts up as palms slap down on tables and countertops. I'm trying to figure out what's going on when an elderly logger in a trapper hat waves me over. His gnarled finger taps the table beside a five-dollar bill. That's when I realize.

It's for me. They're all for me.

My throat goes painfully tight. I spend the next few moments collecting small bills from men who, just yesterday, barely acknowledged my existence. It might seem like a small thing, but it isn't.

Not to me.

Another look at the clock brings me back down to earth. It's past seven. School starts at eight.

I'm jamming my apron into my bag, when I sense someone behind me.

It's the boy from table nine.

His eyes are startling. Silver gray with blue starbursts at the centers. He's tall, too. Over six feet with broad shoulders that suggest he works hard for a living. His hand moves toward me, and I tense. He hesitates before dropping something on the table beside me.

A crumpled twenty-dollar bill.

When he walks past me, the scent of fresh rain and motor oil lingers behind him.

I'm still staring after him when Frankie waves me over to the register. My boss fumbles a cigarette out of his sweat-stained apron and raises it to his lips. "Boy's got some nerve showing up here," he says, violating a dozen health codes with one drag.

"What's his story?"

"Served time for attempted murder. Not long enough if you ask me." Frankie shakes his head, disgusted. "Everyone round here knows he set the fire that killed his folks. Good people. Damn ugly business." His weathered face arranges itself into an expression that could almost be concern. "Do yourself a favor and steer clear of Ian Lawson. That boy is trouble nobody needs."

I nod. What I don't say is that I've spent the last three years working on making myself invisible. Ever since that night in July, I don't wear makeup, or rebel against authority, or drive above the speed limit. Staying out of trouble is pretty much at the top of my priority list.

But the thing about trouble is that it has a way of finding you. Especially when you aren't looking for it.

TWO

pull into the campground just as the early-morning sun is cutting across the water. Even though I'm late, the view still makes me pause. Glory Point is the best seat in the house. A secluded bluff jutting over the sleepy little town and under a blue-blanket sky. In every direction green forests meet crashing Pacific waves. It reminds me of one of those coffee commercials where everyone is happy, and life is a postcard waiting to be written.

Fort Glory, Oregon. Not just another dot on the map. Not just a pit stop on the way to somewhere else.

Home.

Now I just have to convince Mom.

I'm steering toward the trailer when a figure stumbles out of the trees along the ridgeline to my left. A man wearing a nice suit and tie. As I watch, he climbs over the guardrail and walks toward the cliff, stopping just short of the ledge. A coat hangs loosely off his wasted frame. His body is twitching the way addicts sometimes do when they're coming down. He turns.

A chill washes over me when his eyes lock with mine. Before I can figure out why, the man scrambles back over the guardrail. One second, he's there. The next, he's disappearing into the woods. It's bizarre. Is he some wealthy local with a closet drug problem? Another journalist like the woman in the diner? Either way, it's none of my business.

Life is complicated enough without adding other people's problems to my growing list of things to stress about.

On the short, bumpy trip to the trailer, my hands beat restlessly against the wheel. It's not just the weirdo on the ridge. Whenever I think about my appointment at the Hands for Hearths office this afternoon, I can't sit still. If Mom knew what I was planning, she'd have the trailer hitched to the truck before I had time to explain. It's been like this forever. We keep pushing west, never staying in one place long enough for the dust to settle. At first, we moved because Mom was restless. Then that night in July happened, and we did it because we had to. But standing here now with the sun on my skin and the taste of evergreen and sea salt in my mouth, I know that things will be different here.

They'll be better.

The dirt path in front of me opens up to a small clearing surrounded by giant trees. The forest is so thick, you can barely hear the roar of the ocean behind it. The park is mostly deserted. These grounds won't get crowded again until spring, and with any luck, we'll be settled into our new place by then.

I'm locking up the truck when a voice calls out. "You see him?"

I turn to find Rowena Mae camped out on a rickety lawn chair in front of the neighboring trailer. Her skin is a playground for freckles, and her hair is a shade of blond not known to occur in nature. I've only spoken to her twice, but there's something about her that feels comforting in the way strange things sometimes do.

"See who?"

"The man on the bluff," she says. "Fancy clothes. Passed through here a few minutes ago?"

"Yeah, I saw him." I yank the zipper of my jacket up to my chin. "Do you know what he's doing up there?"

"Settin' his mind about the business of dying, I reckon."

"You think he's going to *jump*?"

"Would make the fourth one this week." Rowena scowls. "I told the sheriff she might as well string a net across the water. Save the city a fortune in cleanup."

"Shouldn't we call the police?" Normally, I wouldn't call the cops to save my own life, but nothing about this is normal.

"Already done," Rowena says, letting me off the hook. "Not that it'll make a lick of difference. They've got their hands full down at the station, or haven't you heard?" She thrusts something at me.

My gaze drops from the bright paper in my hand to the box under Rowena's lawn chair. It's full of pink pamphlets.

"You made these?" My thoughts fly to the young man in the diner. Ian. He must be a friend of Rowena's if he's distributing her pamphlets. Rowena doesn't seem like the type of woman to forgive a pesky little thing like attempted murder. There must be more to Ian's story than Frankie let on. I resist the urge to ask. I'm not generally big on personal questions. Mostly because they tend to cut both ways.

Rowena nods and thrusts out her chin. "I knew we were in for it when the birds stopped singing. Happened about three weeks ago. Same day the DARC went back online."

"You mean the collider?" I picture the research facility I pass every day. A few squat warehouses and a handful of tall,

15

randomly scattered cinder-block buildings that are the only eye-sores in this fairy tale of a town. "I don't get what the big deal is."

Rowena snorts. "Where you been, girl? You're standing on top of the most advanced machine ever built by man. Twenty years to plan. Fifteen billion of our tax dollars to build."

"Fifteen billion dollars?" My brain hurts just trying to imagine how many TV dinners or tanks of gas that money could buy. Instead, our government blows it on some glorified science project. "For what, exactly?"

Rowena leans forward in her chair. The rusted slats squeak in protest. "There's more to the DARC than meets the eye. Three hundred feet under this here ground runs a tunnel track twenty miles round. It makes a loop around town and off into the parkland, as far up as the road into Maple. They spent all that money to build their fancy machine, looking for something. But the Europeans had a fancy machine of their own, and they found it first." Her nostrils flare. "The DARC closed down. Stayed that way for three years. Then three weeks ago it goes back online with no warning. Now folks are acting like they've got the devil inside of them."

Gooseflesh breaks out across my arms. I tell myself it has nothing to do with Rowena's ravings. Whatever she says, the DARC is just a machine. It isn't to blame for the way people are acting.

Human beings have never needed excuses to do shitty things to one another.

"And you think the DARC is responsible?" I play along even though I'm more convinced than ever that Rowena is out of her mind. As bizarre as this conversation is, it's still a lot easier to deal with than the one waiting for me inside. For my plan to work,

I'm going to have to lie right to Mom's face. Something I've been dreading even more than our first day at a new school.

"You can't tell me one thing's got nothing to do with the other. People been asking me for proof." She scowls. "I tell 'em to get off their phones. Turn off the damn TV. Sometimes the truth is screaming in your ears. All you got to do is listen."

"I'll keep that in mind," I say, reluctantly turning back to the trailer.

"Wait," Rowena calls out. "Your mother. Helen, is it?"

I turn around, my stomach sinking at the mention of Mom's name. "Yeah." I hold my breath and wait to see where this goes.

"She's got you both working up at the Dusty Rose?"

I nod, and the old woman looks strangely satisfied. "Frankie's a mean ol' bastard, but he pays a fair wage. He looks after his people if they earn it."

"We don't need looking after." My words are sharp. I smile to blunt the edges. "We aren't afraid of hard work."

Rowena's lips twitch. "I bet you aren't." Pale green eyes settle on me with uncomfortable intensity. The old woman tilts her head to the side. "You favor her. Your mother."

I frown. If I look like Mom, it's the way the passing scenery looks through a tinted window. Kind of hazy with the colors on mute. My little brother, Charlie, on the other hand, is my mother with the resolution turned all the way up. "Your brother too." Rowena echoes my thoughts. "What's his name?"

"Charlie. And I'm Rose."

"Father?"

I have to hand it to her. She's not one to throw out lines to fish for information. She's the sort to toss a bomb in the water and see what rises to the surface. "He disappeared."

"Men have a nasty habit of doing that." Rowena snags her coffee mug from the grass beside her and studies me over the rim. "Read the pamphlet. Like I said, folks are acting strange. Best be on your guard."

"Thanks. I will." I offer her a small smile. I can't help it. Most people wouldn't bother with the dire warnings. Especially not for newcomers like us. Rowena may be a little nuts, but she means well. As neighbors go, we've had far worse.

Inside the trailer, I tap Charlie's foot on the way to the bedroom I share with Mom. I grab some jeans and a cable-knit sweater that's as old as I am. Most of my clothes once belonged to my mother. After a hundred washes, they still smell like her. Sunshine and honey.

"Morning, Rose." Mom greets me wearing the diner uniform: a simple pink dress and white apron that makes her eyes glow violet. My mother's eyes are the kind of blue people write songs about.

"What time does your shift start tonight?" she asks.

"Five." I'll be working doubles for the rest of my life, but it'll be worth it if Hands for Hearths accepts our application for a home. At this point, it's a matter of basic necessity. Like our truck, the trailer is on its last leg. It was a relic when Dad bought it. That was nine years ago. Living in it was never the plan. It was a short-term solution while my parents made other arrangements—arrangements that went up in smoke when my dad left one night to buy a lottery ticket and never returned. I've been doing what I can to keep the place livable with his old tools, but there are only so many times you can tape up a leaking pipe before it comes apart in your hands. Most days, I feel like my collection of maps are holding up the walls instead of the other way around. Which leads me to the real reason we have to make it in Fort Glory.

We have no other choice.

"Rose?"

"Yes?" I look at my mother.

"Can you check on Charlie after school? Make sure he's... adjusting?"

We both know what she's really asking. I nod to ease her mind and wish this was one of those towns where the high school and elementary school were right next to each other.

Mom refuses to admit that Charlie is different. I'm not angry with her about it. She means well and she loves us, but I'm tired. *Tired.* And as much as I love her back, I could use a break from all this pretending.

"Why don't you guys swing by the diner after school?" She reaches for me but pulls back at the last minute. "You can tell me how your first day was over a piece of pie."

"There's a cheap mechanic in Maple. I thought I'd check it out before work." I never lie to my mother, and I don't like the way it feels.

"You're a good girl, Rose." She kisses my forehead— something she used to do all the time when I was little. Since I never kissed her back, she must have assumed I didn't like it.

I liked it.

Charlie walks out of the bathroom, his hair curling from the shower. It needs a trim. He's paler than usual, which highlights the dark circles under his eyes. He's also dropping weight when he has none to lose. He isn't eating enough. Isn't sleeping. Whenever I get off late or wake up early, he's just lying on the pullout, staring at the water-stained ceiling. Every so often his lips turn down in a grimace. Almost like he's in pain. He's never done that before, and it makes me worry about him. Even more than usual.

"You ready?" I ask.

Seconds tick by, but I'm used to that. My brother answers every question as if the fate of the world hinges on his response.

"Sure," he says, throwing on his favorite green hoodie. It's way too big and threadbare in places. I've wanted to get rid of it so many times, but Charlie won't let me. It's one of the few things he has left that belonged to our father.

We head for the truck—an '85 Chevy with an extended cab, lovingly named Rusty for reasons that need no clarification. Rowena waves at us from her lawn chair. Movement at the trailer next to hers catches my eye. There's a figure wedged under the hood of one of those muscle cars that always sit on cinder blocks outside of trailers the way white picket fences frame perfect lawns in the suburbs. Only this boy looks like he has plans of driving away. It isn't just the sweat stains on his shirt or the grease under his fingernails. It's the way he's bent over the engine—like he could breathe life into it with his desire to be somewhere, anywhere else.

He turns, and I freeze. It's him. The boy from table nine. Ian.

And he doesn't look remotely surprised to see me.

Ian wipes his face with the hem of his T-shirt and starts putting up his tools in a beautiful toolbox that makes Dad's ancient rollaway seem shabby by comparison. My fingers itch to explore the perfectly designed cubbies. I tear my gaze away before he catches me coveting his tools.

Hinges creak behind me as Mom slips into the passenger

seat. Charlie throws his backpack through the back window and prepares to climb in after it. The door has been jammed forever, which makes getting in and out somewhat of a production. I can't decide which is worse: dropping Charlie off a few hundred yards from Roosevelt Elementary, or letting him climb out like that for everyone to see.

Shadows dot the sky as a flock of geese passes overhead. Charlie watches them intently. "They're going the wrong way."

"Maybe they got turned around." My gaze cuts to the woods, and a shiver runs up my spine. The quiet that was peaceful a moment ago suddenly feels oppressive. It takes me a minute to figure out why. It's the birds. They've gone dead silent.

"No," my brother says. "They hear it too."

"Hear what, Charlie?"

For a second, I think he's going to answer, then he just shakes his head. "Do you feel that?" he asks instead. When I don't answer, he elaborates. "The sky. It's too heavy."

Mom frowns. The silence stretches. Another winged army passes over our heads.

I take one look at Charlie's worried face before I jog back to the trailer. "Just in case." I toss our umbrella on the dash and turn the key in the ignition. There's an awful sound, like chicken bones down a garbage disposal. Panic shoots through me. My appointment with the Hands for Hearths representative is scheduled for four this afternoon. Their office is in the neighboring town of Maple. Fifteen miles away.

I wrench the key in the ignition again only to get the same sound as before. My knuckles gleam white against the wheel. Tears of frustration burn my eyes, but I refuse to cry. Just like I refuse to miss that appointment. I'll walk to Maple if I have to.

When the engine catches on the third try, every muscle in my body goes liquid with relief.

Rowena flags me down as I'm backing out of the park. She chews her lip thoughtfully while she stares at Mom. "I cut hair when I'm not acting as a watchdog for the people. I got some color that might do those roots of yours a world of good, Helen. Come on by, and I'll treat you for free."

"That's kind of you." Mom is practically collapsing into the upholstery in an attempt to make herself invisible.

It wasn't always like this. My mother used to wear lipstick, and sing along to the radio, and look strangers in the eye.

She used to do a lot of things.

Rowena frowns at me. "That truck is an accident waiting to happen. I'll send Ian over later. That boy can fix anything."

"Thanks, but we're all set." Rowena is trying to be nice. I get that. Still, it feels a little like pity and that burns even though I know it shouldn't.

My feelings must show because Rowena snorts. "The weather will turn soon. The road into town is dangerous. Let him take a look, and the boy will tell you what needs doing." I open my mouth to refuse again, but she cuts me off. "Don't let your pride make you foolish, girl. Too many damn fools around here already."

"All right." It's clear she won't be taking no for an answer. "I'll let him look, but I'll pay him for his trouble."

Rowena gives me a nod of grudging respect. "Don't let Ian's manner put you off. He's rough around the edges, but so's gold before it's polished. There's more to a thing than the look of it." She levels Mom with a knowing glance.

"Thank you." I say it again, only this time I really mean it.

Rowena may be pushy, but at least you always know where she stands. In my book, that more than makes up for the crazy.

"You can thank me by spreading the word." Rowena hands me a stack of pink pamphlets. "Knowledge is a weapon, and we've got to arm ourselves. Those big brains at the DARC are knocking on doors best left closed. Sooner or later, they'll get an answer."

I smile politely. Mom is too busy staring at her lap, so I glance in the rearview to share a look with Charlie only to find him nodding solemnly in the backseat.

After dropping Mom off at the diner, I park next to some reddening bushes behind Roosevelt Elementary. A sense of dread fills me at the sight of that rectangular brick building. For a moment, I'm tempted to lock the doors and drive away, but Charlie has to walk through that door, and I have to let him. I just wish it wasn't so hard.

New places aren't easy on Charlie. It usually takes people a few weeks to get used to him. The thing with Charlie is hard to explain. It's not that there's anything wrong with him. It's more like part of him is always off somewhere the rest of us can't follow, which means I sometimes miss him even when he's sitting right beside me.

The wind howls. The maple tree above us releases a handful of autumn confetti. Charlie watches a neon leaf dance to rest on our windshield wiper, and for the thousandth time, I wish I knew what he was thinking. Mom used to say that if heaven is a song, Charlie is the only one who can hear it playing. I'm not sure I believe in heaven, but I do know there's a glow about my brother. The yoke of another world he never fully shed. It lights the space

23

around him, and it makes him different in a way others can't help but notice.

More than anything, it scares the hell out of me.

"Go get 'em." I slap him on the back in an attempt at cheerfulness that is fooling no one. "Keep your head down," I add, though it's pointless. Charlie doesn't go looking for trouble. Trouble hunts him down.

I'm still watching him climb through the window when Charlie freezes with his upper body hanging halfway out of the truck. I follow his gaze to three boys huddled together nearby. One of them moves, and I see it. A bird's nest lying on the sidewalk.

Charlie starts to get out. I twist in the seat and grab his belt. "Don't. It isn't any of our business."

He looks right at me. "Then whose business is it, Rosie?"

My chest tightens. We're officially late and Rusty may not start again, but my brother just asked me to do something, and I can count on one hand the number of times that has happened. I kill the engine.

"Hey!" I jump out of the truck. "Leave that nest alone."

"The mother won't come back if you touch them," Charlie says, as if that settles it. One look at these three tells me this is far from settled. "Please."

"Please," mimics a boy with brown hair gelled into spikes. The others take their cue from him. They close in around us, and I am instantly aware of the chain link at my back.

The bell echoes through the schoolyard.

The ringleader glares at us, an unnerving darkness glittering in his blue eyes. His glare twists into a smirk as he holds out the nest.

I know what's coming even before Charlie moves forward,

his hands outstretched. He's a few feet away when the boy lets it drop.

Eggs shatter.

Charlie gets down on the cement. I wait for the boys to run off and then I kneel with him. Because life can be hard and is usually unfair, but because some things are good, and my brother is one of them.

His shoulders hunch as he picks up a broken shell. "Why?"

"I don't know." I don't know why fathers disappear, or mothers stop wearing lipstick, or little boys with sticks always find someone smaller to poke.

A tear slides down Charlie's cheek. He doesn't cry often, and when he does it's never at what you would expect. Like at the beginning of movies and not at the end, or when one season gives way to another. Charlie doesn't cry when things die, only when they're broken in a way that can never be fixed. Like the egg in his hand.

"Look," I tell him. "There are still two left." I'm wondering how that's possible, when Charlie reaches for them.

"We can save them," he says.

"Leave them for the mother."

"It's too late. She isn't coming back. *Please*, Rosie."

"We've got nowhere to put them," I say, though what I'm thinking is: *They're just eggs. Nobody wants them.*

Charlie places an egg in my palm like it's the most precious gift on earth, and for that brief moment when his hand touches mine, I almost believe it. "Put it in your pocket, near your body so it stays warm. I'll take one and you take the other. We can do it, Rosie. We can keep them safe." He says it with a certainty I will never understand.

25

"But—"

"This." He cups my hands so that our palms form a nest of flesh and bone around the eggs. "*This* is important, Rosie."

Charlie's expression goes dreamy, and suddenly, I know he's seeing something, *hearing* something I don't. Only this time, it isn't something that causes him pain. It's something good.

Seconds pass. Charlie's eyes clear. He smiles at me, and for a few seconds, the world is a lovely place full of strangers holding open doors. I'd do anything for one of those smiles, which is why I place the egg in my pocket and zip up the jacket I won't be able to take off for the rest of the day.

THREE

n the parking lot after school, I study the hinge on the driver's-side door.

It's *clean.*

A mess of brown scrapings crunch under my feet. Apparently, I knocked a few years' worth of rust loose when I slammed the door shut this morning.

I try the engine, and my good luck gets even better. It turns over smoothly, causing a strange lightness to blossom in my chest. The feeling evaporates when Rusty backfires with a *BOOM* that echoes through the parking lot.

A crowd gathers, and I stifle a groan. It's the first bit of attention anyone at this school has paid me all day. Laughter explodes in my ears, but it dies off almost as abruptly as it starts.

When I glance up, Ian is tossing something into the bed of a pickup truck two parking spots in front of Rusty. He's wearing faded jeans and an oil-streaked tee—more blue-collar than bad boy, but one look from him is all it takes to drive off the crowd. It's eerily similar to the scene that plays out at the diner every morning. More than ever, it makes me wonder what his deal is. If he's really guilty of the crimes Frankie accused him of, why would he come back here? Why wouldn't he run far away to some other town where nobody knew his name?

I'm about to restart the engine when something collides with my door.

Startled, I look down into a small face dominated by a pair of massive glasses. The boy crouched beneath my window looks like he wishes he could disappear—something that is highly unlikely due to the thing on his back, a yellow monstrosity that bears more resemblance to a school bus than a school bag.

Brown eyes blink up at me through thick lenses. "Hey."

Before I can come up with a response, a commotion at the front of the school draws my gaze. A group of boys is gathering on the sidewalk. They look pissed.

There's a muffled oath from under my window.

"Friends of yours?" I guess.

"Business acquaintances." The boy can't be any older than thirteen, which means he must've skipped a grade or two to get here.

"What kind of business, exactly?"

"The kind where I write half the football team's term papers in exchange for their not making my life a living hell."

"You must not be doing a good job," I say as the boys scatter to flush out their prey.

"I did *too* good of a job. Now the principal is onto us, and those Neanderthals want to use my body as a punching bag."

Two of the pack break off in our direction. The area is completely open. There's no place to hide.

My hand moves to the door handle and pauses there. I have a rule. It involves not going out of my way to make enemies or friends because both are liabilities I try to avoid. But Fort Glory isn't business as usual. If we're going to be sticking around, it means getting involved, and I'd rather throw in my lot with

Rowena and the stranger hiding behind my car than those creeps at the front of the school.

I wedge the door open. "Climb in." When the boy just stares at me, I repeat, "Get in the truck. Now."

The boy tosses his backpack into my lap and curls up like a cat at my feet. I drum my hands on the wheel. The Hands for Hearths interview is in less than an hour. The elementary school got out ten minutes ago. How long will they keep this up?

Right on cue, the boy opens his bag and produces a book filled with so many highlights, it's practically glowing. The title is the first thing I notice:

THE DEEP ATOMIC RESEARCH COLLIDER (DARC): *Confirming String Theory by Unlocking the Universe's Hidden Dimensions* by Arthur Jackson.

The second thing I notice is the familiar neon pamphlet he's using as a bookmark.

"Some light reading?" I ask.

The boy doesn't look up. "If you consider a work of pure genius by one of the greatest minds since Einstein 'light reading.' Then, yes."

My lip twitches at his tone. "Sounds pretty heavy."

He snorts. "Dr. Jackson's work with the DARC is about to change the way we look at the universe and our place in it."

"Yeah?" I stretch my hands over my head, hoping to ease some of the tension in my shoulders. "If this Dr. Jackson is such a big deal, how come I've never heard of him?" School has never been high on my priority list. That being said, I've always had a soft spot for science. It's something I get from my dad. He had a knack for knowing how things worked. He used to rescue stuff from the dump. Busted TVs. Old appliances. Then he'd take them apart and put them back together again better than before. I could watch him work for hours. It was like magic. No. It was better than magic, because there were *reasons* for everything he did. Rules that never changed. Then one day, he handed me a screwdriver, and I knew that I was born to hold one.

Call me a sucker for anything practical.

The boy shrugs. "Like other visionaries, Dr. Jackson has his haters. You're gonna want to remember his name. He's my uncle," the boy adds, explaining a lot.

"Your uncle works at the DARC?"

"He doesn't just work there. He designed the modifications to the old collider."

"What's the deal with this collider anyway?" I'd be lying if I said I wasn't curious. It's not that Rowena's paranoia is rubbing off on me. It's that I can't help wondering about the machine that is this town's unofficial mascot. If all the hype is real, the DARC is massive. Massive enough to ring the town and a huge chunk of the nearby woods. My head hurts just thinking about how many people it would've taken to build something like that.

My dad would've loved it.

"The DARC is the most powerful particle accelerator in the world," the boy says without skipping a beat. "It sends beams of particles flying around miles of underground tunnels and then slams them together at 99.99 percent the speed of light."

"And people would do this *why*?"

The boy rolls his eyes, but I get the feeling my questions aren't annoying him. If anything, his voice warms. "At that energy level, new particles are created just like they were during the Big Bang. It's like . . ." He searches for the right words. "Figuring how the universe works by learning about its most basic parts."

Unbelievable. Fifteen billion dollars so scientists can smash invisible bits together to try to create even more invisible bits. And according to Rowena, they aren't even the first ones to do it. "I thought they already had a giant collider in Europe," I say. "Why spend all that money to reinvent the wheel?"

"Not to take anything away from the Large Hadron Collider in Switzerland, but the DARC is in another class. It's a little bigger, but a lot stronger. And thanks to Dr. Jackson it has ... other things going for it." The boy shifts. A beam of sunlight touches his brown skin, highlighting the ugly bruise at the corner of his right eye.

The DARC is suddenly the last thing on my mind.

My hands stop drumming. "Is it normally like this around here?" I ask quietly.

The boy catches my drift right away. "No. The last month has been ... rough." The gloomy look he shoots the school makes me want to drive straight to Charlie. "There were three suicides last week and three times as many fights. That's not counting the riot at the football game over the weekend. People are totally losing their shit." It's an eerie echo of Rowena's warning from this morning.

"You think the tabloids are right?" I ask. "That something strange is happening in Fort Glory?"

"You're asking the wrong question." The boy flips a page. "To anyone unbiased it's clear that something strange *is* going on. The more important question is *why*."

"I heard that it has to do with the DARC."

His chin jerks up. "Who said that?"

I nod at the pink pamphlet in his hand.

"Right." He scowls. "Rowena Mae's been spreading her

propaganda about the DARC since it started running again." His lips twist into a smirk. "This is the same woman who insists the government is using the Home Shopping Network to brainwash people."

"Is that right?" I ask, hiding a flash of annoyance. "Because she told me the problems in town all started when the DARC went back online. Seems like a pretty big coincidence. Does your uncle have anything to say about it?"

"Just that it's all superstition and fearmongering. The two greatest enemies of science throughout the ages. If you don't count religion." The answer flies off the tip of his tongue, but his voice is strained. Like he's pushing too hard. Like, maybe, just maybe, he isn't as convinced as he'd like to be.

I'm suddenly more eager than ever to be on my way.

I crack the door. "You're all clear."

Taking the hint, the boy tucks the book into his pack and scrambles out onto the asphalt. "I'm Blaine, by the way. Blaine Jackson."

"Rose."

"Kind of ironic."

"How's that?"

"You work at the Dusty Rose diner, don't you?"

"How do you—"

"Small town." Blaine shrugs as if this fact is the single greatest trial of his existence. "Also, I was there last Friday, and I met your mom. She seems nice."

I flush. My mother *is* nice, but most people are too concerned with what they see on the surface to care about what's going on underneath.

Most people walk through life missing the best parts.

A throaty rumble echoes through the parking lot. It's coming from Ian's truck. He's been sitting in the driver's seat, watching our little drama unfold in his side mirror. I can feel his eyes on me as he pulls out of the lot.

"So, Rose," Blaine says, drawing my attention back to him. "Are you as handy with all tools as you are with a power saw? Not stalking you." He holds up his hands. "I sit behind you in Advanced Woodshop."

"I like to build things," I say.

"That was fairly obvious." Blaine rocks back and forth on his sneakers. Though he's playing it cool, I get the sense he's leading up to something—that it wasn't an accident he chose to hide behind Rusty instead of one of the other cars in the lot.

"I've got a project in the works that requires someone with your specific skill set. I'd make it worth your while."

"How?" My mind flies to our empty savings jar.

"If you're interested in colliders, I'm your best resource." Blaine shrugs. "I interned at the DARC all summer as an assistant to my uncle. If that doesn't interest you I've also got some tutoring money stashed aside. We could work something out." Blaine taps the door with his knuckles and backs away. "Think it over." He glances up at the sky. Worry lines snake across his brow. "But maybe don't take too long."

I know something's wrong the moment I pull up to the school and Charlie isn't waiting for me by the curb. A few years ago, when we were living in Minnesota, Rusty's tank sprang a leak. I had to walk five miles to get gas. It was a snowy day in February.

33

When Mom and I finally arrived at the school, it was dark and cold, and Charlie was still there, half-frozen and waiting right where I'd told him to.

My heart gives an anxious squeeze when I spot his orange backpack abandoned near a clump of bushes. I gave him that backpack when we left Minnesota for Kansas. It looks as new now as it did then, and if you look closely, the tags are still attached to the zipper, carefully tucked away inside the front pocket.

I hop out, leaving Rusty running behind me. I cut through the bushes and come to an abrupt stop on the other side. Charlie is ten feet in front of me, backed against the chain-link fence behind the baseball diamond.

"Are you stupid?" demands the boy from this morning as he pushes Charlie back with a sharp rattle.

Charlie raises his hands. He isn't trying to hit the boy. He isn't even trying to defend himself. He's shifting his arm so it hovers protectively over the bulge in his pocket.

The boy notices. "Give it up."

"Why?" Charlie says, but I'm the only one who knows what he's really asking. Why do people always destroy what they don't understand? Why do we use our hands to break when they should be used for building?

"You just made a big mistake, freak."

The boy punches Charlie in the stomach. My brother goes down hard. He doesn't move his arms from their protective stance, not even to break his fall. I watch his face hit the ground, and everything inside of me clenches.

I lurch forward. Thorns snag at my shirt, trapping me in place. I yank at the fabric with both hands. A few feet away, the boy stands over Charlie.

34

His next kick is a hammer and my world is made of glass.

The boy raises his arm again, but this time I am there. Knuckles collide with my cheekbone, sending shockwaves through my jaw. It hurts. But I'm not thinking about that right now. I'm thinking about my brother in the dirt at my feet, the deep scratch across his forehead and the gravel embedded in his hands as they pat the side of his faded green hoodie.

I turn toward the person responsible. *"Enough."*

The boy pales. He didn't mean to hit me, and he's trying to decide how much trouble he's in. "Whatever." Something in his tone tells me I won't be the last girl he strikes in his lifetime.

"Why?" I repeat Charlie's question. "What did he do to you?"

"He's a freak." The boy's black eyes narrow to knife points. Eyes I could've sworn were blue a few hours ago. "The teacher asked him what he thought about Fort Glory. He said it looked like the inside of a snow globe."

My hands tremble. I want to lash out. I want to hurt this boy the way he hurt Charlie, but it will only make things worse. I know because we've been here before.

"Get lost," I snarl.

The boys run away, laughing. When they're gone, I turn to watch Charlie dig the egg out of his pocket. It's one more problem. One more complication in a life already full of them, but I sag with relief when I see it cradled in his palm.

We don't speak as we climb into Rusty. We both know words won't fix what just happened, just like we both know it will happen again. Rowena and Blaine and all the tabloids might be convinced that some dark force is at work in Fort Glory—a force that's turning the people here violent, but I know the truth: There are boys like that in every town. Boys that become men. One of their kind has sent us packing from state to state, all the way here to Fort Glory.

I am done running.

My cheek stings, but I forget about the pain when I see Charlie curled in on himself, his forehead resting against the glass that's stained white by his breath. My fingers itch to stroke his face the way I used to do when he was little and Mom was working the late shift. I remember watching him sleep and thinking how beautiful he was. How I would do anything to protect him. Only how am I supposed to protect him from the entire world?

Seconds pass while I sit there, my hands on the wheel and Charlie hunched beside me. The image of him on the ground fills my mind. Suddenly, I can't get enough air.

"We can't keep doing this, Charlie. For once, just *once*, can you please try to fit in?"

"Everything has a proper place, Rosie."

"Yeah, well, we're running out of towns to try on for size," I snap, more sharply than I intended. I take a deep breath. "You don't have to win any popularity contests, but couldn't you just try to be—" *Normal.* I stop myself from saying it out loud.

The word hangs between us all the same.

On the drive back to the park, every minute of silence makes me feel worse. I should take it back. I should tell him I didn't mean it, but I bite my tongue and keep driving. I want to build a life here. For us to have a chance at that, I need Charlie to hear what I'm telling him.

It isn't until we're back at the trailer that Charlie speaks. "I'll try, Rosie." He leans into my window, his expression so earnest it tears at my heart. "I promise. I'll try." He gazes at the sky, and a shadow flits across his face. He makes that pained expression he's been making more and more since we came here. "Can I come with you?"

Weeks pass where Charlie barely speaks. Already today he's asked me for three favors. It feels important, but my cheek throbs, and I'm late, and this is just one more thing I can't deal with right now.

"I don't think that's a good idea."

He shifts so that his body is facing the woods. "The music in the dark. It's coming faster now. The cracks are getting wider." He turns back to me, his eyes sadder than I've ever seen them. "I'll be here. Soon. The dark is coming, and I don't want to be alone."

I close my eyes and grip the wheel. "Frankie won't like it. Stay here and do your homework. I'll be back before you know it."

"You promise, Rosie?"

The question is a sucker punch. For a moment, I sit there, emotions clogging my throat. "I'll come back, Charlie. I will *always* come back."

I am not Dad.

Charlie's shoulders relax. "I know. The music in the dark is loud, but it's not as strong as the song inside of us. You'll feel it. Right here." He fists his hands over his chest. "It'll bring you halfway there. The rest you'll have to do on your own. Remember, Rosie. Promise me you'll remember."

I nod even though I have no idea what he's talking about.

Watching him back away from the truck, a small part of me caves. Just like it always does.

"Wait," I call out. "Let me clean that cut."

Charlie shakes his head, his violet eyes anxious. "No, you should go. Right now."

"Are you s—"

"Goodbye, Rosie." Charlie closes my door, ending the conversation.

I use the crank to roll down the window between us, but the words I need jam in my throat.

When I was little, Mom was always offering me pennies for my thoughts. Even back then I could feel it—the wall inside of me that separates the things I feel from the things I can say. Most of the time, I'm glad it's there, but there are moments, like this one, when I'd give anything to blast a hole right through it.

Only, I don't know *how*.

I hit reverse. Charlie stands there, one hand raised and the other still pressed to his chest as he watches me drive away. His face grows smaller and smaller in the rearview. I wait for it to disappear completely. Only then do I allow myself to cry.

I arrive at the Hands for Hearths office with five minutes to spare. For a moment, I sit in my truck, staring at the red door.

We lived near a Hands for Hearths neighborhood in Oklahoma. I can still see the rows of neat houses, hear the hammers as they framed one out a few hundred yards from our trailer. I remember thinking how special that was. To help construct the house that would shelter you and the things that matter most. *Home.* More than a word. More than a place. More than four walls and a roof meant to keep out the rain.

On move-in day, the volunteers held a small party for the family on the front lawn. I'll never forget the father's expression as he opened the door to his home for the first time. It represented everything I wanted to feel. That was five states, three years, seventy-eight paydays ago.

The application feels like a three-hundred-pound anvil sitting at the bottom of my bag.

I smooth out my diner dress and apron. Then I walk up the cement path to the building.

The foyer inside is decorated with framed blueprints. I approach a sixteen-hundred-square-foot ranch with a porch, and I catch my breath because it is so beautiful.

There's a plan just like this hidden behind one of the maps in my room. I keep it with some other things Mom doesn't know about. Things that belong to a ghost.

The worst thing about my father is that I still remember him. You can't miss someone you don't remember, and I still miss him. Every day.

It's strange. I don't recall the exact color of his eyes, or his favorite TV show, or even if he read to me. What I remember is the taste of the butterscotch candies he kept in his pocket and the calluses on his hands as they helped mine hold a hammer. In my memory he's a giant. Seven feet tall with work boots that bent the floorboards. The details of his face have gone sketchy, but when I think of him now, I imagine the lumberjack on the Brawny paper towels we can't afford.

Mom used to keep a photo of him tucked under her mattress. It was taken on their wedding day. My mother in white was a sun whisper; a spot of light so soft and bright it hurt your eyes to look at it. And even though she was lovely in a way that aches, she could never be more beautiful than he was when he was looking at her.

Mom took the picture, but I still have the plans. The ones he drew of the house he was going to build for her. Like his memory, the pencil marks have begun to fade, and the print is barely legible. It was their dream, and he's not here to give it to her.

But I am.

FOUR

Outside the Hands for Hearths office, I grin at the red application folder before I tuck it into my bag. The meeting went much better than I could've hoped, considering I spent the first ten minutes making up excuses for why Mom wasn't there.

Getting her to the main interview on Friday isn't going to be easy.

My mind is so preoccupied with the problem of my mother, it takes me a moment to notice the whistling. High-pitched and whining. I pause a few yards from Rusty and scan the empty street. That's when I notice the sky. I could've sworn it was sunny a second ago. Now the clouds are dark, low, and a sickly shade of green. They're moving fast. Racing each other across the horizon in the direction of Fort Glory like waves drawn in by the tide.

Something tickles my nose. At first, the current is barely noticeable. Like the whistling, it builds until every hair on my body is crackling.

Pop. There's a drastic shift in air pressure. The whistling cracks like glass in my ears, fracturing into a series of jarring notes that slam through my skull.

Oh God. This sound. It's like nothing I've ever heard. A

machine-gun blast in my brain. A vibration in my bones that wants to break me into pieces.

Two men in coveralls burst out of the mechanic shop across the street. Like me, they stare at the sky with their hands pressed over their ears.

I'm sure the noise is going to kill me when, finally, it breaks. There's a *CRACK* like a hundred cannons firing as a thick band of lightning splits the sky. A tremor runs through the ground, shifting the earth under my feet. Car alarms blare. Windows shatter on both sides of the street.

Glass is still raining down on the pavement when another wave of sound hits me dead-on. It rolls through my body and into my brain, burning through my synapses. The sheer force of it bowls me over, and then the pavement is there to meet me. Starbursts of pain explode behind my eyelids.

Gravel bites into my palms, my cheek. I try to lift myself up, but it feels like the entire weight of the sky is pinning me to the asphalt.

Black spots are dancing at the edges of my vision when the pressure in my head finally lets up. When it goes, the pain goes with it.

Cold, clean air fills my lungs. The first breath burns, but by the second, my head has begun to clear. I peel my face off the ground and look over the trees in the direction of Fort Glory. There's no sign of the weird lightning, and the clouds aren't racing anymore. Instead, they hang overhead like downy pillows ready to smother us.

The sky. It's too heavy.

My stomach lurches as my body fights to regain its equilibrium. A quick sweep of the street reinforces the feeling of wrongness. The men from the auto-body shop are sprawled out on the ground. One of them is knocking the side of his head like he's trying get water out of his ears.

Blood drips down the side of his neck onto his stained coveralls.

A moan echoes down the street. A few yards away, a woman in a blazer is kneeling in front of a store window. She stares at her reflection in the glass, her pupils fully dilated and glittering with a darkness that makes my blood run cold. A jagged sob racks her body as she drives her fists into the sidewalk. Again and again and again.

The pavement runs red with her blood.

All around me, people pour out of stores and homes, packing the street and filling the air with their cries. Most of them are focused on the sky. Others stagger around in a daze like the one I can't seem to shake.

I'm still regaining control of my muscles when a man in a postal uniform rushes forward to help the crying woman. Gently, he pulls her away from her reflection in the window. Red nails flash as she claws at his face. The man's shriek pierces the fog around my head.

More confusion erupts in front of the auto-body shop. The two mechanics who were sprawled out a second ago are now back on their feet and trying to kill each other. A crowd gathers around them. People clap and jeer when one of them delivers a vicious jab that sends his opponent to the pavement. The man is still lying there, motionless, when his partner moves to stand over him, a tire iron clutched in his hand. He lets it drop.

That's when I throw up.

The sound of fighting grows louder. The brawl across the

street jumps to the crowd. Violence spreads like wildfire until the road is full of people fighting, running, bleeding.

I wipe my mouth on my sleeve. Smoke fills my lungs, acrid and thick. What's gotten into these people? Most of them are acting as scared and confused as I feel, but a few—the men fighting across the street and the woman with the crazy eyes by the store window—have lost their minds.

Sirens blare in the distance. A cavalcade of police cars races toward us. The relief I feel at the sight of them quickly turns to panic. I have to get out of here. Now. Before they detain me as a witness to manslaughter. And that means I have to get up.

I'm on all fours when the convoy of cruisers reaches us. They hurtle down the road through Maple, past the brawl and the dead man lying in the road and the swarms of injured people. Directly toward Fort Glory.

Mom. Charlie.

Fear is a straight shot of adrenaline, bringing me to my feet.

Glass crunches under my sneakers as I stumble for Rusty. I'm reaching for my bag when fierce barking erupts behind me. A huge golden retriever dragging a leash lunges at the postman. The man's shrill scream cuts through the air as jaws lock around his throat.

I don't watch what happens next. I break into a run. Rusty is a few feet away when something whizzes past my head. The rock smashes out the back window of a nearby sedan, startling me. One wrong step, and the side of my foot smacks into the curb.

Papers fly out of my bag as I hit the ground. Right next to the red Hands for Hearths folder.

I look down at myself. Blood drips from the fresh cuts on my legs onto the hem of my uniform. It's crazy, but suddenly, all I can think about is how stains like that never come out. No matter how many times you run them through the wash.

Another rock zings dangerously close to my ear. I don't pause to see who threw it. Don't stop to wonder why. There are only two things that matter now, and they are fifteen miles down that road.

I drag myself to my feet and sprint for the truck.

The red folder stays with my backpack, abandoned on the sidewalk behind me.

The road to Fort Glory is a minefield of abandoned cars and panicked pedestrians. I drive with one hand on the wheel and the other pressed down on the horn.

Finally, the turnoff for the town comes into view. It is swiftly followed by a wall of red and blue lights. I hit the brakes. The umbrella tumbles off the dash and onto the floor. My heart pounds wildly—like it always does at the sight of police cruisers.

Cars are everywhere, a dozen vehicles and a semi obstructing the way into Fort Glory. Motorists huddle in small groups on the side of the road. A handful of police officers and firemen are spread throughout the crowd, administering first aid, restraining a few disorderlies, talking hurriedly into radios. That's not what worries me.

It's hard to put my finger on—something in the lay of their faces and the hesitant glances they keep shooting over their shoulders in the direction of Fort Glory.

Charlie. Mom.

I kill Rusty's engine and step out onto the road. A woman carrying a toddler rushes past me. More follow her lead. The police are pushing them back. Using force when necessary.

I fight my way through the crowd to the front of the pileup. I stumble when the asphalt under my feet gives way suddenly to grass.

That's when I realize what caused the holdup in the first place.

The road. It just ... *stops.*

Directly ahead of me, a wall of forest stretches out in both directions, blocking the way into town. Not regular trees. Giant redwoods, swallowing everything in their path. Only, that makes no sense. Forests like this grow over hundreds of years.

They don't rise up in a matter of hours.

I'm still trying to understand what I'm seeing when I spot a familiar face. Rowena Mae. She's standing a few feet ahead of me, squared off against a fresh-faced deputy.

"Please return to your car, ma'am," he tells her.

"Not until you tell us what the hell is happening."

"Look." A touch of strain enters the young officer's voice. "I can't tell you something I don't know."

"Somebody here knows something. I suggest you scurry off and find them." Rowena pierces him with a glare before she stalks off toward the trees.

He charges after her. "Wait! You can't go in there. Please, ma'am. Return to the road."

"I'm just going behind that tree. You wouldn't stop an old woman from relieving herself, would you?"

The police officer's radio squawks. He turns it all the way down. "The woods aren't safe."

"This spot isn't going to be safe in about two minutes," Rowena snaps. "I'll come straight back. You're more than wel-come to watch if you like."

In the end, the policeman's orders are no match for Rowena's stubbornness. He turns his back, and Rowena walks away, triumphant. I'm left with half a second to decide.

I follow Rowena behind some trees and out of sight. She spins, and her green eyes show no surprise as they zero in on my face. "I'm getting to the bottom of this. Go back to the road, Rose. What's left of it. There's trouble up ahead, make no mistake. I'm betting it's not the kind you need."

She has no idea how right she is. Drawing attention to myself now could undo everything I've worked so hard for. It would jeopardize our home application, or worse, it'd have the police digging into my closet of skeletons. We can't afford that. I *know* it, but I also know that where a few hours ago there was a road, now there's a forest blocking the way into town.

And my mother and brother are in it.

"I'm coming with you."

Without a word, Rowena heads north toward town. I glance over my shoulder one more time, and then I follow.

The ground is a quagmire of mud that threatens to suction my shoes off my feet. Ahead of me, Rowena huffs and puffs up a steep incline toward the rock rise overlooking Fort Glory. According to the Oregon map of trails I pored over for two weeks before coming here, it's called Devil's Tooth. There were multiple warnings in that book cautioning hikers not to climb.

Rowena stops in front of Devil's Tooth wearing a formidable expression. "Nothing's been right since the birds stopped singing. They felt the darkness coming, and by the looks of things, it's finally here."

I'll be here. Soon. The dark is coming, and I don't want to be alone.

The seed of fear inside of me blossoms into all-out dread.

"Think you can climb to that first ledge if I give you a hand up?" Rowena asks.

The rock wall leers at me. It's about fifty feet tall, with a small lip carved out of the side fifteen feet up. High enough to offer a view over the trees and into town. A fall from that lower ledge wouldn't kill me, but it would do some damage.

My vision blurs. Once when we were living in Georgia and the trailer felt too cramped, I took Charlie to the playground by the park. He went right for the slide. I kept my hands on him the whole way up, but still, he slipped. It was all I could do to wrap my body around his as we went down. We hit the ground on my right arm. It hurt like hell, but it wasn't the pain I couldn't shake. It was the helpless feeling of falling.

I've avoided slides ever since.

I'm about to tell Rowena no when Charlie's voice echoes through my head for the second time.

I'll try, Rosie. I promise. I'll try.

I swallow the saliva in my mouth and meet Rowena's gaze. "I'll try."

"Get up there and take a quick look. Focus on them DARC buildings in the center of town. Whatever disaster caused this, that's where you'll find it." Rowena is surprisingly strong as she braces me. "That's it, girl."

Carefully, I remove my apron, the one holding Charlie's egg, and lay it on the ground. Bits of rock bite into my palms as I pull myself up. One step. Then another. My heart bangs against my ribs. Sweat snakes into my eyes. I'm about six feet off the ground when my left hand slips. There's a flash of pain, and then I'm ten years old again, falling through the air with Charlie enveloped in my arms.

The impact at the bottom drives the air right out of my lungs. Rowena curses under her breath as she helps me sit back up. I raise my hands in front of me. My knuckles are scraped raw, and one of my nails is cracked to the bed. It should hurt, but as strange as it sounds, I don't feel anything. Not even fear.

She whistles through her teeth. "You all right?"

"I'm fine," I lie through a mouthful of copper pennies. My finger is bleeding, but aside from that, nothing seems damaged.

"You're no such thing, girl."

I turn back toward the rise. So high. So, *so* high.

"What are you doing?" she demands.

"Can you give me another leg up?" The danger. The cops. Even the sound fades as I measure the distance to the top. Everything inside of me is screaming that I have to get there. I have to see what's happening on the other side of those trees.

Rowena crosses her arms. It takes all my resolve to keep my voice steady. "My family is in Fort Glory, Rowena." I raise my chin. "If something is happening in the town, I'm going to find out what it is. With or without your help."

"Try not to get yourself killed," Rowena grunts as she bends down to give me another boost.

I start to climb again. Adrenaline floods my veins. The ground is less than three feet below, but it might as well be thirty. The muscles in my legs are shaking. Sweat beads on my brow. Soon, I'm back to where I was when I fell. The next step feels impossible. I close my eyes and picture Charlie's face, streaked with blood and tears and focused on the egg in his hand. I reach up again.

My whole body is thrumming when I finally reach the narrow ledge tucked into the side of the rise. I get my arms over the top before my muscles give out. For a moment, I hang there with my lower body dangling. Unable to move, I catch my breath and stare across the stone at the blue marble sky. Only then do I see the specks littering the clouds, tiny dots of gray that seem to be growing larger by the second. I think they're birds until I realize.

Birds don't move like that.

First there are three. Then three become ten. Then twenty, until the sky is full of metal.

I grip the ledge as dozens of helicopters fall from the sky like clumps of silver fruit. The air is alive with the whirl of blades, a mechanical thunder that sets the rock trembling beneath me. I press myself flat against the side of the wall, a fleck of pink on gray. The swarm passes overhead, so close I can feel the air rush over me in its wake.

"Rose! Are you all right? Rose, what do you see?"

I gaze over the ledge, across the treetops toward Fort Glory, and then I forget all about pink pamphlets and the police and the fifteen-foot drop below me, because I can't understand what I'm seeing. Because it is impossible.

I open my mouth, but there are no words. There are only people. My mother at work in a diner that should be right beyond that bend, her hair pulled back and her scent like a meadow. Charlie. His smile that makes the world a wonderful place. His hand in mine and the egg in my apron pocket.

"It's not there."

"What?" Rowena demands. "The DARC?"

"The town," I say, as if by voicing the thing in front of me, I could somehow understand it. "The town is gone."

FIVE

Nothing.

That's what I see when I look over Fort Glory. No buildings. No cars. Even the steeple of the town church has been uprooted from the horizon.

I blink, but the scene in front of me doesn't change. The forest stays a solid blanket of green stretching all the way to the sea. Ridges and valleys that should be dotted with houses and crisscrossed by streets sit untouched by anything but the pale evening haze.

Fort Glory is gone. Every house. Every sign. Every marker has vanished, leaving behind only forest where the town once stood.

Time slows to a crawl as I stare at the empty valley. The swarm of circling helicopters. I don't know how long I hang there before Rowena's voice cuts through the wind tunnel inside my head.

I look down. Mistake.

The ground swims fifteen feet below me.

Down. I have to get down.

My muscles go rigid. My fingers grip the rock hard enough to break skin. The world is spinning around me like a carnival ride, and the only way to make it stop is to get my feet back onto solid ground.

I'm halfway there when my left toe slips out of its crevice. My knee scrapes the wall, and then I'm falling again. I open my mouth to scream, but the scream never comes.

The picture cuts to black.

My vision returns along with a pain that nails me to the ground. I'm lying on my back. Rowena hovers over me, her mouth moving with distant echoes. She's saying something over and over. It takes me a moment to recognize the sound of my own name.

Even with her help, it's a while before I can sit up.

Rowena's gaze rakes my body before snagging on something down low. "Sweet merciful mother."

I follow her gaze down to my legs and immediately wish I hadn't. The skin of my left knee. It's fluttering like a torn book page.

The forest tilts. I dig my fingers into my thighs like that could stop the world from spinning.

I close my eyes, but the images are still there. An overgrowth of trees where there was a town. A little boy in a green hoodie and orange backpack. A woman whose voice used to sing me to sleep.

Gone.

When I try to speak, my throat closes around their names.

Rowena pushes my head between my knees as I swallow mouthfuls of air that don't reach my lungs. I can't stop picturing Charlie the way he looked waving goodbye outside our trailer. I should've cleaned his cut before I left. I should've gone inside to make sure he was okay.

I should've ... I should've ... I should've ...

A soft sigh echoes through the forest as it starts to rain. Drops splatter my cheeks and roll down my shins to my bloodstained sock. Within moments, my clothes are plastered to my skin, but it's like I'm hovering above my body, unable to feel the cold, or the cuts, or the bruises already forming. The numbness is a shield. If I could just lie down and close my eyes, I could pretend that none of this is happening.

Then Rowena is there, anchoring me to reality with a metal flask in my face. Fumes rise from the bottle.

"What is it?" I ask.

"Drink first. Questions later."

The liquor hits my throat with a raw burn. I cough, but some of the stuff goes down. Warmth spreads through my insides.

"Good girl." Rowena claps me on the back. She hands me my apron, and numbly, I put it on as a flimsy barrier against the cold. And then she's right there in my face, her boozy breath searing my cheek. "What is it, girl? What did you see?"

"It was ... There was ... *nothing.*" My head is buzzing with the alcohol and a thousand thoughts competing for attention.

"What do you mean, nothing?"

"I mean the town's been wiped out."

"Like by a *bomb?*"

"No. Like it never existed." A gaping hole opens up inside of me. It's getting dark, and Charlie doesn't like to fall asleep alone, and I still need to cut his hair for school tomorrow.

Rowena stares unblinking at Devil's Tooth. The expression on her face deepens every wrinkle. "That's it, then. They've finally done it."

Her words take me back in time. To the reporter asking

questions in the diner. To Rowena's strange warnings, and the fear in Blaine's voice when he told me something was wrong with the town. Everything about this morning looks different now. Important in a way I don't yet fully understand.

"What? Done what? Rowena, *please*." I reach out and clasp the fabric of her jeans.

"I don't know." Her hands tremble as she sits down across from me. "God help us all, I don't know."

I take in Rowena's rat's nest of platinum curls. Her tie-dye T-shirt and purple scrunchie. "This isn't possible," I say. The fall must've shaken me up worse than I thought. Or maybe that horrible sound wave back in Maple short-circuited my brain. Either way, I imagined what I saw up there. It's the only explanation. The town isn't gone. It can't be. "Towns don't just disappear."

But the road did. It was there and then it wasn't, and I wasn't the only one who saw it.

"Everything's impossible till it happens." Rowena takes a swig and studies me over the flask. "Go on. Doubt my sanity. But what about your own two eyes? You gonna doubt them, too?"

I dig the heels of my palms into my temples. I shouldn't be here. I need to head back before I get into trouble with the cops. I need to find another way into town before Charlie and Mom wonder where I am.

"I have to go."

Rowena grabs my arm. "I'm not an idiot. I know what people say. They call me batshit, and they tear down my pamphlets, and they cross the street when they see me coming. But I speak the truth, and it ain't my fault if you don't like it." Her grip on me tightens. "Those men at the DARC have been chippin' away at something. Unleashing darkness into Fort Glory little by little. I can't explain it, but I can *feel* it. Ringing in my bones. I've been screaming warnings from the rooftops, but I might as well've been pissin' into the wind, for all the good it's done. Now the dark is here, and it's too damn late."

I'll be here. Soon. The dark is coming, and I don't want to be alone.

No. I refuse to accept that the town is gone. That would be like giving up on my family, and I can't do that. Not ever. I have to believe they're okay. I have to believe I would've felt it if something had happened to Charlie. The way I felt it when he broke his arm in first grade. Like his pain was my pain. The same way I knew something was wrong when I found his backpack sitting on the curb this afternoon.

Because Charlie and I are connected, and if he ever left, he'd take the best part of me with him.

Sobs rise in my throat. I choke them back and thrust them behind the wall inside of me along with all the other feelings that want to overwhelm me. There will be a time to fall apart, but right now, what I need are answers.

"The sound wave," I begin. "Did you hear it?" When Rowena nods, I pull my legs in close to my chest. "It did something to my head, Rowena. Knocked a few wires loose or caused me to hallucinate . . . or *something.*"

"It was the same out on the road. Most folks were confused. Dazed-like. Others turned ugly. Good people who wouldn't normally lift a hand to harm their neighbor. There was something wrong with 'em. Right here." She waves a sun-spotted hand over her eyes. "It was almost like—" She freezes. "Like the devil music in the air had worked its way under their skin."

Can you hear the music, Rosie?

It's what Charlie asked me. Three weeks ago. When all of

the problems started in Fort Glory. When he told me we had to come here.

When the DARC went back online.

A dozen images flash through my mind. The man on the ridge and those boys at the school. The woman at the store window and a pack of dogs turned rabid. The doubt on Blaine's face when he told me the problems in town had nothing to do with the DARC.

"The DARC," I say. "What were they doing with it?"

Rowena scowls. "Couldn't get anybody to give me a straight answer." Pale green eyes take my measure. "We've got to be careful. If this thing is messin' with people's minds we can't trust no one. It means we've got to question everything we see and feel because our own heads might be playing tricks—"

Footsteps sound in the woods behind us. The young policeman from the road stumbles out of the trees. There's another officer with him—older and significantly larger around the middle. His beady eyes dart anxiously about as he follows his young partner into the clearing.

Relief flashes across the younger man's face when he spots us at the base of Devil's Tooth. "You there! Come this way!"

Rowena's mouth hardens as she watches the officers approach.

"The girl's injured. She ain't going nowhere till I've bandaged her up." Rowena retrieves a handkerchief from her pocket. She douses the rag with alcohol and wraps it firmly around my knee. The pain is instant and searing. It helps to clear my head.

The young officer kneels beside me. In an unexpected act of kindness, he places his heavy police jacket over my shaking shoulders. "What happened, miss?"

I train my eyes on the name stitched across the breast pocket: *DEPUTY MILLER*. "I fell."

Silence. When I look up, both Deputy Miller and his partner are fixated on Devil's Tooth.

"Did you see it from up there? The town?"

Deputy Miller's question is so loaded, I half expect it to blow up in my face. I pull the jacket tighter around myself while I decide how best to answer. If I tell them the truth, they'll think I'm crazy, or they'll assume I'm lying. People never believe nobodies like me. It's a lesson I learned the hard way from watching my mother. But if I make something up, there's a good chance Rowena will call me out on it. Either way, they'll bring me in. Ask for identification.

That's one door I can't open.

Deputy Miller's partner breaks his silence. "Tell us what you saw, or you'll be charged with obstruction." His voice matches his body. Big. Deep. At odds with his fear. It sits over the moment like an exclamation point, and it makes me sure of one thing.

These men know something. If they didn't, they wouldn't be here.

"The town is gone." The officers exchange a glance that contains several emotions. Surprise isn't one of them. "You know," I realize. "You know about the town."

Deputy Miller runs a hand through his blond hair. "There are hundreds of reports coming in. We don't have a full picture yet. Probably won't until the National Guard shows up."

The pain in my knee fades to a distant memory as I pull myself up. Rowena's skinny arm wraps around me for support. The deputy's words make no sense to me. Towns don't disappear without a trace. It's not possible, and yet I *saw* it. But if the town disappeared, where did it go?

If Fort Glory is gone, where is my family?

"What about the people?" I reach for Deputy Miller without thinking. His shirt is starchy in my fist. "Whatever happened to the town, those people need help. We have to *do* something."

Gently, Deputy Miller releases my hands from their death grip on his collar. "The choppers have been running flybys since the first reports came in. They would've detected if there were any signs of l—" He backtracks clumsily. "I'm sorry. There's nobody left to help."

Nobody left.

Nobody. Left.

His words knock the breath out of me. I reach out for something to steady myself, and Rowena is there. Her fingers lock around mine. An anchor. A reminder. That we can't trust these officers.

We can't even trust our eyes.

I return her grip full force and straighten to face the deputy. "You *can't* know that. Don't you see? The DARC set something free. It's been playing with people's minds for weeks. It could be messing with the sensors too. We won't know if there's anybody left unless we go and *check*. Tell them, Rowena!"

"The girl's a whack job," the big officer says. "Just like the old lady."

"And you're as ugly as a fence post and twice as dumb, Kyle Jensen." The contempt in Rowena's voice suggests this isn't their first run-in.

"Watch your tongue, old woman. Or you might lose it." A familiar darkness glitters in Jensen's eyes. It sends me back a step.

"Jensen!" Deputy Miller's shock echoes through the forest. "What the hell has gotten into you?"

Rowena opens her mouth, but I clutch her arm tightly. I jerk my chin toward Jensen and watch understanding dawn across her face.

Something *has* gotten into Officer Jensen. Just like it did those people back in Maple.

Right before they almost torched the place.

Deputy Miller steps toward me. My senses shut down one by one until there is only Need. The need to find my mother and brother. The need to make this right. It is driving everything now, including my feet as they take several steps backward.

"We don't have time for this." Jensen reaches for his belt.

"Put that thing away, or I'll shove it where the sun don't shine," Rowena growls when he points the Taser at me.

"Stand down, Jensen." Deputy Miller places his body directly between us. "I said back the hell off! I've got it covered."

Jensen doesn't make another move toward me, but he doesn't put the Taser away, either. He just watches me over the deputy's shoulder with eyes that grow more dilated by the second.

A bubble of static forms around my head. The hairs on the back of my neck bristle in response to some subtle shift around us.

Deputy Miller reaches for me. "Wait." I pull free of his grip. "Do you hear that?"

"What are you—" His eyes widen.

The birds, the wind, even the distant sound of the ocean have gone missing, and the result is a silence so loud it echoes.

Rowena scans the woods behind Devil's Tooth. "Something ain't right."

A breeze stirs, several degrees warmer than the chilly November air. The smell is sharp and faintly chemical. Like chlorine, but harsher. It lifts the rain-dampened curls from my face. Other than the slight wind, the air is the kind of quiet that has you searching the sky for lightning.

Music whispers through the trees behind Devil's Tooth. At first, it sounds like a hundred voices singing over each other, but soon I realize it's only one, playing over and over.

The whisper-music finds me again. This time, it touches something deep inside of me. My body strains toward it with almost physical force. The magnetic pull draws me forward. One step. Then another.

The voice. I know that voice.

I'd know it anywhere.

"Charlie." His name comes out like a prayer. "Oh my God, Rowena." I meet her gaze. "That's Charlie. I hear him." I try to pull away, but Deputy Miller has me in a death grip. "Let go!" I scream.

The deputy drags me backward. Away from Fort Glory. Away from Charlie.

The tightness in my chest becomes painful. My muscles contract like they're trying to reach through my skin to grasp the sound of Charlie's voice.

Deputy Miller offers me an apologetic grimace as his arms reach around my waist. Instinct takes over. My fist smashes into his face.

The deputy stumbles backward. Frozen, I watch the blood drip from his nose onto the collar of his shirt. He straightens to his full height, and suddenly, my aching hand and busted knee are the least of my problems.

The deputy is six feet tall and armed. Now he's also pissed. Hysteria claws its way up my throat. All those years I spent following the rules. All that time I wasted watching my every move.

Gone in a second.

Rowena makes a warning sound. I look up just as Jensen lunges. My back hits the side of Devil's Tooth, and the hissing end of his Taser sails past my ear.

Jensen's lips twist in a snarl. He closes in again, and this time it isn't a Taser in his hand.

It's a gun.

My legs lock at the sight of the weapon. My insides run with liquid fear. He's almost on top of me when someone steps between us.

"Go. Find your brother." Rowena doesn't look at me as she squares off against a man twice her size armed with nothing but a scowl. "I said run, girl!"

I don't make her say it twice. I take off at a dead sprint. A muffled thud echoes behind me. I block it out and run toward the sound of my brother's voice. With every step I take, the tightness in my chest grows stronger.

A narrow path opens up in front of me. It veers hard left. The forest beyond Devil's Tooth is a maze of wood, leaf, and stone. Ferns clog the patches of earth between giant Douglas firs. Their boughs reach for each other hundreds of feet above my head.

Footsteps pound the ground behind me. Over my shoulder, I glimpse Deputy Miller's face, bloody and determined. My lead dwindles with every one of his strides.

I've made it another few steps when the stink of ozone hits me. So sharp it cuts my lungs with every breath. What is it coming from? Where's Charlie? I could've sworn he was somewhere up ahead, but now my chest is on fire, and my head feels like it's stuffed with cotton. My thoughts jumble together until there's only one thing I'm sure of anymore.

I have to keep running.

Branches break right behind me. A hand brushes my dress just as a warm wind rises up around me. A shrill whistle pierces my ears. The same whistling I heard in Maple right before all hell broke loose. Only this time it isn't coming from the sky.

It's coming from deep inside my head.

There's a sound like a bedsheet tearing in half as the world is ripped out from under me. The forest rushes past in a blur of Light. Color. Sound. A scream is yanked from my lips as I'm wrenched sideways by the hook in my chest. A hook made of fire. It rearranges my insides and drags me down an invisible line into the dark.

Pain. Pressure. So much pressure. It breaks me down until I am nothing but millions of cells. Millions of thoughts, searching for the right way to come back together.

The last thing I remember before the darkness takes me is a burning flash of gold and the sound of Charlie's voice, calling out my name.

SIX

CHARLIE

Black.
Not a color.
A place.
Dark ocean of music
roaring behind walls of the world
no one saw
but I could.
I know this place.
The secret it's hiding.
Even here in the dark
I am not alone.
So I wait. I watch. When it comes, I am ready.
Twisting, shimmering. Golden thread winds through the shadows,
running through me like a river. On that river is a song.
Charlie, *it sings to me.*
Charlie, where are you?
That voice.
Once upon a time it read the words and the words were magic. They
belonged to her and she belonged to . . .
ME.
I

I AM someone, somewhere once upon a time she read the words and the
words were Color . . .

> *Green fields.*

>> *Yellow sunflowers.*

>>> *White apron over a Pink dress.*

>>>> *Silver rabbit and a bag of stale*

>>>> *Brown bread.*

Once upon a time she read the words and the words were
Music . . .

Wind-chime laughs

Strangling songs

Quiet prayers in the dark when she thought you were sleeping.

I remember.

I. Remember.

Slowly, slowly the thread glows brighter.

The Black Nothing moves.

It needs the memories in my head. The songs in my ears. My eyes that
have seen Light.

I whisper, Not yet, *and I give it what it came for.*

An eye filled with colors

of the sky set on fire

spilling light through the leaves

dancing shadows across her face.

When the hurting's over, I wind the thread around my hands until it
burns.

I pull it.

Find me.

I need you to find me.

Remember.

I need you to remember.

The Black Nothing is quiet. It has my eye. For now, it's enough.

I don't mind.

The dark doesn't scare me.

And I've never needed eyes to see.

SEVEN

A wall of darkness stretches out in front of me.

Behind it, Charlie hangs suspended. The only bright spot in a world of solid black.

Light shines from somewhere deep inside of him, making him glow like a candle flame.

We reach for each other, but our hands can't push through the barrier between us. It comes alive. Separating into a thousand ribbons of shadow that slither around Charlie's head. He doesn't raise his arms. He doesn't even try to protect himself.

No. That has always been my job.

A vise closes around my throat as I watch the strands of shadow wind tighter until their darkness is strangling him. When they strike his face, I can't do anything.

I can't even scream.

Searing pain rips me out of the nightmare.

My eye. It's on *fire*.

Agony slices through me. I moan and curl in on my side. My hands lift to my right eye.

It's gone. Torn out by the roots. That's the only thing that could hurt this bad.

I brace myself for a gruesome discovery, but there's nothing. Just feathery lashes and the smooth skin of my eyelid.

The relief lasts only until the next wave of pain hits. For a moment, I can't concentrate on anything else. I just lie there in the dirt and focus on breathing. In. Out. In. Out.

Slowly, the burning fades to a lingering ache in my right eye socket.

Minutes pass. I'm afraid to open my eyes. If I can't see, how will I drive? How will I work? If something happens to me, who will take care of my family?

My family.

I sit up so fast, my head splits. With a groan, I drop down and press my cheek to the cool earth. A dozen sensations find me in the silence.

The musk of evergreen and moss.

The clammy press of cotton against my skin.

The hoot of an owl.

My eyes open to total darkness. Slowly, the blackness fades to a hundred shades of blue and gray, revealing the texture and contour of dense forest. Everything comes back to me at once. The weird sound wave. The missing road. Devil's Tooth. The town.

Oh God. The town.

I'm lying at the base of a massive tree. There's a small break in the canopy above, giving me a direct view of a blue velvet sky, studded with diamond stars and streaked with the first hint of dawn.

Dawn?

This time, I manage to sit up. Nerves twitch in my weak eye. Between the dim glow of fading stars and promise of daybreak, I can make out just enough about this place to know I've never been here before. The last thing I remember is running from

Deputy Miller and the odd sensation of being yanked sideways by my chest. Did the deputy hurt me? Did something happen to my eye when I fell? Either way, what am I doing in the middle of the woods? Why aren't I locked up in some cell for punching a cop?

I punched a cop.

I pull the deputy's jacket down over my thighs, and another pain shoots through me. This one from my leg. Rowena's bandanna has slipped down to my ankle. My knee looks like a piece of tattered cloth stretched over hamburger meat. The sight turns my stomach, but for lack of a better option, I grit my teeth and retie the dirty rag.

Purple and pink threads wind their way through the scraps of sky between branches. I'd guess it's around six in the morning. I don't remember spending the night out here, or what happened before I passed out. All I know is that it's been at least thirteen hours since I left Charlie standing outside of our trailer.

Every second that passes is starting to feel like an opportunity I'll never get back.

The wind skates over me with icy fingers. I should pick myself up. I should move, but there's a gaping crater in my chest where Charlie and Mom are supposed to be. I wrap my arms around myself, and it's like I'm one of the paper snowflakes Charlie and I make every Christmas. Insubstantial. Full of holes.

Deputy Miller said the town was gone. He insisted there were no survivors, but what about the voice? I know my brother's voice the way I know my mother's laugh. The way I know my father's plans. It was Charlie. He's still out here somewhere. In these woods. Probably hiding out with Mom. The only thing that matters now is finding them, and to do that, I have to get up.

I struggle to my feet. The ache in my eye has tears streaming down my face. I lean against the trunk and call up the map of Oregon in my mind—the one tacked to the wall over the bed Mom and I share. I've been reading maps for her since I was old enough to sit in the front seat. Looking at them has always made me feel peaceful, and I could use some of that peace right now. Like my dad's blueprints, maps are easy. They don't keep secrets or tell lies. There are no unsolved mysteries. Every line has a meaning. Every question has an answer. You just have to find it.

West. I need to keep the sunrise behind me and head west. Eventually, I'll hit the ocean and then it'll be a simple matter of following the coastline north into town.

Dawn wakes the birds and gives the canopy a silver sheen. The air is pregnant with moisture that cuts right through my bones.

I've been walking for maybe two hours when a soft tinkling reaches my ears.

I follow the sound of running water to a small brook in the forest floor. I slip and slide my way down to the bank and lean out over the stream, getting my first look at myself since I left the Hands for Hearths office yesterday afternoon.

Dirt is streaked across my cheek, which has turned an ugly shade of purple. Scratches cover my neck and arms, but those barely register.

My eye. It looks completely normal. It isn't even red.

My legs go wobbly. I sink down at the edge of the stream, right next to a large boulder. I reach out and cup the cold, clear liquid in my hands. I'm on my third mouthful when a flash of color draws my gaze across the stream.

Twenty yards away, a bit of yellow rope lies abandoned on

the opposite bank. The line runs from the sand, up the slight incline, and over the top of the crest to—a hand. There's a hand hanging over the ledge.

The instinct to flee is almost overpowering. I force myself to ignore it. Running now will only attract attention, and there's a good chance whoever's up there hasn't spotted me yet.

Quietly, I pull on the deputy's jacket and slide behind the boulder, where I wait for the thud of approaching footsteps. The only sounds are the soft hiss of disbanding mist and the gurgle of water. I risk another peek around the boulder. The arm is in the same position, hanging lifelessly over the edge.

It's probably another police officer or one of the National Guardsmen who were supposed to show up yesterday. But what if it's not? What if it's someone else? Someone who needs help?

What if it's Charlie?

I'm across the stream in two seconds flat. Rocks and sharp roots cut into my hands as I scramble up the gentle incline to the giant Douglas fir sitting on top of the ledge. I look around the trunk.

He's lying facedown in the dirt.

Not my brother. A stranger.

My knees go weak. Disappointment. Relief. It all blurs together as I sink down beside the fallen hiker.

Yellow rope runs from his hand, down the long line of his body, back up into the branches of the tree I'm using for cover. A few yards to my left, a gray jacket lies neatly folded on a crag pack.

I let out a breath and shake one muscular shoulder. "Hello?" When he doesn't stir, I ease off his ball cap. Initials are written into the fabric, drenched in blood and so faded, I can hardly make them out.

W. E.?

W. L.?

I drop the cap and focus on the guy wearing it. Dark hair is buzzed short, giving me a good view of the nasty lump on the back of his head.

I check his pulse. Strong and steady. Relief echoes through me for a second before reality sinks in. My small bag of first-aid tricks is no match for a major concussion. He needs help. The kind they provide in the ER. To get him that help I'd have to go back to the road, and that is *not* an option.

My shoulders droop. There's nothing I can do other than leave him here and hope that he wakes up, or that somebody else finds him just like I did.

I'm returning the hand to his side when my chest muscles contract and spasm. Something tugs at my insides, and for one terrifying moment, I feel it happening again. The thing that happened when I was running toward the sound of Charlie's voice behind Devil's Tooth. I brace myself for the hook of fire, the searing pain in my chest, but the sensation of being yanked sideways doesn't come. There's just a soft, steady pressure that's uncomfortable without being painful.

My hands press flat to my chest. The muscles are relaxed—*normal*. It's like the thing with my eye. Only different, because this doesn't make me feel someone has cut out a piece of me. It's more of a pull than a pain. And unlike the agony in my eye, this feeling doesn't fade. If anything, the tug grows stronger until it's impossible to ignore. It makes me feel like a balloon on the end of a string, or a sweater with a loose thread that's being gently tugged by... what?

My knees hit the ground beside the fallen hiker as I realize what this means.

The pain in my eye. The tug in my chest. I'm hallucinating. It could be a lingering effect of my fall from Devil's Tooth. Then again, it could have something to do with whatever they set loose with the DARC.

A force that was turning regular people into psychopaths before the town disappeared.

Fear is a sour taste in my mouth as I look down at the fallen hiker. Soon these woods will be swarming with men trying to figure out what happened to Fort Glory. I need to be long gone before that happens. My family is counting on me, and this guy is a complete stranger, and whatever happened to him, it's really none of my business.

Then whose business is it, Rosie?

Charlie's voice hits me with a tidal wave of memory. It has four years rewinding in my head until I'm back on the side of a lonely Kansas road.

I remember it was evening. I'd been cruising down the highway for hours with no food, no license, and no real idea of where we were headed. I just knew we had to get away from the monster who'd left bruises on my mother. Bruises that spread like the shadows around us.

A rabbit darted across the road. I swerved, but with a few thousand pounds of trailer behind me and Rusty's crap brakes, there was no avoiding it. When I pulled over, the rabbit was dragging its broken legs across the highway.

Charlie hopped out of the truck and carried the dying animal to the side of a sunflower field.

I collapsed on the ground next to Charlie, and the horrors of the last several hours caught up to me. I couldn't get the image out of my head. My mother curled up on the floor. The marks on her body didn't worry me nearly as much as the way she was lying there. Like the animal in Charlie's arms, she was wounded but still breathing. Unlike the rabbit, there was no fight left in her.

My hands clenched into fists. I couldn't stop what happened to my mother any more than I could've avoided hitting that poor animal. But I could make damn sure it never happened again. I would just have to become better, smarter, more capable. Strong enough to fill the shoes Dad left behind, and that meant I had to start doing a lot of things I didn't like.

Teeth gritted, I went back to the trailer for the box above the closet where we kept the last of Dad's things. My hands closed around his old pistol before letting it go in favor of something more subtle.

"Let me have it, Charlie."

Charlie's eyes moved from the dying animal in his hands to the knife in mine.

"It isn't time," he said.

"It's suffering." I meant the words to be gentle. Fear and anger turned them hard. *"Nothing should have to suffer like this."*

We both knew I wasn't talking about the rabbit.

When I'd gone into the trailer, Mom was still lying in the same position. It had been more than sixteen hours since she'd locked us in the bathroom. Fourteen hours since the monster left to buy more booze. Thirteen hours and twenty-seven minutes since I'd wiped the blood off my mother's face, hitched up the trailer, and hit the highway, my eyes anxiously scanning the rearview for the glare of chasing headlights.

"Pain is part of life, Rosie."

I blinked, and my brother was there, one finger gently stroking the creature's matted fur.

"Why?" My voice broke. I spackled it back together. *"Why does it have to be?"*

"Because there is beauty in it, Rosie. If you know where to look."

Charlie held the rabbit, and I cried on the side of that Kansas road. The sun set, cars passed, night came, and still, we stayed. Until my tears dried up, and the rabbit stopped breathing, and we'd buried its mangled body in the hard dirt next to those sunflowers.

I don't remember how long it took, but I remember climbing back into the driver's seat with a new resolve. I wouldn't let our circumstances make us easy targets anymore. Not when asking for help was the same as begging for punishment, and we had had *enough*. I would just have to learn to do anything, *become* anything I had to become to ensure that this never happened again. So I made my promises, and started the engine, and I never looked back again.

Until now.

A switch flips inside of me as I zero in on the man lying on the ground. I don't know what happened to the town, or what's going on with my body, or even if I'm losing my mind. But I know one thing for sure.

Charlie wouldn't leave a rabbit to die alone on the side of the road. He would never forgive me for abandoning a stranger like this.

Carefully, I reach under the hiker's rib cage. It's like trying to move a mountain. The guy is six feet plus of solid muscle. He's also strapped into one of those harnesses rock climbers wear.

All my earlier intentions of gentleness fly out the window. I straddle his hips for leverage, grab one powerful shoulder, and heave.

EIGHT

My eyes lock on the familiar face below me. The shock lasts for less than a second before necessity takes over. Later. I can worry about what Ian Lawson is doing here later. Right now, I have bigger problems.

I reach for Ian's pack and stagger under its weight. The thing is loaded. In the side pocket, my fingers close around something round and hard. I pull it out.

Every bit of blood in my body goes straight to my head.

The compass in my hand is a silver antique with a vintage glass face. I turn it over, already knowing what I'll find. Delicate lines are etched into the tarnished silver, forming an elaborate pattern.

Charlie gave me this compass last December for my seventeenth birthday. He never told me where he got the money, and I never asked because the gift was strange and beautiful, just like him.

How did Ian get this? The compass lives in a tin box, locked away in Rusty's dash. Ian must've taken it, but when? And why? It's not worth much. What possible reason could he have to steal it? Unless he didn't steal it. Unless . . .

Charlie gave it to him.

If Ian saw Charlie out here after the town disappeared, he

might be able to tell me things. Like if Charlie was okay, or if Mom was with him, or even which direction they were headed.

In order to ask him, I'm going to have to stick around long enough for him to wake up.

Eager to speed up the process, I drop the compass into my pocket and keep rummaging through his pack for first aid. Gray light sifts through the trees over my shoulder as I finish cleaning him up. The odd angle of the rays trips an internal alarm. I bolt to my feet.

This isn't right. It can't be past noon, but already the sun is hanging low behind the trees. Judging by the lengthening shadows, it'll be dark within the hour. Somehow, I've lost half a day.

A cold wind rushes over the gorge, whipping my hair across my face. A fresh crop of gooseflesh sprouts across my skin. It isn't just the missing hours, or Fort Glory's disappearance, or the fact that I'm seeing things. By my calculations, this spot can't be more than a few miles from the road. Where are the media choppers and the National Guard? Where are all the people trying to figure out what happened to Fort Glory?

This quiet is wrong. Even if I weren't planning to hang around and grill Ian about the compass, walking through this forest in the dark feels like a really bad idea.

Focus. I have to focus on the problems I can fix.

I dump the rest of the pack on the off chance Ian's managed to fit one of those mini tents along with half of REI. My search turns up a reflective silver tarp.

I lean over Ian's body and study him like I've wanted to do since he first walked into the diner a week ago. It's impossible not to stare. Scars or no scars, the boy is beautiful. Not in the same way Mom or Charlie are. Ian's beauty is more rugged. Back at the diner, I would've put him at nineteen, but this close, there's a vulnerability about him that is almost boyish.

Who am I kidding? Ian is two hundred pounds of lean muscle with a violent criminal record. Compass or no compass, the smart thing to do would be to give him a wide berth.

The tugging in my chest returns full force.

My shoulders droop. If I walk away now, I won't be able to face myself in the mirror or look my brother in the eye when I finally find him.

More important, I'd be blowing my best lead.

An hour later, it's full dark. The tarp is draped over two boulders, anchored with some rope and half a dozen silver clips I found in Ian's pack. Every muscle in my body aches, but on the bright side, the pain in my eye is a distant memory.

All I want to do is collapse, but I assemble a pile of kindling near the opening of our shelter. It takes me three tries before one of the matches finally catches.

I'm gathering the strength to drag Ian under the tarp when a shadow moves in my peripheral vision.

I swing around.

Nothing. Just an endless parade of tree silhouettes.

The blackness to my left stirs again. I inch sideways to keep the invisible threat in front of me. For a second, I wonder if I'm seeing things—if this is like the strange tugging in my chest or the phantom pain in my eye. Not a chance. The woods are too quiet. Even the insects have swallowed their songs. It's out there. Some hidden danger. I can *feel* it. Circling me in the dark.

My trembling hands close around a scraggly branch with a few leaves still clinging to the end. I grip it in my fist. I wait.

There! Two eyes gleam in the shadows. A creature steps out of the trees.

I recognize the bobcat from the descriptions in my guidebooks. The animal isn't huge, but it flashes a set of impressive teeth. The cat slinks toward me, ears pressed back. The guidebook said that bobcats are shy and rarely attack humans, but this one isn't afraid of me or my pathetic excuse for a fire. Is it sick? Rabid?

My hands are shaking so badly, it's hard to keep hold of the branch.

The cat prowls close enough for me to glimpse the darkness glittering in its hazel eyes—the same darkness I saw in Officer Jensen and that dog back in Maple.

Right before it ate a man alive.

Ian groans. The bobcat zeroes in on him. A pink tongue darts out over gleaming teeth.

Every instinct in my body is screaming for me to *run* but my legs are cemented to the spot. Memories fill my head along with the sounds of my mother's cries. I've been here before—forced to choose between facing down a monster and leaving them to someone else.

Ian's eyes flutter open. They lock on mine, confused, searching, and suddenly, I'm trembling as much from anger as from fear.

Rage greets me like a long-lost friend. It floods my system with violence as I dip my stick into the flames. The leaves catch, forming a flimsy torch. Heat licks up the wood into my hands as I focus on the creature in front of me. If it kills Ian, it will take away any knowledge he has that might help me find my family.

I can't let that happen.

The cat growls again. This time, I growl back. I let it see the truth in my eyes. I've faced down worse and survived. Not by running, or hiding, or pretending it isn't happening. By fighting.

Ian stirs as I step over him, forming a barrier between him and the bobcat. The animal takes a test swipe with one paw. It knocks me backward, directly on top of Ian. The branch slips through my fingers as I roll to the side.

The bobcat is on Ian in a burst of deadly speed. Jaws flash as it bends over his throat. I watch it happen and another monster— the one I keep locked behind that wall inside of me—rattles in its cage.

A guttural scream leaves my lips as I grab the torch and stumble back to my feet. I lunge at the cat, swinging wildly. For the first time, the animal gives me its full attention. It prepares to spring, and I prepare to die, and then something happens that neither of us is prepared for.

The cat whines deep in its throat. A new hesitation enters its eyes as they meet mine over the burning end of my torch. Its hackles rise as it turns to stare into the darkness ahead, back arched and fur raised. Whatever it smells doesn't sit well, because the cat takes off through the trees.

The rage drains out of my body. I wilt to the ground next to Ian, who, thanks to my crushing him, is once again out cold.

The forest swims around me. My senses are reeling like I've taken a shot of Rowena's whiskey. All I want is to curl up in a ball and close my eyes, but something is headed this way. Something scary enough to send a deranged bobcat running. I'd rather not be waiting out in the open when it arrives.

By some small miracle, I manage to drag Ian into the shelter. His shoulders span the width of the space. Before, I was nervous at the thought of being so close to him. Now, his solid presence is strangely comforting.

Minutes pass. The woods outside fall back into silence. I think whatever's out there has passed us by when something moves outside.

A person. Streaking across the opening of our shelter.

Every hair on my body is instantly at attention.

I crouch closer to Ian, keeping my gaze on the opening. Logic says it could be Charlie out there, but my heart doesn't believe it. I'm about to call his name, just to be sure. A sound in the dark beats me to it.

Tap. Tap. Taptaptap.

Vibrations pass through the boulder, directly into me.

Tap. Tap. Taptaptap.

The blood freezes in my veins.

That exact pattern of knocks. It's the same one that's played in every one of my nightmares these past three years. The calling card of the monster my family gave up everything to escape.

When I close my eyes, I can still see the glare of headlights as he pulled up beside our trailer. Still count the thirteen seconds it took him to light his smoke and reach our door. That knock was his signature. The first warning that we were in for a bad night.

Tap. Tap. Taptaptap.

The stench of whiskey and cigarettes clogs my nostrils. I gag on the memories and curl into a ball. My rocking digs a shallow trench in the dirt.

Tap. Tap. Taptaptap.

I clap my hands over my ears. This can't be happening. It *can't* be. That monster isn't here, no matter what my senses want me to believe. We're out of his reach. I made sure of that.

Rowena warned me that this could happen. She said the dark force in the town would slowly poison my mind. Like the pain in my eye and the tugging I imagined earlier, this isn't real. It isn't real.

As if to prove me wrong, the tapping starts again.

Desperate for something to hold on to, I reach into the folds of my apron. Charlie's egg rolls into my palm. Solid. Warm. Such a fragile thing, but right now, it feels significant in a way I can't define.

They're just eggs. Nobody wants them.

I'll take one and you take the other. We can do it, Rosie. This. This is important, Rosie.

It's. Important.

More tapping from outside.

I huddle next to Ian and retreat deep inside myself—the only place left to go. A million memories dance through my head until I find one vivid enough to block out the nightmare outside. I focus in on the memory. My whole world collapses down to that day.

We had just moved to Illinois, which made Charlie five and me twelve. Mom had left me in a city park in the wealthiest part of town with three dollars and instructions to mind my brother. I'd felt grown up and hopeful, the way I always did when we tried on someplace new. The Midwestern wind was blowing hard, wafting the scent of candied almonds from a nearby vendor. My stomach grumbled, but then I saw how Charlie was staring at the ducks.

With our two-dollar bags of stale bread, we headed to the pond to feed the birds. I remember it was a cool, drizzly Saturday.

There were a few dancers performing on wet cardboard. I stopped to watch them. It was several minutes before I realized Charlie wasn't beside me. Panic turned the world razor-sharp as I pushed through groups of well-dressed strangers and screamed his name. When I finally spotted him sitting on a bench a few hundred yards away, I was so relieved, I didn't immediately notice the woman.

She was in her forties—practically ancient, and I don't remember a thing about her other than the bag. Dull paisley. She was clutching it to herself as if to stem a gaping wound in her chest. For a long time neither of them moved, and it was like the world was rushing by as the two of them held on to that bench for dear life. And even though I was a kid, I recognized something in their silence that was not meant for breaking. Slowly, quietly, Charlie reached out and pried her fingers from the frayed handles of her bag. He placed the stale bits of bread in her palm. The woman's shoulders shook, and I recognized the song of grief because I'd heard it playing once or twice through the thin walls of our trailer.

Her pain was an eyesore—a truth too uncomfortable to look at, so no one did. No one except Charlie. Birds sang, and people walked past, and my brother sat with a stranger on a park bench, tears rolling down the still slopes of his cheeks. I watched it happen, and for one moment, I swear my brother shone like a spear of light breaking through the clouds from a place that is better than this one. And I knew he was precious in a way that could never be measured, and that I could never lose him again.

I can never lose him.

Tears slide down my face when the memory fades. I'm still squatting in the dark, cold shelter next to an unmoving Ian. The noises are gone, but the weird tugging in my chest is back, along with a strange feeling of peace. It's almost like the thought of my brother's light alone is somehow enough to fend off the darkness.

Thank you, Charlie.

It's my last clear thought before I fall into an exhausted sleep.

NINE

*W*hat are you doing?" I asked you once. It was either too early or too late, but you were staring out the window into the blackness, your hands wrapped around your knees as you rocked back and forth to the music only you could hear.

"I'm listening."

"Listening to what?"

"The dark."

I climbed up onto the pullout couch because the wind was howling outside, and the heat didn't work. But mostly, because I'd realized long ago that the warmest place on earth was the space right beside you.

"Are you afraid of the dark?" I pressed my shoulder into yours.

You shook your head. "Without the dark, there are no stars, Rosie."

"Then what are you afraid of?" I asked.

"Forgetting."

I jerk awake. My first thought is that it's cold. My second thought is that it's not as cold as it should be.

Heat sears my side where it's pushed up against something hard. I turn over. Directly into Ian's chest.

I scramble into a sitting position. Ian is lying so still, I have to place my palm over his mouth to assure myself he's actually breathing. A callused hand shoots out to grab my wrist, and suddenly, I'm looking down into a pair of starburst eyes.

Ian sits up. The sleeping bag slips down his torso to pool around his waist. And then it's just me and him in a few square feet of claustrophobia.

When I lean back, Ian's grip on me tightens. The wildness in his eyes pins me right to the boulder at my back.

"Let go," I choke out. "You're hurting me."

Ian blinks once and releases me. The shirt strains across his chest as he raises a hand to his head.

I don't move. Don't even breathe. Ian looks twice as big sitting across from me as he did sprawled out on the ground. He's a criminal and he's huge and we're close. Way too close sitting like this. Too late, I realize he might not be in his right mind—that the dark force Rowena warned me about could've gotten to him like it did that bobcat or those people back in Maple. Like it's been trying to get to me.

If so, I just made the biggest mistake of my life.

I scoot sideways. I've almost reached the opening when Ian looks up. His eyes widen when they lock onto my face. He moves forward.

Dirt flies as I launch myself outside. I'm at the edge of the trees when a deep moan stops me in my tracks.

"Shit," Ian says, stopping on all fours in the shelter entrance.

I slip behind a tree and listen to him empty his stomach into the bushes. An unwelcome twinge of sympathy sneaks through my fear.

What am I thinking? Running off into these creepy woods with zero supplies and even less of an idea of where I'm going? Ian might've broken into my truck, but that makes him a thief.

Not a serial killer. Also, there's a chance Charlie gave him my compass *after* the town disappeared. Am I really going to blow my only lead because I'm afraid of some guy who can't even stand up without assistance?

The retching on the other side of the tree is replaced by a low groan. It makes up my mind for me. Ian couldn't hurt me right now even if he tried. He has supplies, and he had my compass, and even if he never crossed paths with Charlie, there's a chance he saw something that could help me find my family. Either way, I like my odds better here with him than out there in those woods with whatever's stalking me.

When I slip back around the tree, Ian is sitting against the boulder. Sweat glistens on his brow. Gathering my courage, I circle the campsite to where I stashed his canteen and place it on the ground in front of him.

I think he's passed out again, when his eyes pop open, hitting me like high beams in the moonlight. He reaches for the canteen.

"Thanks." Ian's voice is low and rich with just a touch of gravel. He rinses out his mouth with the first swallow before draining the rest.

"You've got a concussion and a nasty gash on your palm," I say to fill the silence. "The bandages are fine for now, but you'll need stitches." I wait for him to say something. He doesn't. "Do you remember what happened?" I ask at last.

"I fell."

It's the exact same non-answer I gave the deputy back at Devil's Tooth. Under any other circumstances, I might find that funny.

A deep line cuts across Ian's brow as he takes in our surroundings. It's easy to guess what he's thinking.

"The tree's up that way." I point in the vague direction of the stream.

"How'd I get here?"

"I dragged you."

Ian's gaze snaps back to mine. It lingers there for a second before his attention shifts to our camp. The improvised shelter and dying fire. The paw prints in the dirt.

"There was a bobcat." He says it like he's asking for backup. "It felt like a dream..."

"Not a dream. It's gone now. Something scared it off."

"What?"

"I'm not sure. I...I think there might be someone out here with us." Or we're completely alone, and I imagined the person just like I've imagined everything else. Not that this is the right time to get into it.

Ian studies me for a long moment.

"How'd it happen? The fall, I mean?" I ask to redirect his focus away from me. Ian's got the back and shoulders of a seasoned climber. His crag pack is the real deal too. Something must've gone seriously wrong for him to get hurt like that.

I have a sneaking suspicion I know what it was.

"I heard a sound. It was..." Ian rubs a palm over his face. "The clouds started racing across the sky. There was a crack of lightning."

I inch closer. "Then what?" From up in that tree, Ian might've had a view of town. If something happened at the DARC, he would've had a front-row seat.

Ian leans back against the boulder. "I don't remember."

My chest deflates. I slump down a safe distance away. "I was in Maple when the sound wave hit. People lost it. There was something wrong with them. You could see it. Right here." I point to my eyes and repress a shudder at the memories. "I was headed back to Fort Glory when I got stuck on the road."

Ian sits up and winces at the sudden movement. "How? Your battery fail?"

"Uh, no." A warning bell rings in the back of my mind. How does Ian know about Rusty's crappy battery? He also has a strange habit of turning up wherever I go. At the diner and the campground this morning. Then later at the high school. Now here in the woods with my compass in his bag. Rowena said she didn't believe in coincidences.

Well, neither do I.

"There was a problem. With the road," I hedge, while I decide how best to draw him out. "The cops were pushing us back. Rowena thought—"

"Rowena was with you? She's okay?" Ian's questions come rapid-fire. "She's my grandmother," he explains when I just stare at him.

The last time I saw Rowena she was facing down Officer Jensen so that I could get away. I decide to keep that particular piece of information to myself. "It was her idea to hike to Devil's Tooth. She wanted to see what was happening in the town. She was convinced that it had something to do with the DARC."

Ian's face gives nothing away. "Doesn't explain what you're doing here."

"When the police found us, they ordered us to evacuate." I hug Deputy Miller's jacket tighter around my knees.

"But you didn't?"

I shake my head. "I couldn't. Not after what I saw."

A slight pause. "What's that?"

Instinctively, I know the next few words will decide everything between us. If I tell Ian the truth, he may return the favor. Or he may decide I've lost my mind. It's a risk, but I picture Charlie kneeling on the side of that Kansas road, and I decide that it's a risk worth taking.

"The town is gone."

I wait for Ian to call me crazy. To hurl insults or insist that I'm a liar—like anybody else would in his place. Instead he just closes his eyes. "Yeah."

"You saw it?"

"I saw something over the town. Hiding it." He probes the bandages on the back of his head.

A weight I didn't know I was carrying slides off my shoulders. If Ian saw something from up in that tree, he might actually be able to help me. "Tell me."

His head falls back against the boulder. "I don't know how to describe it. Other than scary as hell."

It's a cop-out answer. Ian is hiding something. Not just whatever he saw up in that tree. I've been sure of it ever since he mentioned Rusty's battery. It's had me playing yesterday's events over and over inside my head, questioning every decision, second-guessing every turn that could have brought me anywhere other than here.

Rusty's miraculous recovery. The rust shavings on the asphalt. My compass in Ian's backpack. These are the things I keep coming back to.

"Did you fix my truck?" I ask.

Ian's silence is as good as an answer.

"Why?" I demand.

Ian rubs the back of his neck. "Because you looked like you could use a break."

"Try again."

An invisible current sparks the air between us. "Because your brother asked me to."

"Charlie? What—When?" I'm crawling toward Ian before I realize what I'm doing. One look from him stops me in my tracks.

"Yesterday morning. I was working on my car when he asked me to replace your battery. He said he needed it to run. That you were—" Ian shifts. "That it was important. It wasn't a big deal. The battery was easy to get. I did most of the work when you were in school."

This. This is important, Rosie.

Charlie knew. Somehow, Charlie knew what would happen to Fort Glory, and he made sure I'd be long gone when it did. If he hadn't asked for Ian's help, Rusty might've died before I could get out of town. I could've been lost with the rest of them.

But if Charlie knew, why did he want to come here in the first place? If Charlie knew, why didn't he try harder to save himself?

"You did all that for a stranger? Some kid you didn't even know?" My fingers find Charlie's egg in my jacket. My brother has a way of seeing right to the heart of a person. Of all the people in Fort Glory, he asked Ian for help. *Ian.*

There had to be a reason.

I take a deep breath, let go of the egg, and hold up my compass. "I found this in your bag."

Ian meets my gaze without a trace of guilt. "Your brother gave that to me."

"When?" I know what he's going to say before he says it, and still, the words are a blow.

"Yesterday morning. When he asked me to fix your car."

The truth settles on me like a weight. If Ian hasn't seen Charlie since yesterday morning, it means I've wasted all this time for nothing. I run my thumb over the beautiful etching one more time before I toss it over.

"Keep it." Ian tosses the compass right back. "I only took that because it seemed important to the kid."

My fingers close around tarnished metal. Why would Charlie give my compass to Ian? And why would Ian go out of his way to help us when, according to everyone, he's a violent lowlife? None of this makes sense, and I'm suddenly so damn tired of trying to figure it out.

"Your face."

"What?" The directness of Ian's gaze leaves me feeling strangely flustered. It's a minute before I realize what he's talking about. I touch the bruise on my cheek. "It's nothing."

"Doesn't look like nothing."

"Some kids at school were giving Charlie a hard time." I shrug. "It was an accident."

"You do that a lot?" Ian asks.

"Do what?"

"Fight other people's battles for them?"

I look at him sharply. "What were you doing out here before you fell?" He's not the only one who can ask personal questions.

"Getting the hell out of town before I suffocated."

I blink at him. Most people hide what they really mean under layers and layers of bullshit.

Clearly, Ian Lawson isn't most people.

"If you hate Fort Glory so much, why'd you come back?" I ask when my thoughts become too loud for the dragging silence between us.

"To say goodbye." Ian's hand moves to his head, almost like it's searching for something. Whatever he's looking for, he doesn't find it. His frown transforms into an expression of loss that hits me right in the chest.

Ian pushes to his feet, but it's too much, too fast. He drops down with a grunt.

I crawl past him into the shelter. By the time common sense catches up to me, I'm already standing right in front of him.

The second Ian sees the Mariners cap in my hands, the tension drains out of him. "Thank you."

Somehow, I know he's talking about more than just the hat. "You're welcome."

The silence stretches out between us. Ian rubs a hand across his jaw. "You shouldn't be out here alone. I'll take you back to the road in the morning."

"The road is gone." This time, I give him the truth without worrying how he'll take it. "Just like the town. Otherwise I'd be there already."

Ian grips the bill of his cap in his injured hand. "Where does it stop?"

It's hard to tell from his tone whether he believes me. Honestly, right now I don't care.

"Just after the turnoff to Fort Glory. Where that giant bill-board used to be. Now there's nothing but trees and every clown with a badge within a ten-mile radius."

"That's where I'll take you, then," Ian decides.

I bite my tongue to keep from snapping. Ian doesn't get it yet. But he will.

"I'm not going to the road. I'm going back to Fort Glory to find my family."

Ian pulls on his cap. "The thing I saw over the town. Storms I understand, but this...this wasn't natural. It was like a death funnel or a whirlpool in the sky straight out of your nightmares." He shakes his head like he can't believe what he's saying. "The town didn't stand a chance. Neither will you if you go back out there."

"You can't be sure of that," I insist. "Don't you see? The DARC unleashed something. A force that's been manipulating our minds for weeks. When I looked at the town from Devil's Tooth there was no monster storm. There was nothing but forest."

"So you're saying you saw one thing, I saw another, and we both can't be right," Ian concludes.

I nod, relieved he's getting this. "We don't know what's real and what's not. We won't know unless we go to Fort Glory and *check*."

"Whatever this is, it's over our heads," Ian says at last. "Let the authorities handle it."

His words burrow right under my skin, because I've been here before. When Dad went missing. I remember sitting next to Mom in an uncomfortable metal chair, trying to understand how the case officer could stand there, calmly drinking his coffee while my whole world was falling apart. The feeling I got back then was an awful lot like the feeling I had when I fell from the slide with Charlie in my arms. Or yesterday when I lost my grip on Devil's Tooth. Like I was headed for an impact and was powerless to stop it.

But I am not powerless now.

Charlie and Mom will be nothing more to the cops than two names on a long list. It's the way it is, but that doesn't mean I have to accept it. And I won't. Not this time.

"Is that what you would do if it was your family? Would you trust strangers to find them for you?"

Ian's expression softens. Or maybe it's just the shadows playing tricks on me. "I'm sorry. About your mom and brother."

His sympathy breaches the protective barriers I've built around myself. A little bit of truth seeps through. "I heard him," I say softly. "I heard Charlie calling to me in the woods behind Devil's Tooth. Right before something knocked me out." Without thinking, I press my fist against my chest, directly over the source of the strange tugging.

Suddenly, there's not enough air on the planet to ease the burning in my lungs.

"Is that what you believe, or is it what you want to believe?" Ian asks.

My stomach sinks because I know what he's driving at. Things are weird out here. Like the tugging and the pain in my eye, there's a distinct possibility Charlie's voice was a figment of my imagination. Only I don't believe it. I can't.

"It doesn't matter. There's still a chance he's out here somewhere, and I'm not leaving until I find him."

Even as I say the words, I know how impossible they sound. I have no idea what happened to the town, or what it has to do with the DARC, or how I'm supposed to find my family. I just know I have to *try*.

Ian stands in front of me. A trail of blood runs from the bandage, down his neck, to his collar. He jerks his thumb toward the shelter. "Get some sleep. We'll deal with the rest in the morning."

"Thanks, but I'll stay out here." Where I can take off at the first opportunity.

Ian shoots me a look that says he wasn't born yesterday. "You built the shelter. You sleep in it." Though their features are nothing alike, the stubborn expression on his face suddenly reminds me a lot of Rowena.

I roll my eyes and crawl inside. Ian tosses me a sleeping bag from his pack and proceeds to make himself a bed directly in front of the only exit. Unless he passes out again, I'm stuck.

Which is completely the point.

Heat creeps up my neck. I don't care if his intentions are good. That doesn't give Ian the right to order me around. I've been taking care of myself since I was nine, and I've survived this long without anyone's protection.

Ian tosses me an extra blanket. I yank it toward myself and settle down in the corner, where I can keep my eyes on him. I'll wait him out. As soon as he falls asleep, I'll figure out a way past him.

I settle myself down on the ground, using the deputy's jacket as a pillow. It's surprisingly comfortable.

More movement from outside.

There's the sharp crackle of a fire. Warmth wraps around me and despite my best intentions, I crash-land into sleep before I even feel myself falling.

TEN

Something nudges my foot.

I sit up so fast the world spins.

Ian squats in the shelter opening, wearing a gray jacket and an impossibly alert expression for someone who's recently suffered head trauma. He offers me some trail mix.

"Breakfast."

My stomach groans at the sight of food. I snatch the bag out of his hand and tear into it like I haven't eaten in days. Which, I guess, I haven't.

The morning is chilly and overcast. Mist drapes the forest and blankets the ground in thick white clouds that smell like earth and growing things.

There's a sharp *snap* as Ian pulls the roof off our makeshift shelter. Other than some stiffness, he doesn't appear to be in pain. My eyes drift to the scars on his hands. It occurs to me that he might just be good at hiding it.

"How do you feel?" I ask.

"I'll live." Ian thrusts the tarp into his pack and lifts it like it weighs nothing. "The easiest path to the road will take us a mile southeast of here. We should reach it in an hour."

I crush the empty bag in my fist. "The road is gone. We've been over this."

Ian straightens. "Look, I'm not saying you're lying about what you saw."

"Then what are you saying? That I'm delusional? That I'm losing my mind?"

"I'm saying that you're hurt, and you don't know what happened to you," Ian responds with irritating calm. "It's possible you got confused."

Deep down, I'm terrified he might be right, but admitting that out loud would be like surrendering to his plan.

That isn't going to happen.

"This coming from the guy who spent most of yesterday unconscious?" I stand and face Ian across the campground. "Believe me or don't. Either way, I'm leaving."

Ian grips the straps of his pack as if he'd like nothing better than to get rid of me.

"You'll move faster without me," I continue, but he's already shaking his head. Frustration bubbles up inside of me. This entire conversation is a massive waste of time. "Are you prepared to knock me out and drag me? Because that's what it's going to take."

"I'll do what I have to do." Emotion flickers across his face before he turns away. "Or haven't you heard?"

He's doing his best to intimidate me with his reputation, but the way his shoulders droop makes me feel a pang of sympathy for him in spite of everything. It sucks when every stranger has a fully formed opinion of you. It makes you feel like who you are doesn't matter nearly as much as what they think of you.

A thought hits me out of nowhere: What if that's what this is about? By rescuing me like some lost little girl, Ian could be hoping to prove to the world that he's not the monster everybody assumes he is. It's the only thing that makes sense. People don't just go out of their way for strangers. Not unless they want something in return.

The possibility that Ian is using me to make a point burns, but then it does something much more useful.

It gives me an idea.

"I'll make you a deal," I say, before I can change my mind. "You say the town isn't safe. I say the road is gone. How about we see who's right?"

Ian frowns. "What are the terms?"

My brain flies into overdrive. "We get to higher ground. Somewhere with a decent view. If that storm is still hanging over the town, I'll agree that it's a lost cause and we walk back to what's left of the road."

Ian's eyes narrow. "And if it's not?"

I lift my chin. "You guide me back to Fort Glory."

Ian palms the bill of his hat. The gesture is second nature. I doubt he even knows he's doing it. "There's a ridge a quarter mile southeast of here that should work," he says at last. "We could be there in half an hour."

Southeast? "But that will still take us back toward the road," I say quickly.

Ian shrugs. "It's the only easy climb within a mile. I'll agree to your terms, but only on this condition."

I frown at him. I could call his bluff. Start walking toward Fort Glory and force his hand. But then I'd be no better off than I was before. Ian has a pack full of supplies. More important, he knows these woods. I've got a better chance of making it to Fort Glory with him as a guide, even if it means taking a minor detour.

When I nod, Ian looks relieved. Like he wasn't exactly sure what his move would've been if I'd said no.

Eager to get going, I grab a rope and spool it around my arm. Something moves in the corner of my vision. I spin around. The terror of last night returns to me along with a cold sweat. "Did you see any signs of the person?" I ask. "The one who scared off the bobcat?"

Ian pauses in the middle of folding the tarp. "I couldn't find any tracks, but that doesn't mean we're alone."

Newspaper headlines from the past few weeks run through my head. The murders. The violence. The riots. If someone else is out here with us, there's a good chance they aren't friendly.

Ian stamps out the fire without waiting for the embers to burn down. This place must be giving him the creeps too, because we finish packing up camp in no time and start working our way southeast.

Every step sends a stabbing pain through my knee. To distract myself, I hum a song in my head. The one Mom used to sing to us every night before bed. I can still remember the last time I heard it. It was after Dad disappeared, but before everything fell apart. Mom said we needed to go somewhere nobody knew us. Somewhere we could reinvent ourselves into whoever we wanted. She was like that back then. A million songs and half-realized ideas in a shell of beautiful disappointment.

But it was more than that. I saw the truth in the way she searched the face of every passing stranger. She was still hoping to find him. I was only thirteen, but already I knew this was an invitation for more pain. Memories fade for a reason, and when things disappear, they don't ever come back.

Back to the song and the last time I heard it. I remember it was that quiet hour just before sunset that brings out the dreamy shades you never notice during the day. Mom was hanging the wash out on the line. Clothes flapped, and she sang that song to herself, and the world stopped to admire the picture my mother made.

A man walked over. He took off his hat and gestured at Rusty's broken taillight. My mother smiled at him, and I knew that our taillight would be fixed by tomorrow. That we'd be seeing a lot more of this man before we moved on. I didn't like the look of him.

Guys like this crawled out of the woodwork wherever she went. She'd accept their help in exchange for kind words and attention, never letting them get too close. Never letting them see the emptiness behind the smile.

My fists shook in my lap. *"We don't need him. I can do it. I can fix the light."*

It wasn't until Charlie answered that I realized I'd spoken out loud.

"She knows you can."

"Then why?"

Charlie didn't ask me what I meant. He knew.

Charlie always knew.

"Because it's not the taillight that needs fixing, Rosie."

Ian clears his throat. It takes me a moment to realize we've stopped walking.

"I thought you might need a rest," Ian says to break the awkward silence.

"Yeah. Okay." But he just keeps standing there, staring at me. "What?" I demand.

"You were singing."

My cheeks are instantly on fire. I must really be losing it if I let my guard down like that.

Now that it's down, I'm having a hard time pulling it back up.

Images run through my head. My mother in the kitchen, forearms coated in flour. Waves of white fabric crashing around her ankles as she danced with Charlie strapped in the sling across her chest.

Suddenly, I miss her so much it hurts. The mother who would brush my hair, sing me songs, and let me walk around in her high heels.

My throat burns, and then I'm blinking much too fast.

"My bunkmate used to sing in his sleep," Ian says abruptly. "At least you can carry a tune."

It surprises a small smile out of me. Then the full meaning of his words sinks in. "How long were you—?" I backtrack in a hurry. "Sorry. It's none of my business."

Ian shrugs off my apology. "Eighteen months. It happened. It's over." He takes in my sweaty face and nods toward a massive tree stump a few feet away. "Sit. Before you keel over."

Too tired to disagree, I collapse onto the stump and wrap my arms around my waist. It's not even December, but already the weather has taken a sharp turn toward winter. My heart gives a little squeeze. Charlie's green hoodie will be useless against this cold.

I stretch out, and Rowena's bandanna slips down my knee, making me wince.

"What's wrong?" Ian asks over my shoulder.

"It's—"

"Nothing?" He recycles my words from last night. "Let me see."

I let my hands fall aside. Lines form around Ian's eyes. "You should've said something." He digs through his pack for gauze and rubbing alcohol before he kneels in front of me.

"Don't."

Ian's hands still a few inches from my knee, and it's like that moment in the diner all over again. "This needs to be cleaned," he says slowly. "It's going to hurt like hell."

"I'll do it."

"It's hard to inflict that kind of pain on yourself. It'll be easier if you let me."

He's being kind. Just like he was a few minutes ago when he tried to distract me with that story about his bunkmate. The last thing I want is to throw that kindness back in his face, but I am not my mother.

If something's broken, I want to be the one to fix it.

"This is my mess. I'll clean it up."

Ian's eyes meet mine and hold.

Slowly, he leans forward to lay out the supplies on the stump beside me. His arm brushes mine, and my pulse races. He stands quickly—almost like he can hear it. Without a word, he backs away to give me space.

While I clean the wound, Ian studies scraps of sky through the trees. I wonder if he's thinking the same thing I am. A town vanished into thin air while the world was watching. Where are the helicopters? Where are the drones doing flyby missions? These woods should be swarming with activity, but we could easily be the last two people on earth.

I'm bandaging up my knee when Ian drops down beside me.

"How much farther?" I ask. I'm already starting to regret this bargain I've made. Every step we take away from Fort Glory increases the tightness in my chest. Deal or no deal, if we don't get there soon I'm going to have to find a way to ditch him.

"Not much." He presses the tip of his switchblade into the wood and starts to carve. An intricate design takes shape under his hand. It takes me a moment to realize what it is. A pattern like the one on the back of my compass.

"It's weird, right?" I ask. "This quiet?"

A flicker of surprise shows in his eyes as they slide sidelong to me. "It's usually not a good sign when the animals run for cover."

The sun rises behind the canopy as we set out again. Ian gradually increases his pace until I'm forced to jog to keep up. My lungs are starting to burn when he finally turns around.

"We should've seen the ridge by now."

"Are you sure?" I ask.

"We've been walking southeast for almost two hours. Even if we missed the ridge, we should've crossed the road."

Not willing to get into that particular argument again, I let it pass. "Do we head back to the stream? Retrace our steps?" On jelly legs, I stumble over to an old stump and crumple.

"I don't know." Ian finds the lump at the back of his head. "Things aren't how they should be."

While he contemplates our next move, I attempt to catch my breath. My fingers brush over something grainy on the wood. It's rough and textured. Like sawdust or pencil shavings, or . . .

The hairs on my arms rise straight up in the air.

"Ian. Come here."

"I need to find a landmark," he says to himself. "Something to pin down our location."

"I'm serious. You need to look at this."

He walks over, and I know the moment he sees it. His whole body goes rigid.

There. Under my left hand. A delicate series of lines. The carving is so fresh, the depressions in the wood are still green.

"We've been walking in circles," I say.

ELEVEN

That's impossible." Ian stares at the lines as if he could force them to make sense by sheer strength of will.

"Then how do you explain this?" I run my hands over the carving.

"I must've gotten turned around." Ian grabs the bill of his cap. His hand stays there a solid thirty seconds before he lets it drop. He's making a conscious effort not to scare me. It isn't working. My gut tells me Ian is too careful to have led us in a giant circle. Just like it's telling me we shouldn't be here now.

That feeling is back. The itch between my shoulder blades that insists something is very, *very* wrong here. It makes me want to drop everything and sprint the rest of the way to Fort Glory, screaming my brother's name. Only, now I have no idea which direction to run.

"Hold up." I reach into my bag for my compass. At the sight of it, the uneasy feeling inside turns into something sharper. "This doesn't make sense," I say as I watch the needle turn round and round. Round and round. "This compass is old, but the last time I checked, it still worked."

"It isn't working now." Ian leads us through the forest, down the exact same path we took before. The signs of our passage are everywhere. Broken ferns. The shells of Ian's sunflower seeds.

We've been going for about an hour when Ian stops so suddenly, I plow into the wall of his back, getting a noseful of cotton that smells of bleach, and rain, and boy.

I peek around his shoulders and there it is. An old stump with a series of graceful lines freshly carved down the center.

"What's going on?" I ask.

"I don't know." Ian's admission makes things real in a way they weren't before. I scan the woods and fight a growing sense of hopelessness. I'm used to uphill battles, but this is different. This feels like the entire universe is conspiring against us.

"I grew up in these woods." Ian fiddles with the straps of his pack. "We should've reached the road by now. Even if the road is gone, we shouldn't have circled back here. It's almost like—"

"Like what?"

"Like we're stuck in a cage without bars."

Ian waits for me to freak out. Maybe that'd be a normal reaction to something like this, but I don't need a compass to tell me we shouldn't have passed this spot twice. We're stuck here—wherever here is. Having a meltdown isn't going to change it.

Ian's pack thuds to the ground, making me jump inside my skin. He strips off his jacket until he's standing there in a tight gray T-shirt and climbing harness, a spool of neon cord in his hand.

"What are you doing?" I ask.

He approaches a towering tree. "I need to get higher. It's the only way to know for sure about the road and the town." Ian attaches a weighted clip to the rope. In one fluid motion, he tosses it toward the lowest branch, some thirty feet above our heads. It's an insane throw. Like trying to thread a needle at a distance. Ian hits it on the first try. The clip sails over the branch and back down to us. Ian attaches one end of the rope to the front of his harness before looping the other around the line leading up into the tree, making not one, but two devilish-looking knots.

Pain shoots through my knee. A reminder of my recent fall from Devil's Tooth. This tree is higher than that. A lot higher. My legs wobble as I measure the distance to the nearest branch. "Is this safe?" I ask.

"Compared to what?" Ian adjusts the bill of his cap and faces me. "Don't move from this spot. I'm serious, Rose. If you're not down here when I get back, we're going to have some real problems."

If this had happened an hour ago, I would've been hatching an escape before Ian's feet even left the ground. Things are different now. At some point, we stepped out of reality and into one of those *Twilight Zone* episodes Charlie and I used to watch back when our TV still worked. If I cut and run for Fort Glory now, there's a good chance I'll never find it.

"I'm not going anywhere."

"Hold this." Ian loops a spool of extra rope over my shoulder before he turns to the tree.

He leans back in the harness and wraps both his hands around the bit of free rope hanging loose from his elaborate system of knots. He yanks with all his strength. The rope shortens manually, catching on the knots and lifting him up several inches. Muscles strain in his forearms as he arcs his back and jerks the rope again.

Pull by pull, he works himself up the trunk. I've never seen anybody move like that. Didn't even know it was possible. Ian climbs as if the rope is an extension of his body, and for a moment,

I completely forget about the yards of empty air stretching between him and the ground.

Ian reaches the first solid branch and anchors himself to it. From there he moves faster, relying less on the rope and more on his own strength and agility to work up through the branches. He disappears into the canopy, and the danger of this plan hits me all over again. I might not be the one fifty feet high, but I still feel vulnerable down here. Exposed.

My scalp prickles. I search the forest. Nothing but trees in every direction.

A dull buzzing reaches my ears. It's soft at first, but grows louder by the second. It reminds me a little of the whistling I heard back in Maple before things went south. Only, this sound is layered. So vibrant it's almost... *alive.*

I take a step backward. My breath comes out in a rush as my spine slams against the trunk.

I'm about to call out to Ian, when the buzzing erupts in an explosion of feathers. Hundreds of birds shoot through the forest. I throw up my arms to shield my face as they dive past, stirring my hair with their wings.

Leaves and twigs rain down on my shoulders as the flock passes through the branches overhead. Ian's muffled curses echo above me.

The bird cries have barely died down when the next wave begins. An army of squirrels, rats, and other forest creatures. They dart out of the trees in a blur of tails and gleaming eyes, all coming from the same direction. North.

From Fort Glory.

Claws pinch my foot as something scuttles over my sneaker. My cry echoes through the forest.

"Rose! Are you okay?" The rope jerks as Ian abruptly starts back down.

Before I can answer, a flash of activity draws my eyes deeper into the woods. A herd is on the move. Elk. Hundreds of them. A few are bulls with racks that could total a truck.

And they're headed straight toward me.

I scan the forest. There's no shelter in sight. No rocks or fallen logs to use for cover.

Branches strain above me. "Stay there!" There's a flash of leg as Ian emerges from canopy. "I'll lift you up!" Muscles glide under his shirt as he works his way down to me fast—much faster than is safe.

It's still not fast enough.

Ian is less than twenty feet away, but it might as well be twenty miles. Musk clogs my nostrils. The strike of hooves becomes a thunder rolling straight through my chest.

I run.

The forest blurs in my peripheral vision. Leaves tickle my arms and branches rake across my face as I sprint through the trees, desperate to outpace the herd at my back.

Sweat drips into my eyes. I don't know how long I've been running when a tree root comes out of nowhere to snag my ankle.

I hit the ground on all fours. There's a boulder a few feet away. I drag myself over to it and prepare to be trampled by a thousand hooves. But the thunder of the herd doesn't get any closer. It pulls farther and farther away. As it fades, another noise rises up to take its place.

The rush of water.

I think I'm hallucinating until I smell the river. A blast of silt and brine on the breeze. I stumble to my feet.

The growl of running water turns into a roar as I lurch forward. Within moments, the river has drowned out every sound but one.

A voice.

Young and afraid. It cuts me right to the bone.

"Help," my brother calls to me. "Help."

TWELVE

My heart is a drum in my ears as I follow Charlie's cries to a bluff carved out of the forest. There's a fifteen-foot drop to the river below. It batters the rocks, sending up ribbons of white spray that splatter the ledge under my feet.

I see her right away. The little girl's red coat is hard to miss.

A knot forms in the pit of my stomach when I realize my mistake. All the strength goes out of me. I'm dropping down to the bluff when the scene in front of me crystalizes.

The girl is in trouble. She's clinging to a boulder in the middle of the river as the water rushes past her on all sides. She's eleven. Maybe twelve. It's hard to tell how deep the water is around her. With a current this strong, it doesn't really matter.

The girl loses her grip on the wet stone. She slides a few inches deeper into the water. Even from this distance, I can see her arms shaking. Every second she clings to that rock is an act of pure willpower.

I scramble down the side of the bluff to the riverbank. "Hold on!"

Wide hazel eyes meet mine. The girl's lips are two blue slashes in a deathly pale face. She's in bad shape. She's going to lose this fight with the river soon. Unless I can figure out a way to get her out of there.

Several yards above the girl's boulder, a tree lies on its side, forming a rough bridge over the water. I strip off my jacket and apron and lay them down on the sand. On second thought, I pick up Ian's rope and make my way to the tangled mass of roots at the base of the fallen tree.

Bits of rotted bark slough off under my fingernails as I pull myself up onto the log. It's not high—barely more than a few feet above the river. Nothing like Devil's Tooth. Too bad my body doesn't seem to realize that. Tremors run through my arms. I glance around one more time for another way. When that fails, I force myself into a crawl.

The ground disappears beneath me as I inch my way toward the girl in the middle of the river. Icy foam shoots into my eyes. The rushing water below pulls at me with almost magnetic force. I keep my gaze locked on the wood under my hands until I'm roughly halfway across. I let out a breath and look down.

"I'm going to get you out of there," I tell the girl five feet below.

She's wet to her skin and shaking like a leaf, but she grits her teeth, lifts her chin, and nods. It's gutsy. A burst of admiration cuts through my fear.

I'm racking my brain for some way out of this when I remember the rope around my shoulders. I pull it over my neck and quickly work it into a loop around my waist. To my left, a rough knob sticks out of the trunk. With steady fingers, I fashion the other end into a lasso and slip it over the knob.

In the few seconds this takes, the girl's condition goes from bad to worse. Her mouth hangs slack. She isn't shaking anymore.

She rests her cheek against the stone and closes her eyes. I stare down at this little girl, wet and ragged and fighting to survive, and suddenly, it isn't a stranger I see. It's Charlie. The bruise on his face and the cuts on his knuckles as he held on to that egg in his hand.

"What's your name?" I ask, shoving my fear behind the wall inside of me where it won't get in the way.

She makes a courageous effort to focus. "B-B-Becca."

"I've got you, Becca, okay?"

Her eyes roll back before fluttering closed again. Helplessly, I watch her arms give out until she's submerged up to the waist. Tremors rack her body, but she just holds on to that rock with a bravery most grown adults can't match. And it won't do her a damn bit of good.

My fingers dig into the rotting wood so hard it hurts.

Something moves on the ledge above me. My head jerks up, and then three things happen at once.

Becca lets go.

I scream her name.

And someone claps me right between the shoulder blades, pushing me headfirst into the river.

I hit the water, and the water hits right back. Cold. It's so cold. On instinct, I reach out and yank Becca toward me. We break the surface in a rush of foam and light. The current is a battering ram. The rope around my waist the only thing keeping us from being swept away. I search with my toes, but the bottom is too far down to reach. Becca is totally limp in my arms. It's taking every bit of my strength to keep both of our heads above water.

Black spots are dancing at the edges of my vision when the sound of my name reaches me over the roar.

"Rose."

I look up and Ian is there. One of his hands grips the rope while the other anchors him to the tree bridge.

"Listen to me, Rose." Ian's voice cuts right through the chaos. "I'm going to pull you up. Don't let her go. Do you hear me?"

He doesn't wait for an answer. The rope around my waist gives a vicious tug. For one terrifying moment, Becca and I hang suspended over the roiling river. Her body is a dead weight, wrenching my arms out of their sockets, and then Ian has me by the back of my dress.

My stomach hits the rotting bark, and I heave up a gallon of river water. Dimly, I register Ian scooping Becca into his arms. I close my eyes, too exhausted to do anything but breathe.

The log creaks under the sudden addition of weight. A few seconds later, Ian lifts me up. For a moment, I'm floating, and then my back touches silty riverbed. When my vision finally stops spinning, it's centered on Ian's furious face.

"What the hell were you thinking?" The question is dead calm, but the hands on my arms are shaking. Or maybe that's just me.

"I—I heard someone scream. I thought it was Charlie." I glance over to where Becca is lying on her side under Ian's tarp. The knot in my stomach loosens when I notice the silver material rise and fall with her breath. "She was trapped on a rock. I thought I could help."

"By *jumping in?*"

For the first time since he pulled me out, I notice Ian's appearance. Scratches cover his face and hands. Twigs and mud cling to his clothes like he rolled through several barns to get here. The only clean thing on him is that old hat. It's ridiculous. *He's* ridiculous, sitting there half-soaked, furious, scolding me, and I couldn't care less. Right now, I couldn't care less about any of it.

A giggle bubbles up in my throat, and it feels *good*. So good because even though I'm wet and freezing and lost in every imaginable way, Becca and I are both alive.

And for once, I am not alone.

Ian stares at me as if I've completely lost my mind. "Sorry," I gasp. "But you should see yourself right now."

The corner of his mouth twitches. "You might not want to talk."

My laughter ends in a wet cough, and Ian's expression turns dead serious. "Did it cross your mind to wait for me before you dove headfirst into the rapids?"

I frown at him because it *didn't* cross my mind. Not once.

"I didn't jump in on purpose. Someone pushed me in. I'm serious," I insist when Ian just stares at me. "I thought I saw someone on the ridge, and then I felt a hand on my back, shoving me over."

It was the same person who scared off the bobcat yesterday. It had to be. Which means I'm not completely losing my mind.

It's only partially reassuring.

Someone is following us. But what could they possibly gain by pushing me into the river? More important, what will happen if they find Charlie before I do?

Desperation creeps in on me again without warning. "The road," I say, sitting straight up.

Ian rises to his feet. "These woods look identical to the woods outside Fort Glory. Same landmarks and everything. But once you get past the city limits, heading toward Maple, everything just...stops."

His words bring me up short. "What do you mean it *stops?*"

"I mean the road never starts again. There's no police block-ade. No pileup of abandoned cars like the one you described. It's like the trees go on and on in that direction, but they don't look *right.*" He pulls his cap back down over his brow as he searches for the right words. "It reminds me of one of those paintings. The ones with the staircases that never really get anywhere."

A chill creeps up my spine. "What about the town?"

Lines of sadness frame his eyes. "Every trace of it is still cov-ered by that storm I told you about. It's bigger than it was yester-day. Whatever it is, it's growing." The pause that follows suggests I won't like what comes next. "Remember how I told you there's an eye at the center? It's stirring up all sorts of weather. Those animals had the right idea. I've never seen clouds like these before."

Just like that, the missing road becomes the least of our problems.

I'm about to ask Ian where that leaves us, when a warbling voice cuts me off.

"Ian?"

Ian turns toward the little girl. She's sitting up, shivering in the mud, her gaze locked on him.

A hint of confusion flashes across his face.

Becca slumps. "Don't you recognize me?" There's something in her tone. A touch of hurt that goes deep.

Ian's complexion grows two shades lighter. "Becs?"

My heart twists at the expression on his face. It's relief and sadness and regret all at once. The moment feels intensely per-sonal, but it's too late to look away now.

"I missed you," the little girl says.

Ian takes a halting step forward. "I'm surprised you still remember me." His voice is oddly thick.

"I couldn't forget you. Not ever." When she smiles, it's like the sun decided to shine through the dark.

Ian walks across the beach to kneel beside her. Becca watches him approach with flushed cheeks. It's obvious she adores him. That she has for a long time. She reaches for him. The tips of her pale fingers brush his stubble. He cups her trembling hand against his jaw like he's afraid her bones will shatter.

"When'd you cut your hair?" Becca's smile turns crooked, and I get a glimpse of the fire I saw when she was holding on to that rock for dear life.

Ian runs a hand over his buzzed head. "What do you think?"

"It looks stupid."

Ian laughs. It's the sound of pure relief.

Blue-tinted lips curve into a smile. It lights her whole face for a moment before something stirs in her eyes. A familiar darkness that makes the hairs on the back of my neck bristle.

"Ian—" I don't get to finish the warning.

"You didn't see me," the little girl says. The joy bleeds from her expression. "You didn't even know me."

"It's been a while," Ian says. "You look—older."

"Two years." As she speaks, the darkness in her pupils bleeds into the whites. "You didn't say goodbye."

Ian flinches like she slapped him. "Becs, I'm sorry. I—"

Becca claps her hands over her ears. The movement is so violent, her whole body starts to shake.

I kneel beside her. "We need to get you dry," I say, but it's obvious she doesn't hear me.

She doesn't hear anything.

Fingers claw at her scalp. "You didn't see me. You didn't say goodbye." She crumples.

My heart clenches as she hits the sand at my feet. Right next to a clump of bloody hair.

Ian is beside Becca in an instant.

"How long was she in the water?" He gathers her into his lap. Darkness glitters in her blown pupils. It douses the last traces of hazel in a sea of pure black.

"I ... I don't know."

Ian's hands are steady as they move from Becca's waist to her neck, but there's panic in his eyes when they meet mine. "She's going hypothermic."

"Her eyes," I say. "They're dark like the people I told you about. The ones in the town right before they went—"

"I know." His Adam's apple bobs once. "But I don't know how to fix it. All I know is we've got to get her warm, or she'll die."

Things become really simple, really fast. "Tell me what to do."

"Find some kindling. Anything dry we can burn." Ian sheds his jacket and rips the shirt over his head. With one arm, he pulls Becca against his bare chest. "I have to keep her warm. Can you get what we need?"

I don't waste energy on an answer. The riverbank is a tangled web of driftwood. I gather what I can, but my arms are shaking so badly from my dip in the river, most of it never makes it to the pile.

"Switch with me," I say.

Ian nods. I slide in front of him and gather Becca in my arms.

"Take off your clothes."

"What?" I crane my neck to look up at him.

"You both need body heat. Skin-to-skin contact is the best thing for that." He kneels in front of me and drapes his jacket around my shoulders. It's nearly big enough to cover me and Becca both. Ian bunches the material under my chin. "I need you to trust me."

I get the sense he knows exactly what he's asking.

I nod, and Ian quickly turns away to finish building the fire.

Using the jacket as a shield, I pull off my clothes and Becca's until we're both in our underwear. Her skin is ice-cold, but within seconds, miraculous warmth flows between us. Heat sinks into me with pins and needles.

A shiver runs down my spine as I pull Becca closer. She's not moving anymore, but her eyes are open. Clouded over with blackness. Just like Officer Jensen and all those people who lost it before Fort Glory disappeared.

We already saw how that worked out for them.

No sooner does the thought cross my mind than Becca moans. Fingers curl into claws as she tears at herself again.

Horror leaves me paralyzed. Another bloody clump of hair hits the beach beside me, and then I stop thinking. I grab Becca's hands.

It happens out of nowhere. A hook of fire sinks into my guts, tearing a groan from my lips.

This feeling. *Oh God.* It's the same one that hit me in the woods behind Devil's Tooth. Right before I blacked out and woke up here in—

The hook digs in deeper. The forest blurs as I am ripped sideways. Away from Ian and my body holding on to Becca on the riverbank. Toward an ocean of darkness hovering at the edge of my mind. It rises up, yawning and deep. Waves of terrible notes crash over me. Their roar fills my head, tearing at me with barbed teeth until I can't breathe. Can't *think*.

The closer I get to the black ocean, the louder it gets. I'm almost over the edge when something jerks me back.

The dark ocean releases my mind with the snap of a rubber band.

"Rose!"

Ian is leaning over me. Judging by the hoarseness in his voice, he's been calling my name for a while.

"What happened?" I ask groggily.

"You tried to stop Becca. The second you touched her hand, your face went blank. I kept calling your name, but you were gone."

I struggle to sit up. "I saw something. Or some place. It was like… an ocean of darkness somewhere at the edge of my mind. It was… loud."

"I know," Ian says.

"What? How?"

His eyes dart to Becca, lying in my arms. "I didn't know what else to do, so I tried to pull your hands apart." Beads of sweat stand out on his brow despite the freezing cold. "That's when I saw it. It only lasted for a second." Judging by the look on his face, a second was more than enough.

"What do you think it was?" I ask.

"No idea. But now's not the time to figure it out."

I nod. Becca's gone quiet again. I take a deep breath and pull back her lids. The blackness has faded into her pupils, revealing hazel irises shot through with red.

Gathering my courage, I reach for her hand.

Nothing but the cold press of her skin against mine.

I'm slumping back down to the sand when a white fleck lands on the tip of my nose. It melts within seconds, but the uneasy feeling it leaves behind lasts much longer.

"Here." When I look up, Ian is standing over me, holding out my jacket. "Let Becca keep mine."

"What about you?"

"I'll be fine."

No, he won't. None of us will be.

"I just saw a snowflake," I tell him. The cold is bad enough. We won't survive an hour out here in the snow.

I'm no good to Mom or Charlie if I'm dead.

"How long before that storm wall hits us?" I ask.

"Not long," Ian says, confirming that we are in serious, serious trouble. "It shouldn't be this cold. Or this dark," he adds with another ominous glance at the sky.

"The same thing happened yesterday. It went from morning to night and skipped right over afternoon."

Ian nods in acceptance. We've both seen too many strange things to question the truth. Wherever this place is, however we got here, the rules we know no longer apply.

I hug Becca closer. "We can't stay out here."

Ian's eyes dart to the little girl in my arms. "The Boy Scouts have a camp on a local lake. There are a few cabins and a wash-house. It's still there. I saw it from up in the tree."

"How far?" I demand.

"A mile or two north. The trip would take us closer to the storm. We'd be racing it to the camp."

"We can't go back. We already tried that, and it didn't work."

Ian fingers the lump on the back of his head. His hands drop to his sides. "There's a good chance I'll lead us in circles all night."

A snowflake lands on Becca's eyelash.

We don't have all night.

"We have to try."

Ian shakes his head. "It's too dangerous."

"Compared to what?" I throw his words from a few hours ago back at him.

Becca needs more than a tarp. She needs something with four walls and a roof. If Ian is right about the storm moving in, we'll *all* need real shelter to survive the night.

The bizarre tugging starts again in the center of my chest, flooding me with a strange certainty. I decide to put my faith in it. And Ian.

"You can find it," I tell him stubbornly.

Surprise flickers across Ian's face. It makes me wonder how long it's been since anybody took a chance on him. A few more beats pass before he tosses me a bundle of dry clothes. "They'll swallow you, but they're all I've got."

Grateful, I duck behind a rock to change. Charlie's egg rolls out of my jacket pocket and into my palm. I grip it gently and pray that wherever they are, Charlie and Mom are safe from this storm.

When I step back out onto the riverbank, Ian is easing Becca into a fireman's carry. Her hip brushes the back of his head. He sways on his feet and steadies himself against a rock as tremors run up his arms.

He hasn't said a word about his concussion, so I just assumed it wasn't bothering him.

I assumed wrong.

Ian bends at the waist. I think he's going to be sick, when he pulls himself upright again.

"You said it was a mile or two to the campsite." I try and fail to hide the hitch in my voice. "Can you make it that far?"

Ian's hand drops from the tree. "I'm going to have to," he says.

It starts to snow.

THIRTEEN

CHARLIE

I hear her first.

Little light, crying in the dark.

I follow the cries to an island in the Black Nothing.

"Is someone there?" *asks the little light.*

"Yes."

More crying. Not sad now. Happy.

The little light glows brighter. "I see you," *it says.* "Do you see me?"

"I see you."

Starshine on my face.

"What happened to your eye?" *asks the little light.*

"I gave it to the Black Nothing so I could keep the lights burning. Why are you crying?"

"I thought I was all alone."

"You are never alone. What's your name?" *I ask the little light. Not so little anymore.*

"My name?"

"The song? The one inside of you? Do you hear it?"

A moment. "Yes." *Amazement.* "Yes, I hear it."

"What's it singing?"

"Sarah." *The light grows brighter.* "My name is Sarah, and I want to go home."

"My name is Charlie, and I'm going to help you."

"I'm scared, Charlie."

"What are you afraid of, little light?"

"The dark," *she whispers.* "I'm afraid of the dark."

"You don't have to be afraid. Here, I'll show you."

I take her hand. A silver thread shoots from mine to hers, connecting us. Solid. Bright.

The little light named Sarah gasps when she sees the things I see.

Two thousand two hundred thirteen stars shining in the Black Nothing. Snow globes of song. All the millions of threads connecting them.

"They're so pretty." *She touches a thread.* "Where do they come from?"

"They've always been there. You just couldn't see them before."

"Why?" *she asks.*

"Because they live in the places eyes can't touch."

"But yours can?"

"Not my eyes," *I tell her.*

"What, then?"

"I'm going to teach you," *I say.* "But first I have to do something."

I touch the golden thread. The one running through me. I send some notes down the golden river to the one at the other end.

A reminder.

A gift.

The Black Nothing moves in around us. When it comes, I pay the price.

The Black Nothing steals the roll of the ocean.

The colors of a million leaves about to die.

Skies full of falling snow.

Pain explodes like fireworks.

Flashes of color.

Bursts of light.

Her face.

The last thing I see before the lights go out.

The Black Nothing takes my eye, and Sarah cries. When it leaves, I take her hand.

"It's over now, little light. Time to go."

"Where are we going?"

"To catch more stars."

FOURTEEN

The outlines of a few cabins have solidified through the trees when it strikes.

A searing pain in my eye. Not the right one. The left one this time.

I stumble. The ground breaks my fall. Cold. Hard. It knocks the wind out of me. And then there is nothing but the pain.

Hands on my shoulders. Ian's. His voice echoes in the vacuum of my head. I fold myself around my broken parts. This agony. It's like nothing I've ever felt. It is going to kill me. I know it. And I'd be okay with that if it weren't for one thing.

Charlie.

His name is the only word I can remember. His memory is the only thing sharp enough to cut through this pain. His image fills my head, and for a second, I can see him right there in front of me. Suspended behind a wall of darkness. That's when I know that I'm really dying. And it's okay. It's okay so long as my brother's face is the last thing I see.

I reach for him. My fingers dig into the snow between us. I can't touch him, so I do the only thing I can. I make his face my focal point for however long this lasts. Only, Charlie's face is different than I remember. His mouth is pressed thin. His brow is twisted in agony. And his eyes.

Charlie's eyes are black holes in his beautiful face.

This is wrong. It's the last thought I have before the shadows at the edges of my vision break toward me.

Consciousness returns with a slap. The first thing I'm aware of is the pain. It's not as sharp as it was before. My entire body trembles with relief.

I press my face into the snow. Like that could somehow put out the blazing inferno in my left eye socket. I don't know how long I lie like this before I hear it.

Glass shattering somewhere in the distance.

I crack my eyes open. It's full-on night, but there's a strange light filtering through the trees. It reflects off the snow, lending a soft glow to the forest. The silence is heavy. Peaceful. Like someone wrapped the world in a thick blanket.

Snow falls in big, fat flakes. It wouldn't be the worst thing to fall asleep right here. The temptation lasts for less than a moment before the image of Charlie is there to drive it back. I picture him. Not the way he was the last time I saw him. The way he appeared to me just a moment ago. Surrounded by darkness. In torment.

Hallucination or not, it felt *real*. Charlie could be out there right now, alone and lost and waiting for me to find him. Which means that as tired as I am, I can't just lie here.

I have to get up.

Stabbing pain cuts through my eye as I lift my head from the ground. There's no sign of Ian. He must've left to get Becca to safety. I don't blame him. In his place, I would've done the same.

The cabins are still visible up ahead, but the snow is getting heavier. If I'm going to move, it has to be now.

I grit my teeth and drag myself forward. After a few minutes, I manage to raise myself up onto all fours. I don't know how long I've been crawling when a pair of strong hands wrap under my arms.

"I've got you, Rose. I've got you." Ian lifts me to his side. Together we stumble to the closest cabin. Ian kicks the door open.

I collapse on the threshold. Behind me, the door slams shut on the wind.

Within seconds, Ian's hands are on my shoulder, turning me over to face him. "Are you all right? Talk to me, Rose. *Please.*"

"My eye," I manage.

Ian's gaze moves to my hand, where it protectively cups the socket. "Let me see." He says it gently, but the command is unmistakable. When I don't comply, Ian's palm moves so that it is hovering directly above mine. He doesn't force my hand down. He doesn't even touch me. He just asks me again for permission without words.

I let my hand drop. Ian leans in close enough that I can make out the unique starbursts at the center of his eyes. He studies me for a few breaths before he gives me back my space.

"There's no obvious injury." Chest heaving, Ian collapses on the ground across from me. There's a slight tremor in his hand as he rubs it over his face. "I'm sorry I left you. I couldn't carry you both, and I thought you stood the better chance of making it until I got back."

"You don't have to apologize."

He doesn't seem to hear me. "I would've gotten to you sooner. You'd made it halfway to the cabin by the time I realized you weren't where I left you." The touch of admiration in his voice is quickly drowned out by something else. "What happened back there?"

"I'm not sure, but it's happened to me before." I tell Ian about the phantom pain. It's easier to think now that the agony has been replaced by a low-grade ache. The whole experience this time around was a little more intense. I suppress a shiver at the thought of it happening again.

"Back in the woods. When you were trying to talk to me. Did you notice—? Were my eyes—"

"No." Ian catches my drift right away. "They didn't go dark like Becca's did at the river."

My shoulders relax. This isn't Rowena's dark force threatening to turn me into a psychopath. This is something else.

The thought is not as comforting as it could be.

Ian doesn't give himself long to rest. As soon as he's convinced I'm not dying, he starts grabbing anything flammable he can get his hands on. Within moments, he's got a fire going in one of the two hearths. Gently, he places Becca on a pallet directly in front of the flames.

I scoot closer to her. My gaze sails out of the window. The blizzard is gaining strength outside. The wind is an angry monster, howling in the dark.

This is the worst storm I've ever seen. It's not just the wind and the snow. Since we left the river, the temperature has taken a nosedive. Even next to the fire, I can feel the chill creeping in. It's the kind of cold that mingles the air with the taste of metal on your tongue.

And it's only getting colder.

Becca shivers beside me. I wrap another blanket around her.

Wood splits as Ian rips apart a bunk for more firewood. He's using his bare hands to break the boards into pieces. The bloody splinters in his palms tell me everything I need to know about the danger we're in.

Paper shreds, followed by the quick strike of a match. Ian lights a fire in the second hearth. He bends over the flame, shielding it from the air blasting through the window he broke to get in here. When he leans back, the skin around his lips is a glaring shade of white.

The temperature inside the cabin drops a few more degrees.

Ian glances around us, searching for some untapped source of warmth. There's nothing. Only the storm outside trying to get in. The sound of cracking draws both our gazes to the windows. The glass. It's splintering against the cold. As we watch, jagged lines of frost spider over the panes in deadly diamond webs.

I've never seen glass do that before.

Ian's fires aren't enough. The cabin walls are crappy insulation. We're going to freeze to death in here if we can't find a way to keep what little heat we have from escaping.

My gaze sweeps the cabin. A table sits in the center of the room, surrounded by two dozen bunks pressed up against the pine walls. There's a closet, too. I toss the moldy blanket aside and approach the door. The handle doesn't budge. Locked. Or frozen solid.

"You should come back to the fire." Ian pulls Becca into his lap. He inches dangerously close to the flames, his broad shoulders visibly trembling.

"The fire isn't going to cut it." I force the words past chattering teeth. "We can't survive much longer like this."

"No. We can't." Ian doesn't lie. Not even to spare me worry. A tinge of gratitude chisels itself through the ice in my bones.

"I have an idea," I tell him. "But I need your muscle and some tools to make it happen."

Ian studies me for a long moment. I'm asking him to give up

what little warmth he's got in order to help me carry out some vague plan. I think he's going to blow me off, but instead, he puts Becca down.

One solid ram with his shoulder, and the closet door snaps open.

The space inside is a treasure trove of supplies. My heart leaps when I spot the metal toolbox on the top shelf.

Back in the main cabin, I grab a small handsaw with shaking hands and move down the line of bunks.

Ian speaks up behind me. "What are you thinking?"

"We can use one of these bunks to cover the broken window. Keep the wind out. If we pile the mattresses around us, it'll give us a few layers of insulation. Maybe enough to get us through the night." It's getting harder and harder to talk. My lips have gone numb, and every breath sends a stabbing pain through my lungs.

"It's a good idea." Ian holds out a blue-fingered hand.

It takes me a moment to realize what he's asking for.

"I know how to use a saw." I tighten my grip so that the freezing handle burns my skin.

"I got that. But I'm taller."

Under any other circumstances, I would never let this slide. But it's already getting hard to move my fingers. Soon, my hands will be useless. We need to do this. Now.

I turn the saw over, and Ian hops up onto the top bunk.

He's got good hands. Before long, one side of the bunk crashes down. Then the other. Together, we drag the wooden frame to the broken window.

"Hold up the mattress while I secure it with these." My breath is a white stain in the air. I can't feel my face anymore.

Ian glances dubiously at the spare bed slats in my arms.

"Trust me," I add, because I may not know jack about building a fire, but I'm Mark Montgomery's daughter. I sure as hell know how to build a wall.

Ian nods, and then it becomes too cold for words. My frozen hands are clumsy. Luckily, the work requires more muscle than finesse. Within minutes, the window is covered. The difference is immediate. Without the wind sucking out all the heat, the warmth of the fires begins to build. Feeling returns to my fingers. I take my first full breath in minutes.

By the time we're on the last window, the worst of the danger has passed. Our project becomes more about comfort than survival. In the stillness of the cabin, the rest of the world falls away like it always does when I work.

I'm almost finished when I notice Ian watching me.

"What?" I spit out a nail.

"You went someplace for a minute." Ian grabs another slat. "Must be better than here if it makes you smile like that."

My cheeks burn. "I like fixing things." I switch up my grip so the hammer rests against my calluses.

Ian studies the wood under his hands. "You should do it more."

"What? Manual labor?" I joke to cover up the fact that I suddenly have no idea what to do with my hands.

"Smile."

His words send another blast of heat through my face.

Ian clears his throat and looks back at our improvised wall. "Where'd you learn to do this?"

Slowly, I fit another slat across the back of the mattress. "My dad. He could make anything." I can't remember the last time I talked about my father. The old ache of missing him opens up in my chest, but instead of burying it away like usual, this time I put it to words. "I used to watch him work for hours. It always made me feel safe."

A pressure valve releases inside of me. It's such a small thing, but for a second, it's almost like I have part of him back.

"Lucky for us you take after him," Ian says.

The pride I feel at his words evaporates when a sobering thought occurs to me.

Ian leans toward me. "What is it?"

"Charlie. He's out there somewhere." My palm squeezes the hammer in a death grip.

"Rose," Ian says, forcing my gaze back to his. "If Charlie's half as resourceful as you are, he'll have figured out a way to ride this out."

"He shouldn't be alone." I give voice to the ugly thoughts inside of me. The ones I've been carrying like a cross ever since the town disappeared. "I never should've left him."

"You couldn't have known this would happen."

I shake my head. "Charlie tried to tell me." Maybe it's because I'm tired, and we nearly died, and the world is spinning completely out of control except for Ian, standing next to me so very solid and real. But I let myself admit part of the truth if only because the weight of it will crush me if I don't.

"There's a Hands for Hearths affiliate in Maple. That's where I was when everything happened. I thought ... that things could be different here. Better, you know?" Once the words start, they won't stop. "I wanted Charlie to have a real bed to sleep in and a place to put his stuff that's not a trash bag behind the pullout. I wanted a kitchen for Mom and a bedroom with an actual door for her to close when she needs to be alone."

A few beats pass.

"And what did you want for you?" Ian asks quietly.

"I wanted—"

More than a word. More than a place. More than four walls and a roof meant to keep out the rain.

"Rest." I don't realize it's the truth until I say it out loud. We've been on the move for so long, chasing ghosts and running from mistakes, and I just needed it to *stop*.

Not that any of that matters now.

"How old are you?" Ian asks. That frown is back between his brows. The one that makes me wonder what he sees when he looks at me that troubles him so much.

"Seventeen."

He considers his words. "Seems like a lot to take on."

"If I don't, who will?"

Ian doesn't say anything, but I have the strangest feeling he *gets* it. Whatever else he is, Ian Lawson isn't a coward. If he was, he never would've come back to a town that had blackballed him. He wouldn't have shown up at the diner, day after day, just to make a point.

"What happened to him?" Ian asks at last. "Your dad?"

I drive in one last nail. "He left one day and never came back. Technically he's a 'missing person,' but that's just a nice way for the cops to say he bailed on us." It didn't matter how many times we told them.

My father loved us. He would never leave. Something took him from us.

Ian grabs the hammer by the head. "The police don't know shit," he says in a dead-on impersonation of Rowena.

My laugh startles us both. Ian turns back to the wall we built, but not before I notice his mouth tilt up at the corners. *He wanted to make me laugh*, I realize. The thought warms me, and it makes me feel like I've won something out here in the middle of nowhere. Like Ian and I are allies. Maybe even friends.

I can't remember the last time I had one of those.

I sit back down in front of the fire next to Becca. Behind the mattresses, the glass rattles. Wood creaks and rafters groan. I can feel each blast of the wind in the pit of my stomach.

"It's getting bad out there." I hate the way my voice cracks. We lived in Kansas once when a tornado passed right through our trailer park. With nowhere to hide, Charlie and I watched it come for us through the bedroom window. I remember holding on to him so tightly it hurt, vowing that if it hit us, they'd find our bodies a mile away, still attached to one another.

This is worse. From the sounds outside, you'd think the sky was cracking open.

And this time, I'm not there to hold Charlie's hand.

Ian feeds more wood into the fire. When he settles back onto his elbows, his gaze wanders to the girl sleeping under a heap of blankets.

"How do you know Becca?" I ask, to distract myself from the noises outside.

"My father used to do some work for her family." Ian studies the building flames. "It was a long time ago."

"She seems ... attached to you," I say, hoping to draw him out a little.

His expression softens. "The last time I saw her she was riding around on a bike with purple streamers."

"What was she like?"

"Funny." Ian runs a hand under his cap. "She was always

stuffing cereal in my shoes or putting fake 'for sale' signs on my car." His lips quirk.

I remember Becca's crooked smile on the beach—a glimmer of this girl from Ian's memory. It's easy to see why he loves her.

"I checked on her a few minutes ago," I say. "Her eyes are back to normal. Whatever was messing with her head back at the river, I'm pretty sure we've got her back."

Ian nods but says nothing.

I decide on the direct approach. "What do you think is going on?"

Ian takes his time answering. "Something happened to the town, and we got caught up in the middle."

"Do you think it has to do with the DARC?"

"Maybe." He shrugs. "All I know is, wherever we are, it seems pretty determined to kill us."

"The weather isn't our only problem," I point out. "That thing that got Becca back at the river is still in here with us."

Ian grabs another board from the pile and snaps it in half. "We'll have to watch ourselves." He waits for me to look at him. "If you feel something weird coming on again, speak up. I'm serious, Rose. Don't try to tough it out."

I lean back to study him, eyebrows lifting. "Because you're such a shining example of openness."

Ian massages his neck. "This is different. This is about survival." His expression darkens. "If I feel myself going over the deep end, I'll give you a heads-up." He looks away. "It might just buy you enough time."

"To do what exactly?"

He meets my gaze dead-on. "Run."

Oh.

138

I release a sharp breath and nod. "Fine. I'll tell you if I start to feel psychotic, if you promise to return the favor."

Ian stares at my hand hovering in the air between us. A second passes before his callused palm swallows mine. Starburst eyes zero in on me, and a jolt of electricity runs straight up my spine.

He misreads my shiver. "You don't have to be afraid of me, Rose."

After everything that's happened, he's still worried about frightening me. It's one more piece of evidence proving he isn't the monster people assume he is. A monster wouldn't worry about my feelings or help a little boy just because he asked. A monster wouldn't have dragged me through the snow or carried Becca like she was made of glass.

"I know."

Ian drops my hand, and I instantly feel the loss of warmth. There's something about him. A stillness that is somehow charged. Like the seconds of quiet between lightning and thunder. Mom told me once that every person was a strange land with their own strange weather. It makes me wonder if the secret landscape inside of us looks just a little bit the same.

Thoughts of storms bring mine back to the one outside. It hits me that I haven't heard the wind for a while. Quickly, I move to the mattress blocking the window.

Outside, the storm is breaking up. Already the snow has stopped, and the clouds are clearing, leaving behind a patchwork sky. Light bathes the landscape and illuminates a lake ringed by trees. When he was little, Charlie loved nights like this. He'd sit for hours with his nose pressed against the glass and a smile on his face like the stars were spelling out secrets only he could read.

Ian moves in close beside me. We're huddled next to the window like we need its light to breathe, and even though I don't want to break the strange connection that's been growing between us since the river, there's still one question I have to ask.

"Why did you fix my car? I mean, I know Charlie asked you to, but that doesn't explain why you did it."

Ian flexes his injured hand. "Your brother is different."

Different. I hate that word. I especially hate how people use it when they really mean something else. My feelings must show, because Ian shakes his head.

"That's not what I meant." He palms the bill of his cap. "It was something about the way he looked at me." When he turns to me, the expression on his face makes my heart snag in my chest. "I . . . I can't remember the last time someone asked me for a favor."

I'm still searching for a response when boards creak outside.

A sharp rap on the door has the terror from last night flooding back to me. I want to retreat inside myself like I did then, but the incessant pounding says whoever's out there isn't going away. It could be the person who pushed me into a raging river a few short hours ago.

It could be Charlie.

The strange tugging starts up in the center of my chest. This time, I don't hesitate. I let it guide me until I'm standing directly in front of Becca.

The next three heartbeats hang suspended, and then the peace crashes down with a *bang*. Right along with the front door.

FIFTEEN

"Crap!" The intruder stumbles and hits the floor.

Something about the high-pitched, nasal voice strikes a familiar chord.

Ian reaches for the person lying just inside the door, but I get there first.

Brown eyes blink at me through thick frames as I help the stranger off the ground.

Blaine's entire face lights up when he sees me. An unexpected warmth winds through my chest at the sight of him. He's a little piece of normal out here in these woods. More important, I can't remember the last time someone was this obviously happy to see me.

Blaine springs to his feet and moves in close to my side. His nostrils flare as he takes in the boarded-up windows. The mess of tools on the floor. The partially deconstructed bunks. "I haven't been in here since Scout camp in the fourth grade." His voice cracks at the edges. "Like what you've done with the place."

"Are you okay?" I ask.

"Not really." The side of his arm brushes mine.

"What are you doing here?" I ask.

"I was out for an evening stroll. I saw the smoke from your fire and thought I'd drop in."

"You think this is funny?" Ian speaks up.

The arm pressed against mine starts to tremble. "Nothing about this is funny."

"It's okay." I shoot Ian a warning glare and lead Blaine to the fire. He follows me like a puppy. When I sit, he hovers awkwardly over my shoulder, like he isn't sure what he's supposed to do.

I pat the blanket beside me.

Blaine drops down to the dusty floor and proceeds to tap his knuckles against the wood in a *rat-tat* pattern. "What's with her?" He nods at the sleeping girl by the fire.

"We found her in the river." Becca's hair has fallen across her face. I push it back, and Blaine's eyes bug.

The tapping stops. "Is that Rebecca. As in *Kennedy*?"

"Um, maybe?"

Blaine's eyebrows arch as he glances at Ian. "Fascinating."

Ian's glare has the younger boy cringing against me. I'm missing something here. What's Ian's connection to Becca, and why did it make Blaine react like that? A dozen new questions pop up in my mind. They'll all have to wait.

"What are you really doing here?" I ask.

"Hiding." It's just one word, but somehow, it's loaded with enough emotion to blow the roof right off this cabin.

"Have you tried going back to town?" I ask.

Blaine shakes his head. "Not yet. I tried to go home yesterday. My family lives a few miles outside of town, on the far side of the road. I kept walking and walking." His lips tremble. "But no matter how far I walked I never got there."

Ian and I share a look. Blaine is too wrapped up in his own story to notice. "I've been trying to get up the guts to head back into town all day, but that freak cold front came through almost killing me and..." He trails off.

"And what?" I press.

"And I was afraid of what I'd find," Blaine says, finally meeting my eyes.

Time collapses until I'm back in the high school parking lot listening to Blaine brag about how everything was about to change. The book in his lap and Rowena's pamphlet in his hand. Back then he'd struck me as a little bit strange and a lot lonely, but everything about that day looks different now. Including Blaine.

"Why were you afraid of going back to town?" I ask.

Silence.

"Please." I reach out and grab his hand. "We just want to know what's happening. Where did everyone go?"

Blaine blinks at me. "Go? What do you mean *go?*"

"The town is lost," Ian says. "It's completely covered up by some freak storm that seems to be growing wider. From what I can tell, the four of us are stuck with it in a six-mile-wide patch of woods that are all that's left of the world."

Blaine, who has been vibrating nervous energy since he first stumbled in here, goes completely still. "You said six miles?"

Ian shrugs. "Give or take. The land runs in a circle from the storm over town all the way to the woods, near where the road to Maple should be."

Blaine's face loses all color. "Oh God. Oh God."

"What is it?" My grasp on his hand tightens. "Blaine, what's going on?"

"It's called Murphy's Law. Otherwise known as everything going to complete and utter shit."

"You have two seconds to start making sense." Ian's shadow falls over us, and Blaine shrinks back. After what I saw in that parking lot, his reaction makes a sad sort of sense.

I motion for Ian to back off. He rolls his eyes but retreats to a safer distance.

"Explain it to us." I try for a gentle tone even though all I want is to shake him until he spills his guts.

Blaine's throat bobs once. "This patch of woods you're talking about. Approximately six and a half miles in diameter. Twenty miles in circumference. Just under thirty-two miles in total area. It's an exact match to the underground dimensions of the DARC."

My heart is suddenly beating so hard I can barely hear myself think.

Every clue, every bit of evidence has been pointing back to one place.

"What was it, Blaine? What was your uncle doing with the DARC?" I ask.

Blaine's gaze meets mine. "I can't tell you."

My stomach sinks.

The terror on his face melts away, leaving behind pure resolve. "But come with me, and I'll show you."

Blaine leads us across the campground to a shack on the lakeshore. Clouds are thin wisps across the black sky above us. As we walk, Blaine shoots repeated glances at me from under the brim of his oversize trapper hat.

The shack door opens, and a wall of warmth hits me. There's a portable furnace in the corner hooked up to a battery pack surrounded by wires. A few cables lead to an open laptop, while others are attached to a coffee maker, hot plate, and a half dozen other appliances.

My focus switches to the pine walls. They're covered with newspaper articles and pages ripped out of scientific journals. Some of them are familiar. About Fort Glory and the recent crime wave. Others talk about the collider in Switzerland and the DARC here in town.

Blaine walks to a desk littered with empty soda cans, candy wrappers, and books. They're piled high in corners and lying on dusty shelves. The titles are even stranger than the clippings on the wall.

Warped Passages: Unraveling the Mysteries of the Universe's Hidden Dimensions.

The Hidden Reality: Parallel Universes and the Deep Laws of the Cosmos.

Parallel Worlds: A Journey Through Creation, Higher Dimensions, and the Future of the Cosmos.

The Little Book of String Theory.

A flash of bright pink on the desk catches my eye. I stare at Rowena's pamphlet and the feeling of déjà vu almost bowls me over. "What is this place, Blaine?"

"Did you know my dad is the local pastor?" he asks, avoiding my question.

"So?" I ask.

"So my parents believe in the Good Book. As in, God created the world in six days. Let's just say they don't approve of my choice of reading material." He's talking fast. Like he recently drank a can of Red Bull and inhaled a Pixy Stix, but mostly, I think he's just relieved not to be alone.

"My dad used to drag me out here with his Scout troop. He thought it'd be good for me to 'get my hands dirty.'" Blaine places the words in air quotes. A flicker of old hurt crosses his face. "They haven't used this cabin in ten years. I knew I could stash my stuff here without anybody messing with it. I've been using it as a quasi office since eighth grade."

A drop of moisture draws my attention to the sagging ceiling. Something clicks. "This is the job you were talking about at school. You wanted me to fix this shed up for you."

Blaine pulls off the trapper hat. Static stands his curls on end. "There are a few leaks in the roof. My books kept getting wet." He says it like it's a disaster of epic proportion. "I figured you were desperate enough to help without asking a bunch of questions."

"What makes you think I'm desperate?"

Blaine rolls his eyes. "High school student working graveyard shifts at the Dusty Rose? Doesn't take a rocket scientist to do that math." His expression falls when he sees my face. "Sorry. I wasn't trying to be a jerk. Honest."

"You said you were an intern at the DARC," I say, letting it slide. "What did you do there?"

"Made copies. Delivered coffee. Cutting-edge shit like that."

"What does any of this have to do with the town?" Ian breaks his silence.

Blaine reaches for something on the desk—a book. The same book he was reading in the parking lot the first day I met him.

THE DEEP ATOMIC RESEARCH COLLIDER (DARC): Confirming String Theory by Unlocking the Universe's Hidden Dimensions by Arthur Jackson.

"What is it?" I ask.

"The closest thing I have to a Bible," Blaine says. "My uncle is a genius and a revolutionary. He says I take after him. He even gave me a shout-out in the dedication, see?" Blaine displays the title page and personalized signature like it's his most prized possession.

At our blank expressions, the book drops back into his lap. "The thing you have to understand about physics is that it is *competitive.* When funding for the DARC was approved in the nineties, it was supposed to blow the Large Hadron Collider in Switzerland out of the water. But none of that ended up mattering because the team in Europe got there first. *They* discovered the Higgs boson, or God particle. This is like..." He searches for a way to make us understand. "The holy grail of particle physics. And when they did that, all the money and hopes wrapped up in the DARC went bust. That's when my uncle got involved. He believed the DARC didn't have to compete with the European collider. He believed the DARC could be made into something completely new. We're talking next-level shit."

"In other words, go big or go home," Ian says.

Blaine nods. "The Large Hadron Collider in Switzerland excelled at finding new particles, but my uncle was hunting something more elusive. Something that, if he found it, would change *everything.*" He pauses for dramatic emphasis. "Extra dimensions."

The silence lasts a beat too long.

"We're talking parallel universes?" Ian sounds as doubtful as I feel.

"Yes. No. It's more complicated than that." Blaine starts to pace. "For years, scientists have been trying to create a theory of everything, unifying the four fundamental forces of nature into a set of equations that would reveal the inner workings of the universe. The problem is that we can't make the math work. Not unless we account for there being more dimensions than we can actually see. Specifically, eleven."

"And you're saying the work your uncle was doing with the DARC would prove the existence of these extra dimensions?" I ask.

Blaine's excitement is electric. "Think of our world as a tiny stage. Now imagine that most of reality lies behind a curtain, completely hidden from us. My uncle was using the DARC to punch a tiny hole into that curtain, offering us our first glimpse backstage. Depending on how close these extra dimensions are, he believed it might even be possible to open a portal to an entirely new world."

Ian leans against the door, effectively blocking the only exit. "Your uncle sounds like a crackpot."

"Funny," Blaine says, displaying a glimmer of nerve. "People said the same thing about Aristotle. Copernicus. Einstein. Perhaps you've heard of them."

"The people who funded the DARC obviously thought it was possible, or they wouldn't have put up the money," I say.

Blaine nods. "Like I said, the idea of extra dimensions isn't new. It's not that physicists don't believe these dimensions exist. It's that they've never been able to *prove* it."

Ian studies the clippings on the wall. "And this is what he's been doing since the DARC went back online last month?"

"Yes."

"Which is exactly how long things have been going haywire in Fort Glory?" I follow up.

"The last time I saw my uncle was on Monday at his office.

He was practically *giddy.*" Blaine shakes his head. "I'd never seen him like that before. He told me their sensors had detected a pulse during the DARC's last run. He was sure it was a signature of an extra dimension. A small trace that had slipped through before the cracks closed. It was proof that they were getting close."

Can you hear the music, Rosie?

The hairs on my arms stand up straight. "What kind of pulse?"

"He called it a dark pulse. *Dark* as in they didn't know where it was coming from." Blaine runs a hand through his hair, standing it on end. "I wanted to be happy for him, but it was too coincidental. I asked if it could have something to do with the way people were losing it."

I lean forward. "What did he say?"

"He shut down. Told me not to give in to the superstition and hysteria."

"But you didn't believe him?" I ask.

"I believe in following the evidence to its logical conclusion."

"And what conclusion is that?" Ian presses.

"That my uncle was doing exactly what he set out to do. That for weeks he's been successfully chipping away at the wall between the dimensions we see and the ones we don't." Blaine swallows. "Only he was so focused on getting that door open, he didn't ask himself the most important question of all: What would be waiting on the other side?"

"None of this explains what happened to the town," Ian says when the silence becomes unbearable.

"I know." Blaine's shoulders droop. "All I know is that everything is so messed up." He tosses the book, and it falls open on the floor. Ian's face takes on a strange intensity as he picks it up. I glance down at the open pages in his hands. One depicts a simple black-and-white diagram resembling an hourglass. A funnel with two open mouths and a bottleneck. The other is a three-dimensional, full-color rendering of what looks like the same thing.

Ian doesn't raise his eyes from the pages. "What's this?"

Blaine looks over his shoulder. "An Einstein-Rosen bridge. Aka white hole or wormhole." When neither Ian nor I show any sign of understanding, Blaine sighs. "Basically, it's a black hole with an entrance and an exit. It's a stellar version of the submicroscopic hole my uncle was trying to punch with the DARC."

Ian looks up at me. "The thing I told you about, hovering over the town. This is what it looks like."

For the first time all evening, Blaine forgets to be afraid. "Say what?"

"I was climbing when everything went to hell," Ian explains. "I saw something where the town should've been. It looked a lot like that thing right there."

"You saw a wormhole?" Blaine's voice reaches a painful octave. "Over the town?"

Ian rubs the back of his neck. "The effect was a little different in person, but yeah. Maybe."

"Oh God." Blaine stands up so fast, he upsets a stack of notebooks on the desk. "Don't you see what this means? It explains everything. Where we are. What happened to the town. *Everything*."

"Slow down, Blaine," I plead. "Help us understand."

"The DARC!" Blaine cries. "It succeeded in punching a hole

to another dimension. Only, that opening didn't stay on a quantum scale as planned. Somehow, it must've inflated out of control, growing into the wormhole you saw. One that leads to the source of the dark pulse." His hands drop to his sides. "It shouldn't be possible."

"Tell that to the town," Ian says.

Blaine blanches. His sorrow fills the cabin. It's real and it's suffocating, and it reminds me that I'm not the only one who lost someone when the town disappeared. He turns to the wall, but not before I see the tears on his cheeks.

I take a few steps toward him. Blaine draws a shuddering breath that freezes me in place. Suddenly, I'm not sure how to close the distance between us, or even if he'd want me to. So I wait for him to pull himself back together, and when he does I say, "There has to be something we can do."

"There isn't." He wipes his eyes with his sleeve. "We can't help anybody, and nobody can help us."

Fingernails bite into my palms. "I don't accept that."

"Doesn't change anything. Our town will still be gone, and we'll still be stuck here at the edge of the greatest achievement and, simultaneously, the worst disaster in recorded human history." Blaine slides down to the floor to hug his knees.

"Stuck where? What is this place?" Ian asks.

Grimly, Blaine holds up the diagram of the wormhole. "The world we know may seem solid, but it isn't. It's actually flexible—like this paper." Blaine folds the piece of paper, tucking the edge back into the binding so that the page forms a balloon in the middle of the book. "When the wormhole inflated out of control, it must've created a Fold in the fabric of space-time. Think of it as a bite-sized pocket of reality around the wormhole containing it—a safety mechanism put in place by the universe to protect itself. The three of us had the bad luck to be in the woods when it happened. Too far away from town to be sucked into the wormhole itself, but close enough to get caught up in the Fold around it. That's where we are."

"You're saying we're stuck in some weird bubble dimension with the wormhole that ate the town?" Ian asks for clarification.

Blaine nods miserably. "It's a piece of our universe that's bent out of shape. The rules will be different here. The environment more unstable. If you haven't picked up on that already. And it'll just keep getting worse."

His words leave me reeling. It's not just what he says but *how* he says it. Totally defeated. Like there's no way out of this. For any of us.

The cabin walls close in around me, and I sit down hard on the floor beside him. All this time, I've had a plan. Get to Fort Glory. Find Mom and Charlie. Get out again. But if Blaine is right, even if I find my family, there'll be nowhere safe to take them. It means that I can't chart my way out of this. No matter how hard I try, I can't fix it.

My hands drop uselessly to my sides. "There has to be a way out." I say it like I could make it true.

"There isn't. We're stuck in a loop with no entrance or exit." Blaine rests his head against the wall like it's become too heavy to hold up without assistance. "I'm guessing the wormhole over Fort Glory will keep pushing out until it takes over the Fold, and then the whole thing will just sort of... collapse in on itself. Theoretically," he adds, as if it in any way softens the blow.

His words buzz through my brain. Half of what he's saying goes right over my head, but one point I heard loud and clear.

My heart pounds in my chest as I rise to my feet. "You're wrong," I say. "There is a way into the Fold."

"And you know this because you've got a doctorate in theoretical physics you've conveniently failed to mention." One look at my face, and Blaine's instantly falls. "Sorry. I wasn't... I didn't mean it like that."

"No," I say slowly. "I know because it's how I got here."

SIXTEEN

D o you feel that?" you asked, turning away from the window. We had pulled off the road, behind a low rise in Yellowstone National Park. The sky stretched out above us in every direction. It was beautiful and so vast, it made me feel small, but not in the way I hated.

I wanted to lie in the grass until the dark fell around us and the stars danced over our heads. Instead, I continued plotting a course west.

"Do you feel it, Rosie?" you asked again.

"Feel what?" I kept my eyes glued to the map in my lap. The map didn't need me or say things I didn't understand. The map didn't fill the trailer with strangled night sounds or bleed as a reminder of all the ways I'd failed.

A groan rose from the front seat. We'd pulled over an hour ago so Mom could sleep while I came up with a plan.

It hurt to leave. Even when there was nobody left to say goodbye to. Even when bad things happened and staying was worse than running, I still wanted for something I couldn't quite name. I broke a little more each time. Pieces of me littered the highways from here to North Carolina.

It wasn't all bad, I told myself as I studied the squiggles, and numbers, and names of places I wanted to know. Running away also meant running toward. New roads. New signs. New people we could become.

"Listen," you said in that way of yours that gave me no choice.

I strained my ears, but whatever music was playing for you wasn't meant for me. "I don't—"

You reached out and placed your hand on my throat. I could feel our pulses marching together through a thin layer of skin. "Close your eyes."

I did. Because I loved you and because you asked me to. And because, deep down, I wanted to hear whatever it was you heard. For just one moment, I wanted some of the light that filled you to spill into me and chase away the darkness.

The sounds came to me slowly. Wind and deep breathing and distant highway music. And then everything faded away, because I finally knew what you were trying to tell me.

The air caught in my lungs. I was afraid to move. Afraid to shatter the peace that had fallen over us.

You smiled at me, your gift complete.

We looked up at the exact moment the snow started to fall. It danced from the clouds, light as feathers. We sat like that for hours, watching it purify the world outside our window until everything was new and clean.

Slowly, quietly, you reached for my hand, and the song inside of you poured into me.

I cried, tears of joy, not sadness, because for one moment, I too was beautiful.

"This changes things." Blaine stares at Deputy Miller's jacket like it's the most fascinating thing he's ever seen. He's been like this since I told him about hiking to Devil's Tooth with Rowena. About hearing Charlie's voice, the hook of fire in my chest, and the feeling of being yanked sideways.

"How?" I ask.

"I'm not sure."

It's not what I want to hear. "But if I fell into the Fold, there must be an opening between here and our world, right? If we could find it, couldn't we try to, I don't know, fall back out again?"

A deep trench cuts across his brow. "That would be like trying to find a needle in a universe-size haystack. The opening between the Fold and our world, *if* it exists, might not even lie in any of the four dimensions we have physical access to."

I'm about to ask what the hell that means when something moves in my peripheral vision.

A shadow. Streaking across the window.

I'm across the cabin floor in two seconds flat.

"What is it?" Ian asks, joining me at the window.

"There's someone out there."

"Are you sure?"

It's dark, and we're all on edge, but I know what I saw. "I'm sure."

"Rose is right. We're not alone." Blaine is wound so tight he's practically humming. "I've been hearing noises, outside. Like, voices. But whenever I look, there's nobody there."

Ian and I lock gazes. "Someone's been messing with us too," he says. "They ran in front of our tent last night and shoved Rose into the river earlier today."

Blaine pales. "So we should probably assume they don't come in peace."

"There could be more than one other person trapped in the Fold with us. It could be Charlie," I say, even though I don't really believe it. Charlie wouldn't haunt our steps like a ghost or try to spy on us. He wouldn't hide.

Not from me.

"That wormhole is an open door that swings two ways,"

Blaine says. "The dark pulse is only going to get stronger as it floods in. It could've sent whoever's out there over the edge. We could be dealing with some suburban housewife turned psycho killer."

I meet Ian's eyes, and for once, I know exactly what he's thinking.

Becca.

Ian bolts for the door. Blaine opens his mouth, but I push past him before he can ask for an explanation.

Outside, it takes my eyes a moment to find Ian in the darkness. He's sprinting full out toward a spot of pulsing brightness up ahead. Orange firelight bleeding around the cracked door of the cabin where we left Becca.

We didn't we leave it like that.

I sprint into the cabin and grind to a halt. Air leaves my lungs in a rush when I see Ian kneeling at the hearth beside Becca.

Footsteps pound the floorboard behind me

Blaine bursts in. "A little. Warning. Next time?" He bends over at the waist.

I block out the sound of his wheezing and walk over to the others. "I'll sit with her," I tell Ian, sinking down beside him. "Go. Make sure whoever's out there stays out." I need Ian focused on the threat outside. Not the one inside Becca's head.

With a lingering glance at Becca, Ian moves to do a quick sweep of the cabin while Blaine stands watch at the window.

Becca moans and rolls toward me. The covers twist around her legs. I lean over and pull the blankets back up.

My hands freeze in midair.

Becca's face. It's scary pale. But that's not what has my stomach twisting into a pretzel.

Bones protrude over hollow cheeks. Dark bruises form circles around her closed eyes. She looks frail. Sick.

She looks how Charlie looked before the town disappeared.

The realization sets my thoughts racing. A thousand questions bang around inside my head as I finish covering Becca up. There's something there. Some epiphany lurking just under the surface of my mind. If I could just quiet down the noise in my head long enough to *think*.

"Any sign of them?" I ask when I join the others at the window.

Ian shakes his head. "Whoever they are, they don't want to be seen."

The clouds move past the moon, flooding the clearing with light.

There's a flash of movement in the dark to our left. A shadow streaking from the edge of the woods to the shack we just left.

The wind blows. Something crashes in the dark behind the shack.

I go rigid. I can't help it. Whoever's out there, every instinct in my body is screaming we don't want to mess with them.

"I told you we weren't alone," Blaine whines, every trace of smugness gone. "I've been hearing them all day. Whoever they are, they're clearly deranged."

This time, I don't argue with him. Anyone in their right mind would've shown themselves by now. They wouldn't be taking every available opportunity to terrorize a bunch of kids.

"We have a bigger problem," I say. I don't try to explain. Instead, I lead them over to the hearth. Ian's shoulders stiffen when I pull back the blanket covering Becca.

"She's lost ten pounds since this morning," I say.

"You did fish her out of a river," Blaine says.

"Hypothermia wouldn't make her waste away. It also wouldn't do this." I pull back one of Becca's eyelids, displaying the dilated pupil.

"It's the dark pulse, isn't it?" Ian's question is directed at Blaine. For once, there's no ready answer on the tip of his tongue.

"We need to head for the outer edge of the Fold," I say, gaining both of their undivided attention. "As far away from the wormhole and the source of the dark pulse as we can get. It might be the only way to help Becca."

It's not a total lie. If the dark pulse is more concentrated near the town, its effects will probably be stronger there too. Getting Becca farther away may be the only way to save her. But that's not the real reason I want to go there.

I study Becca sleeping by the fire. The thinness of her body. The occasional grimaces that wrinkle her smooth brow.

Flashes of pain like the ones that had been crossing Charlie's face ever since we moved here.

Can you hear the music, Rosie?

Charlie can hear the dark pulse. He could hear it all along. Which means, all this time, I've been looking for him in the wrong place.

If the dark pulse is stronger near the wormhole, the noise for Charlie could be almost deafening. However Charlie escaped the wormhole, he wouldn't stay right near the source of the chaos. He's too smart for that. He'd head to the outer edge of the Fold.

Just like we need to do.

I lift my chin. "We have to leave. The sooner the better."

Ian's eyes stay locked on Becca. "Will heading farther out slow down what's happening to her?"

"Maybe." Blaine hesitates. "Maybe not."

Ian's hands hang uselessly at his sides for a moment before they reach up and grip the bill of his cap. "There are a few sleds in the closet. We can pack them up with supplies and haul out at first light."

"And risk running into the psycho stalking us?" Blaine asks.

"We don't have a choice," I say. "Not if getting out of here is the only way to help Becca."

"What about Charlie?" Ian asks me.

"You were right about the town," I tell him. "It's been taken over by the wormhole. Charlie would've had to run from it." I draw a breath to steady myself, but when I close my eyes, the image is there. The one of Charlie in the dark.

Blaine looks between us. "Your brother was in the town when the wormhole opened up?" When I nod, Blaine assumes an expression I don't like one bit. It's like his face is apologizing in advance for his mouth. "This wormhole isn't some elevator ride to an alternate, hospitable reality. Wherever it leads isn't pleasant." His eyes slide away from mine. "If Charlie was in Fort Glory, he's gone. I'm sorry."

Blaine's words fly right over my head. I don't know anything about physics, dark pulses, or wormholes, but I know my brother.

"You're wrong. I can feel him. Right here." I fist my hands over the memory of the tugging in my chest.

Blaine's eyebrows draw together. "You're telling me your brother managed to avoid the wormhole that devoured Fort Glory and everyone in it. And you know this because you *feel* it?"

He doesn't believe me. It stings even though it shouldn't. Not after everything that happened with my dad. But this is different. This is Charlie.

Charlie who can hear the dark pulse. Charlie who's always been halfway caught up in a world I can't see. I always knew there was something about him. Something special. It has to be connected to how he was able to escape when nobody else could. It *has* to be.

"You said it yourself," I say, searching for a way to make them understand. "We don't know how things work in the Fold. There could be some other force at play. What if—"

"Enough!" Blaine's face crumples before he turns it to the wall. His voice drops to barely a whisper. "My family wasn't perfect, but I loved them. I'd give anything to believe they're still out there somewhere." Blaine wipes his runny nose. "I want it so badly I can't think straight. Which is exactly why I can't let my brain go there just because it's what my heart wants to believe. That isn't how science *works*."

Blaine faces me, that ridiculous trapper hat clutched in his hands, and suddenly, it isn't the kid with the thick glasses and massive backpack I see. It's a scared-shitless little boy who misses his family.

"I realize it doesn't make sense," I say softly. "But I'm not asking you to believe me. It doesn't change what we have to do."

Ian nods. "We can load up and head out before dawn. With any luck that'll be early enough to ditch our tail."

There's still one major flaw with this plan.

"With the weather like this, we're going to need someplace safe to stay," Blaine says, seizing on it right away.

He's right. It's a problem. So I work it the way I work everything else. By taking it apart into pieces and fitting them back together in a way that makes sense.

A moment passes before the solution comes to me. "Glory Caverns." The guidebook I studied for two weeks before coming here had a small write-up about the caverns. They're supposed to be a well-kept local secret. "If I'm remembering right, they're about five miles southeast of town. That should put them inside the boundary of the Fold, opposite the wormhole. If we can find—"

"I know where they are." Ian's voice is strangely tight. I study him sideways. If he knew about the caverns all along, why didn't he suggest them in the first place?

"Creepy cave to wait for the end of times?" Blaine sighs, drawing his knees up to his chin. "My dad would've so loved this." *

SEVENTEEN

CHARLIE

"What about that one?" *asks the little light named Sarah.*

Up ahead, a star.

Brighter than the others.

Weary and wise.

Too old to be afraid.

"Come with us," *I say to the wise old light.*

"I am tired."

"It's hard to shine in the dark," *I say.* "But it isn't time to go out. Not yet."

The wise old light sighs.

"Come with us," *says the little light named Sarah to the old light named Winnie.*

"Where are we going?" *Winnie asks.*

I spin the silver thread between us. "To gather the lights in a silver net and bring them home."

Sarah reaches for Winnie's hand, showing her the silver thread between us. All the thousands of stars.

Fireflies trapped in glass jars to keep out the dark.

Winne cries when she sees. "How many are there?"

"Two thousand two hundred thirteen. We counted," *the little light named Sarah says proudly.* "Charlie is keeping them lit. We're gathering them up so they'll be ready."

"Ready for what?" *Winnie asks.*

"Someone special," *I tell her.*

The Black Nothing presses in around us.

It wants the stars. It can't have them.

Not yet.

I reach for the thread inside me. The one that leads to another place.

Light music to drown out the dark.

Golden Light feeds the silver threads, making them dazzle. It helps me to remember.

Salt spray, sea-foam, and sand between my toes.

Digging.

Her hands next to mine. Fingers touching. Chapped lips and dirty knees.

A single shell. Buried treasure.

I give it to her.

Round and white. Perfect snowflake in her hand.

The way she smiles.

Sand dollar, *she tells me.* It is special. Like you, *she says.*

Like you.

Like you.

Like you.

She builds a castle and she tells me we'll have one someday. A castle made of wood.

She packs the walls with promises, not with her lips but with her eyes.

So beautiful.

Cold. Wet.

I reach into the river and pull it toward me.

Cold wet.

I reach through the Black Nothing.

Through the curtains and doorways in my head. All the spaces in between.

I press my finger into the sand.

I write her name.

She's on the other side. I feel her.

So close.

I want to walk the rest of the way through, but I can't be with her and keep the lights on.

I have to stay.

To keep the stars from burning out.

So I leave something behind.

Something for her to find.

And I slip back into the dark.

The Black Nothing screams.

The scream goes on forever.

I want to hide.

Under the covers in my mind.

But I think of the lights.

Of her face over mine.

The words she said to me.

Once upon a time.

Breathe, Charlie. Just keep breathing.

So I do.

I breathe.

I stay.

When the Black Nothing comes,

I give it my hand.

EIGHTEEN

We stop at the edge of a clearing frosted over with ice. My muscles scream as the rope goes slack across my chest.

I take a few sips of water before raising the canteen to Becca's lips. She woke up this morning about an hour into our trek. Just sat up on the sled and started talking like nothing had happened. It makes me hope that getting her farther out might actually be making a difference. It's one thing we have going for us.

Maybe the only thing.

There's been no sign of Charlie since we set out for the caverns. I've searched every patch of woods, combed every inch of ground for his prints. Nothing. For the first time, I realize how big the Fold really is. Thirty square miles is a lot of ground to cover. If Blaine is right about this place collapsing, we don't have forever to find him. We might not even have days.

A stab of anxiety shoots through me. I ignore it and focus on putting one foot in front of the other. My shoes sink into the tracks Ian left behind. Despite the cold, he's been shedding layers all morning. A band of hard muscle shows above his belt line as he pulls the sweater over his head.

"You good?"

I blink, and he is standing directly in front of me. "Huh? I mean, yeah. I'm fine."

Ian wipes his face with the bottom of his shirt. "Take a breather. You've earned it."

Every part of me is simultaneously wet, cold, and burning with exhaustion, but all I can think about is Charlie the way he looked in that vision. The deadness in his eyes. The pain on his face.

"I'm okay," I tell him.

For a minute, it looks like Ian is going to argue. Instead, he readjusts the rope so it isn't cutting into my ribs and sets off again. Sweat forms a narrow triangle down his back. He's doing most of the work, pulling the supply sled and cutting the trail for the rest of us, but he hasn't slowed down all day. It's like he can't feel the cold, or the strain, or the fear. Like he's found some way above them.

"I have to pee," Becca announces. When I stop, she slides off the sled. "Thanks," she says, and hobbles through the snow. I'm watching her disappear behind a bush when a voice wheezes out behind me.

"Watch your back around Lawson."

When I turn, Blaine's glasses are fogged, and twigs cover the tie-dye sweatshirt he dug out of the camp's lost and found.

"He's not so bad." I motion for Ian to wait up ahead.

"That kid is a *Dateline* special waiting to happen."

"You don't know him," I cut back. "You just know what people say about him."

"You're right. I don't know if he started the fire that killed both his parents or if he laughed like a psycho while the flames ate them alive. But I'm not talking about some sketchball rumor. I'm talking about what he did to the mayor's son."

Stomach acid rises into my throat. "What's that?"

"He almost put the kid in a coma. Probably would've killed him if the police hadn't pulled him off."

"You were there?" A rock forms in the pit of my stomach.

"No, but I went with my dad to the hospital afterward. Official pastoral duties." Blaine blows into his mittens. "The kid looked like someone put him through a meat grinder. Don't get me wrong. Jeremy is a class-A douchebag, but nobody deserves that."

I avoid Blaine's gaze and find Ian up ahead, where he's cutting back some bushes with his knife, making the trail a little easier for us. He sends me a wave when he catches me watching him and quickly ducks his head. It makes me wonder how many other good deeds he does when he thinks nobody's looking.

My chest goes strangely tight. "If it was that bad, why'd they let Ian out of jail?" I ask.

Blaine raises an eyebrow. "The DA offered a plea bargain. It reduced Ian's sentence."

"Why would they do that?" The question comes out too loud, but Blaine doesn't seem to notice.

He shrugs. "Maybe the mayor's family didn't want the publicity of a trial. Maybe because everyone who saw what Ian did refused to come forward."

Everything he's saying only confirms what seventeen years have taught me about people.

"Why are you telling me this?"

He grips the straps of his pack. "That afternoon in the parking lot. What you did for me. It was cool. Girls like you never—What I mean is…you seemed different, like, sort of lonely or…crap. I didn't mean that like it sounded." Blaine claps his gloves together and breathes into his hands. "I just thought that maybe, I don't know. We could be friends. Or something."

It's the most inarticulate thing I've ever heard him say. I'd hug him if I didn't think we'd both die of embarrassment.

"Anyways," he blazes on, red-faced. "I just figured I owe you one for—"

"Yes, Blaine. I'd like to be your friend."

His eyes go wide between thick frames. "Really? I mean, yeah. Um. Awesome."

"But you don't have to worry about me, okay? I can take care of myself. And if it wasn't for Ian, none of us would be here." I don't know where my certainty comes from, but I'm sure Ian isn't dangerous. The same way I'm sure that Charlie is out here somewhere. It's a feeling down deep in my gut. Lately, those feelings seem more real to me than the real world around me.

Blaine doesn't look entirely convinced. "All I'm saying is you might want to think twice before you go off alone with him. Ian's got baggage. You never know when the dark pulse might unload it on us."

It's nothing I haven't already thought of. As long as the dark pulse is in here with us, we're all a potential threat.

Some of us more than others.

Becca reemerges. I shoot Blaine a brief nod to let him know I heard him before I help her back onto the sled. We've been pushing forward another twenty minutes when Ian stops at the top of a knoll. Needing a break from pulling, I drop the rope and trudge up the hill. I'm halfway to the top when a strange ache blossoms in my chest.

The tugging. I've been noticing it more and more. At first, it weirded me out, but lately it's become more of a comfort than a nuisance. I can't explain it, but it makes me feel less alone.

The sensation in my chest intensifies as I join Ian at the edge of another clearing. I'm about to ask him if he feels it too, when I notice his face. He's staring down at the clearing like whatever he sees is about to change everything. His eyes meet mine, and I know it already has.

The wind blows through the trees, freezing the sweat to my skin.

Time slows as my gaze runs across the acres of pristine snow, narrowing in on a small section of discoloration in the perfect smoothness. At first, I can't decide what I'm supposed to be seeing. Then my eyes adjust to the scale, and I can make out the narrow lines of a single word written into the snow.

Not just any word.

A name.

ROSIE.

NINETEEN

Shhh." I pressed my hand over your mouth. You hardly ever spoke, but touching you made me feel better, and I needed that with the engine revving outside. I could identify the truck by that roar as easily as I could by the bright orange flames painted across the hood. Vinyl seats. Ashtray smell.

The monster was back. His kind never took no for an answer.

Tap. Tap. Taptaptap.

"I want what you promised." His voice shredded through paper-thin walls.

"I didn't promise anything." Wood grated across linoleum as our mother dragged our only chair over to the front door.

"You took my money."

"It was a gift!" There were tears in her voice, but I made myself hard against them. I'd told her not to take the money. I'd told her this would happen.

"He's just trying to be kind," she'd said when we'd first met him a few weeks ago and he'd fixed our taillight. "People do things like that sometimes, Rose. Because they want to help."

"Not people like that." I'd seen the man's eyes. They were full of something. It wasn't kindness.

"Don't worry so much." She had smiled. "It'll give you wrinkles."

I worried anyway. I worried because gifts like this had strings attached, and sometimes those strings found a way around your neck.

I closed my eyes. Nothing could block out the strike of fists against flimsy wood.

Soft hands pulled me to my feet and into the bathroom where you were crouched by the toilet. Mom kneeled in front of us, and the expression she wore was one I had never seen. It was love, and it was pain, and it made my chest ache with emotions I didn't have words for.

She handed me a book. "Read this to your brother," she said in a whisper. "Lock this door when I leave." She grabbed me by the chin. Nails dug into skin. "No matter what happens. Don't open this door. Do you hear me, Rose?" She waited for me to nod. She left.

You held the book, and I held you, and the world broke in half along with the front door. I closed my eyes.

"Give me what you owe me," said the monster in the dark. "Give me what I paid for."

"Leave. Now and there'll be no trouble."

"I'm not leaving without the money."

Soft thuds and the click of glass. The lid came off our savings jar with a clatter. I knew. It wouldn't be enough.

"Two hundred and fifteen dollars?"

"It's everything I have."

"Not my problem. Give me what I want, or I'll tell everyone what you are. Who do you think they'll believe? You think they'll let you keep those kids if you're homeless?"

"I won't do it," our mother said. And then stronger: "No!"

In spite of everything, I felt a flash of pride.

But in the end the word was like the door. Too small a thing to stand against the weight of this evil.

Everything got quiet. So, so quiet. And then came the singing. Soft and low and aching. I listened to it, and I knew that life would never be the same. That none of us would be. And I cursed our father for disappearing, and our mother for her beauty and her faith in people who didn't deserve it. I picked up the book and read about a dog that belonged to himself. I read about his pipe and his house and his bowl of soup for dinner, and I swore that someday I'd be like him. Someday I'd have a house with a kitchen and a door to withstand heavy feet.

I would build that house. It would belong to me, and I would belong to it.

I read until you fell asleep in my arms, and the monster left, and the singing was replaced by a silent crying louder than any sound I'd ever heard.

My eyes devour every detail of the word in the snow. The shape of the *R*. The curve of the *S*. The memory of a hand trembling as I taught it how to write.

Air leaves my lungs in a rush.

"Rose, what is it?" Ian demands.

"It's Charlie." A grin breaks out across my face. Ian's eyes widen when I turn it on him. "He wrote this, Ian. That means..." *Oh God.* "Charlie!" I sprint into the clearing, halting just short of my name. "Charlie!"

"Rose, stop."

My heart is pounding like a jackhammer. Somehow, someway, Charlie is *alive*.

Wonder fills me as I stare at the proof in the snow. I sink to my knees in front of it, and the knot I've been carrying around inside of me finally starts to unwind. I can't explain how Charlie escaped the wormhole that took Fort Glory, or how I've been able to feel his presence here in the Fold, but I know Charlie. This is his way of telling me he's still out there.

That, maybe, they all are.

I close my eyes, and the tugging is right there in the center of my chest. All at once, I can feel my brother's presence lingering in this clearing like the scent of Mom's perfume. It makes me miss him so much I can barely breathe.

Ian's hand drops onto my shoulder. "If Charlie was still here, he would've shown himself by now. He's probably gone to find shelter. The weather is turning again."

For the first time in minutes, I become aware of my surroundings. The light around us is fading fast, and the cloud cover is getting thicker by the minute. It's warmer than it was when we started out this morning. The snow is already turning wet and heavy under our feet.

The rush of finding Charlie's message is still pulsing through my blood when the sharpest tug yet draws my eyes to my name in the snow. Desperate for some kind of physical connection to my brother, I reach for the familiar letters. My palm presses into the cold snow, directly between the *O* and the *S*.

It happens without warning. A wave of agony hits me with the force of a sledgehammer.

There's a flash of gold, and then my hand is on fire. So hot it feels like the bones will melt right through the skin.

Darkness rushes toward me from the edges of my vision, a curtain falling on the world. It's almost blinded me completely when I see him.

Charlie.

Trapped behind a wall of darkness. His body gives off a soft glow, the only source of light in the pitch-black.

His head is bent. His entire body pitched as he grips something against his chest.

Darkness bleeds from the wall. Tentacles of shadow. They reach for him.

Run. The command is a scream trapped inside of my head.

But Charlie doesn't run. He doesn't even hide. He just grits his teeth and offers something to the dark.

His hand.

The shadows writhe around it, smothering its soft glow.

My heart stutters. Charlie looks up, almost like he can hear it.

The blood turns to ice in my veins.

Charlie's eyes. The violet eyes he got from our mother are two black spots in his beautiful face.

The light in my brother's hand starts to flicker. His lips part in a silent scream.

I stare at the place where Charlie's hand was just a moment ago. It's dark. Like the wall around him. Like his eyes.

Gone.

The realization sends a crack through my foundation. And then I'm collapsing in on myself like a house made of paper.

The darkness rushes toward me. I watch it come and this time, I can't fight it.

I reach out to Charlie one more time.

I'm still reaching when all the colors run to black.

TWENTY

My searching hand connects with something hard.

Charlie!

My eyes won't work, so I go by touch alone. He feels solid. Warm.

Whole.

I dig my face into Charlie's neck and breathe in his scent. Oranges and snow. Honey and oil.

Oil?

Something shifts. The darkness goes gray at the edges. And then I'm not holding on to Charlie anymore. He's holding me. He strokes my hair and whispers reassurances into my ear.

Cold. It's so cold.

Stubble scratches my cheek.

No. That isn't right.

My eyes flutter open to cement sky.

I lean back to the sight of Ian's anxious face.

"Damnit, Rose." He breathes the words into my hair. My body relaxes into his embrace for a second before another wave of pain crashes into me.

Oh God.

With a groan, I pull my burning hand into my chest.

Ian's grip on me tightens. "It's okay. You're gonna be okay. Just breathe, Rose. Breathe through it."

A memory echoes through my head. The same words coming out of my mouth three years ago.

Breathe, Charlie. Just keep breathing.

Another wave of pain drives the past back behind the wall inside of me. Where it belongs. Swell after swell rocks through me as I lie in Ian's arms. Each one a little less intense until I can finally sit up on my own. The first thing I do when I regain control of my body is crane my neck to see around Ian's wide shoulders. It's still there. Solid letters in the snow.

Every muscle in my body goes limp.

It was real. I didn't imagine it.

"It's the pain again?" Ian asks.

I nod, my gaze still locked on my name as I rub at the lingering ache in my bones.

"You blacked out for a minute." Ian helps me sit all the way up. "Scared the hell out of me."

A warmth that has nothing to do with the rapidly changing weather spreads through my belly. It's almost enough to make me forget about the throbbing in my hand. "Were my eyes—?"

"Normal. Just like last time." Ian's touch is surprisingly gentle as he cups my elbows. "Can you walk?" When I nod, he lifts me to my feet. "Come on. Let's get back to the others."

Blaine is on me the second we come back into view. "You look like a ghost. Why do you look like a ghost?" His voice drives a spike straight through my temple.

"Let her breathe, will you?" Becca offers me the canteen. I take it gratefully. Her eyes dip to my trembling hand, but she doesn't say a word. If I didn't already like the kid, that would've clinched it.

Blaine bounces back and forth on his feet. It's obviously taking every ounce of his self-control to keep his mouth shut. I can't decide if he's concerned for my safety, or terrified that he'll end up stuck out here alone with Ian if I somehow drop dead.

Which is looking more and more like an actual possibility.

I sit down hard on the wooden seat and concentrate on breathing. My hand still throbs, but it isn't the pain that's stealing my air. It's the image burned on the back of my eyelids. The one of Charlie reaching out to me. The pain on his face and those blacked-out parts of him. He needs me. I can feel it. The knowledge is a thousand-pound weight crushing my chest. It's getting harder to breathe. Harder to think. All I know is that I have to find him. Now. Before whoever is hunting us decides to switch to easier prey. Before I lose my mind completely, or the dark pulse erases Charlie the way it is slowly erasing Becca.

Before there's nothing left.

I grind my teeth to keep them from chattering. My heart beats out of control against my ribs. I might be imagining all of this. It might be my mind searching for a way to rationalize the pain, but I don't think so.

Certainty flows through me along with the strange tugging in my chest.

A pair of fingers snap inches from my nose.

"Earth to Rose."

Blaine's anxious face comes back into focus.

"What's the deal with your hand?" he asks.

With effort, I let it drop down to my side. "It's fine."

"She's getting flashes of pain," Ian speaks up. "They're not tied to the dark pulse. Her eyes are totally normal when they hit." He pauses. "I think they're getting worse."

I shoot Ian a look, but he just stares right back, daring me to disagree. I haven't said a word about the pain getting worse, but Ian must've noticed. Just like he notices everything. "You were talking to someone," he says. "When you blacked out. It was like you were somewhere else."

"It's nothing." Ian's gaze turns sharp on my face, but I pretend not to notice. "There was pain, and now it's gone, and that's all I remember."

I ignore the little twinge I feel at the lie. The visions of Charlie *are* important. But whenever I try to find the words to describe them, the wall inside of me rises up to block my throat. Besides, Blaine and Ian already think I've got a blind spot when it comes to my brother. Going into detail about hallucinations of him disappearing piece by piece isn't going to help.

The pain. The visions. The tugging. All of it is tied together in a way I can't figure out, but I will. The same way I figure out everything else.

On my own.

A rush of adrenaline flows through my veins. I take one more deep breath, and then I stand to face the others. "My brother is here, and I can finally prove it." I lead them to the edge of the clearing. "It's a message," I say. "To let me know he's still alive."

Blaine studies the letters in the snow for a long moment before he says, "Tell me about Charlie."

Ten years of protective instinct kick in without warning. "Why?"

"Roughly two thousand people disappeared when things went south at the DARC. So far, there's only one known survivor.

That makes all information on the subject of Charlie Montgomery relevant." Intelligent eyes narrow thoughtfully on my face. "Something makes you think he could pull this off. I need to know what it is."

"Charlie isn't like anybody else," I say. "There's this light around him. He doesn't see things the way we do. He doesn't look at people and think how terrible they are. He only sees how good they can be, and when he's looking at you, just for a minute, you believe it too."

"Okay, I get it. He's good people," Blaine says.

I gnaw the inside of my cheek to keep from groaning. How am I supposed to explain something I don't even understand? I rack my brain, but the words I'm searching for aren't there.

They never are when I need them.

"It's more than that," Ian says. He tosses his pack onto the supply sled. "There was something about him—about the way he looked at me." His eyes meet mine briefly. "It made me wonder if there was more to the world than what I could see."

My shoulders slump because that's it. Exactly.

"As unexpectedly poetic as that is," Blaine says, "I'm not sure how it's relevant."

"It's relevant," I say. "Charlie could hear the dark pulse, Blaine. He's called it music. It's been hurting him. Ever since we moved to Fort Glory."

Blaine eyes narrow on me with laser focus. "Explain."

When I'm done, Blaine stares at my name in the snow. "If Charlie can hear the dark pulse—if he somehow evaded the wormhole, we need to know *how*." He glances up at me. "We have to find him."

I don't realize how much I needed to hear those words until

180

he says them. My face goes hot as tears prick the corners of my eyes.

"There's another storm blowing in," Ian says, drawing attention away from me.

I quickly wipe my face while I look up at the sky. It's getting steadily darker. Either time in the Fold is pulling another fast one on us, or something nasty is headed this way.

I study the clearing one last time. If Charlie was here, he would've heard me call for him by now. He's probably gone to wait out the weather in whatever shelter he's used to survive these past few days. There's nothing left for me here.

Ian tosses me the rope to the supply sled, switching it up so that he's the one pulling Becca. His impatience is contagious. This weather is scary.

We resume the trek. The rope digs into my shoulders. My back. It's getting harder and harder to lift my legs. Ian doesn't say a word, but it's obvious I'm slowing him down.

"Go ahead," I say the second time he doubles back for me. "Take Blaine and Becca and head for the caverns. She needs that shelter more than any of us."

Ian looks up at the sky. The clouds are tinted lime green.

His mouth sets in a hard line. "They aren't far. When I've got them settled I'll come back for you and the supplies. Just follow my tracks. Don't leave the trail I cut. For any reason, okay?" Ian waits for my nod before he pulls ahead. Within minutes he's vanished into the trees up ahead.

I keep walking. One painful foot at a time. Thoughts of Charlie chase me the whole way. I can't escape the feeling that he's close. Like we're back at the trailer and he's just in the next room. Separated from me by a flimsy wall. The sensation is so intense, I keep expecting to see him. Behind every tree. Around every turn in the path Ian cut. But whenever I look, there's nothing there.

After a few more minutes, I pause to catch my breath. I'm reaching back for the canteen when something in the snow draws my attention.

A single set of footprints.

They lead down to the bottom of the narrow ravine a dozen yards to my right.

Lightning flashes in the distance.

My hands move to the rope and freeze. Ian told me not to leave the path for any reason. But this isn't just any reason. This is Charlie.

The rope falls to the snow behind me as I make my way down to the bottom of the ravine. The grade isn't steep. My right hand is still tender, so I brace myself with my left. I'm about a quarter of the way down when my feet slip out from under me. I finish the descent in an inelegant slide, coming to a stop directly next to a little stream. I'm so intent on Charlie's footprints, it takes me a minute to realize.

I am not alone.

A boy stands on the opposite side of the creek. Not Charlie. A soldier in uniform. He's young—not much older than I am— with sharp, handsome features and short-cropped black hair. Something metallic gleams in his hand.

I rocket to my feet.

The boy lifts his weapon, and then I'm staring down the barrel of a gun.

My heart slams into my throat as I come face-to-face with

the person who's been following us. The one who pushed me into the river.

I resist the urge to back up. Any sudden movement could set him off. The soldier doesn't look deranged; all the same, the dark pulse must have control of him. Why else would he draw his gun?

My eyes dart to the ridge. Twelve yards of icy slope. I might be able to beat him to the top, but what if he decides to put a bullet in my back instead?

A dozen questions are still running through my mind when the soldier takes a step forward, making the decision for me.

I trip over my feet in my hurry to back up. The soldier frowns and follows my gaze to the weapon in his hands. He quickly lowers the gun.

I make my move.

"Wait!" he calls out as I turn and sprint up the gulch. Boots splash through water behind me.

I've made it ten yards when a gloved hand closes around my ankle. My leg flies out from under me as the soldier drags me toward him on my stomach. I kick and scream and spin around to face him. His body presses mine into the snow.

"Stop," he says.

I lash out. He blocks the punch. In one swift move, he has both of my arms pinned over my head. "Cut it out. I'm not going to hurt you."

"You *are* hurting me." His weight is crushing, and his fingers dig into my wrists.

Hazel eyes widen. The soldier raises himself up onto his elbows and quickly drops my hands. It's not something a crazy person would do, but I don't give myself time to think about that.

My next blow catches him off guard. The soldier swears and sits back. It's the opening I need. I wriggle free and lurch to my feet.

I'm halfway up the ridge when he calls out. "Rose?"

When I turn, the soldier is sitting right where I left him. "It's you, isn't it?" He rises slowly to his feet. "Rose Montgomery?"

Blood pounds in my ears. "How do you know my name? Why have you been following us?"

"Following you? I haven't been—" The soldier's eyes dart over my shoulder. Every muscle in his body goes rigid.

Ian's approach is soundless, but somehow, I know it's him. As soon as he reaches my side, the tension seeps out of me.

"You're here." The relief in my voice takes us both by surprise.

Ian frowns at me. "I didn't feel right leaving you, so I turned back. Are you okay?" A muscle jumps in his jaw when he sees the grip marks on my wrist where the soldier grabbed me.

"Fine. He surprised me, but Ian. He knows who I am."

Ian's gaze swings to the soldier. Something dark slithers across his features, and suddenly, I'm looking at a completely different person. Someone who's capable of all the awful things people accuse him of.

"I'm sorry I scared you," the soldier says, ignoring Ian completely. "But I needed to find out if it was really you."

"What do you mean?" I ask.

"You're Rose Ellen Montgomery, right?" the soldier asks. "Seventeen-year-old transfer student to the local high school? You live with your mother, Helen, and your little brother, Charles, in a trailer last seen on Glory Point."

"How do you know that?" All at once, I feel like I'm in one

of those interrogation rooms with the one-way mirrors. "Why have you been following us?"

"I already told you. I haven't been following you, and as it happens, I know a lot about you, Rose."

I study the soldier's dirt-streaked face. If he hasn't been following us, who has? More important, what's he doing here? Unless...

"Charlie." I take a step forward. "My brother. Have you seen him? Did he tell you about me?"

The soldier shakes his head. "I'm sorry. You're the first person I've seen since yesterday."

"What about the town?" Ian cuts in. "Do you know anything about that?"

The soldier gathers himself before he looks at Ian. "Since Fort Glory disappeared three days ago, there's been nothing. No signs of the town. No traces of the two thousand plus people who lived there. There's talk that it had something to do with the DARC, but really, there've been no actual leads. Except one."

I take a step backward. "What? Why are you looking at me like that?"

"The same day Fort Glory disappeared, a girl went missing. Word is she vanished into thin air. Right in front of some local cops."

My stomach sinks into the soles of my sneakers.

"The story blew up," the soldier continues. "People went nuts trying to connect the girl to the DARC. To the town." He shakes his head. "*That's* how I know you. Because, Rose Montgomery, your face is plastered on every newspaper and television screen in the world."

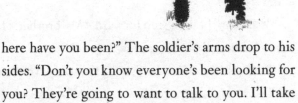

TWENTY-ONE

Where have you been?" The soldier's arms drop to his sides. "Don't you know everyone's been looking for you? They're going to want to talk to you. I'll take you—"

"You aren't taking her anywhere."

The raw anger in Ian's voice has me doing a double take. Ian doesn't lose his cool. Ever. There's something going on here. Some subtext I'm missing.

The soldier smiles. It isn't remotely friendly. "That's what I've missed most about you, Lawson. Your fabulous people skills."

"You know each other," I say. It's not a question.

Before either of them can reply, Becca's voice drifts down to us. "Jeremy?"

The soldier freezes.

"Jer?" Becca's dark head pops over the ledge. At the sight of her, Jeremy's whole face transforms. The gun falls from his hands as he scrambles up the muddy slope and drops to his knees in front of Becca. He doesn't touch her. He just looks at her like he's afraid she'll disappear, and then her arms are around his neck, and they're holding each other while Ian and I look on, forgotten.

"Thank God you're all right. They told me you were gone, but I didn't...I couldn't—"

"It's okay, Jer." Becca strokes his head, and even though I don't know him, it kills me a little to watch this big, tough soldier come apart in her frail arms.

Jeremy pulls back without letting go. "What happened? Are you hurt?"

"I'm fine. Rose and Ian have been taking care of me."

Jeremy nods at me briefly over her shoulder. "Mom and Dad?"

A tear slips down Becca's cheek. Whatever Jeremy feels, to his credit, he locks it up tight. "It's okay." He brushes away the tear with a dirty thumb. "We're together now."

"About that," Blaine says. He's sitting at the top of the gorge with his scrawny legs dangling over the edge. "How exactly did you get here?"

Jeremy squints up at Blaine. "Do I know you?"

"You're kidding, right?" Blaine slides over the ledge and starts picking his way down. "Science fair. Two years ago. You and your idiot friends cut my string theory display to pieces and then humiliated me when I won first prize in spite of you."

Recognition lights Jeremy's face. "Pastor Jackson's son?"

"My name is Blaine." His voice vibrates with an anger I didn't think he had in him. "Not that anybody calls me that anymore. I'm now known as Blaine the Brain. Thanks for that, by the way."

"I'm sorry. I'm...not that guy anymore." Jeremy's tan cheeks turn ruddy.

"How convenient," Blaine snaps. "How about you just answer the question?"

"Yeah, okay." Jeremy runs a hand through his black hair. "I

was moving through the woods when there was a pain in my chest. It felt like my insides were on fire. I must've fallen, because that's the last thing I remember before waking up a few hours ago."

My gaze locks with Blaine's. "It's the same thing that happened to me when I fell into the Fold. There's a way in. There has to be." My heart takes a wild gallop through my chest. If we can figure out how Jeremy and I got in here, maybe we can figure out a way to get back out.

"You said you were in the woods. What were you doing there?" I ask.

"My commander told me Becs had skipped out of school the day the town disappeared and that nobody had seen her since." Jeremy's hold on Becca tightens. "I thought there was a chance she'd gone to the river. That she was lost, or—" His Adam's apple bobs. "I got in my truck. It's like the end of the world out there. People are getting out of the state. Others are pouring in. Scientists and military. The government set up a perimeter around the town, but I know these woods." His eyes dart to Ian and quickly away. "I found a way past it."

"You were looking for Becca?" I ask.

Jeremy nods. "I was calling for her in the forest when I heard something. It sounded like a voice before it turned into whistling. That's when the tugging started. It got so bad I couldn't think about anything else."

Becca leans into Jeremy, and he takes her hand. I watch them together, and my own hands feel cold. Empty. I'm raising them to my lips when something clicks into place.

My fingers freeze halfway to my mouth. "Jeremy came here looking for Becca. Just like I came back for Charlie. There's something—something about our connection to them that allowed us to pass into the Fold."

Blaine doesn't say a word, but I can almost hear the gears in his head shifting to make room for this new info.

"The Fold?" Jeremy frowns.

"We'll explain later," I say. Visibility is almost down to zero. There's a weird current in the air that has the flyaways dancing at my temples. "We have to find shelter."

Jeremy pulls Becca to her feet beside him. "We're heading back to the road. Come with us."

"You can't go back to the road," I tell him.

"Listen to her, Jer," Becca pleads, but it's obvious Jeremy isn't ready to hear it.

"Look," he says. "I get why you might be worried about what'll happen if you go back with me."

"What's he talking about?" Blaine demands. "Why would you be afraid to go back to the road?"

A sinkhole opens up in my stomach.

Jeremy said they'd been looking for me for days. That every media outlet in the world had been trying to dig up information—

My eyes lock with Jeremy's.

"It'll be okay." He makes me the same promise he made Becca. He delivers it with so much conviction I almost believe him. "But you have to come back with me."

I shake my head. Whatever they've discovered about my past, whatever Jeremy knows or doesn't know, it's irrelevant.

"Listen to me," I say. "What you described earlier? That thing that happened to you? It happened to me too. I haven't been hiding, Jeremy. I've been trapped in here. We all have."

"I won't force you to come with us, but trust me. If you stay here, you are making a massive mistake." He reaches for Becca's hand.

"Jer, you're not listening." She tries to pull loose. "Jer, stop!"

"Let her go." Ian blocks his path.

"Back off, Lawson." Jeremy tries to move around him. Their shoulders collide. The impact sends Jeremy back a step.

"Move." Jeremy's voice is low and furious.

"Or what?" Ian growls. "Your daddy isn't here this time to cover your ass."

"Don't give me that shit. This isn't about my father or what happened to you. This is about Wi—"

Ian's fist connects with Jeremy's jaw, snapping his head backward. Blood spurts from his mouth. Becca screams as Jeremy stumbles.

He spits out a mouthful of blood and straightens to face Ian. "You want to do this now? Let's do it." Jeremy undoes the buckle across his chest. The rucksack hits the ground behind him.

Becca moves to interfere. I yank her back. The way Ian and Jeremy are looking at each other, it's like they could drown the whole world in the bad blood between them. They're both pissed off and stubborn, and it's going to get somebody hurt.

I'll be damned if that person is Becca.

I look down at the little girl in my arms. Once, when Charlie was five, I spent an evening catching the last fireflies of the season in a glass jar. I'd wanted him to have a little piece of summer by his bed, but I realized my mistake the moment I tried to give it to him. The expression on Charlie's face when he saw those bugs behind glass is the same expression Becca wears as she watches her brother and Ian now.

My grip on Becca tightens. "This is ridiculous," I snap. "You're both acting like idiots."

Jeremy's smile is a blade. "I can't help it if this asshole keeps trying to kill me."

His words send my mind flying back over the last three days. To every loaded look. Blaine's story about the mayor's son.

All the things Ian didn't say.

"Your dad is the mayor of Fort Glory?" I ask Becca. "Jeremy is the kid Ian assaulted two years ago?"

Becca nods. "They were best friends until they ruined everything. Now they're gonna do it again."

"Stay back, Becca," Jeremy says, but Becca just struggles harder to break out of my arms. "Now!" Jeremy's shout echoes through the forest.

Becca's chin warbles. "You want to kill each other? Fine." She wrenches free from my grip and walks off to stand beside Blaine.

Lightning flashes again—faster now as Ian and Jeremy start to circle each other in the snow. It's pointless and it's juvenile, and worst of all, it's wasting precious time we don't have.

"Ian, cut it out." I grab hold of his arm.

Ian's gaze drops to my hand before it lifts to my face.

Ice floods my veins.

His eyes. They're almost completely black.

I let out a quick breath and step backward. My muscles are tense, ready to bolt. I'm halfway to the trees when I notice Blaine hiding on the other side of the supply sled. That stupid hat of his a twisted lump in his hands. Beside him, Becca stands with her arms around her waist like they're the only thing keeping her from flying apart.

The thuds of fists on flesh ring through the forest as Jeremy launches himself at Ian. They're going at it like the two mechanics in Maple, and there's not a doubt in my mind that this is going to end the same way.

I look at the woods over my shoulder and then back at Blaine and Becca, hiding behind the sled.

I let out a breath and force my hands to unclench.

The fight. The storm. My pounding heart. I block out everything and focus on the problem, and then I do what I do best.

I find a way around it.

Blaine's eyes are puffy and red-rimmed as they watch me approach. "They're going to rip each other to pieces," he says.

"It's the dark pulse," I say. "It's getting to them."

"They could've picked a more convenient time to go postal." Blaine shoots the sky an ominous glance just as another band of lightning cuts across it. "This dry lightning," he says. "It isn't normal."

Just like the blizzard and the intense cold front weren't normal. It's coming too fast without any thunder to break it up. It makes the world feel like a movie cut into frames with no sound.

"We need to leave. Right now," Blaine says, echoing my thoughts perfectly.

"We can't find the caverns without Ian," I say. "I think I know how to get through to him. But I'm going to need both of you."

More thuds. More grunts of pain.

Becca meets my gaze. Tears are streaming down her face, but her mouth sets in a stubborn line. The same one I saw when she was clinging to that rock in the river. "Tell me what you need," she says.

I don't waste any time.

When I turn around, Ian and Jeremy are on the ground. They're so intent on killing each other they don't even notice when I upend Ian's pack. The thing I need is shoved at the bottom.

I light the flare. There's an explosion of crimson smoke as it shoots through the canopy. A red missile, slashing the sky above us.

Jeremy and Ian fly apart. It's just a second, but it's all I need. I suck in a breath and step directly between them.

Both boys surge to their feet. It takes Ian's darkness-shot eyes a full minute to focus on me.

"Get out of the way, Rose." Ian's voice is as angry as I've ever heard it, but still, I feel a flood of relief. He *knows* me. The dark pulse is working on him, but it doesn't own him. Not yet.

"I'm done watching this. You want Jeremy bad enough, you're going to have to go through me."

The coldness in Ian's eyes cuts right through me. "This isn't your business."

His words light a fire inside of me. I take a step toward him, and he meets me halfway, drowning me in his shadow. We're so close now, we're practically breathing the same air. My pulse stutters. The little voice is back in my head—the one that has kept me alive until now.

Run! it screams. *Run!*

Instead, my feet grow roots to the earth. "What happens to you concerns me," I snap. "What happens to Blaine concerns me too. And what about Becca? Are you going to force her to watch this?"

At the mention of Becca's name, the darkness in Ian's eyes retreats just a fraction.

It's Blaine's cue. He doesn't miss it.

Blaine's voice carries loudly in the eerie silence. "You guys! Come quick! It's Becca!"

She's lying on the ground at his feet, her red jacket a bright smear on the snow.

Ian gets to her first. Blood trickles from a cut on his brow. He's pulling the jacket over his head when Jeremy pushes him aside.

"Get your hands off her!" The soldier's lip is split, and his left eye is already starting to blacken. He pulls his own jacket over his head.

Ian's expression shuts down as he backs up, his jacket bunched in his hands.

"He's just trying to help," I say.

Jeremy covers Becca with his coat, revealing the tight tan T-shirt underneath. "Becca doesn't need his help. She's none of his fucking business."

"Yeah?" Ian speaks up behind me. "You weren't the one who fished her out of a freezing river, so don't tell me it's not my fucking business."

They square off against each other again, and suddenly, all I can see is Becca shivering in the snow, giving the performance of her life. I saw Charlie like this once. Back then I would've sold my soul to be there when he needed me. Just like Becca needs Jeremy and Ian now. Only they're too hung up on each other to notice.

She deserves better.

I wedge myself between them and hit their chests with every bit of strength I've got. Years of bussing loaded trays finally pay off because I have their undivided attention. "You can kill each other later. Right now Becca needs you. Both of you." I zero in

194

on the one piece of common ground they share. Their love for this little girl.

The darkness breaks in their eyes, but I don't let it fool me. One wrong move could send them spiraling again. I need to keep their focus on me. On Becca. On anything but each other.

"Ian, you pull the supply sled. And you"—I point to Jeremy—"get Becca on the second sled. I can't pull it another step and Blaine's not strong enough. That leaves the two of you."

Jeremy shoots Ian a look that could wither paint, but then he just drops to his knees beside his sister. "Tell me what happened."

"Later," I say. "We need to get to those caverns before the lightning hits us."

I meet Ian's gaze. Relief floods me when I see the beautiful starbursts of his eyes. His jaw is locked, but he nods. We need Jeremy. He knows it. Even if he doesn't like it.

Another barrage of lightning sets the forest pulsing.

Jeremy stares at the gun in my hand. "The woods around Fort Glory were crawling with feds. That flare should've brought them running." He swallows hard and looks up at me, his face pale. "We're really on our own out here."

"You think?" Blaine says acidly. "Like Rose said, there's nobody around except for her brother and some crazy—" His words cut off. "Do you hear that?"

"Hear what?" I ask.

Ian's shoulder brushes mine. Without realizing it, we've moved to stand shoulder to shoulder.

"There's somebody out there." Blaine rubs furiously at his ears. "I just heard them. Laughing."

The only sound I can make out is the wind rushing through

the trees. It's been picking up steadily with the lightning, turning every gust of air into a low moan.

The image of my name written in the snow flashes through my mind. Hope flares to life inside of me.

"Charlie!"

My words are swallowed up by the wind. I scan the woods, desperate for any sign of my brother. Sharp bursts of lightning reveal the surrounding forest in short flashes of green. And then, there it is.

Movement. On the ridgeline a hundred yards to the left.

The back of a green hoodie disappearing over the slope.

I lurch forward, but a gust of wind drives me back. Ian steadies me with one hand on my waist. "It's Charlie," I say, excitement catapulting my words over the wind. "Come on!" When I start forward, Ian's grip on me tightens. I spin around to face him. "Let go! We have to catch him before he gets away!"

Ian studies the swaying canopy. "That lightning is almost on top of us."

"I don't care." I push him back. It's like trying to move a mountain.

"Rose." Ian's grip on me loosens, and I wrench myself free. "If we go after him now, we'll never catch him."

It takes every ounce of my self-control not to snarl. "How can you know that?"

Ian's eyes meet mine. No more swirling black. Something worse.

Sympathy.

"Because he doesn't want to be found."

His words rip the ground out from under me, and then I'm falling with my feet planted firmly on the earth. "What?"

"The dark pulse," Ian says gently. "It must've gotten to him. Why else would he run from you? Why else would he have done any of the things he's done?"

The implication is clear. Ian thinks Charlie is the one following us.

He thinks Charlie terrorized us that first night and pushed me into the river.

I shake my head. "He didn't. He wouldn't—"

"He isn't himself. You can't know what he would and wouldn't do. If you go after him now, you'll only drive him deeper into the storm. It'll get you both killed."

I back away from Ian, my mind racing to come up with some other explanation for why Charlie would run. There's nothing but the memories of those visions playing over and over inside my head. Haunting me. What if they weren't proof that I'm losing my mind? What if they were a sign? That the dark pulse is taking my brother piece by piece. That I have to find him soon or risk losing him forever.

My fingers knead my chest, directly over the place where the tugging should be. How long has it been since I felt it?

"He'll follow us." Ian reaches for something in the side zipper of his pack and places it on my palm. "He's drawn to you. So, work with that. *Use* the bond between you."

I look down at the object in my hand. A roll of tape in fluorescent blue.

"How, exactly?" Blaine asks.

My fingers close around the tape. This time, I'm the one who answers.

"To lead him somewhere safe."

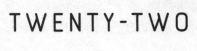

TWENTY-TWO

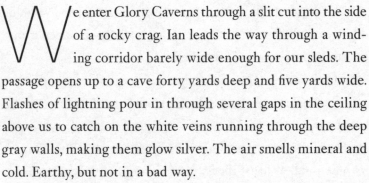

We enter Glory Caverns through a slit cut into the side of a rocky crag. Ian leads the way through a winding corridor barely wide enough for our sleds. The passage opens up to a cave forty yards deep and five yards wide. Flashes of lightning pour in through several gaps in the ceiling above us to catch on the white veins running through the deep gray walls, making them glow silver. The air smells mineral and cold. Earthy, but not in a bad way.

Ian moves to a rounded alcove set into the wall on one side. He spreads out several blankets before unrolling his sleeping bag for Jeremy to lay Becca down. They don't say a word to each other. They just play off one another's movements with a perfect symmetry that says they've done this many, many times before.

Jeremy rips off his pack and quickly pulls at Becca's wet boots. She's still pretending to be unconscious. I've got to hand it to her. The girl knows how to follow through.

I wait till Ian and Jeremy are occupied before I tap her. "Becca, you can wake up now."

She doesn't stir.

A frown dissects Blaine's brow as he settles down across from me. "Becca," he says. "Drop the act."

Becca doesn't answer. She doesn't even move.

"What is it?" Ian asks over an armful of kindling.

"Becca won't wake up." The words catch in my throat. My insides twist as I stare down at Becca lying lifelessly at my feet. I assumed she was getting better since we started heading to the far side of the Fold, but she doesn't look better. If anything, she looks worse.

"Rose told her to pretend to be passed out," Blaine explains. "To keep you two idiots from turning each other into tenderized beef."

"You told her to fake it?" Jeremy's voice echoes off the walls. "There's nothing wrong with her?"

"Obviously it wasn't all an act, or we wouldn't be having this conversation," Blaine snaps.

"You lied." Ian doesn't raise his voice, but the accusation still hits me like a slap.

"It was a shitty thing to do," Jeremy echoes.

It burns me that *this* is the one thing they can agree on. I draw my shoulders back. "You don't get to look at me like that. Not after the stunt you two pulled. You didn't leave me with a choice."

Neither of them tries to deny it.

Jeremy leans over his sister. "What's wrong with her?"

My chest constricts. Becca's eyes have sunken deeper into her head. Even her dark curls have lost some of their shine since yesterday.

Jeremy reaches for his pack and pulls out a med kit with a large red cross stitched into the green canvas. For the first time, I notice the matching red cross patched to his shoulder.

"Nothing in that bag of yours is going to help," Blaine says miserably.

"What does that mean?" The desperation and frustration on Jeremy's face mirror everything I've been feeling these past three days. "What the hell is happening out here?"

"What do you know about the DARC?" I begin.

"Just the basics." Jeremy shakes his head. "Nobody knows how it's connected to what happened to the town. Every theory is crazier than the last."

No theory could be harder to believe than the truth. "Blaine's uncle was using the DARC to open a door to a higher dimension," I explain. "Only he didn't realize something was creeping through. A dark pulse that's been slowly affecting the people in town, unleashing their inner crazy."

"Becca isn't crazy," Jeremy says stubbornly. "She's sick."

"We still haven't figured out exactly how the dark pulse works," Blaine admits.

"Aren't you supposed to be some sort of genius?" Jeremy snaps.

"Skipping a grade doesn't make me a genius," Blaine informs him acidly. "It makes me a nerd."

"I might have an idea," I say, before they can go at it again.

Suddenly, everyone is looking right at me. My throat goes tight, and I'm overcome with an intense desire to fade into the wall. When Blaine motions for me to continue, I search for words to explain the thought that's been forming in my mind since I had that vision of Charlie in the clearing. Since I saw Becca's body wither away in front of our eyes.

"We're in the Fold now, right? Stuck with a wormhole open to some bizarre dimension that's leaking a toxic force." My gaze rests on Becca's shriveling frame. "What if this is a more extreme version of what we've already seen? What if, in the Fold, the dark pulse isn't just messing with our minds? What if it's messing with our bodies, too?"

Blaine's fingers tap against his knees. "We humans tend to separate the mind from the body, the physical from the metaphysical, but physics isn't that cut-and-dried." His hands stop drumming. "The Fold could've taken the purely psychological and given it a physical edge."

"And it could affect any one of us," I add, my heart hammering my ribs when I think of Charlie alone in those woods.

I study Becca's gaunt frame. Jeremy's jacket has slipped off her shoulders, revealing jutting collarbones. She can't last much longer like this. And what about Charlie? How many more pieces can he lose before there's nothing left? I pull the jacket back up to Becca's neck, and a vise clamps around my heart.

Silence echoes through the cave as everyone processes what this means. For Becca. For Charlie. For all of us.

"How do we make it stop? How do we save Becca?" Jeremy asks at last.

"We have to get out of the Fold. Away from the dark pulse." I infuse my voice with all the confidence I can fake. "Charlie is the only one who escaped the wormhole. If we want to do the same, we have to find him."

I don't know if it's true or even if I fully believe it. But it's not like anybody else is throwing out better ideas, and if it means getting help for my brother, it's worth taking the risk of being wrong. I ignore the stab of guilt, and I tell myself it doesn't matter if I can prove it. Right now, all that matters is if I can *sell* it.

Machine-gun blasts of lightning send shadows dancing across the cave walls. There's a loud crack from outside that launches my heart straight up into my throat. The thought of Charlie in this storm makes it hard to breathe. So I stow it away with all the others that want to break me. Right behind the wall inside of me.

It's getting damn crowded back there.

"We'll take shifts watching out for Charlie," Ian suggests. "When he shows, we'll be ready to grab him."

I rise to my feet. "I'll take first watch."

Jeremy snags my wrist. "Stay for a minute."

Ian's nostrils flare at the sight of Jeremy's hand on mine. When I shake my head, Ian wrenches his gaze away and makes for the corridor.

"I'll keep Lawson company." With a scathing look at Jeremy, Blaine slams the trapper hat back down on his head. I watch them disappear into the darkened corridor and fight the urge to follow. As much as I want to wait for my brother, I can still read between the lines.

Jeremy has something to say to me, and he doesn't want an audience.

It's quiet for a few minutes before Jeremy finally speaks. "Blaine told me about what you did for Becca at the river." He pauses. "Thank you."

I frown at him. "It was mostly Ian. He … really cares about her."

Jeremy rubs the purpling bruise on his jaw. "Keeping Becca out of trouble has always been a full-time job, but I guess you know that already."

"She's a sweet kid."

A lopsided smile touches his lips. "I remember when all the other girls were into Barbies, Becs was obsessed with that old movie, you know, the one about the southern chick who could have any guy she wanted but was scheming on her cousin."

"*Gone with the Wind?*"

"Right. Anyways, Becs got this, like, old-fashioned ball gown for her birthday. She wore it every day. Drove my mom nuts. It got so bad the teacher called my parents to ask them to talk some sense into her." He smiles. "She just kept wearing that damn dress and watching that movie over and over, always with the same dopey look on her face."

I'm guessing it's the same look she wears whenever Ian is around.

"It's weird how the things you love most about someone are sometimes the same things you wish you could change," I say, reaching into my pocket.

Jeremy raises a brow when he sees Charlie's egg in my hand. "Do I even want to know?"

"It's my brother's."

Jeremy's expression turns somber. "I'm sorry. About what happened to him." He reaches down to brush a curl out of Becca's face.

"At least he and Becca are alive." My mother's face flashes though my mind. The memory of her smile. My throat burns. "Not everyone was so lucky."

For a moment, neither of us speaks, and it's like his parents and my mother are right here in the cave with us.

"You said that it would be better if I came back to the road with you. Why?" I ask.

"There were stories about you. On the news." Jeremy shifts uncomfortably. "They're saying the police want you for questioning."

"Are you going to tell the others?" I hate how desperate I sound.

"I'm not telling Lawson shit."

The stubbornness in his voice has my eyebrow lifting. "The two of you are equally impossible, you realize that, right?"

Jeremy flashes me a crooked grin that must have the girls falling all over themselves. "I like you, Rose Montgomery." He stands and offers me his hand. After a second's hesitation, I take it. "But maybe don't tell Lawson. He might decide to kill me after all."

Heat spreads across my cheeks. "It's not like that. He's just—"

Ian walks into the caverns carrying a load of firewood. I drop Jeremy's hand and take a step back before I can question the impulse. Jeremy's eyebrow makes a break for his hairline.

"Where's Blaine?" I ask, groping for something to say.

"Standing watch at the entrance," Ian says, his eyes moving between me and Jeremy. "No sign of Charlie yet, but we'll keep a lookout posted all night." He puts the wood down. When he straightens, his head nearly brushes the cavern ceiling.

"Ian's got a concussion," I tell Jeremy. "And the cut on his hand needs stitches."

The soldier grabs his med kit and moves forward, all business. Ian freezes him out with a stare.

Jeremy rolls his eyes. "I get it. You hate my guts. Now that we're clear on that, how about you stop being a stubborn ass for five seconds and let me help you."

"Like you helped me the last two years?" Ian's nostrils flare in disgust. "While you were off getting a new life, I was rotting in prison."

"I was in Ranger School. It was an ass kicking. Not a tropical vacation."

"Is that why you turned your back on Becca? You were too busy earning patches like some glorified Boy Scout?"

All the anger drains out of Jeremy, leaving him pale and drawn. "I didn't know she needed me."

"How? Are you blind?"

"Because I never came back."

Ian blinks. "What?"

"You heard me. After what happened with Wi—" Jeremy's Adam's apple bobs like he's trying to swallow a massive lump in his throat. He gags and coughs.

"Jeremy. Are you okay?" I step toward him.

He clears his throat and shoots me a quick nod. "There are things you don't know," he tells Ian. "If you'd just let me—" His face goes red as he dissolves into another coughing fit.

It must be the air in here, thick with mildew and smoke. I move quickly to his side and pat him on the back until his lungs clear. Jeremy draws a shaky breath, but Ian doesn't give him the chance to pick up where he left off. "Shut your mouth or I'll shut it for you."

Jeremy wipes his chin with the back of his sleeve. A vicious glint enters his eyes as he throws his arms wide. "Be my guest, Lawson. Do your old man proud. Prove everybody right about you."

Ian flinches. Jeremy looks like he wants to take the words back, but they're out there now, poisoning the cavern air.

"I'll do it," I say, causing both of them to glance my way.

"Do what?" Jeremy asks.

I walk up and grab the suture kit out of his hand. The two of them are wired like bombs set to explode. I have to keep them apart, and this is the only way I can think of.

"I'll stitch Ian up," I say. "But I'm going to need more light than we have in here."

"I know a place," Ian says at last.

I follow him to the back of the cavern where the walls narrow to a gap a foot wide. We squeeze through, into a smaller cavern cut in a circle so seamless, it appears man-made. Above me, lightning flashes through a rough skylight. It catches on the green-and-silver rivers running through the rock. I run my fingers over the stone. Perfectly smooth.

"These caverns were made by rainwater." Ian's voice comes from directly behind me. "It carved them out over a few hundred thousand years."

"How do you know so much about the caverns?"

"My brother and I used to come here." His voice is hushed. It must be this place. It has a strange kind of magic.

The cool dampness of the caverns washes over me. I close my eyes and concentrate on the rhythmic dripping of water on rock nearby. For the first time since I woke up in the woods, I take a full breath.

"You have a brother?" I ask, finding Ian in the shadows.

He studies the walls as if he's half expecting them to answer for him. "Will. His name is Will."

He cuts across the circular room to the opposite wall. It takes me a moment to figure out what he's looking at. Light marks on the otherwise dark stone. Words carved into the wall with a knife or a chisel.

W & I L.

Will and Ian Lawson.

I run my finger over the timeworn grooves.

"Will did it," Ian says before I can ask. "Summer before fifth grade. He must've been thirteen. We'd been out here for a week with a few blankets and a backpack full of stolen candy, living large." A ghost of a smile touches his lips.

"Weren't your parents worried?"

Just like that, the smile is gone. He starts to pull away, and suddenly, I don't want him to.

"Where is Will now?" I ask quickly. "Do you ever see him?"

He shakes his head. "When he—" Ian palms his hat. "When he took off, he was leaving behind more than just the town."

"Do you miss him?"

"Every single day."

"I bet he'll be proud."

Ian gapes at me like he can't believe I just used the word *proud* and his name in the same sentence. There's an awkward pause that threatens to drag on forever. I rush to fill it. "It couldn't have been easy, coming back to Fort Glory. I'm glad you did. None of us would be here without you."

Ian's expression softens. "Do you always see the best in people?"

Never. "I see what's there."

Ian looks at me. *Right at me.* And then it's just the two of us in this cavern carved by water and time, and the words I shouldn't have said.

I clear my throat. "Sit down under the skylight. I can work as long as the lightning keeps up." I open the suture kit and set out the contents.

Ian's eyes are luminous in the low light. "You were serious."

"I'm always serious." I lift my chin. "Give me your arm."

A few seconds pass before Ian does as he's told. The heat coming off him is intense—or maybe I'm just hyperaware of how close we are. It's been a long time since I let anyone get near me like this.

It's been a long time since anybody wanted to be.

"Do you know what you're doing?" Ian asks, watching me.

"A few years ago, Charlie had an accident. He was cut up pretty bad."

The "accident" happened a week after the first time we tried to run. When the monster found us, I was sure he was going to kill Mom. Instead, Charlie got a glass bottle to the chin. My hands didn't shake when I'd sewed him up, but afterward, I locked myself in the bathroom and threw up everything in my stomach.

The needle in my hand hovers over Ian's palm. "This is going to hurt," I say.

"It's just pain."

My eyes fly to the scars on his jaw. His eyebrow. His knuckles. They tell me that pain is a subject with which Ian Lawson is intimately familiar.

I jab the tip into his skin. The thread goes slick with his blood. Revulsion rises up inside of me, but I lock it up behind my wall, and I repeat the motion. Over and over because that's the only way this ends.

When I'm finally done, I wipe at the bloody stitches and release Ian's hand. "This thing with Jeremy," I begin. "You have to get it under control. I don't know what he did to hurt you but—"

"Hurt *me*?" Ian shakes his head. "You must be the only person alive who sees it that way."

I sit up a little straighter. "If it makes any difference, I think he's willing to do whatever it takes to make peace."

Ian snorts. "This is what he does. He uses that Kennedy

charm to gain your trust, so when he starts drinking before class, or harassing freshmen, or peddling dope because he's bored with his perfect life, you're too blind to see it."

"Then why were you ever friends?"

Ian brushes the carving on the wall. "Because when he's not screwing up your life or being a general ass, Jeremy makes you laugh. Even when there's nothing to laugh about." His jaw sets in an obstinate line. "He's selfish, and irresponsible, and impossible not to love, and you're falling for it, just like everyone else does."

My face burns. "I'm not falling for anything," I lie. "I'm just saying we can't afford another incident like the one earlier. Maybe Jeremy's changed since you knew him."

"People don't change. Some things can't be fixed, Rose."

I frown at him, because suddenly, I'm not sure what we're talking about.

"I can feel it," Ian says after a moment. "All the shit stirring inside of me." He meets my gaze head-on, revealing the swirling black at the center of his pupils.

A reminder that the true danger in the Fold isn't the storms in the sky.

It's the storms inside of us.

TWENTY-THREE

The wind cuts straight through my blankets.

I wake up inside the cavern opening, where I spent most of the night scanning the woods. Blaine showed up to relieve me around midnight, but I was never leaving this spot.

Not while Charlie was out in that dry lightning alone.

My heart lifts at the sight of clear sky outside. Charlie would've had to wait for the weather to turn before he tried to track us.

We made it nice and easy for him.

Blue tape marks the trees all the way here to the caverns. A trail of fluorescent breadcrumbs that will lead him right to us.

A wheezing sound draws my gaze to the right, where Blaine is snoring loudly enough to disturb the local wildlife.

I reach down and pat a scrawny shoulder.

Blaine groans and rolls over. "What? What's wrong?"

"For starters, you're a lousy lookout."

Blaine rescues his glasses from the long slide down his nose. Between his slightly glazed expression and his gravity defiant bedhead, he looks like he's been chewing live wires. "Sorry."

"We survived the night without your help." I smile at him. I can't help it. Charlie is alive, I have a plan to bring him in, and for once, the weather in the Fold is cooperating.

Morning rays pierce the cavern. My eyes land on something lying inside the corridor.

The water dripping down the cavern walls. The birdsongs outside. They all fade to white noise.

I push past Blaine and come to a grinding halt beside Becca.

She's lying in the middle of the passageway. Her oversize pants are bunched around her calves. The too-long sleeves of her sweatshirt swallow her hands. I drop to the ground, push back her hair, and recoil.

Becca's cheekbones protrude like razors from a skeletal face. Another ten pounds have melted off her during the night. Now there's nothing but bones held together by loose skin and too much fabric.

Blaine makes a strangled sound over my shoulder. He's looking at me like Charlie used to look at me when he was little, and hungry, and Mom was too sad to get up. Like he's waiting for me to do something, to fix this. Only I don't know how.

I don't know how.

Becca moans. Helpless tears burn their way up my throat. I force them back behind the wall inside of me and I focus on what needs to be done.

"Go." Somehow, the word comes out dead-even. "Get Jeremy."

Blaine takes off for the main cavern.

I lay Becca down and place my ear over her heart. The beat is too sluggish. Her shallow breathing barely lifts her chest. The only lively things about her are her eyes, twitching restlessly behind her lids.

Her whole body starts to tremble in my arms.

Footsteps in the corridor. Jeremy freezes when he sees Becca lying on the floor.

"What do we do?" My voice bounces off the cavern walls.

Jeremy doesn't answer. He doesn't even move. He just stands there, staring at what's left of his little sister.

I get off the ground and move until I'm blocking his view. "We might be able to help her, but I need you to tell me what to do. *Tell me, Jeremy.*" I grip his shoulders.

Becca moans again. A whispery, pitiful sound.

Jeremy's muscles go rigid under my hands. He drops to his knees beside Becca. When he looks up at me again his mouth is set in a hard line. "We need to get some liquid into her," he says.

"Will this work?" Blaine tosses him a bottle of Gatorade we picked up at the camp.

Jeremy tears off the cap and raises it to Becca's lips. The red syrupy drink runs down her chin. It comes right back up again in a burst of breath and spittle.

Blaine squeaks, and steps out of range.

Sticky droplets of saliva cover Jeremy's face. He doesn't pause to wipe them off.

The bottle is a few inches from Becca's lips when her eyes fly open. Her pupils are two black holes that swallow the light. My insides squirm away from that darkness. Like it's somehow contagious, but I think of the little girl on the stone floor in front of me. The one who wears ridiculous ball gowns and stuffs cereal in Ian's shoes. I hold my ground.

A violent shudder racks Becca's body. Her spine arcs off the cave floor, and for a few seconds, the world stops spinning.

She slumps back down.

"What's happening?" Blaine cries.

"She's seizing." Jeremy's calm is quickly surrendering ground to fear.

Another seizure grips Becca. This time, Jeremy manages to slip his arm under the back of her head, cushioning it. He doesn't move, not even when he takes a flying elbow to the face. Sorrow shines in his eyes. "I don't know what to do."

My throat is raw from holding back tears. One streaks down my cheek. I swipe it with the back of my sleeve. "It's the dark pulse," I say. "It has her." I've seen that ocean of blackness before. That's how I know there's nothing Jeremy or anyone else can do to help Becca now.

Yes, there is, says a voice at the back of my head.

I stare down at my hand on Becca's sweater. Slowly, I roll up her sleeve, revealing skeletal white fingers.

"What're you doing?" Blaine asks over my shoulder.

I don't bother trying to explain. The black ocean I saw when I touched Becca on the riverbank still doesn't make sense to me. All I know is that the dark pulse is pulling Becca away from us. Just like it is pulling Charlie.

And there may be just one chance left to save them.

We have to meet the darkness where it lives and fight to get them back.

The next seizure has Becca's body arching like a bow about the snap. Arms shoots out, catching Jeremy across the mouth.

"We're losing her," he says brokenly. Blood drips from his lips, down onto her curls where they're matted against his chest. He cradles her to him. The sight tears at me.

I held Charlie like this once. Like he was my axis when the world was spinning around us. I still remember the slippery feel of his blood on my hands. The way my entire existence hung on every rise and fall of his chest. Fragments of that night still cut me whenever I try to get a deep breath, and Charlie *survived*.

213

What happens to Jeremy if Becca doesn't survive this? Because she won't.

Not unless I stop watching for once in my life, and actually *do* something.

I reach for her fingers. The moment our hands touch, the muscles in my chest coil into a hook of pain and pressure. It conducts me down a power line into a world without Color. Without Light. Without any Sound but one.

Dark pulse.

It roars through my head, splintering me apart from the inside until there is only pain and darkness and a noise so huge, it leaves no room for thoughts.

Wave after wave smashes into me. It gnaws at me with a need that feels almost like hunger. I rear back, but the undertow has me now. A scream tears through my head as it pulls me down the side of a cliff, into the black abyss waiting down below.

The darkness rises up over my head. My lungs scream for air, but there is only emptiness. Thicker than air and harder than water. I am drowning in it when a soft glow reaches me from somewhere down below. A person illuminated against the black.

Becca.

She's sitting on a ledge carved out of the dark, hugging her knees and rocking back and forth like a child trapped in a nightmare.

Becca's face goes out of focus. The already faint glow around her starts to fade. Just like in the visions I've had. The ones of Charlie. Only this isn't a vision.

Everything about this is real.

I reach down to her, but my arms don't budge. They don't budge because they aren't *here*. My mind might be stuck in this black world with Becca, but my body is still sitting on the cave floor. I can feel a thread tethering me to it like Ian's safety cord. It's keeping me from falling over the edge into the dark ocean below, but it's also holding me in place so I can't reach Becca. And there's nothing I can do to fight it, because whatever this place is, it's solid for Becca in a way that it isn't for me.

That's because this isn't your darkness. It's hers.

The thought marches through my mind uninvited. Right on cue, the hook of fire flares to life inside of me.

No! I resist it with everything I've got, but still, it reels me in like a fish on a line.

I start to fall out of the dark.

"Becca!" I don't know whether I think her name or say it. Either way, the word shimmers. A drop of brilliant light. I watch it glitter down a gossamer line in the dark. That's when I realize.

There's another thread. A pink thread linking me to Becca. It's thinner, weaker than the one trying to pull me back to my body, but it's real, and it's there, and it means Becca's not completely out of reach.

I concentrate every bit of my focus on the rosy thread between us. All at once, a dozen images dance up the blushing line into me.

A little girl with black curls and hazel eyes, blowing out the candles on a strawberry cream cake. Her parents too preoccupied with their phones to notice. She's allergic to strawberries.

That same girl wedged between them at the dinner table, listening to them talk about her as if she isn't there.

Sitting on a bus in a blue ball gown, alone even though every other seat is taken. Wondering how she can feel so conspicuous, and at the same time, be completely invisible.

Clutching a pen as she writes page after page of letters to her brother. Letters that never receive an answer.

Watching Gone with the Wind *a thousand times and waiting for a happy ending that will never come.*

Because she is invisible.

Because she will never know what it's like to fall in love. To be cherished. To be seen.

The images stop coming, and then it's just Becca, rocking below me on a ledge here in this black nothingness, her outline so muted I can barely make it out.

The tug on my mind yanks me hard. I start to slip back to my body and the real world. In slow motion, I watch Becca grow smaller and smaller in the distance until she's almost gone.

A scream builds in my mind. I'm going to lose her. I'm going to watch her disappear right in front of me. Like the town. Like Charlie. Like my dad and everything else that has ever mattered.

Something snaps inside of me.

Remember. Help her to remember.

The words drifts through my mind like smoke. Remember what? I don't know what I'm supposed to remember, or how I'm supposed to save Becca, or beat this unbeatable dark.

Without the dark, there are no stars, Rosie.

And then I'm not alone. I can't explain it, but I can feel someone else in here with us. Giving off a frequency that somehow cancels out the dark one in my head. Lending their song and their light to mine so that it plays just a little bit louder. Shines just a little brighter. Bright enough to catch on the thread shimmering between me and Becca.

Showing me a way where before there was only darkness.

I focus in on the thread between us. A wisp of color in a colorless world. The last bit of something holding me to this place. To her. I might not be able to swim to Becca, or grab her, or even speak to her. But maybe I don't have to do any of those things. If I can see what's in her head, maybe, just maybe, she can see what's in mine.

Becca's light gutters as I pour myself into the thread and watch as all the words I can't say turn into notes of music that are somehow also images. They vibrate and shimmer down the blushing line into her.

I show her the look on Jeremy's face when he heard Becca's voice at the gulch. His desperate love as he rocked her and begged her to come back.

Ian watching her sleep in the cabin. The way he smiled when he talked about her, like the world was that much brighter because she was in it. Maybe even bright enough to be bearable.

I let her see herself through my eyes. A survivor clinging to a boulder in the middle of a raging river. The girl who watched *Gone with the Wind* a thousand times, and fell in love with her brother's best friend, and never once stopped believing in happy endings.

Strong. Alive with hope. Beautiful.

Not invisible.

Never invisible.

The thread between us blazes. Rosy fire shoots between us. Solid. Real. And then Becca isn't hiding in the darkness.

The darkness is hiding from her.

I'm here, Becs. I'm right here.

Until I'm not anymore. The tether to my body yanks me back. There's a moment of mind-numbing pain before my eyes snap open to blinding light.

I take in the scene around me in rapid blinks.

Cavern walls painted silver by the rising sun.

Scrawny arms around my waist. *Blaine.* The tear tracks on his cheeks and the blood vessels in his eyes as they widen on me.

Jeremy, cradling his sister's body.

Ian. Standing in the corridor, face frozen and arms loaded down with firewood.

And then nothing matters but the little girl in Jeremy's arms. Because she's awake, and she's looking at me with wide, hazel eyes. I scan her from head to toe. There's more flesh on her bones than there was a few minutes ago. It's almost like the thread between us fed her more than light.

It fed her some of her life back.

Becca smiles, and the pink thread between us—the one I can no longer see but can somehow feel—forms a knot deep inside my chest. Permanent. Irreversible.

"You came," she says. "He told me you would come."

My entire body goes still. "Who?"

"The boy," she says. "The one singing in the dark."

TWENTY-FOUR

"harlie was there. Charlie was in the abyss." My voice is way too loud in the small space. I jump to my feet, every muscle in my body coiled tight.

I don't know how it's possible. I don't know how I felt Charlie in there with me in that dark place, but I did and it was real and what Becca just said *proves* it.

"Abyss?" Blaine blinks at me. "What abyss?"

I tell him exactly what I saw when I went after Becca. Just now and a few days ago, on the riverbank. The ocean of darkness. The threads. Everything.

"You saw it too?" Blaine asks Ian.

"When I touched their hands back at the river." Ian stacks the wood on the ground. "Any idea what it was?"

"The Black Nothing."

Everybody turns to Becca. She shrugs. "That's what Charlie called it."

My heart is suddenly so high in my throat, I swear I can taste it beating. "What else did Charlie say?"

Becca frowns. "At first, there was just darkness and noise. I could feel it taking away my good memories, leaving the bad. I thought I was alone until he came." She takes a shuddering breath. "He touched my hand, and it was like . . . a song flowed through his fingertips. One that kept the dark pulse out." She marvels at her hand. "He gave me pictures to chase away the bad ones in my head."

A shiver runs through her. "He showed me a woman. She was lying on the ground and...I wanted to look away but then you were there, Rosie. You kept telling the woman that it would be okay. And that's when I knew you would come for me just like you came for her. I just had to hold on."

Jeremy shifts beside me. I turn away from the speculation on his face only to find Ian staring right at me.

"What happened next?" I ask, to shift their attention away from me.

Becca's mouth goes soft. "Then he showed me the stars and all the threads between them." Her voice drops to a whisper. "He wanted me to know."

Every hair on my arm stands straight up. "Know what?"

"That we don't have to be afraid. Not of the dark."

"Are you afraid of the dark?" I asked you, pressing my shoulder into yours.

You shook your head. "Without the dark, there are no stars, Rosie."

"Then what are you afraid of?" I asked.

What are you afraid of?

"And when he left, you were there. Really there," Becca says, cutting into my thoughts. "And I could see the thread shining between us like all the webs between the stars." She looks right at me. "He knows you saw him yesterday. He wants to come to you, but he can't." Her expression turns fierce. "You have to come to him."

My pulse starts to pound. Watching Charlie run away from me yesterday in the woods almost broke me, but a part of him must have known me. That means his mind isn't completely lost to the dark pulse. I can still save him.

I can still save him.

"*Okaay,*" Blaine says, yanking me out of my own head. "Since all three of you saw it, this Black Nothing has to be a real place. I'd bet money it's the same place my uncle unlocked with the DARC. A hidden dimension beyond the ones we can sense."

"And this hidden dimension is where the dark pulse lives," I say, my mind scrambling to keep up with my racing thoughts.

Blaine nods. "The dark pulse is blending the line between the physical and the metaphysical. It's separating our consciousness from our bodies, drawing our minds into the Black Nothing before the wormhole can finish the job. And if we're right, it's been living right next to us this whole time, just out of reach."

"Until your uncle sent our town into the Black Nothing and unleashed its dark pulse on the world," Jeremy says.

Blaine snaps a response, but I'm not listening anymore. His explanation has me sailing back in time. Not just over the last three days. To that night three weeks ago.

"Can you hear the music, Rosie?"

"Where is it coming from?"

"From the dark. It's always there, but now it's getting louder. It shouldn't be this loud."

It shouldn't be this loud.

"Charlie said the dark pulse was always there, but that it had gotten louder," I say. "He knew where it was coming from almost like ... like he could see it." It was in the things he said. How he acted. "Charlie warned me about the town. He's known about the Black Nothing all along. He knew it was a bad place."

"I don't get it," Jeremy says. "A lot of people were sucked into the wormhole when Fort Glory disappeared. Why is Charlie the only one who's been able to escape? And how did Becca see him in the Black Nothing when we all know he's here in the Fold with us?"

They're good questions. Over the past few days, I've learned more about my brother and the things he can do than I'd figured out in ten years of living right beside him. But none of that matters if I can't also figure out *how* he's doing it. That's what we need to understand if we're going to get out of here.

I turn to Blaine for an answer. The boy starts to pace. Just watching him think makes me dizzy.

"The extra dimensions," he says. "What if Rose is right and Charlie can somehow see them? What if he didn't need the DARC to cut a hole through the curtain of our world because he already had a backstage pass?" Blaine's eyes widen. "It would explain how he's so perceptive. Why he's never fully present."

"You're grasping at threads," Jeremy says, causing Blaine to go completely still.

"The expression is 'grasping at straws,' but as it happens, yes. That's *exactly* what I'm doing." Blaine reaches for his uncle's book. "The core assumption of string theory is that all matter is made up of tiny strings vibrating and rotating at different frequencies."

"Strings? As in threads?" I ask, my pulse racing.

Blaine nods. "Michio Kaku uses a metaphor that compares the superstrings in string theory to violin strings. All mathematics represent their musical notation. Physics is basically the melodies of those notes, making the universe one great big string symphony."

"We're talking music? In extra dimensions?" Ian asks.

"It can't be an accident," Blaine says, awestruck. "The threads you saw. They're the key. I don't know what they are, but Charlie obviously does. *They're* what allowed Rose to go into the Black Nothing and bring Becca back. *They're* the loophole Charlie exploited to escape what happened to the town. The one he's using to travel back and forth between the Fold and the Black Nothing. The same loophole that brought Rose and Jeremy into the Fold in the first place. That makes them our ticket out of here."

Excitement is building in the cave. A sense of hope.

We're onto something. How else would Charlie be doing the things he's doing? Haven't I always known he was in touch with something I wasn't—that the world through his eyes was somehow different than the one I saw?

"There's another possibility," Ian says after a moment. "Charlie's acting like the dark pulse has control of him. What if it has trapped his mind in the Black Nothing while his body is still stuck in the Fold with us?"

His words fall through me like a stone down a well. The blood drains from my face.

"Damnit," Blaine hisses. "You might be right."

I steady myself against the cave wall. It's rough to the touch, but I close my eyes and grip the stone so hard it hurts. "We have to find Charlie." I focus on the only part of this I can control. The only part that matters. "If he can see these extra dimensions, maybe he can find a path through them, back to our world. Maybe he could show us how to work these threads and slip out of here."

My words echo through the cave.

"We can set a trap for him," Ian suggests. "Use you to draw him out. It's the best use of our limited resources."

"No." I push myself off the wall and face him. "We split up. Some of us search the Fold while the others wait to see if Charlie follows our trail here." Visions of Charlie flash through my mind. I press my hand against the sudden pain in my chest. "You heard Becca. He can't come to me. I have to go to *him*."

"That's not going to be easy," Ian says. "There are over thirty square miles of territory he could be holed up in. If the weather stays like this, we'll be risking our lives every time we step outside."

I clench my fists. "We don't have a choice."

"I'm with Rose on this," Jeremy says.

Ian's nostrils flare. "What about the dark pulse?" he asks me, taking a page out of Becca's book and ignoring Jeremy completely. "It'll get stronger the closer we get to the wormhole over Fort Glory."

I focus on the problem, turning it over in my mind. "We work in teams," I say at last. "Watch each other's eyes to make sure nobody is about to go dark."

"We can start at the edge of the Fold and push in from there," Jeremy adds.

I nod at him. My heart is a drumbeat in my ears because we can do this. Working together we *can* find Charlie.

We have to.

I glance over at Ian just in time to catch the flash of his back before he disappears into the corridor.

"Forget Lawson. We don't need his permission."

I turn on Jeremy, my spine stiffening. "No. But we could definitely use his help."

Birds are filling the forest with morning songs when I follow Ian out of the caverns. He stops at the edge of the misty woods with his back to me, posture rigid.

One look at his hunched shoulders and the arguments turn

to ash in my mouth. I take a hesitant step toward him. "Ian, what's wrong?"

His shoulders rise and fall once. He pulls off his cap and turns to face me.

A gasp escapes my lips. The skin over his right brow. It's red and blistering. The burn mark runs at a slant across his temple, like someone branded the side of his face with a hot poker.

I reach out. My fingers stop an inch shy of touching him. "What happened?"

Ian stares at the mist-threaded woods. My hand drops softly to his chest, and his whole body relaxes. "I don't know."

"What do you mean, you don't know?"

His gaze lifts from my hand to my face. "It was there when I woke up."

I struggle to get my breathing back under control. The dark pulse almost killed Becca. It's stealing Charlie, piece by piece, and now it's after Ian, too. Heat licks up my neck into my face. I want to lash out. To fight something. But how do you fight something you can't even hear?

Weak light filters through the trees. It highlights the strong lines of Ian's face and glitters on the tips of his eyelashes, white with frost. "I have these dreams sometimes."

His words are little monsters that sneak into my head. "What kind of dreams?"

He flexes his hand and stares at the white scars crisscrossing his knuckles. "I don't remember, but when I wake up, I'm always so angry. Sometimes I swear I'm going to combust."

"When's the last time you had one of these dreams?"

"Last night."

I force myself to remain outwardly calm. Last night, Ian got so angry he felt like he would catch fire. Today, there's a burn mark across his face.

"Do you want to tell me about it?" I ask.

"Do you want to tell me about the crying woman Becca saw?" Ian shoots back.

My eyes widen. I start to back away. A callused palm drops onto my hand, capturing it against Ian's breast.

"The woman you were taking care of. It was your mom, wasn't it?"

My hand is on fire where his skin touches mine. I don't say anything. I don't have to.

"How old were you?"

"Fourteen."

"She's lucky to have you."

My chin jerks. "My mother isn't lucky. She's broken."

Ian frowns down at me. "She's sad. That's not the same thing."

Memories hit me hard. Mom covered in flour up to the elbows. Her favorite apron and a smile on. Those days were some of the best because when Mom cooked, she would sing. Her voice made you feel like you could fly if you wanted to.

I never wanted to. All I ever wanted was to stay right there. With her.

In the end, she was the one who left.

"I'm sorry, Rose."

My shoulders round. "It happened. It's over."

"Is it?"

My eyes fly to the burn mark on Ian's face. One more ugly reminder that bad things happen to people, whether or not they deserve them. That some scars never truly fade.

No. It's not over. The Fold is stirring up the ugliness inside of us, bringing it floating to the surface. Even now, I can feel the dark pulse chipping away at that wall inside of me. Trying to crack it open.

It terrifies me because I know exactly what's waiting on the other side.

"Hey." Ian anchors me to the present with his fingers on my chin. "We're going to find Charlie. When we do, you're going to bring his mind back. Just like you did for Becca."

"What if I can't?" My voice quivers.

"You will."

"How can you be so sure?"

"Because it's what you do," Ian says simply. "Step up when people need you."

Heat floods my face. "Do you always see the best in people?" I ask to distract from the fact that my cheeks are red and my pulse is suddenly racing out of control.

In spite of everything, Ian's lip twitches. "Only when it's you."

My mouth drops open.

Ian's brow furrows as he takes a quick step backward. I watch the flush creeping up his neck, and my stomach does a sharp somersault.

The silence between us lasts a beat too long. My brain is scrambling for some way to break it, when a rumble echoes through the forest.

The earth comes alive under our feet.

The force of the tremor knocks me sideways, and then it's all I can do just to stay vertical.

The ground pitches, sending my heart slamming into my

throat. Vibrations roll through the canopy, releasing a rain of debris onto my back. Gasping, I throw my arms up over my head and hit the soft ground on my knees. I curl into a ball.

Time plays tricks with my head. I'm not sure how long I lie there before the earthquake fades to a few mild aftershocks.

I drag myself to my feet. A cold sweat breaks out across my brow as I search for Ian in the chaos. My chest muscles loosen when I spot him a few feet away. He's on his knees. Struggling to get up.

My breath comes in ragged blasts and my legs are wobbly like I just ran ten miles, but I stumble over to him and reach down.

Ian takes my hand. His grip is like a vise. I'm not sure which one of us is holding on tighter.

With a grunt, I haul him to his feet.

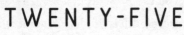

TWENTY-FIVE

The Fold is getting more unstable. This whole place is about to fall apart." The tremble in my voice is a weak echo of the aftershocks still running through the ground.

Ian doesn't respond, but I can read him much better now than I could a few days ago. He's worried. We've got enough stacked against us without adding seismic events to the list.

We have to get out of the Fold. Before it implodes, or the dark pulse takes us, or any of a thousand other things can go wrong. Which brings this conversation back full circle.

I square myself up to face him. "We have to go after Charlie."

Ian's shoulders droop. "I went looking for him this morning after the storm broke. There's no sign of him by the caverns."

It's no surprise. I haven't felt Charlie's presence or the weird tugging since last night. My gut tells me we have to head deeper into the Fold to find him.

"I'll get the others." I start back for the caverns.

"Wait."

I turn.

"The temperature is rising fast, but the ground is still too cold," Ian says. "There's a fog coming in. A quarter mile from here it's a complete whiteout. I barely found my way back. Anyone who goes out there now won't be so lucky."

"I don't care. Charlie *needs* me. He's hurt, Ian. Maybe dying." For the first time, I let some of the desperation sneak past the wall and into my voice.

Ian studies my face. "Charlie has made it this long," he says. "He can make it a few more hours till the fog clears."

I grind my teeth so hard my jaw aches. Ian doesn't get it. He thinks this is about me and my obsession to find Charlie. Maybe he's even a little bit right about that. But he doesn't know the *reason* for it. And whose fault is that? I was so sure keeping the visions to myself was the right move. I was so positive the others would think I was losing it if I told them the truth. But what if the problem was never them?

What if the problem was me?

A piece of hair falls into my face. I yank it back behind my ear and study the bits of sky between the trees. I've spent the last three years running from what other people think. About Mom and Charlie. About me and the ghosts in my rearview. And what has it ever gotten me but a few maps tacked up on the wall and an existence of just barely getting by? Now even that is gone.

What do I have left to lose?

I set my jaw and meet Ian's gaze head-on. "The phantom pains. Every time they come on, I've been getting visions of Charlie. The dark pulse is killing him, Ian. Taking him piece by piece. If I don't find him soon, he'll be gone. I can't let that happen. I *won't.*" The truth slides off me along with a weight I didn't realize I was carrying. My relief lasts only until I catch the dangerous flash in Ian's eyes.

"Why didn't you say something?"

"I thought you and Blaine would think I was losing it. I

couldn't afford to make you doubt me." I take a step toward him. "Look, maybe I should've told you before, but I'm telling you now. I haven't seen Charlie since last night. I have to know if he survived the storm. I can't feel him anymore, Ian, and it's *killing* me."

Ian's eyes sail past me to the white tendrils of fog creeping toward us through the trees. His expression wavers for a moment before it hardens. "I know you want to find your brother, but there are ways to help Charlie that won't get anyone killed. Forget it, Rose."

His dismissal sets off a hurricane inside of me. Bitter words hang on the tip of my tongue. I'm about to let them fall when I catch a flash of green over Ian's shoulder: the back of Charlie's hoodie, before he disappears behind a tree a hundred yards from the caverns.

I don't move. I don't even blink while I wait for Charlie to show himself again. He doesn't.

I open my mouth to call out but stop myself at the last second. Ian made his position clear. He won't risk the fog. Not even after everything I've told him. Arguing with him about it will take time, and I've already wasted too much.

"Okay." I force my eyes away from Charlie's hiding spot. "We'll wait out the fog if you think it's best." The words stick in my craw, but somehow, I force them out.

Tension leaves Ian's shoulders. "As soon as the fog lifts, I'll help you search for Charlie. Believe me, Rose. This is the right call." Ian motions for me to go ahead.

I gnaw the inside of my cheek. If I refuse, he'll see right through me. So I do the only thing I can. I glance at the woods one more time, and then I turn my back on my brother and walk into the caverns.

Every step I take tightens the throbbing knot in the center of my chest.

Time. What I need is time. Enough to build a lead so that Ian can't track me down. Now I just have to figure out a way to buy it.

When we enter, everyone is holed up in their own separate corners. Blaine is flipping through his uncle's book for the thousandth time. I want to scream that the answers he's looking for aren't in those pages. They're hiding behind a tree about two hundred yards from this cavern.

I need a distraction and I need it fast. Maybe if I could—

"I have to go to the bathroom," Becca announces in the silence.

"There's a hole in the back you can use," Jeremy says.

She wrinkles her nose. "No thanks. I'll squat in the woods. Like a civilized person."

"It's not safe for you to be outside alone," Ian says calmly.

"I won't be alone. Rose will come with me. Won't you, Rosie?"

Rosie.

My throat goes tight when she reaches for me. Her fingers are slippery in mine. When he was little, Charlie's palms were always sweaty. It was like the light inside of him was trying to burn a hole right through his skin. My chest aches because I can't remember the last time I held his hand.

"Sure." I try to keep my voice level. I must do a bad job because Ian's gaze turns hot on my face.

He starts to say something, but Becca cuts him off. "It

might be the end of the world, but I'm not peeing where you can hear me."

A moment passes before Ian gives in. "Stay near the cavern mouth," he warns. "Five minutes."

Five minutes. It's not a lot of time, but it's enough. It has to be.

Becca trots out of the cavern ahead of me. We pass Ian on the way. His hand brushes mine. "Thank you," he whispers.

"For what?" My gaze is already moving ahead. To the fog outside, where it beckons me with crooked fingers.

"For trusting me. I'll help you find your brother. I promise. But when we do it, we do it the right way."

His words send a twinge of guilt through me. I ignore it. "See you in five."

Outside, the mist is getting thicker. I wait till the cavern mouth is behind us before I turn to Becca. "I have to go."

"I know." When I just stare at her, she rolls her eyes. "You really think I need your help to pee? I'm here to cover you."

For a second, I don't know what to say. "They won't be happy you helped me," I warn her.

"Too bad. They don't get to tell me what to do. Not after they left me for two years with not even a phone call." Her expression turns fierce. "Jeremy and Ian think they know everything, but they don't know about Charlie. He saved the lights in the Black Nothing. He can save us, too. But first you have to save him."

A crooked curl drops across her brow. Charlie has one just like it.

I'm overcome with the desire to wrap my arms around this

strange little girl. Instead, I settle for brushing that misbehaving curl out of her face. "Thank you."

Becca nods. That stubborn furrow pops up between her brows, making her look exactly like her brother. "Go. Find Charlie. Bring him back so he can bring us home."

TWENTY-SIX

CHARLIE

The Black Nothing is full of stars.

One by one we catch them.

One by one we gather them in a net of silver thread.

Some lights are easy to keep burning.

Others need more help.

One by one we find them.

One by one they remember their songs, take the silver thread, and See.

"I don't understand," *says a weak light, dimmer than the others.* "I don't understand how this could have happened."

"You're the one who made the door," *I say.* "The door that let the dark through?"

The dim light grows dimmer still. "It's not possible. I don't know what went wrong."

"It's not your fault," *I say.* "You couldn't have known. The door you made. The music in the dark fed it in from the other side."

"Music in the dark?"

"Can't you hear it all around you?"

"The dark pulse? Yes. Yes, I hear it." *The light shudders.* "What is this place?"

"The Black Nothing. Shadow world behind the curtain."

"Another dimension?" *the flickering light asks, flashing a little brighter.* "Hyperspace?"

I don't know this word, but I understand the feeling.

"Yes."

"Are there are more worlds like this one? Worlds we can't see?"

"The Black Nothing is where the dark song lives. There are other songs. Other places that make the music inside of us."

"And you can see them?" *asks the dim light.*

I nod. "Do you want me to show you?"

The trembling light touches the silver thread. He gasps when he sees.

The hallways running through my head.

Doors stacked on doors.

All the threads running through them.

"What are they?" *asks the trembling light.* "Where do they come from?"

"They live all around and inside of us. Deep in the places eyes can't touch."

The flickering light cries softly. He understands. "Tell me what to do. Tell me how to fix this."

"We can't," *I tell the flickering light.* "Not us."

"When will she come, the one you told us about?" *asks the little light named Sarah.* "When can we go home?"

"She will find the dark when she's ready," *I tell her.* "And when she follows the golden thread to me, she'll find us all."

Golden thread anchoring a silver net full of stars.

Silver balloon on a golden string.

Remember, *I wish on the golden thread, giving it a little tug.* I need you to remember.

A funny little dog on the cover of a book.

Who wore a hat made of straw.

Someday, you told me. *Someday we'll have that too.*

Funny little girl.

You said it again and then you cupped your hands over my ears. You didn't want me to hear the singing through the wall. I didn't tell you.

I hear everything.

Someday, you promised when it was over and the world was screaming quiet.

I heard you.

Please. Please, hear me now.

Hear me.

Feel me.

Find me.

Right where I told you to.

Remember.

Remember your promise.

I wish the words upon the golden thread, and I see her at the other end.

Searching for me.

Always searching

in the wrong places.

Hurry, Rosie. Hurry.

The Black Nothing reaches for me.

Faster now. Stronger, because it knows.

I am afraid.

When it comes

I give it my ear.

TWENTY-SEVEN

A flash of movement up ahead.

I stumble toward it through the trees. White bands of mist creep through the forest. The fog doesn't roll. It *reaches* for me like the fingers of a hand about to close. Gooseflesh breaks out across my arms, but then I catch sight of Charlie up ahead.

I work my way toward him through the fog, my stomach churning. Dread. Relief. It's all mixed together now. Charlie is alive and he's close. All the same, I don't need a compass to tell me where we're headed.

Back to Fort Glory and the wormhole hovering over it.

I've been walking for a few minutes when I feel it. The air. It's getting warmer. More of the brown of the forest peeks through the white crust. Drops of melting snow splatter my head and shoulders. Soft *thunk*s sound around me as sheets of ice slide off branches, covering any tracks Charlie may have left behind. Not that I'd be able to see them in this soup.

At first, the mist was a veil covering the ground and draping the canopy. Now it's a tsunami, drowning everything in white. The air is thick enough to drink. It gets so bad, I can't see the trees until I'm about to smack right into them.

I'm walking completely blind now, using my hands to guide

me. Minutes have passed since I last saw Charlie. He could've changed his trajectory. He could've doubled back. He could be standing three feet in front of me, and I wouldn't have a clue.

My scalp prickles. When did the forest get so quiet? It's that first night out in the woods all over again. I can't shake the feeling that I'm being watched.

"Charlie? Are you there?"

Something moves in the fog directly ahead. A streak of gray behind a wall of white.

My limbs lock in place as the visions play in an endless loop through my head. If there's any truth to them, the Charlie waiting for me in that fog might be nothing like the brother I left behind in the park. The thought drives a nail right through my heart.

I take a step forward. "Charlie. I know you're out there."

The fog swallows my voice. Silence. It hangs heavy for a moment before a sound reaches me from up ahead. The scuffle of feet. Or the brush of a jacket against a tree. I work my way toward it in the complete whiteout.

Another noise. This one from the right. I spin and barely avoid stumbling into a bramble of bushes.

The sound comes again. This time from directly ahead of me.

Charlie is close. So close I swear I can feel his breath on my cheeks.

Every nerve in my body comes alive as I extend my arm through the curtain of fog. Its wetness parts at my touch. Something brushes against the pad of my fingertip. Featherlight. I take one more step toward it.

"Charlie, plea—"

My foot comes down on empty air. I rear back, but I'm too

239

far off balance. The world shifts sideways as I fall forward into white nothingness.

My shoulders hit the earth with a wet squelch. I roll. Again and again and again. Soft dirt gives under my nails. I think I'm going to tumble right off the face of the earth, when my side slams into something hard.

I fold myself around the small boulder. My ribs ache from the impact, but the pain fades when I glimpse what waits for me on the other end of this drop.

The sinkhole is a gaping wound in the forest floor.

The world spins around me as I search its murky depths.

Deep. So, so deep.

Fear floods my veins with a burst of adrenaline. I'm halfway down the incline that leads to the open mouth of the sinkhole. Solid ground lies less than fifteen feet above me. The grade isn't steep. Barely forty degrees. I can make it on my hands and knees if I get myself into the right position.

At the slightest shift of my weight, the dirt around me starts a violent cascade into the open mouth of the sinkhole. I freeze.

This soil. It's too soft. The entire section of earth below me could give at any moment. I can't move, but I also can't stay here. If the sinkhole grows much more, it'll take me with it, and then I'll have lost my only chance to get out of here.

I look down into the endless darkness below. My limbs start to shake. Hot tears burn my throat because I've been this person before. Scared. Helpless. *Weak.* I swore to myself on the side of that Kansas road that I would never be this person again. I've kept that promise even when I thought it would kill me.

I refuse to break it now.

My vision narrows until I can see nothing but the firm ledge above me. I pull myself up toward the lip of the sinkhole. The earth is soft and wet. It crumbles in my hands when I try to use it as an anchor.

Every movement sends a fresh wave of dark soil tumbling toward me. It gets in my mouth. My nose. I time my breaths to avoid inhaling lungfuls of dirt, but it still coats the back of my tongue with grit.

Inch by inch, I drag myself out of the hole until I'm a few feet from the top. I've almost got myself onto solid ground when it happens.

The pain bursts out of nowhere.

Fireworks in my head.

My ear. My ear is a bomb detonating through my skull. I scream. The sound fractures me into a million pieces that break apart in the wind.

I lose my grip. The ground. They sky. Everything blurs together in a cyclone of white as I roll into the open mouth of the sinkhole. I'm near the edge when something wraps around my waist, jerking me to a stop.

The tree roots jut out of the soil like an open hand, cradling me in its palm.

Waves of pain leave me twitching in the bed of dirt, moss, and rotted wood.

The tremors in my body set the roots groaning beneath me, but I'm past fear now. Past reason. I am past anything but the pain. It is driving me out of the world on a wave of shadows when I see him.

Charlie.

Suspended behind a wall of darkness. Hovering right in front of me just like Becca was in the Black Nothing. Except that

Charlie isn't lying on a ledge somewhere in the distance. He's so close I can almost touch him. Only, I can't move my arms. Can't feel my lips. Every bit of my strength is focused on holding back the shadows lurking at the edges of my vision.

Charlie's body is bent. Like before, he straightens, almost as if he can sense me there.

The sight of him is a crack through the foundation of my world.

Charlie's hand. His eyes. *His ear.* They're all lost to the darkness.

But that isn't the part that kills me. It's the expression on what's left of his beautiful face. Something buried deep under the pain. The thing he doesn't want me to see. The one thing he could never hide. Not from me.

Fear.

My brother is afraid, and it makes me want to tear out of my own skin if that's the only way to reach him.

"Charlie." My voice is a rusty hinge.

His body trembles. The way it did that night three years ago. The night I thought I would lose him forever, but instead, I lost myself.

Breathe, Charlie, I said. *Please don't stop breathing.*

Charlie's voice sails through my head.

I heard you, Rosie.

Please. Please, hear me now.

"I hear you, Charlie. Please." My lips crack and bleed around my tongue. It hurts to talk. Hurts to breathe. But I concentrate on his face and I push the words past the pain. "Please. Don't leave me."

Find me.

Right where I told you to.

Remember.

Remember your promise.

Tears run. His. Mine. I don't even know anymore.

"How? Tell me how."

The darkness closes in. Not the darkness that's slowly killing Charlie. The darkness waiting in the wings of my vision.

It starts to pull me under.

No! I push it back and focus in on the pain—the only thing that's real. The only thing left connecting me to Charlie. It burns through my synapses. It lights a fire in my nerves that parts my lips in a silent scream. Even as it kills me, I tell myself I can handle it. I can handle anything.

Just, please. Let me stay here with him a little longer.

Black spots dance in front of my eyes. Charlie's lips move with silent words. I'm trying to make them out when the shadows rush in. This time, there is no stopping them.

The blackness sweeps past me in a wave. It carries me.

Away from the sinkhole.

Away from my brother.

It strips me down in layers until there is only one thing left: the thing hidden behind that wall inside of me. Something buried so deep I could almost forget it's there.

But the darkness knows.

It knows the darkness too.

TWENTY-EIGHT

M y eyes fly open to the sight of trees swaying over my head. The sky behind them is a sickly green that perfectly reflects how I'm feeling.

I draw myself up onto all fours and retch.

A broad hand strokes my back.

I peek through the curtain of my hair to find Ian leaning over me, his face a mask of concern. My heart lifts at the sight of him.

"Are you all right?" His voice is raw. Like he's been yelling.

I nod and sit up slowly. The drumming ache in my head makes it hard to get my bearings. My eyes slide past Ian to the giant sinkhole lurking a few feet behind him.

I scramble backward, right into a fallen log.

"It's okay. You're okay." Ian crouches down in front of me.

The edges of my vision go blurry. I close my eyes and wait for it to pass. Only then do I risk another look at the sinkhole. Ian's rope lies in a heap at the edge. A few yards of it are still wrapped around my waist. That answers the question of how I got out. A dozen others pop up to take its place.

I ask the most pressing one first. "How long was I out?"

"It's been two hours since you left. It took me that long to find you." I wait for him to chew me out. To tell me how stupid I was, but he just tugs my elbow. "Let's go."

I lean away from him. "I saw Charlie at the caverns. I followed him this far before the pain hit again. He was here. He might still be close."

Ian doesn't say anything. He's either too tired or too furious with me or both. Right now, I don't care. I don't care about anything but Charlie.

"He's dying, Ian. I saw it with my own eyes. Every second that passes, the dark pulse is eating away at him. Just like it did with Becca. Only he has nobody to bring him back the way we did for her."

"We'll talk about it at the caverns." Ian doesn't make eye contact. He just starts jamming equipment into his bag.

Maybe I should be grateful to him for saving my life. For coming to get me when I blew him off, but right now, all I can picture is Charlie the way he looked in the dark. The blacked-out parts of him. The fear on his face he couldn't hide.

I drag myself to my feet. "I'm not going back without Charlie." I've taken a few stumbling steps when Ian catches up to me.

His grip on my arm is painful.

"Let me go!" I wrench free of his grasp.

"We have to leave. Right now." The wind howls through the trees, sending Ian's chin jerking skyward.

Something's wrong. I can tell from the way he's shooting anxious glances at the branches overhead. He's trying not to alarm me, but he's fidgeting. Ian Lawson doesn't fidget.

I'm officially alarmed.

"What's going on?" I demand.

"The Fold. It's heating up too quickly. Do you know what happens when a cold front meets a warm front?"

My mind flashes back to that trailer park in Kansas, but then

I think of Charlie, and I square my shoulders. "Whatever's coming, I won't hide in a cave while my brother faces it alone."

"Then you're going to die," Ian says bluntly.

"We're all going to die here!" I shout the words over the rising wind. "I'm done waiting for the Fold to kill me, Ian. I'm going after Charlie." I don't drop his gaze. I need him to see me. I need him to understand.

I am done being scared.

I am done running.

I am done with *all* of it.

Ian doesn't back down, and this time, neither do I. Seconds pass before the thud of heavy boots interrupts our stare-down.

A figure crests the ridge to our left.

I swivel to face the person approaching us. They pause at the top of a ridge, their shoulders bent, face turned toward the ground. My heart thrums once. Twice. The figure straightens. All my hopes crash and burn in a pile of ash.

"Jeremy?" I say.

"Good. Lawson tracked you down." Jeremy joins us at the edge of the sinkhole.

"What are you doing here?" Ian's voice is low and furious. "I told you to stay back with the others."

"Yeah, well, Rose isn't the only one who thinks your orders suck." Jeremy brushes some brambles clinging to his uniform. "I couldn't sit in that cave with Becca pretending I don't exist and Blaine inventing new ways to tell me I'm a moron."

"So you just left them there? Alone?" Ian demands.

"They're safer in that cavern than we are out here. Have you checked the sky lately?" Jeremy grins at me. "If you'd told me you were planning on taking off, I would've come with you. Any sign of Charlie?"

I fill him in on what happened in the fog. When I'm done, thunder rumbles in the distance.

"We've got to go," Ian says.

Jeremy throws an arm over my shoulder in a not-so-subtle attempt to piss Ian off. "Go if you're scared. Rose and I will catch up with you once we find Charlie."

"I'm not leaving her out here with you." Ian's voice sends shivers up my spine.

Another gust of wind rocks the forest, revealing scraps of sky through swaying branches. Overhead, dark clouds march in to the beat of distant thunder.

"Rose is a big girl," Jeremy says. "She can make up her own mind."

"Is that what you tell yourself to sleep at night?" Ian asks calmly. Too calmly. "It's not your fault the pills you pushed destroyed lives? It was their choice to take them. Not yours?"

Jeremy's arm drops from my shoulders. "Shut up."

Ian takes one step forward. I move on instinct, blocking his path. "Enough, Ian."

A sudden shift draws my gaze to the treetops. The light behind the canopy. It's fading like someone hit the dimmer switch. Shadows lengthen and stretch all around us. The wind tapers off until it dies down completely. The stillness hovers like a sword above our heads.

When Ian doesn't respond, I plead with Jeremy instead. "If we're going to find Charlie, we have to do it now. Come on." I tug on Jeremy's arm. He doesn't budge.

"Is that what you told yourself when Will came to you?" Ian continues like I'm not even there. "That he was a big boy? He could handle it?"

"What do you want from me? Do you want to hear that I'm sorry? That I hate myself?" Tears streak angry paths through the dirt on Jeremy's cheeks. "Because I am so fucking sorry, Ian." Jeremy's voice seems to shatter.

"Your apologies can't give me the past two years of my life back. They won't bring—" Ian's chest hitches.

"I know," Jeremy pleads desperately. "But you don't know the whole—" The words are drowned out by a fit of coughing. Once it starts, it doesn't stop.

"Jeremy!" I pat him on the back to clear his lungs. I think the coughing will go on forever, when Jeremy's eyes fly open.

Darkness swirls in his growing pupils.

Not now. Please, please not now.

"Jeremy." I reach for his hand, searching for some of that Kennedy warmth, wanting to give it back.

He steps away from me. The darkness leaks out of his pupils into his irises, staining them black. "I can't take it anymore," he tells Ian. "I can't take you punishing me over and over for something I can't change. If I could go back and do it differently, don't you think I—" A violent hacking takes him over. It ends in a choked gurgle. Jeremy kneads a fist against his chest. "There are things you need to know."

"So tell him," I say quickly. If Jeremy can get out the words, maybe he'll step back from the ledge he's teetering on. Maybe he'll be able to *breathe.*

We can't afford to lose Jeremy now. Not with Charlie so close.

Not with the storm bearing down. And if Jeremy goes, I have a terrible feeling he'll be taking Ian with him.

"I've been trying," Jeremy cries. "But the words get stuck in my throat, like, physically stuck. And whenever I try to push them out, it feels like I'm coughing up razor blades."

His words creep up my spine. "It's the dark pulse," I say. "It's working on Jeremy physically." Just like it did Becca. And Charlie. "Don't say anything else. Please, Jer. You'll only make it worse."

"I don't care." Tears leak through butterfly lashes. The hacking starts up again. Tremors bend him over at the waist, and his face turns an alarming shade of red.

"Shut it." Ian's voice is cold, but there's a touch of something that wasn't there before. Worry.

"No," Jeremy rasps. "I'm going to tell you what happened, and you're going to lis—" The next wave of coughing brings him to his knees. When he looks up again, his jaw is set in an obstinate line. "You're going to listen," he finishes, spitting out a mouthful of saliva. "Even if it kills me."

He smiles. Blood stains his teeth.

"Ian." His name comes out panicked.

But Ian isn't listening to me. He stares at Jeremy bleeding on the ground in front of him like it wouldn't be the worst thing to watch his friend choke to death on whatever dark truth has driven this wedge between them.

"Ian!"

This time, he looks at me with swirling pupils.

I take a few steps backward. Ian watches me go, a frown cutting across his brow. Muscles tense in his neck, his arms. Like it's taking everything in him not to follow me. The darkness in his eyes breaks for half a second, and I can almost hear his voice yelling in my head.

Run. Before it's too late.

Ian makes a sound deep in his throat and twists away from me. His hand moves to grip his hat, knuckles gleaming white against the faded bill.

I watch him hold on to that last piece of himself, and something moves deep inside of me. I don't know what to call it or what it means, but I know one thing for certain.

It won't run. Not from this.

Ian follows my approach with inky eyes. He jerks his head. One last warning. I ignore it and move until I'm standing right in front of him. "Think of Becca," I say, the only thing I can think of to get through to him.

Seconds fall like dominoes. The light comes back into Ian's eyes. He nods, and the relief has my knees going soft.

Ian drags Jeremy to his feet and pushes him in the direction of the caverns. "Move your ass, Kennedy."

"Just leave me." Jeremy drops back down to the ground. A two-hundred-pound child throwing a tantrum. "We both know it's what you want to do."

A crack of lightning flashes in the sky as Ian grabs Jeremy by the front of his uniform and hoists him to his feet. "And tell Becca I left you out here to die?" He grunts. "Not happening."

Jeremy shoves Ian off. "Screw you."

Another rumble of thunder. This one closer. When I try to take Ian's place, Jeremy pushes me away. "I didn't know what he was going to do," he tells me desperately. Blood and spittle fly out of his mouth to speckle my arms where they hold on to him.

"Jeremy, please!" I beg, but he's past the point of no return.

His eyes are open, every last trace of hazel drowned in a sea of pure black.

"I should've come clean with you," he tells Ian. "I should've told my old man to go to hell when he tried to brush my part under the rug. I couldn't stop him from pressing the charges, but I swear, I never spoke against you." Every word sounds like it's torn out of his throat by a pair of pliers. "He signed me up for boot camp. Told me his lawyers would make it worse for you if I didn't go quietly. I convinced myself I was doing it for you, but I was a coward. I was afraid to embarrass my family, or let Will down or have you hate me, and now it's too late to fix any of it. It's too fucking late." Agony contorts Jeremy features. The coughing escalates into frantic hacking.

Jeremy's arms thrash, one last desperate strain for air. Then he slumps to the ground, utterly still.

I lean over and place my cheek against his chest. Panic sends my eyes shooting to Ian's. "He's not breathing."

The words are barely out before Ian is on Jeremy's other side. He tilts his head back to open his airway and places both hands over Jeremy's breast bone. He starts to push. One. Two. Three dozen times.

Ian covers Jeremy's mouth with his own. The soldier's chest rises and falls with each breath Ian gives him. It doesn't rise again.

"Come on, Jeremy." Ian restarts compressions, throwing his whole body into it. "Come. On."

Four more breaths. Two more waits that end in disappointment.

"Don't you do it. Don't you fucking die on me." Ian pushes. Again and again and again. I sit on the ground next to them, hands folded in a prayer that won't come. There are no prayers now. No words. There is just this moment and the weight of Ian's desperation about to cave in Jeremy's chest.

Tears stream down my face as I watch Ian try to beat the life back into his friend.

More breaths. More compressions. More rolling thunder in the dark.

"Breathe." Another flash of lightning highlights the sheen of sweat covering Ian's face. "Goddammit, Jeremy. *Breathe!*"

A gasp sounds through the woods as Jeremy draws a ragged breath. Then another. He's still unconscious, but at least he's breathing.

Ian slumps to the ground beside him.

It starts to rain. Stinging drops cut vertical trajectories through the canopy, driving the reality of the situation right into our faces. The sky has turned the color of an old bruise.

The air crackles. Branches creak and groan as microbursts shred through the forests.

Ian rips off his jacket and lays it over Jeremy's body. "Go back to the cavern." He raises his voice to be heard over the rain. "We'll be right behind you."

"You can't carry him the whole way," I yell back. Jeremy weighs almost as much as Ian does. Besides, we both know the storm isn't the worst danger facing Jeremy now. "If we don't go in there after him, he'll fade into the Black Nothing," I say. "His body won't matter because his mind will be gone."

I reach for Jeremy's hand. Ian catches my wrist. "This isn't your mess. It's mine. I have to clean it up."

Words crowd my mouth. I want to tell him to forget it. That it's too big of a risk, but he has to do this, and I have to let him.

But it's hard. Trusting is hard. And it never gets any easier.

"You'll feel a thread pulling you back to your body," I tell him. "Concentrate on finding the other one. The one between you and Jeremy." I squeeze his hand. "Find it and bring him back."

Ian meets my eyes through the driving rain. His face moves with an emotion I can't place. "Promise me you'll find cover if the storm gets worse." His grip on my hand tightens. "Say the words, Rose." He looks at me like I'm the only thing he sees.

"I promise."

Ian offers me a tense nod. He drops my hand and swaps it out for Jeremy's. As soon as their skin touches, Ian's face contorts in agony before going completely blank.

"Ian." I shake him. "Ian!" He doesn't respond.

And the driving rain around us turns to hail.

Drops of ice the size of golf balls shred through the canopy, releasing a rain of leaves and branches from up above. Pain lights up my back and shoulders. I raise my hands to protect my face. A piece of hail hits Jeremy on the forehead, opening up a cut over his eye. Another splits Ian's knuckles where they grip Jeremy's hand. The sight of their blood running together acts like a bucket of ice water, bringing me to my senses.

Stinging shards slice into my cheek as I scramble for Ian's pack. Folded at the bottom is a familiar flap of silver.

Hail becomes sheets of freezing rain as I shake out the tarp. I can barely see, so I go by touch, tucking the free end under Jeremy's body while I hold up the other side, forming a crude tent over the two of them.

Gusts of air tear through the trees, flinging dirt into my eyes and threatening to rip the tarp out of my fingers. The wind runs wild through the forest, playing the branches overhead to an ominous tune of creaks and groans.

The sound of splitting wood fills my ears. Several branches fly from the treetops to hit the ground behind us.

Branches that could easily cave in a titanium roof.

My gaze cuts to Jeremy and Ian lying helpless beside me. Ian made me promise to leave if things got bad, but it's too late for that now. The Fold has cracked my world wide open. It isn't just the dark pulse. Blaine and Becca. Jeremy and Ian. I can feel the fragile bonds between us growing stronger with every passing minute. Tying me right to the spot.

I risk a quick glimpse at the sky just as a thick band of lightning splits the world in half. The flash is accompanied by a crack of thunder that sets the ground trembling beneath me. It happens again, and I realize what it is. Not thunder. Not another earthquake. The sound of a massive tree hitting the ground nearby.

My breathing comes in short bursts.

Another tree hits the forest floor, close enough to set my back teeth ringing.

Ian and Jeremy have been gone too long. We're never making it out of here. Not unless I find some way to bring them back.

The world breaks down into a series of stimuli.

The scent of ozone and dirt.

The cold rain on my face and the slap of the wind as I let go of the tarp.

The warmth of Ian's and Jeremy's skin as I grab hold of both of their hands, forming a circle in the center of the storm.

The hook rises out of the chaos around me to coat my insides in liquid fire, and then the Black Nothing is there, just like I knew it would be.

I fall sideways into the dark.

The dark pulse slams into me. The sound is enough to make me wish I was dead. Once I can think past it, I focus on what's around me.

Down below, Jeremy is curled in on himself in the Black Nothing. The light around him is holding steady, fed by a deep blue thread that runs through him from somewhere to my right.

Ian.

I can feel him there, a solid, steady presence. The only bearable thing in this darkness. I reach for him with my mind, and at once, a storm of images assaults me.

Two boys playing in the woods in the back of a white house with crumbling shutters. The quiet one carrying a trash bag because he's not supposed to leave until all the beer cans are cleaned up. The black-haired one pretending he doesn't notice the peeling paint, or the car on cinder blocks, or the way his friend tries to hide his shame and his bruises under the bill of a hat.

The same two boys a few years later, following an older boy to a pool in the middle of the woods, because for two of them, these woods feel so much safer than home. Their laughter echoing through the clearing. The black-haired boy's attempts to distract the brothers from their scars glinting in the sun by diving backward off the waterfall without paying attention to the rocks below.

A thirteen-year-old Jeremy with skinny arms and shaggy hair, doing something stupid that gets him yet another detention. But not before making Ian laugh so hard his split lip starts to bleed. Jeremy's grin of satisfaction as he's removed from class, and Ian's voice following him out into the hall, calling him a dumbass.

Ian as a teenager, scaling the side of a mansion in the dead of night before climbing through Jeremy's window. Jeremy tossing him a pillow and a towel with a grumbled warning about leaving blood on the sink before

255

pulling the inflatable mattress out from under his bed. Waking up the next day and acting as if nothing had happened.

Jeremy going to the caverns to look for Ian when he doesn't show up at school. Saying something stupid to push Ian's buttons. The sound of flesh hitting stone as he tackles Ian to the ground. Not because he wants to fight, but because he knows Ian needs to.

The images stop, and suddenly, I'm hurtling out of the abyss and back to the middle of the storm.

Something hits me across the face. The tarp, flapping wildly in the wind.

I push it down to see Ian blinking at me. My heart lifts even higher when Jeremy groans at his feet. He's battered. They both are. But they're alive, and they're *here.*

Ian's eyes move from the raging storm to the flapping tarp to me. "You can yell at me later," I tell him. "Right now, let's move."

Ian nods. "Come on, Kennedy." He throws one arm around Jeremy.

"Careful," Jeremy groans as Ian helps him to his feet. "I'm starting to think you don't actually hate me."

Ian laughs, and in spite of the blood flying from his mouth and the world falling apart around us, Jeremy actually grins.

They've both lost their minds.

Another crack of lightning cuts through the forest. During the flash, I catch a glimpse of the clouds rolling toward us. A wall of solid black, twisting in a circular motion.

I've seen clouds move like that before.

A narrow funnel drops down from the sky.

I break into a run. Ian and Jeremy stay close beside me. Debris flies through the air. Ragged blasts of air hit us on all sides.

The light has bled out of the sky. It's hard to see what's in front of me. Almost impossible to keep my feet.

I have to keep my feet. I have to—

An earsplitting howl fills my head. Gusts of wind hit me like hammers, driving me sideways into Ian's solid weight. He catches me with both hands and we tumble across the forest floor.

My head is still reeling when someone reaches down to yank me up. Jeremy. Together, Ian and I climb to our feet.

The sound of roots being torn from the earth comes from directly behind us.

I stumble back into a run even though I know it's useless. The tornado is too close. The caverns too far. We'll never make it.

My eyes dart frantically around the forest. They zero in on a tree lying on its side a few dozen yards away. Directly underneath it, a trench snakes through the ground. It could be a few feet deep or it could be a mile.

It's a chance I'm willing to take.

I yank on Ian's sleeve and drag him toward the tree. Jeremy follows right on our heels.

We're almost at the trench when Ian pulls me in close to his side. The wind tears a cry from his lips. He staggers. A moment later, he's standing straight again, pushing me ahead of him into the ditch.

I roll several feet down to the bottom and come to a stop under the solid trunk. Needles prick my neck and the smell of sap fills my nostrils as I press my body flat to the earth. A moment later, Jeremy is crawling over me. Seconds tick by, but Ian doesn't show.

I'm about to crawl out after him when he rolls down into the trench, slamming to a stop beside me. Something crashes into the tree from up above, releasing a flood of needles onto our backs. Ian throws his body over mine, pinning me to the dirt with his weight. The world comes apart over our heads.

Branches break. Trees fall. The wind screams.

It feels like the whole forest is crashing down on top of us. We're not going to make it. We're going to die right here in this trench.

I'll never see Charlie's face again.

The thought fills me with sadness just as there's another massive *thunk* on the trunk. More needles fall. It goes on and on and on, until, gradually, it stops.

The howl turns into a gentle keening. The ground stops shaking.

I lie there for a few minutes longer, not daring to lift my head.

Jeremy sits up beside me. "The sky. It's starting to clear."

An exhausted smile splits my face as I nudge Ian. "You can get off now."

He doesn't move.

I try again, but Ian doesn't stir. Something hot and wet seeps into my back.

My heart skips like a stone across a pond. "Jeremy! Help!"

Jeremy has Ian off me in seconds. The first thing I see when I turn over is Jeremy's terrified face.

The second thing I see is the ten-inch sliver of bloody wood sticking straight out of Ian's chest.

TWENTY-NINE

We stumble into the cave an hour after dark.

Blaine is on us the moment we come into sight. His knuckles gleam white around the handle of Jeremy's gun. His face appears to have aged two years since this morning.

"Where have you *been*? We were hit by a crazy storm and we thought—" His expression transforms from relief, to anger, to fear once he gets a good look at Ian, hanging between us.

"Quick," I say. "Get some water boiling and as many rags as we can spare."

Blaine sprints ahead while Jeremy and I half carry, half drag Ian into the circular room at the back of the cavern.

Blaine builds the fire back up while I grab the scissors from Jeremy's kit and kneel beside Ian's motionless form. He regained consciousness a few minutes after the storm passed. Even weak from blood loss, he managed to stay awake for most of the trip back. If he hadn't pulled most of his own weight, we never would've gotten him back here.

I peel the bloody shirt from Ian's chest. An ugly wound glares up at me in the firelight. Ian's shoulder is stabbed clean through by a jagged shard of wood ten inches long and as wide as my thumb.

Blaine sucks air between his teeth. "What happened?"

I open my mouth, but words don't come. All I can do is stare at Ian, lying on the stone floor. His face is so pale, I can trace the blue veins fanning out over his closed lids. He looks more like a ghost than a boy, and it's my fault. All of this is my fault.

He told you this would happen. But you wouldn't listen. You didn't listen.

"Tornado," Jeremy answers when I don't.

Silent tears stream down Becca's face. "Is he going to die?"

"No," Jeremy tells her. "It went through his shoulder. He's going to be okay. He's going to be okay," he repeats. Jeremy removes a scalpel from his med kit and moves toward Ian.

Blaine comes out of nowhere to block his path. "What are you gonna to do?"

"I'm going to cut that shard out."

Blaine's eyes lock on the scalpel. "The two of you have been trying to kill each other since we first saw you. Why should we let you anywhere near him?"

At the sight of Blaine's trembling lips, Jeremy softens. "That's over. I swear it. I'll take care of Ian like he's my own brother." Jeremy's voice goes quiet. "He was. Once."

Blaine doesn't back down. He wasn't in the forest with us when the world was falling apart. He didn't see what I saw.

"Let him through," I tell Blaine softly.

The younger boy hesitates for a moment, but then he does what I ask.

Jeremy drops to his knees next to Ian and wraps his hands around the piece of wood. "What do you need us to do?" I ask, joining him.

"Blaine, can you grab those rags...please?" Jeremy adds gently.

Blaine returns with an armful of random clothing we picked up at the camp. "This good?"

"Perfect," Jeremy says, and Blaine holds his head a little higher.

"As soon as I get this clear, I need you to put pressure on the wound," Jeremy tells me.

It's happening before any of us are ready. Jeremy yanks the wood out of Ian's shoulder. Blood spurts. I grit my teeth and press the cloth to Ian's shoulder, using my fingers to plug the wound.

Time passes. I'm not sure how much. Jeremy removes splinters, douses the wound with antiseptic, and stitches it up. Becca hands him towel after towel while Blaine removes the dirty rags, for once not feeling the need to comment or give Jeremy shit for being a moron.

And then the wound is wrapped, and Ian is sleeping, and Jeremy is telling Blaine and Becca about what happened to us. The cave echoes with their voices, but the words are lost in the vacuum around my head. I block out the wind and the cold and focus all of my attention on the rise and fall of Ian's chest as I match my breaths to his.

The fire has burned down to embers when something wakes me. A cry in the dark.

I crawl out from under my blankets and pad toward the circular room at the back of the cave.

Cold air drifts in through the single skylight. Ian is propped up against the wall, his long legs sprawled out in front of him.

With his head tipped back and eyes closed, he looks almost peaceful. I allow myself a few seconds to study him like this before I turn to leave.

"Don't go." When I glance back, Ian's eyes are wide open.

He's awake. My shoulders relax. I should let him rest, but there's something I have to say, and this might be my only chance.

I join Ian against the wall. We're close, sitting side by side. Not close enough for our arms to touch, but close enough that I can feel his every breath. His chest is bare except for the mass of white bandages across his left shoulder. The firelight turns his skin a warm honey color.

I keep my gaze fixed on the far wall. Words tangle on my tongue, but I take a deep breath and force them out. "I'm sorry. Charlie is my responsibility. I had no right to ask you or Jeremy to risk—"

"Do you regret it?"

There are many things I regret, but going after Charlie isn't one of them. "No."

"Then save your apologies." Silence. "You're not in this alone," Ian says quietly. "As soon as the sun rises, every single one of us will help you look for your brother. All you have to do is ask."

He makes it sound so easy.

I press back against the cavern wall. Its cool dampness sinks into my skin. Ever since Dad went missing, it's been just me, Mom, and Charlie. I've been so focused on carrying the extra weight, maybe I forgot that the world was bigger than the three of us.

My gaze runs over Ian, sitting beside me. The pale hollows of his cheeks. The dried blood still crusted to his muscular chest. The scars he tries so hard to hide.

With a lurch, the walls I've built around myself push out a few feet in every direction.

I take a steadying breath. This isn't just about my family anymore. Other people are involved now, and one of them almost died today because I was too busy looking ahead to spot the danger about to sideswipe us. Just like I was too obsessed with getting to that Hands for Hearths meeting to hear Charlie's warnings when they could've made a difference.

I can't change any of that now. But maybe I don't have to keep making the same mistakes over and over.

"How are you holding up?" I ask, to distract myself from the unwelcome thoughts in my head. Like the memory of Ian's blood, soaking the back of my shirt. Or the way my heart stopped when I saw the stick jutting out of his shoulder.

When he doesn't answer, I shift sideways. The firelight glints off a strip of seared flesh spanning the width of his forearm. A burn so fresh it's still glistening.

Everything inside of me goes deathly still. "What happened?"

"Same thing as before. I could feel myself getting angrier until I was burning. And then I woke up and that was there."

"Are you okay?" I ask.

"It's—"

"It's just pain, right?" I look up into his eyes. Mistake. His breath brushes my cheek, and then I'm staring at his mouth.

"Pain comes from here." Ian taps my temple. The callused tip of his finger skims my skin. "You can block it out if you have to."

"How?" I don't recognize the thin sound of my own voice.

"By going somewhere else." Ian studies the inscription on the wall, and suddenly I'm back in the Black Nothing, watching two brothers jump off a waterfall into a hidden pool. The sunlight glinting off the scars covering their bodies. A topography of violence years in the making.

As if sensing the direction of my thoughts, Ian stiffens. I wish I could leave it alone, but there are greater things on the line right now than his privacy. The dark pulse is going to keep wearing him down. Building 101. Everything has a breaking point.

Even Ian.

I angle my body so that I am fully facing him. "When you went into the Black Nothing after Jeremy, I touched you. I . . . saw things."

"I know."

"How?"

Ian runs a hand over his naked scalp. "I felt you like a light on somewhere in my head, and it . . . helped." He draws an unsteady breath. "Rose—"

"I have scars too. Ones I wouldn't want anyone to see." My words trip over themselves in their rush to be spoken. "Everybody has a right to their secrets. Yours are safe with me."

Ian relaxes against the wall. His good shoulder presses against mine. The fire crackles, and the wind howls outside, and for one moment, I'm less alone than I've been in a long, long time.

"You look like him. Will, I mean. I saw you two swimming in the pool where we found Becca."

"My old man hated it when we took off like that." Ian stares at his hand. "It was worth the punishment. Most of the time."

A shiver runs through me. "Ian, I didn't mean—I wasn't trying to—" But I kind of was.

He grips my knee. "If something like that happens again, you should be prepared for what you might see. I don't want you to think—" He swallows. "There are things I need to tell you."

The tortured look on his face almost undoes me.

"It wasn't always like this. I don't know why I feel the need to tell you that. It's just…" He meets my eyes, pleading. "I need you to know that there were good times, too. Times I wouldn't trade for anything." His expression turns fierce. "So don't feel sorry for me."

"Okay." We both know it's a lie.

There are no words for how sorry I feel.

"When Dad was drafted into the minor leagues out of high school, my parents practically left Fort Glory on a parade float. Then Dad threw out his shoulder, and it was all over. They came back. Dad got a job as a mechanic, started drinking. Things weren't great, but they were okay. For a while."

"What happened?"

"Will." Ian rubs his eyes. "The kid was superhuman. He could do anything. *Anything.* But the only thing he really loved was baseball. He never left home without his hat and a glove in his back pocket." Ian pulls off the Mariners cap and runs his fingers over the faded blue fabric. "Scouts were sniffing around him when he was still in Little League. My dad saw Will heading for the future that should've been his. It made him ugly." Pain flashes across Ian's face. "Will took the brunt of it. Maybe it was easier for him because he knew it wasn't permanent. Baseball was his ticket out of this shithole—the one thing he had that nobody could touch, and that bastard knew it."

Cords bulge at Ian's neck. "One night, Dad came after me. I don't remember why. Will got between us. It wasn't the first time he'd stuck up for me, but it was the first time he did it with his head held up." Ian swallows. "So our father crushed Will's future under the heel of his boot. Seventeen bones in his right hand, one by one."

When Ian looks at me, his eyes glisten with a sorrow that dares me to look away. "Broken bones heal. Broken dreams are the real killer."

It's a moment before I can speak. "What happened to him?"

Ian stares at the writing on the wall, his gaze unfocused, and I know that his brother is here with us in this cave, inscribing their names on a rock while Ian laughs beside him. Two lost boys hiding from the world.

"He started hitting Jeremy up for pills. Painkillers, mostly. They both hid it from me, but I should've seen the signs. Will stopped going to school. Stopped doing his PT. Stopped giving a shit. And then a week before my parents died, he asked Jeremy for something harder." Ian shrugs. "I guess he got tired of waiting for my father to kill him. The next day I found him facedown in a pool of his own vomit with his glove in his good hand. He'd been dead for hours."

Ian's words gut me. I don't tell him I'm sorry. I don't ask him to be strong, or brave, or to forget, because even though forgetting is a break from pain, it's only a way to defer it with interest. So I sit quietly while grief runs through him.

When Ian's breathing evens out, he shifts so that his face is inches from mine. "I was so angry at Jeremy. When I found out about the drugs, I lost it. If the police hadn't shown up, I would've killed him, and then I would've hated myself, because it wasn't his fault. He looked up to Will. Idolized him. He would've done anything he asked, but he never would've given him the drugs if he knew what Will was up to. And it wasn't his job to figure it out because Will wasn't his brother. He was mine."

"It wasn't his fault," I agree. But it wasn't Ian's, either. The person responsible isn't around anymore to take the blame.

As if reading my mind, Ian's expression grows taut. "Do you think I set the fire that killed my parents?"

"Does it matter?"

"Yes," Ian says, and my stomach does a sharp flip-flop. "What you think matters. To me."

I search his face like it's a map I have this one second to memorize. "You wouldn't hurt someone unless you had a reason. But you would do it if you had to." *Not because you're bad. Because you're like me.*

Because you are like me.

Ian sags against the wall. "Right after Will—" He swallows hard. "Dad was passed out on the couch when I left for Rowena's. I saw a cigarette butt sticking out of his mouth, and I *prayed* for it to fall so I wouldn't have to kill him. Because I wanted to. God, Rose, I wanted to. I didn't feel like I could breathe while he was still alive."

The pain in his voice cuts straight through me. "It wasn't your fault."

"When I came home and saw the flames in the windows, eating our house, every last memory, I was *happy*. Then I remembered Mom." He stares uncomprehendingly at the scars on his hands. "I tried to break out her window. I punched it over and over, but it didn't do a goddamn thing."

"Ian, I—"

"I hated them." His head hangs between his knees. He covers it with his arms. "I hated my dad for breaking Will, and her for letting him, and most of all, I hated Will for leaving me alone. And now they're all dead."

My mouth is full of words I won't say. No matter what he thinks, Ian isn't responsible for what happened to his family. They made their own choices. But he's not ready for that truth, and he may never be.

Ian turns toward me. "You know what burns the most? After everything that bastard did to us, I still turned out just like him. Things got rough and my answer was to almost kill someone."

I reach for him without thinking. "It's not the same. You're nothing like him. It's a choice, Ian. Maybe we don't get a say in the way people see us, but we choose who we *are*. We build ourselves up out of the scrap around us, and what we look like at the end is on us and no one else."

"You really believe that?" His breathing is heavy, his lips parted, his eyes bottomless and beautiful and locked onto my mouth.

A rush of air. Someone moving forward.

I turn my head. The way Ian looks at me. Like he sees all the parts I keep hidden, and still thinks I'm worth a damn. It makes me want to show him things I shouldn't.

Stop being a coward. Stop running. Say it. Say the words.
The truth.

But the truth gets stuck behind the wall inside of me along with the words I can't say. The only words that have ever really mattered.

"Rose." When I look up, Ian is watching me, every emotion safely locked back in its drawer. "I felt Charlie. When I went into the Black Nothing for Jeremy."

My breath leaves me in a rush. "What happened?"

"There was a moment. When I first got there. The noise in my head was so bad. I thought I was losing it." Ian's fingers probe the burn on his arm. "Then Charlie was there. It was exactly like Becca described. He made the pain stop, and he took me out of the darkness in my head and showed me something else." Ian glances at me sideways. "A field of blue flowers. They...reminded me of you."

I know the exact field he's talking about. It was lying behind a cheap motel in Tennessee. There were bugs in the carpet and mysterious stains in the shower, but none of that mattered when Charlie and I saw the ocean of blue petals outside. Mom said they were wishing flowers, and that we should make the most of them. So I did. I wished for a house on the ocean for Charlie and a porch swing for Mom. The smell of sawdust and the rough texture of wood under my fingertips.

"What did you wish for?" I asked Charlie when Mom fell asleep, and he and I were watching drops of moonlight water the flowers outside.

He smiled and shook his head. I thought he was keeping secrets, but only now am I starting to understand what Charlie was really saying as we lay side by side on a lumpy mattress and stared at an empty blue field. I thought we had nothing, but in that moment, we had each other and our mother sleeping in the bed next to us.

We had everything, only I was too blind to see it.

"Where was it?" Ian asks.

"Someplace we stayed once. A happy place. I'll never forget those flowers."

Ian nods. He looks at the fire and then back at me. "They were beautiful."

Of course they were. They were the exact color of my mother's eyes.

When I was little, every night before I went to sleep I'd kneel and I'd pray: *Please, God, make me beautiful. Just like her.*

Just. Like. Her.

I'd spend hours in the bathroom with her makeup littering the sink, painting myself into a pretty picture. Red lips. Dark lashes. She caught me once. My hair was sticking straight up where I'd coated it strand by strand with mascara.

"What were you doing?" she asked as she dabbed my temples with a warm washcloth. She leaned forward. I breathed her in. Violets and honey. Fingers in my hair, her laugh like a song, and I knew that I would never again be happier than I was in that moment.

"Trying to look like you."

Her hands froze.

I gazed at my beautiful mother, and my fingers itched to pick up the broken pieces and nail them back together. Only, I didn't have the tools.

She kneeled on the floor in front of me. *"Someday, Rosie, you'll look at me and you'll see what everyone else does. When that happens I'll have this memory to remind me of who I was to you in this moment."* She brushed back my hair and turned me away. I didn't say it then, but I knew she was wrong.

She wasn't.

The day she was talking about came less than three years later. She had just worked a double, and Mom was so tired she could barely push the grocery cart. The circles were like bruises under her eyes, and still everybody was staring. The monster had

270

been busy, spreading lies. He did it every time we moved on. Every time he found us. To make us miserable and keep my mother in her place. Like most rumors, these had taken on a life of their own.

Mom moved to the makeup aisle for some of the drugstore lipstick she always wore. It was a little thing, but it made her happy. My father loved it. I remember he was always telling her that, and then he was always kissing it off her lips so she would have to put on more. She still wore it every day. Like she wanted to be ready when he came back home to kiss it off again.

There was a woman browsing the cosmetics next to us. She clucked her tongue when Mom picked out the reddest shade they had. And suddenly, I was looking through a stranger's eyes, at a woman whose clothes were too tight, and whose smile was too wide, and whose face was too good to be true. I was ashamed.

She knew. I don't know how, but my mother glanced at me and she knew. She didn't say a word. She just put the lipstick back on the shelf, and she never wore it again.

And I was relieved.

THIRTY

CHARLIE

One light left. Deep in the Black Nothing. Faded star with a golden tail.

So much darkness. The star is drowning in it.

It's been drowning for a while.

"I'm here," *I tell the faded star.* "You don't have to be afraid."

It flickers. Beautiful, sad star. "Charlie?"

It knows me.

I know it too.

"Hi, Mom."

She cries when I wrap the new thread around her. Silver blanket. The Black Nothing beats against it. It's getting harder to move. Harder to keep all the little lights burning.

I have to keep them burning. Just a little longer.

I can.

I can.

"Come with me, Mom."

"What about Rose? Where's Rose?"

"Right here." *I touch the golden thread inside me and it comes alive with Light Music in the dark.*

Slow dances in the kitchen, arms coated with flour.

Red lips. White pearls of laughter in glass bottles hidden deep in your pockets. Eyes to make the sky jealous.

The smell of sunshine. Honey. Fields of blue wishing flowers.

I pull on the golden thread, and the Light inside of me—the one that's keeping the stars lit—starts to die.

Remember, Rosie.

Please remember.

Hurry, Rosie.

Please, please hurry.

I smell the flowers one last time. When the Black Nothing comes, I give it my nose.

THIRTY-ONE

open my eyes to solid cave wall. I'm back in the sleeping bag we borrowed from the camp.

When I sit up, a blanket slips off my shoulders. Ian's blanket. I breathe in his scent, and something shifts deep inside of me.

Sunlight pours into the cavern through a hole up above.

Just like that, I'm wide awake.

A few feet away, Jeremy slops something into a tin bowl.

"How long has the sun been up?" I don't bother with greetings.

"Not long. I just have to change Ian's bandage, and then we'll be ready to go in ten. Is that fast enough or are you going to take off on us again?" When I shake my head, Jeremy grins. "Excellent." He thrusts the bowl at me. "Do me a favor. While I deal with our patient, bring this to Becca and make sure she eats some of it. She won't do it if I'm the one asking."

My eagerness to get going is almost painful, but I take the bowl and join Becca where she's idly sketching inside the corridor. Behind her, Blaine mutters something under his breath and tosses in his sleeping bag.

"Hungry?" I drop down beside her.

"Who wants to know?"

I suppress a sigh and place the bowl in front of her. "I understand why you're angry. Jeremy embarrassed you." *In front of Ian.* "But if he acted like a jerk, it's because he's worried about you. So maybe you could cut him a break."

"It's not just that." She tosses the chalk. "He left, Rosie. He never wrote. Never called. I can't just pretend it didn't happen."

An image flitters through my head. Becca in the Black Nothing. Writing letter after letter that receive no answer.

"Maybe not," I agree. "But if Charlie were here, I wouldn't waste the time I had with him no matter how mad I was." My eyes drift back to the corridor just as Blaine sits up like he's been shot out of sleep with a cannon.

"What was that?" he cries.

"What was what?" I ask.

Blaine blinks at us, looking even more harassed than usual. "I thought you whispered something."

"You must've been dreaming," I say.

He cocks his head sideways like he's trying to shake water out of his ear. It's not the first time I've seen him do this. I'll have to ask Jeremy to check on him when we get back to the caverns.

After we find Charlie.

"We're leaving in five," I tell him.

Blaine grimaces. "I'd better find a tree before we commence our death march." He disappears down the corridor. Less than thirty seconds pass before I hear Blaine's voice, calling for me.

Hot, muggy air hits me when I bolt outside, Becca right on my heels. My eyes fly around the clearing until I locate Blaine. He's standing in one piece facing the woods.

I relax long enough to take in the morning around me. The storm has completely cleared. So has the snow, thanks to the recent heat wave.

My gaze moves to the east, where the horizon is backlit by an orange glow and hung with steely clouds. I assume it's the sunset, until I realize.

The sun doesn't set in the east.

My eyes fly back to the horizon. To the strange light and the heavy clouds.

Not clouds.

Smoke.

"What's that?" Becca points to the encroaching light.

"Wildfire."

Ian's voice comes from behind us. He's standing with Jeremy outside the cavern entrance, his left shoulder immobilized in a sling.

Seeing him after everything that happened last night gives me a little jolt. "How long until that gets here?" I ask, ignoring it.

"It's a few miles off, but fire can move fast when the wind is driving it."

"We have to put ourselves out of its path," I say, my mind racing. "We can head for the river. It's a natural firewall. Worst-case scenario, we cross and wait it out."

"But that will take us closer to Fort Glory and the wormhole." Blaine's voice turns shrill. "The dark pulse will be stronger there. We've already had to rescue two people from the Black Nothing. If we head right into this thing, how far do you think we'll get before the rest of us go full dark?"

"It's not like we have a choice," Jeremy points out.

"Did I ask for your opinion?" Blaine snaps.

"Right," Jeremy cuts back. "Because I'm a jock, and I had friends, and that automatically makes me an idiot. Well check this, smart-ass, I'm not the one proposing we sit here like a bunch of marshmallows waiting to be toasted."

"Give it a rest!" I say. The others look at me in shock, but my mind is in overdrive, and I just need one second to *think*.

Being trapped in a shrinking bubble with a raging fire isn't ideal, but it just might work to our advantage in one important way. "The fire," I say, meeting Ian's gaze. "Charlie will have to run from it too."

Ian catches my drift right away. His eyes widen. "It will drive him right toward us."

Blaine fidgets beside me. "I don't know if—"

"Jesus Christ," Jeremy groans. "Man up, dude. You don't have to lead the charge, but stop being such a coward."

Blaine flinches like he's been slapped. The guilt and shame I glimpsed that first night in the cabin are suddenly *right there* on his face. Like he still blames himself for what happened to the town even though there's no way he could have stopped it.

"Shut up, Jeremy." Becca moves to stand beside Blaine. The look she shoots her brother cows him just a little. It reminds me that there's an iron rod running through Becca, and it makes me think that of the two of them, she is made of the stronger stuff.

I keep waiting for Blaine to call Jeremy out. To tell him he's a Neanderthal in his usual, vibrant fashion, but he just shrinks in on himself, smaller and more uncertain than I've ever seen him. "Okay." He rubs at his ear again.

Something's definitely up. As soon as we get to the river, I'll have Jeremy check him out. Right now, we have to move.

This fire could be our best chance of catching Charlie, but only if we time it right.

"Grab what you can," I say. "We're out of here in two minutes."

We scatter, gathering anything useful that fits into our pockets. I'm throwing the hatchet and a few tools through the loops of my pants when Becca moves to stand in front of me.

"You almost forgot this." She holds up something.

Charlie's egg.

It's wrapped in a protective casement of twigs, held together with twine and lined with cloth to form an improvised container.

"Ian helped me make it," Becca says proudly. "You can give it to Charlie when you see him. He'll want to know you kept it safe for him."

I stare at the egg in her hand.

Put it in your pocket, near your body so it stays warm. I'll take one and you take the other. We can do it. We can keep them safe.

I'm reaching for the egg when it happens. A tingle in my bones is the only warning I get before the pain hits with blunt force.

I fall to the hard floor on my knees.

My nose. Someone is carving it out of my face with a hot knife.

The world tilts until I am staring up at the cavern ceiling. Dust motes dance in the rays of sunlight breaking through the rock. I fixate on them as someone yells for help. Becca. Her face appears over mine. I can't focus on what she's saying. I can't focus on anything but the wall of darkness closing in. Because I know what it holds.

Charlie.

I think his name and then there he is. Right where Becca was just a moment before.

A scream tears from my throat.

My brother is almost unrecognizable. There are more holes to him now than substance. More shadows than light.

He's leaning toward me, reaching out with his one good hand. This time, he doesn't try to hide his fear. That's how I know we're almost out of time. That if I can't break through this darkness, if I can't find a way to breach this wall to reach him, he will disappear forever.

Just like the town.

Just like my father.

Just like everything that has ever mattered to me.

I strain toward Charlie even as he strains toward me. So close yet out of reach. Right in front of me, and yet, too far away.

His mouth moves. He keeps saying something over and over. I can't figure out what it is, and it makes me so angry, for a moment I forget even about the pain.

When the pain finds me again, it does so with a vengeance.

It drives a sword through the center of my face.

It sets my mind on fire until the whole world is made of flames.

When they burn out, they take me with them.

My eyes fly open to the sight of the canopy gliding over my head.

I'm lying on a sled, being pulled through the forest. When I sit up, the sled stops moving.

A few clicks of a harness and Ian is at my side. He gives me a quick inspection before he drops down beside me. "You've really got to stop doing that to me," he says, running a hand under his cap.

"It's not by choice." My voice is rusty. My body aches like it's been lying in the same position for a week. "How long was I out?"

"Half an hour this time." Ian says it like it's an eternity.

"Where are the others?"

"Refilling their canteens at a stream up ahead. We'll need water when the heat gets worse, and there's no more till the river. I said I'd wait here with you."

Everything comes back to me at once.

I throw my legs over the edge of the sled. "The fire?"

"Getting closer." Ian eases me back down with a hand. "We couldn't afford to wait for you to wake up, so we dragged out the sled. There's been no sign of Charlie," he adds, anticipating my next question. "Can you walk?"

The pain in my face hasn't entirely faded, but my legs work fine. For now.

The attacks are happening more and more frequently and taking longer to let up. The next time the pain takes me out, there might not be any handy sled lying around to save my friends from having to make some tough choices.

I struggle to my feet. "I can walk."

Ian nods. "We'll move faster without the sled."

We don't say a word to each other while we wait for the others to return. The silence between us is somehow loud. Ian meets my eyes, and I let out the breath I've been holding.

There's no regret. No awkwardness. Just an expression I see more and more whenever he looks at me.

Ian's smile breaks like the dawn. Shy at first, and then with a burst of light that's nearly blinding. It's a gift. Like Charlie's egg,

I would cover it in protective wrapping if I could. But it doesn't work like that. All I can do is take his trust for what it is and offer something in return.

The truth.

I open my mouth, but something fills it.

Hot and coppery. I reach out and touch my nose. My fingers come away bright red.

Ian jumps back and pulls something from his pocket. A handkerchief. He raises it to my nose with one hand and gently tips my head back with the other. The calluses on his palms are rough and warm against the nape of my neck.

When I look up, Ian's face is inches from mine. His eyes widen. His gaze dips to my mouth, and just like that, my skin is tingling like I've been chewing tinfoil.

"Thank you," I manage.

The side of Ian's mouth ticks up. "I know my way around a busted nose."

"For pulling me in the sled, I mean. I ... know it cost you time."

"You stayed for me once." Ian pushes a curl out of my face and tucks it firmly behind my ear. "That was before you even knew me."

My heart is suddenly beating so hard, I'm sure that he can hear it. "Turns out you're not nearly as scary as people say."

I regret the words as soon as they're out of my mouth. Ian pretends he doesn't care what people think, but I know better.

His face clouds over. He starts to drop the handkerchief, but I grab his hand to keep him close.

"They don't know you, Ian. They're wrong. About everything."

Slowly, deliberately, Ian swaps out my hands for his. "They think I'm trash, and they think I'm dangerous. They're right." He lets me go.

"You're not giving yourself enough credit."

A muscle twitches in his jaw. "I know what I am, Rose."

The bloody rag falls onto my lap, forgotten. "So you've made mistakes. So what? Nobody's perfect. Does that mean that none of us deserves a chance at happiness?"

Ian's eyes meet mine and hold. "Some people deserve to be happy."

Blood rushes to my face. There are so many things I want to say to that, but Ian speaks before I get the chance. "Bad things happen, Rose. Sometimes those bad things are people."

"What if you had to?" My voice is dangerously thin. "What if you had no other choice?"

Somehow, Ian seems to know we're no longer talking about him.

I'm opening my mouth to spill my guts when something moves in the corner of my vision. A flash of green fifty yards to my left. I track it through the trees. Relief loosens every muscle in my body.

I force my eyes away from the movement in the trees back to Ian. He's searching my face, his expression as concerned as I've ever seen it. He doesn't see what I saw. He doesn't know.

Everything is going to be okay.

"Rose, what is it?"

Joy courses through me. So sweet it unfurls in a smile across my face.

"It's Charlie. He's following us."

THIRTY-TWO

We cut a trail toward the river. Like yesterday, the air gets hotter the closer we get to Fort Glory. It presses in on us from every angle, muffling even the sharp hiss of Blaine's wheezing.

Urgency settles over us along with the muggy heat. We've been going for less than half an hour when the wind picks up. Ian's shoulders stiffen. I smell it too.

Smoke.

We increase our pace. We're moving at a steady clip, but the scent of the encroaching fire grows stronger by the minute. There's a heavy *thunk* behind us.

Blaine lies on his back, steam fogging his glasses. "Can't. Breathe."

Becca is bent over at the waist beside him, clutching her side. We ditched the sled back at the stream. We can't push them beyond their limits, but we also can't let that fire catch up to us before we reach the river.

Another gust of wind blows through the trees. This time it carries more than a trace of smoke. It carries a dry heat that scorches the moisture right out of the air.

"They need rest," I tell Ian quietly. "Or they won't make it much farther."

"I'm going as fast as I can, okay?" Blaine snaps.

I frown at him. "You're doing fine. This isn't just about you. We could all use a breather."

"Just stay off my case."

Ian looks at me sharply. Blaine has *never* talked to me like that. The pressure is getting to him. To all of us.

Jeremy hands me a canteen. I force down a few swallows before holding it out to Blaine. He doesn't take it.

"Do you hear that?" he whispers, head cocked to one side.

Seconds pass. The only sound is the wind chiming through the trees and a low rumble of the fire headed toward us.

Blaine scrambles to face the woods behind him. "There it is again!"

I turn and catch a flash of movement fifty yards behind us. Charlie's back before he disappears behind a tree.

Ian looks at me. I nod at his unspoken question. We haven't told the others about Charlie yet. We didn't want them accidentally tipping him off. But Blaine is half-terrified out of his mind, and it's making everyone jumpy.

"It's Charlie," I tell them. "He's following us." It's been nearly impossible to pretend he isn't there. I've wanted to turn around so many times, but I just keep reminding myself that every step we take toward the river is a step closer to bringing Charlie in.

Blaine grabs my wrist. "For how long?"

I look down into his anxious face. The elation I feel at having Charlie close fizzles right out.

"Since the stream." I tear my gaze away from Blaine's gaping pupils. "He's trailing us about sixty yards back."

"So what're we waiting for?" Jeremy takes a step forward.

"Don't!" He turns at the sound of my voice. I force myself to lower it. "If we chase him, we'll only drive him back toward the fire. We keep moving. Let him follow us to the river. Then we can grab him when he least expects it."

Ian signals his agreement by starting off again. I match my steps to his and resist the urge to look over my shoulder. If Charlie suspects we're onto him, it'll make him that much harder to catch. I sneak a quick glance at Ian's face. His jaw is clenched tight, and there's a hitch in his stride. Every few minutes, he takes a sharp breath.

I want to ask him how his shoulder is, but this is Ian we're talking about.

I save my breath.

The wind picks up, cloaking the scent of evergreen with the stench of burning timber. Already, the music of the fire has become the steady roar of an approaching train. If we don't reach that river before it reaches us—

A sound cuts through my thoughts. A muffled cry.

Ian staggers and pitches forward.

He hits the ground with a *thunk*.

I drop my knees beside him. "Ian!"

Blood stains his lower lip where he's bitten through the skin. His eyes fly open and I forget to breathe.

Even in the shade of the trees his pupils are twice as large as they should be.

He blinks once. Twice. Fighting hard for control. Always fighting. His gaze narrows on my face hovering over him. He relaxes. "It's okay. I'm . . . Help me up?"

I reach under Ian's shoulder and lift. He snarls, and we drop back down to the ground.

"What is it? What's wrong?" I ask, afraid to hurt him, but more afraid to let go.

Ian grits his teeth and pulls his shirt loose from the front of his body, revealing a nasty burn that runs from his collarbone all the way across his left breast. My hands go still on his arm.

"How many are there?" I ask him.

"I'm fine."

"Like hell you are," I snap. "You can't even stand up without assistance. Answer the question."

Jaw clenched, Ian uses his good arm to pull the shirt over his head. He fights the material for a few seconds, and then I can't bear to watch him struggle any longer. I help guide the shirt over his head. I know it's bad even before Becca gasps, but nothing could prepare me for the extent of the damage.

Ian's body. A body that climbs trees and scales walls. A body that can build camps and fires, and still be so gentle when it wants to be. His body is *ruined*. Burn marks cover his back. His shoulders. His upper arms. A roadwork of vicious red welts scattered across the map of scars he already has.

"Why didn't you say something?" My voice trembles with sadness and anger and a dozen other emotions that won't fit neatly where I shove them.

"Because he's a dumbass and a martyr, that's why." Anger fashions Jeremy's words into darts.

Ian's eyes flick to mine and quickly away. "What could you have done?"

"That's not the point." I move aside so Jeremy can do a quick inspection of the wounds.

"How bad is it?" I ask.

"He'll live," Jeremy announces flatly, and keeps right on walking.

I help Ian up, and we press on toward the river, each of us fully aware of the fire closing in and the quiet shadow trailing us at a distance. Thick tendrils of gray smoke are working their way through the trees. After ten more minutes, Ian stops. I think it's the burns again, but one look at his face tells me it isn't pain that's bothering him now.

"What is that?" I ask, because I feel it too.

"The wind," Ian says. "It's shifting toward us."

"We're all going to die." Blaine's assessment only adds to the feeling of dread in the pit of my stomach.

"The fire will spread faster now," I say. "We have to keep moving."

Nobody needs to be told twice.

As we walk, the wisps of smoke become billowing clouds of black that roll in over our heads, snuffing out the sun. It's getting harder to see.

I'm leading the way around a giant boulder when Blaine calls out, "Wait!"

Despite the heat and the smoke scorching my skin, a shiver runs down my spine at his tone. There's something off about it. Something distinctly *not Blaine.*

"What's the problem now?" Jeremy demands.

Beads of sweat stand out on Blaine's brow. "I . . . I . . ."

"Seriously?" Jeremy snaps. "Is it possible for you to be any more of a chickenshit?"

Blaine flinches. "Go ahead." His voice quavers. "Keep calling me names."

"I'm sorry if I've offended your precious snowflake feelings," Jeremy snaps back. "I guess I'm overly focused on surviving the next ten minutes."

"Shut up!" Blaine's body is coiled tight enough to snap.

"Blaine. Please, we have to keep moving." I take a step toward him but stop when I see the unmistakable glint in his dilated eyes.

I freeze in place.

"You heard her. Move your ass," Jeremy says, unwittingly making things worse.

Blaine's shoulders shake despite the heat all around us. "Don't yell at me!"

"I wasn't yelling," Jeremy says. Blaine just cringes and presses his hands to his ears.

The darkness in his pupils swirls like ink in water.

Ian steps up to my side, the quiet tension in his body signaling his understanding without words. The dark pulse is wearing Blaine down. It's probably been wearing him down for a while, only none of us noticed. He's hovering right on the edge. We can't afford for him to go over. Not with Charlie so close and the fire closing in.

I silently signal for Jeremy to back up. When he does, I step forward to take his place. "Whatever you're hearing…," I say. "Whatever's bothering you, we'll fix it. I promise, but right now, we have to move."

Blaine's lips twist in a grimace. "No. I don't want to. I don't *want* to."

"I hear you." I make my voice as gentle as I can. Blaine's hurting and scared. One wrong move could send him running. "I won't force you. I'm just asking you. As your friend. Come with me. Please."

A beat passes before Blaine's shoulders slump. "All right."

Nobody moves while I lead Blaine around the boulder. A pocket of fresh air waits for us on the other side. I devour it in greedy gasps. The rock forms a natural barrier from the smoke, letting me see clearly for the first time in minutes. I'm covertly scanning the woods behind us for any trace of Charlie when the sound of crying draws my gaze back to Blaine.

He's standing a dozen yards from the rest of us, tears streaking through the dirt on his face. "They won't leave me alone. Why won't they leave me alone?"

"Who won't leave you alone?" I ask, my hackles rising.

"The voices. The ones that have been following us." His bottom lip quivers—a stark reminder that for all of his fierce intelligence, Blaine is just a kid.

He clasps his hands over his ears. "Can't you hear them?" His words are a whisper.

I force myself to walk toward him slowly. I've cut the distance in half when a bird swoops between us. More follow, diving below the smoke line and filling the air with startled shrieks.

Blaine stares at the birds, his head snapping back and forth. Another flash of pain crosses his face. "You don't know me. Stop calling me that! Stop calling me that!" His voice hinges on a scream. He clasps his hands over his ears again. Something leaks between his fingers.

Blood.

"What's happening?" Becca whispers.

"Get him to the river," Ian instructs Jeremy over her head. "We'll deal with this there."

Jeremy nods and approaches Blaine, who focuses in on him with raw terror. "Stop! Please!" he begs. Desperate. *Small.* "Leave me alone. Please, just leave me alone." More blood drips down his scrawny neck. For every step Jeremy takes forward, Blaine takes two back.

My mind flashes back to that afternoon in the school parking lot, watching Blaine hide from a group of older boys out for his blood. The ugly bruise on his cheek. The way he looked at me, like his heart was steeled for rejection even while his mouth was asking for help. That damn book he carries around like a shield of armor, and the shy hope in his eyes when I said I'd be his friend.

I move toward him. "It's not real. Whatever the voices are saying, it's not real." I say the words even though I don't really believe them. The voices may be a figment of Blaine's imagination, but the blood running down his arms is every bit as real as the fire headed toward us. As real as the Black Nothing that stole Charlie's mind, the wasting that took Becca, and the burns on Ian's back.

Blaine's chest rises and falls like the beating of a bird's wing. His glasses are gone, lost at some point. He backs up, and his spine slams into a tree trunk.

Another blast of hot air washes over us, carrying bits of ash and glowing embers.

"Let's go." Jeremy moves forward, but Blaine dances out of reach.

"No! I am not a loser. I am not a freak!" He wipes at his tears, leaving a bloody streak across his cheeks.

"Nobody thinks that. None of us would even be here if it wasn't for you," I say while Jeremy closes the distance between them. It's down to a few feet when Jeremy lunges.

"Come on, man," Jeremy grunts, making a grab for him.

"My. Name. Is. BLAINE!" The sheer volume of his outrage stops Jeremy in his tracks. We stand there, frozen, as Blaine starts to run.

Away from us and voices in his head.

Directly into the fire.

THIRTY-THREE

laine disappears into one of the inky black clouds ahead. Swearing loudly, Jeremy yanks his T-shirt over his mouth and dives in after him. I follow, desperate to keep them both in my sights.

I can't breathe. Can't see more than three feet in front of my face. Everything is dark and swirling and hot. So hot. Jeremy vanishes into the gray haze. I strain to hear his footsteps, but the crackle of the fire has become a roar drowning out every other sound.

A light cuts through the smoke up ahead, outlining Jeremy's body. My heart leaps when I see Blaine in his arms. He is fighting, kicking, clawing at Jeremy with everything he's got. A wall of flames rises up behind them. A barrier of fire that reaches all the way to the sky. It's less than fifty yards away and quickly gaining ground. The flames act like a sickness, shooting out from the wall, spreading through the underbrush to infect even more trees. The wildfire is every shade of orange and red and blue, beautiful in the way only truly deadly things can be.

I'm still staring at it, mesmerized, when a nearby tree catches fire. Flames shoot up the trunk, a thousand angry tongues lapping at the bark. The flames explode skyward, turning the tree into a blazing column. It rocks me sideways, directly into the person emerging out of the smoke.

Ian catches me with his good arm. Together we go sprawling across the charred earth.

Another tree goes up in smoke. This one closer. Ian throws his body on top of mine. Bits of debris and smoldering ash land on my arms, searing through the fabric.

Jeremy falls to his knees a few feet away. He's still holding on to Blaine, trying to drag him below the smoke line. I scour the woods over Ian's shoulder, searching for any sign of Becca or Charlie. There's nothing but gray vapor in every direction. Ian must've sent Becca ahead to the river.

They'll survive.

It's the one thought I cling to as I haul myself up to my knees.

The smoke is everywhere. My tongue feels like cardboard. My mouth tastes of cinders and blood metal. Spots dance at the corners of my vision. The world is starting to go dark when Ian grabs my arm and yanks me down to a layer of breathable air just above the ground. Behind him, Jeremy is doing the same for Blaine, who is still struggling madly to get free.

Blaine's nails rake down the side of Jeremy's cheek. Embers dance through the air all around them like fire jewels, setting Jeremy's uniform smoking. He bats at them with one hand while the other keeps Blaine firmly pressed to the ground.

"We've got to get out of here!" I yell over the growl of approaching flames.

The fire breaks toward us in a wall of flame, illuminating Jeremy's face, streaked with dirt and terror. His eyes widen at the incoming blaze, but he just sets his jaw and turns his back on the flames. Jeremy's legs falter when he lifts Blaine over his shoulder. I think he's going to go down, but at the last second, he finds his feet. He starts to run.

Ian and I follow, cutting an angle away from the fire's path.

I feel the river before I see it. A moist coolness that soothes my parched and aching skin. I draw in a clean breath. Then another. My lungs drink in the untainted sweetness. The low rush of water rises above the growl of the fire. Hope sends a fresh burst of adrenaline to my legs. We're almost there when a loud *thud* sounds out behind me.

Jeremy and Blaine hit the ground. The impact sends them sprawling in opposite directions. I double back to help Jeremy up, but he shoves me off, coughing and clawing at his chest as if he could somehow dig out the soot he's inhaled. Nearby, Blaine staggers to his feet, his black eyes spinning and locked onto the trees ahead.

"Blaine, stop!"

My warning comes too late. I watch Blaine sprint through a curtain of ferns. There's a moment of terrible silence, and then a single scream echoes through the forest.

Dread twists my stomach as I claw my way through ferns to the edge of a ravine. It cuts through the land in front of us, two steep walls of dirt and rock covered in ivy and a layer of emerald moss that does nothing to blunt its sharpness. Thirty feet below, the river flows through the gulch framed by two thin strands of beach and divided by a sandbar in the middle.

My eyes snag on a spot of bright color against the dull sand.

For a moment, I can't do anything but stare at Blaine's body.

Small. Motionless. The acute angle of his limbs not adding up in my mind. A sharp cry brings my gaze up.

To a lone buzzard making lazy circles in the sky.

The world collapses until it is no bigger than the sight of Blaine's body lying broken on the ground.

The buzzard lands on the ravine floor, right next to Blaine's book—the one written by his uncle, his hero—its neon pages scattered across the beach.

The buzzard hops closer. It stabs at the ground near Blaine's head, releasing a wave of pure violence through me.

Kill it. I will kill anything that touches him.

The rage inside of me drowns out everything. The fire. My terror of the sharp drop in front of me. A scream tears from my throat as I throw myself onto the ground and over the ledge.

Ian makes a grab for me, but he's too slow. I start to slide. My fingers dig into the dirt as gravity pulls me in a barely controlled fall down the side of the slope.

A ribbon of fear winds its way through my rage. Fast. I'm going too fast. Wind rushes past me, and my muscles burn as they try to keep me from tumbling head over feet.

A sharp rock looms directly in my path. I grasp for something to slow myself down. My fingers close around a stocky shrub. Pain wrenches my shoulders, but I manage to hold on.

"Rose! Stay where you are." Twenty feet above me, Jeremy hefts himself over the ledge. A few yards below him, Ian is already free climbing down the side of the ravine. Angry burns roll and split over his muscles as he makes his way toward me one-handed.

I let out a shaking breath and look down. The ravine floor is less than ten feet below. Blaine is lying in the exact same spot. I can't tell yet if he's breathing.

I squeeze my eyes shut and let go.

The impact at the bottom sends shock waves through my limbs. Too stunned to stand, I crawl toward Blaine.

His left forearm is bent at an impossible angle. Blood stains his right shin, but thankfully, it looks more like a simple break than a compound fracture. With trembling hands, I reach for his throat.

Rocks spray the ravine floor, and then Ian is beside me.

"He's alive." Tears of gratitude stream down my face.

Ian sucks air through his teeth. "That arm is in bad shape."

I'm more worried about the things we can't see. For all we know, Blaine could've broken his spine. And then there's the dark pulse. It has full control of him now. If the Black Nothing takes his mind, it won't matter what we do with his body. There won't be any bringing him back.

"Come on." I stuff down my panic. "Help me move him."

A *hmmmph* echoes through the ravine as Jeremy hits the bottom.

"Stop!" He jogs over, his handsome face as serious as I've ever seen it. "Keep his head still. If his back is broken, it could be fatal to move him."

I scan the ravine for some way out of this. We have no idea how bad Blaine's injuries are, or if he can be moved. We don't know if Becca and Charlie made it to the river, how soon the fire will reach us, or if the Black Nothing has already stolen Blaine's sanity completely, trapping his mind in the dark.

Before I can verbalize any of these thoughts, there's a flash of black curls. Becca emerges around a bend in the ravine. She's limping badly, but she's here and she's safe.

One of the knots inside me comes undone.

Horror twists her features when she spots Blaine. "What happened?"

"He lost it," Jeremy says. "Ran right over the ledge."

"We've got to get him back," I say.

"Let me check him first," Jeremy begins.

I hold him off. "If we don't go after him now, the Black Nothing will own him. Then nothing you do will make any difference."

"What about the fire? And Charlie? Have you seen him?" Becca asks, scanning the ridge above us, where it's already leaking smoke into the ravine.

"Charlie will show up." Conviction flows through me from some invisible source. I can sense him. Like a bolt of pressure in my chest that keeps ratcheting tighter the closer we get to Fort Glory. He's close. I know it's true the way I've known everything else in the Fold. Without having to understand why.

"One of us will follow Blaine into the Black Nothing," I say. "The rest will figure out a way across this river. So when Charlie comes, we'll be ready."

Jeremy stares at Blaine lying motionless on the riverbank. "I'll do it. I'll go in after him."

There is no diplomatic way to say this so I don't even try. "The threads depend on the connection between you being solid." Blaine and Jeremy can barely stand to be in the same room together. There definitely isn't enough space for both of them in Blaine's head. "You might not be the best person for this, Jer."

"That's exactly why I have to do it," he tells me. "I owe Blaine. I screwed up, but I won't run away. Not this time." Jeremy's eyes stray to Ian before returning to my face. He makes a grab for my hand. "I can save him, Rose. I can do this. It has to be me."

We can do it, Rosie.

We can keep them safe.

We can.

Jeremy's gaze is a magnet, pulling me in. This is his chance. His opportunity to make up for some of the shitty things he's done, and as hard as it is to let go, to trust someone else with something this important, I can't take it from him.

"Okay," I say.

Jeremy nods and turns to Becca. "It'll be all right, Becs. I'll come back. I promise."

She returns his shaky smile with one that is full strength. "I know."

Jeremy squeezes her hand before reaching for Blaine's. His brow contorts in agony, and then his expression dissolves into pure blankness.

Becca sits on the beach, as close as she can get to Jeremy without actually touching him. She hugs her knees and waits for her brother, trusting in his promise to bring Blaine back, because sometimes, trust is all you can do.

I join Ian where he stands at the edge of the river, facing the opposite bank thirty feet away.

I study the raging river in front of me and try to work out a way across it that won't leave anyone behind. Most especially Charlie. My mind goes through an inventory of the materials at our disposal. It's a depressingly short list. "The canal is narrower here than it was where we found Becca," I realize.

"That just means the current will be stronger," Ian says. "There's no way we can swim it."

"Maybe we don't have to." I nod at the sandbar forming a narrow island in the center of the river. "If we can get to that strip, it might be enough to protect us from the wildfire. We can anchor your rope to that driftwood over there and pull ourselves across. I'll stay behind for Charlie. When he shows I'll grab him, and you pull us over."

"Jer!" Becca cries out behind us before Ian can comment on my plan.

I turn to see Jeremy's eyes open. He takes in the world in rapid blinks. With a groan he pulls himself over Blaine, who is just starting to stir.

I scramble over and drop down beside them. Blaine lets out a low moan saturated with pain. My breath hitches when I place my hand across his chest to keep him still. "Shhh. It's okay, Blaine. It's going to be okay."

More words. Promises I'm not sure I can keep.

Tears flow under the bridge of Blaine's lashes as he turns toward the sound of my voice.

Blaine turned his neck.

Across from me, Jeremy's soot-stained face lights up. "Don't talk. Just listen to me." Jeremy places his hands on both sides of Blaine's head. "I'm going to tap your leg. Right above the knee. Blink once if you can feel my hand."

Blaine blinks, and my spirits lift. If his back isn't broken, we can move him. If we can move him, he might just make it out of this ravine alive.

"Good. That's really good," Jeremy says. "You've got a few broken bones, but you're gonna be fine. You hear me, Blaine? You're gonna be fine."

At that moment, the fire reaches the edge of the ravine above us. The trees go up like votive candles. Flaming branches crash and roll down onto the narrow beach. Bits of burning bark ignite the vines curving down the side of the ravine. They start to writhe.

"We need to get him across," Jeremy says.

"I know." I'll help them get Blaine to safety, but there's no way I'm leaving this beach without—

Movement on the ridge above us.

My heart takes one giant leap as a figure in a green hoodie emerges from the trees.

Charlie. His name forms on my lips.

And dies there.

The world goes in and out of focus, and then I'm on my feet without remembering how I got there. My mind is tripping over itself to understand the thing it's seeing.

Because it is impossible.

I stumble toward my brother on legs that feel like they don't belong to me. I'm almost at the edge of the ravine when someone steps in front of me. Ian. He grips my shoulders and leans in close. His mouth is moving, but I can't make out the words. I can't hear anything but the banging of thoughts inside my head.

I move around him and find Charlie up above us. My brother is walking toward us through the fire. Not running. Not screaming in agony. *Walking.* The smoke forms a screen, hiding his face, but his green hoodie is a beacon among the flames. They twist and turn around him. Almost like they're afraid to touch him.

"He's not burning." My voice is raw with smoke and wonder.

"Who?" Ian steps in close to my side.

I point. Ian follows my finger to the edge of the ravine above us. A flicker of fear flashes over his face. He sees it too.

No human can walk through flames and survive. But Charlie is doing it. He's moving through the blaze, making no effort to rush or even shield himself as he sets a course right for us.

"Who do you see?" Ian's voice is a warning bell sounding deep in my head, but whatever it's trying to tell me, I can't focus on it right now.

"Charlie. He's here." I swing toward my friends only to find them all staring at me with uniform expressions of worry and confusion.

Terror is a knife slipping between my ribs.

"Rose," Ian says gently. "There's nobody there."

THIRTY-FOUR

The figure walks through the fire to the edge of the ravine. Flames shield him from view as he starts the long slide down.

Loose tendrils of smoke drift over the beach, keeping him concealed until he reemerges at the bottom of the incline, a smoky silhouette facing me across ten feet of smoldering riverbank.

A gust of wind howls through the ravine, creating a break in the smoke line. I steel myself to meet my brother for the first time since the town disappeared—since the dark pulse cracked his mind, but no vision could prepare me for the sight of the face, peering at me through the miasma of gray.

Because there isn't one.

The thing in front of me isn't a person. It's a monster. A human figure wearing stained jeans and a green hoodie. The shadow-thing's face eddies and ripples, giving a sense of movement and expression without any clear features. The harder I look, the more I think there's a real person underneath the shadow skin, trying desperately to break free.

A whimper escapes my lips as I lurch down the beach to a small pool of standing water. I kneel beside the pool and gaze down at my own reflection.

Light brown hair. Pale face, painted with soot and a handful of bruises. Faded blue eyes, and at their centers, two swirling whirlpools of bottomless black.

Tears leak down my cheeks and drop into the pool.

Plop. Plop. Plop.

The water takes on a rosy tint.

I touch my wet cheeks. My shoulders start to tremble. "Is this real?" I tear my gaze away from my bloody fingers. The worry lines around Ian's mouth say it all.

I'm crying blood.

"What's happening? Where's Charlie?" Becca asks. "What's wrong with Rose?"

I stare at the shadow.

The shadow stares back.

"He isn't real?" I ask the question even though I already know the answer.

"Tell me exactly what you see." Ian helps me to my feet.

So I do. I tell them about the shadow creature standing on the riverbank, quietly watching us with eyes it doesn't have. It hasn't moved for the past several minutes. It wants something. It has wanted something all along.

This time, it isn't leaving until it gets what it came for.

The wind gusts around the shadow bringing its stench across the sand. It hits me with the full force of memory.

Whiskey and cigarettes.

Copper. Powder. Fear.

I want to take off screaming, but I'm stuck here between a deadly forest fire and the wormhole.

For the first time in my life, there is nowhere left to run.

"It's in my head, isn't it?" I ask. "It's the dark pulse messing with me?"

"Do you know why it's taking this shape?" Ian asks.

His question has my mind whirling. With everybody else, the dark pulse has manifested as something specific to them. It made Becca's body almost as invisible as she felt. It gagged Jeremy with every word he never said but should have. It blew out Blaine's eardrums with the voices from his past, the ones that called him names and insisted he wasn't good enough.

And Ian. It's burning him up with the anger he fights so hard to control. The anger that turns him into someone I don't know.

All of these manifestations. There's a pattern to them. But this shadow and these red tears don't follow it. They're the pieces that won't fit. No matter how hard I try to force them.

I'm so tired of trying.

"I don't know." My voice breaks. "I don't know why my mind is showing me this."

CREAK.

Another tree collapses on the ridge. It topples over the ledge, down onto the beach a few feet away.

A storm of burning embers shower over us.

"We've got to get across," Jeremy says.

Ian tosses me the harness. "Put that on." He rips the sling from his arm and removes every bandage except the one actually covering his wound. From his pack, he takes some chalk and covers his palms.

Before my mind can put these pieces together, Ian breaks into a run. Using speed, he propels himself up the incline and vaults onto the side of the boulder. His good shoulder bulges as it takes most of his weight. He hangs there for an agonizing second before he swings sideways. His feet hit the rock and then he's scrambling over the ledge to the top. A moment later, his body

304

rockets over the river. Momentum sends him rolling onto the sandbar.

He stands slowly, motioning me forward with his good hand.

On autopilot, I hook myself into the harness, adjusting it to my legs. Grief and sorrow turn my limbs to lead as I wade into the river. The current batters me on all sides, but it's like I can't even feel it. I can't feel anything.

The fire. The current. None of it matters anymore because Charlie isn't here.

Charlie was *never* here.

Every time Charlie has shown himself, *every time* starting with that first night in the Fold, I've been the only one to see him. The voice Blaine heard in the woods and outside the cabin. We assumed it was Charlie, but it was the dark pulse working on Blaine. Just like this shadow creature is the dark pulse working on me. He isn't real. He was *never* real.

Which means there is no way out of this now. For any of us.

Somehow, I make it safely to the island in the middle of the river. Becca follows next. Jeremy uses Ian's discarded sling to immobilize Blaine's arm before he hooks himself into the harness. Blaine moans as Jeremy walks into the river holding him against his chest. It takes all three of us to pull them across.

Becca and I are dragging a shivering Blaine up onto the sand when the fire hits the beach. The flames hiss and scream where they kiss the water.

"What's the shadow doing now?" Becca asks me.

"Nothing. It's—"

The shadow stirs. It lifts one dirt-crusted finger and points. Directly at me.

No. Not at me. Behind me.

The tugging starts almost immediately. A yank on my insides that tries to spin me around. I keep my eyes on the shadow monster.

"Rose, what's happening?" Ian demands.

"It's pointing across the river."

The shadow seems to smile, which is weird since it doesn't have a mouth. It inclines its head over my shoulder. The pull on me grows stronger.

I turn.

"Oh shit." Jeremy swallows.

There's something on the horizon. At the end of the trees, everything just... *stops.* The shapes and textures of the forest blend together in an eerie haze that makes the whole world seem out of focus.

My eyes struggle to make sense of what they're seeing. It isn't fog or even mist. It looks like the static you get when your TV loses picture. Like the forest has broken down into a million pixels searching for the right way to come back together.

At the center, a hulking mass of matter twists and churns— an iridescent whirlpool of Color. Light. Sound. It reaches up into the clouds.

The wormhole creeps toward us through the trees.

I turn my back on the wormhole and face the shadow. It isn't on the beach where it was just a few seconds ago. Instead, it's waiting on the opposite bank. The one on the same side as the wormhole.

I meet its veiled gaze, and the tugging flares back to life in the center of my chest. A pressure that comes from somewhere deep inside of me, and at the same time, somewhere too far to reach. Charlie's familiar frequency slides through my mind like a skeleton key, unlocking door after door.

Everything that's happened. Everything I've seen and felt since I fell into the Fold comes flying back to me. A hundred images. A hundred moments crash together and break apart again, over and over in a kaleidoscope of memory.

"Are you afraid of the dark?" I pressed my shoulder into yours.

You shook your head. "Without the dark, there are no stars, Rosie."

"Then what are you afraid of?" I asked.

"Forgetting."

Forgetting.

Forgetting.

Then the answer is hanging right there in front of me. Where it's been this whole time.

Understanding burns through my brain. "I know."

"Know what?" Jeremy studies me like he's trying to ascertain my level of sanity.

"Where Charlie is. I know what he's been trying to tell me. That we don't have to be afraid. Not of the dark." I repeat the words Becca said two days ago. "Even in the dark we aren't alone."

"What?" Blaine rasps from his sandy bed beside us.

I meet his pain-shot eyes. "I'm the only one who's seen Charlie in the Fold, and the thing I've been seeing... *that* isn't my brother." My shoulders tremble uncontrollably, but my voice gets stronger with every word. "The visions I've been having. They were the reality all along. It was Charlie. In the Black Nothing. He wasn't trying to tell me how to find him. All this time, he's been trying to *show* me."

I should've figured it out sooner. The dark pulse can prey on our inner demons, but it can't create demons where none exist. Charlie would never terrorize me. He would never push me into a river. Because it isn't *in* him.

I sit up straight when I realize what this means. "There's no darkness in Charlie. That means there isn't anything for the Black Nothing to amplify. He's got access to something in there. A force that's working against the dark pulse. I could feel it when I was in there with him, lighting the threads between us. Whatever he's tapped into, it's allowed him to beat back the dark and survive. It's how he's been able to help us and keep his own light from disappearing."

"He's the brightest light," Becca says. "When he showed me the stars, he was the brightest one of all."

"Wait. You're saying the stars he showed you in the Black Nothing weren't stars? They were actual people?" Jeremy demands.

Becca smiles. "Two thousand two hundred thirteen. Charlie caught them in a net of silver thread. He's keeping them turned on."

Ian meets my eyes. "Two thousand two hundred and thirteen. That's almost the exact population of Fort Glory."

"They're in there." Jeremy inhales sharply. "They're *all* in there. Charlie's shielding them with this force we all felt. The one that works against the dark pulse."

And I know exactly what it's costing him.

"It's the threads," I say. "He's using them to do it. To do everything. Just because we can't see them doesn't mean they aren't here. Linking us to each other. I can feel the thread that connects me to Charlie right here." I put my hand against my chest, directly over my beating heart. "He's been using it this whole time to reach me. The tugs. The memories. Everything I've been feeling. They were all Charlie's ways of trying to get me to understand."

"Understand what?" Ian asks quietly.

I meet his eyes. "That the only way to him is through the darkness. *My* darkness."

I gasp as another memory sails out of the shadows of my mind. The last words Charlie said to me.

"The music in the dark is loud, but it's not as strong as the song inside of us. You'll feel it. Right here." He fisted his hand over his chest. "It'll bring you halfway there. The rest you'll have to do on your own. Remember, Rosie. Promise me you'll remember."

"He told me," I breathe. "He told me this would happen. He's waiting for me in the Black Nothing. On that special ledge of the darkness carved out just for the two of us."

I don't say the rest. Ian figures it out anyway.

"You want to follow this *thing.* You want to follow it into the Black Nothing or the wormhole or wherever the hell it decides to take you." It's not a question.

I let my eyes move to the shadow. *Fake.* To the river, and the ravine walls, and my friends forming a circle around me. *Solid. Real. Strong.*

"I have to face the Black Nothing. The part that is mine and Charlie's. I have to go to the one place I can *see* the thread between us, and I have to use it to pull him back."

"We aren't sending you out there to be erased. I don't care what your gut says," Ian grinds out.

"What if Rose is right?" Jeremy asks. "What if it's the only way?"

"Then we make another one."

"My darkness is right there, Ian." I point at the shadow monster, where it's patiently waiting. "One way or another, I'm going wherever it leads."

"So you want to gamble your life on the chance that the thread between you and Charlie is strong enough to survive the force that wiped Fort Glory off the map?" There's a quiver in Ian's voice that has the others staring. They haven't been with him at three in the morning when his dreams are bad and his eyes are full of horrors and tears he doesn't know how to cry.

They don't know him, I realize. *But I do*.

"I have to believe I can find Charlie. And once I do, you—*all* of you—can pull me back. Just like we did before."

"This is crazy. Even if you find him, there's no guarantee we can bring you back."

"I have to do this, Ian."

"No. You don't. Walking into the Black Nothing in the hope of finding Charlie is just asking to be erased."

"It's not your choice," I tell him quietly.

"You think I don't know that?" Ian cries. "That doesn't mean I'm just going to let you throw your life away on some scheme that has zero chance of succeeding." He grabs my arm. His fingers dig into skin. The darkness in his eyes seems to stretch and yawn toward me.

I react on instinct. My rage at everything—the past, the present, the choices I'm always being forced to make—erupts like a long-dormant volcano. I push him hard enough to send him a few steps backward. The hurt and shock on his face almost destroys me.

Jeremy puts his hands on Ian and gently nudges him back. "Easy, bro."

"I am *not* your brother."

"Fine. But whatever your problem is, this isn't the way to fix it."

My anger leaves me in a whoosh of exhaustion. "Sometimes all we have are bad choices, Ian," I tell him. "This is the only one I can live with."

"Bullshit. This isn't a choice. This is a surrender. We're never going to see our families again. Every one of us knows it." Ian steps in close. "But I think the truth is too real for you, Rose. I think you'd rather walk right off a ledge into the abyss than face it."

"Harsh, Ian," Becca says, but she has no idea how harsh it is. She has no idea what Ian is really calling me. A coward. A quitter. But even though I know Ian's darkest secrets, he doesn't know mine. He doesn't know what I would do to protect the people I love. What I've already done.

The shadow monster seems to smile. It points again.

Charlie. This shadow. I know where they are trying to take me. Into the darkness I see whenever I close my eyes.

The darkness I've spent the last three years running from.

I am done running.

Blaine speaks before I can. "Go." Pain twists his features. "Find Charlie."

You should go. Right now. Goodbye, Rosie.

I take in the wall of fire in front of us. The wormhole at our backs.

Jeremy straightens. "I'll stay with Blaine," he says, reading my hesitation.

"Me too," Becca pipes up.

"The fire—"

"Forget about the fire," Jeremy growls. "Charlie is our only shot. If you don't find him, we're all going to die, and all of this will have been for nothing." Before I can object, Jeremy heaves me to my feet and leads me toward the bank of the sandbar. There are boulders on this side, spaced close enough that I could probably leapfrog to the other side.

Jeremy grabs my shoulders. "You can do this, Rose."

Put it in your pocket, near your body so it stays warm. I'll take one and you take the other. We can do it, Rosie. We can keep them safe.

We can.

"I've got her back," Ian says.

Jeremy meets Ian's gaze over my shoulder. "I know."

"Jeremy—" I begin.

"Find Charlie. Get us out of here. If the fire comes I'll find some way to get them across. I swear to God, Rose, I won't leave them. Not this time." Jeremy makes me this promise, and then he turns back to Blaine and Becca and the fire desperately trying to make its way over the water.

I watch Jeremy tend to Blaine's leg, and another thread, one deep inside of me, flares to life with a violent tug.

We've run out of time. There are no more detours. No more chances to find our way. All we have is this moment. This one possible road to fix things.

And that road runs through Charlie.

I reach into my pocket and pull out Charlie's egg in its homemade casing. A little piece of my brother. I ask Becca to hold it for me, and when she agrees, I turn back to the shadow.

It beckons again, and this time, I follow.

THIRTY-FIVE

t takes forever for me and Ian to cross the river and drag ourselves out of the ravine. When we reach the top, the wormhole
hangs on the horizon, towering over the trees.

I don't know what time it is. I don't know how long we have
before the wormhole gets here, or where the shadow monster is
leading us. My mind is still stuck on the image of Blaine lying
helpless on that sandbar with Becca beside him. Jeremy standing guard over them both. Ten yards of river their only defense
against a wall of fire.

The shadow wearing a green hoodie makes a beeline for the
wormhole. The air on this side of the river is mostly fresh. Moss
blankets the forest floor in emerald green. It reminds me of the
woods around the campground, so beautiful and familiar it makes
me ache.

Ian hasn't said a word since we left the river, but I can feel
his anger like a living thing between us. He thinks this is crazy.
The only reason he's going along with it is because he knows I'm
doing it with or without him.

"It's still walking," I say, as much to break the silence as to
keep him informed. My words drag through the air. It's just him
and me now. There are no more excuses. No more reasons to

stall. My darkness is lurking somewhere up ahead, and I won't let Ian walk into it blind.

"Ian, I—"

He turns on me suddenly. His chest heaving, his face flushed with anger so hot, it blasts me from several yards away.

"What's wrong?" I ask, startled.

"You." He flings the word at me like a grenade. "You are very clearly what is wrong with me. It never stops with you. How much is enough, Rose? How much do you have to suffer before you can forgive yourself for whatever it is you think you've done?"

His questions cut deep. There is too much truth in them. "I didn't ask for any of this." Hurt laces my voice. "Nobody is forcing you to be here. So either tell me what's pissing you off or leave it alone."

"You want the truth?" Ian eats up the ground between us in two easy strides. "You want to know why I'm here? You want to know what Charlie said to me the day Fort Glory disappeared? Because I wish I could forget."

I back up so quickly, my spine collides with a tree trunk. Bitter triumph flashes across Ian's face. "You don't, do you? Isn't that why you've been running? Isn't that why you won't tell me about whatever darkness is chasing you even when we're about to walk right into it?"

My heart hammers my rib cage. "Did Charlie tell you?"

Ian studies my arms where they've wrapped around my middle. He softens. "Not about what happened to you. But you don't have to be Blaine to figure it out."

Ian grips my shoulders. "So I'm asking you to let it go. Whatever truth you're holding. Let it go. Even if you think it's going to level everything around you, because if that happens, we'll deal with it like we've dealt with everything else. Because we have to, and because we *can*, and because it's worth it. I'm willing to ride it out if you are."

"You don't know what you're asking."

His voice goes quiet. "I do. That's *why* I'm asking. You're not alone anymore. You have friends now. People who... people who care. People who are willing to deal with your shit, no matter how bad it is." Ian cups both of my cheeks in his hands. I feel his touch all the way down in my toes. "I want to help you. *Please.* Let me help you."

My words are all breath. "I don't want..."

His heat burns holes through my skin. "What don't you want? *Say* it."

I don't want you to look at me the way you look at yourself. I don't want you to learn to hate me, when I am just starting to love you.

"I don't want to lose you when you find out who I really am."

"You won't lose me." He says it with complete conviction. "And I know exactly who you are. You're brave, and kind, and you take care of what's yours. You're good with hammers, and half-crazy old ladies, and little girls who miss their brothers. I know you try to fix the things around you, even when those broken things are people. I know you make the world a more livable place, just by being in it."

Ian kisses me. His lips are cold and his mouth is hot and he tastes like smoke and pine.

I gasp against his mouth, and then his hands are moving from my face down my sides, to the small of my back where they press me against him.

When Ian pulls away, I'm not ready. My lips tingle, and my cheeks are raw from his stubble. One hand splays across my jaw as he searches my face. A flicker of doubt enters his starburst eyes, but whatever he's afraid of, he won't let it stop him. Not Ian.

"You asked me what Charlie said to me that morning in the park. He said that you were important. He asked me to take care of you because you were special, and because you were the only one who could help fix me. He said that if I was lucky, maybe I could help fix you, too."

I look at the boy who carried Becca like she was made of glass. The boy who walked into danger with his friends even though he thought they were doomed to fail. And I know that I love him because he's good in a way that has nothing to do with being perfect, and everything to do with being Ian. But that doesn't mean things won't go wrong. It doesn't mean he won't get hurt, or get tired of trying, or disappear one day without a trace. But he's worth the risk.

The wormhole lurks.

The shadow waits.

And I do what I should've done days ago. What I've wanted to do ever since I met him.

I blast a small hole through that wall inside of me, and I tell Ian the truth.

THIRTY-SIX

CHARLIE

Nothing left
but Pain and a few
drops of Light.
All the stars,
they flicker.
Their cries
fill my head.
I want to say,
Don't be afraid.
But I am.
Please, Rosie.
Words
floating down
golden thread.
The Black Nothing cries.
It wants the grass
on bare skin
dusted with calluses,
tickling kisses,
pressed to bottoms
of chubby feet.
Remember.

One last
drop of Light.
But I can't
hold on.
I can't.
The Black Nothing comes.
And then I don't
have legs.

THIRTY-SEVEN

C ome on." Ian takes my hand. "Let's get this over with."

We follow the shadow to a small clearing about a quarter of a mile from the wormhole. The shadow stops. Relief echoes through me. Somehow, I know we've come as far as we can go.

The shadow smiles its mouthless smile. I turn away from its rippling face, not ready to see what it wants to show me. There is still one thing I have to do.

I reach up and touch Ian's cheek. I can feel them clearly now. The dark pulse in the air, drawing my mind toward the Black Nothing. The thread in my chest tugging me toward Charlie, like it has been since I first fell into the Fold.

Ian cradles my palm against his cheek. "I'll be there with you. No matter what, I'll be there to bring you back."

"You have to give me enough time. If you pull me back too soon, I won't be able to find Charlie."

Emotions flash across Ian's face. He couldn't stop what happened to Will or to his parents, but he can stop me from doing this.

"If I wait too long, you may never come back." The way he says it leaves no doubt. Right now. In this moment. Letting me face the Black Nothing alone will be the hardest thing Ian Lawson has ever done. Because as hard as it is to leave, it is ten times worse for the one who stays behind.

His breath hitches as Ian lays my palm across his chest, flat over his heart where it tries to beat itself into my hand.

"It's just pain," I breathe into the shrinking space between us.

"It's not pain." Ian presses his mouth to mine.

And that's when I finally understand what my mother was trying to tell me that day when she kneeled in front of me and wiped the mascara out of my hair. What Charlie meant when he held a dying rabbit on the side of a Kansas road.

To love is to open yourself up to pain. The deepest pain there is. But it is worth feeling.

Ian Lawson tells me he loves me, and then he proves it.

He lets me go.

I approach the shadow. Every step I take increases the tugging in my chest. It has thrown my entire body off balance when a storm of birds fly out of the treetops above us.

The ground vibrates.

I stop ten feet from the shadow. The vibrations travel through the soles of my shoes up into my limbs. The tremble becomes a shake that sets my back teeth clacking. The earth starts to move in ways it shouldn't.

Not if it wants to stay in one piece.

Ian calls my name, and then time slows down and speeds up all at once.

The land under my feet pitches sideways, taking my legs with it. The fall seems to last forever. By the time I hit the ground, everything looks different.

What was flat forest a few moments ago is now an uneven patchwork quilt of land squares that don't fit together. My eyes seek out Ian. He's lying a few dozen yards away, dragging himself toward me on his stomach.

I crawl toward him. We've almost reached each other when a fault line splits the ground under my hands. I scramble backward. There's an earsplitting *crack* as the fault line widens from a centimeter to a foot.

It keeps growing.

When the dust settles, Ian and I face each other across a gaping chasm ten feet across.

Ian grips the bill of his cap as he measures the distance between us.

Too far. It's much too far.

He starts to back up.

"Ian, don't—"

He breaks into a run.

He's almost at the edge of the gap when the patch of earth beneath him starts to slide. Ian grinds to a halt. His eyes meet mine just as the ground he's standing on falls away. And then he's...gone.

A scream leaves my lips. I lunge toward the empty space where Ian used to be. My heart spasms when I spot him, lying on a ledge of earth thirty feet below. He climbs to his feet, shaky but in one piece. The relief of seeing him alive lasts only a few seconds.

The earth pitches again, knocking me onto my back. This time when the ground cries, the whole world answers.

Another fault line splits open behind me. My legs dangle

over the ledge. The next quake sets the earth in front of me shooting skyward. I fall sideways.

My temple hits the ground, sending thoughts cartwheeling through my head. When they finally settle, I am lying on a narrow ledge between the sharp drop-off that leads to Ian and a wall of solid earth that reaches up toward the sky.

Thirty feet above my head, the shadow smiles.

An invitation.

A challenge.

"Rose!" Ian calls to me. "Wait there! I'm coming!" He starts pulling himself up the wall with his good arm. He's made it a third of the way when the dirt crumbles, sending him sliding back down to the bottom.

I realize the truth before I read it in his eyes.

From here on out, I am on my own.

I lift my gaze to the shadow where it waits, and the small part of me that isn't afraid knows that this is how it was always meant to be. That every twist and turn in the map of my life has been leading me to this moment. This one wall I have to conquer.

I take a step toward it.

"Rose, don't!" Ian says from down below. "I'll figure out a way. I just need a little more time."

I crane my neck to watch the shadow where it stands on a ledge thirty feet above my head. Somewhere, behind that shadow, my brother is waiting for me. Alone. Scared. Almost out of light.

He has been waiting long enough.

"I can do it." I force the words through my closing throat. "I can make the climb."

Ian's hands bunch at his sides. "Your last attempt didn't work out so well."

As if I needed the reminder.

"I can do this," I call out. "But I need you to coach me. Please, Ian." My voice cracks. "I need your help."

Ian knows exactly what those words cost me. The knowledge is right there on his face.

His jaw sets in a hard line as Ian pulls the harness from his body and tries to toss it up to me with his good arm. It hits the side of the dirt wall a few feet below the mark before tumbling back down to his ledge. Ian attempts the throw again. And again, but the harness is heavy, and with his bad shoulder, the throw is beyond him.

Ian stares at the harness in his hands before raising his eyes to mine. "You'll have to free climb it."

My chin trembles as I nod.

"You won't have a safety line," Ian says. "I'll try to spot your holds, but if you get stuck, don't force it. Better to come back down than to fall from that height."

The bottom drops out of my stomach.

"Rose."

I tear my eyes away from the wall and look at Ian.

"You've got this."

I force my knees to unlock. With one last nod at Ian, I approach the wall.

Flashbacks of Devil's Tooth run through my head. That wall was not nearly as high as this one, and I didn't make it.

I didn't make it.

The tugging flares to life inside my chest, flooding me with a strange sense of calm. This time will be different. This time, *I am* different. Unlike Devil's Tooth, I am not facing this wall alone. I have Ian down below. I have Becca, Jeremy, and Blaine on that strip of burning sand by the river. And Charlie. I have Charlie waiting for me somewhere at the top.

I refuse to let them down.

A network of roots lies exposed in front of me. I study the interconnected system like it's one of my maps. I chart my course up to the top.

I reach for the wall. My toes dig into the earth, making a solid groove. When my weight is securely braced, I reach up again.

Moss and weeds cling to the side of the rise along with a few clumps of grass. Bits of sharp wood cut into my fingers as I work my way up, using the roots as anchors. Ian coaches me through the first few holds, but as I make my way higher, he goes silent.

Hand by hand. Inch by inch the ground falls away. The thoughts in my head go quiet until it's just the wall under my hands, the breath in my lungs, and the tugging in my chest, coaxing me higher.

After a few minutes, I make the mistake of checking to see how far I've come. The small ledge where I started swims twenty feet below. Fear slams into me with a vertigo that sets the world spinning. It's another minute before I get the shaking back under control.

No more looking down.

The last few feet are the slickest. The earth is all topsoil. It's almost impossible to get a good grip. There are fewer roots—no more easy holds, so I have to make them, carving them out with the tip of my sneaker. I've finally glimpsed the ledge above me when a familiar shudder runs through my limbs.

Aftershocks echo through the ground, sending clumps of grass tumbling from up above. Terror clogs my throat as I hold

324

on for dear life. More dirt falls past me in brown sheets. A scream leaves my lips. The earth under my hands gives an inch before jerking to stop.

Blood pounds in my ears. I can barely hear myself think, but somehow, Ian's voice cuts through. "That wall is caving in! There's a solid root at your two o'clock. It'll hold you. But you have to let go and reach for it."

I force my gaze up and there it is: a thick root bent like an elbow about a foot above my head and slightly to the right. Just below the ledge.

Far. It's too far.

The wall under my hands slides another inch, and my heart jumps right up into my throat.

"You can make it, Rose." Ian's voice comes at me through a long, dark tunnel.

"I. Can't."

"You can." Ian's words hold no doubt. "You have to believe you can."

We can do it, Rosie.

We can keep them safe.

We can.

Charlie's voice echoes through my head. The earth trembles again, and then the world fades away piece by piece until there is no ground and no sky. No up and no down. There is only me, and my brother, and this wall standing between us.

The tips of my sneakers dig into the cliff face as I push up with all my strength. The surface gives out beneath me. I close my eyes, let go of my hold, and *reach*.

My fingers close around the root. The side of my body hits the wall with a *THUD*.

My feet scissor air for a terrifying moment before they make contact with the wall. Every muscle in my body screams as I use the root to pull myself up that last foot of dirt and scramble over the side, onto the ledge. I lie there on my stomach, panting. When I can finally move, the first thing I do is crawl over and look down at Ian. He grins at me from sixty feet below, his face streaked with sweat and so much pride, it makes my heart hurt.

Something calls to me over my shoulder. Slowly, I shift my attention to the shadow.

I've taken a few stumbling steps toward it when I feel a familiar tingle in my bones.

No. Not again.

The pain is a wave, towing me under.

Agony has me collapsing in on myself like a dying star. When I fall, the darkness is there to catch me.

Dimly, I hear someone screaming. Ian. In the vacuum of the pain, every sound is magnified: The beating of my heart. The scrape of Ian's nails as they dig through dirt that won't hold his weight. The silent laughter of the shadow as it watches me writhe.

And then I can feel him. Right there in the center of my chest.

Charlie.

When I force my eyes open, my brother is hanging directly in front of me, suspended behind a wall of darkness just like he has been in every vision. Only now, I know exactly what I'm looking at.

Charlie in the Black Nothing. The dark pulse bleeding him dry of the light that makes him different. The light that makes him *him*.

My hands ache to stroke his face, but I can't move. Can't do anything but watch the darkness eat another piece of my brother.

Until there is more wall than boy.

More shadow than light.

I'm afraid that if I blink, he'll disappear completely. I can't let that happen. I *won't*. Because he is mine and I am his, and if he disappears, I want to disappear with him.

Please, Rosie.

Remember.

The words echo through me, and then I'm back in the park at Glory Point, making my brother a promise through the driver's-side window. I remember the moment. All the things I said, and all the things I didn't. The vow I made.

If I want to keep it, I'm going to have to figure out a way to get up.

The pain is a nail, driving me into the ground. My bottom half is on fire. So I do what Ian does. I let my mind go somewhere else. To a field of blue wishing flowers. And I drag myself forward with my arms. Inch by painful inch.

Under my chest, the ground starts to tremble again.

The Fold. It's collapsing.

And Charlie. Charlie is fading.

His light. The light inside of him is almost gone.

I drag myself forward until I am lying at the bloodstained feet of the shadow.

Pain steals my breath. It feels like I'm fighting the weight of the entire universe as I force my head up. My eyes lock with the shadow's. The darkness ripples and moves until it isn't a blank void wearing a familiar green hoodie staring back at me. It's a person.

I meet her faded blue eyes. Study the familiar brown hair and the sallow skin, streaked with blood and tears. The mouth wide open in a silent scream of rage.

The shadow wearing my face reaches down to me.

With the last of my strength, I take my own bloody hand.

THIRTY-EIGHT

Falling.

I am falling through shadow, into a tunnel of darkness and light. Tiny spots of brightness streak past me. I wonder briefly if they're stars before the thought dissolves in a blur of motion.

Fast. So fast it wears me down to specks of dust that scatter across the universe. I can feel it all around me. Everything that was. Everything that is and will ever be. It hangs there in front of me, and for a moment, I can almost see it.

The order behind the chaos.

The reason and the meaning.

The answer to every question.

It's *right there*. Until it's not.

The tunnel takes a sharp turn into blackness. My body comes to a screeching halt.

An ocean of solid black stretches out in every direction. A vacuum of Light. Color. Life.

The Black Nothing.

It's the same as it was before, only different, because this time I am not looking over the edge. This time, I am deep inside its belly.

All around me, the dark pulse jangles in the air. The pitch is painful. The notes jarring through my bones. Beyond it, the emptiness beckons with crazy force. I can feel the dark pulse picking at the strands of my mind, slowly unwinding them one by one. My thoughts slip away from me in bursts of notes. Glowing drops of light. Too many. Too fast.

Help.

The word is a scream yanked from my mind.

I'm lying on a ledge carved out of the darkness, illuminated by an anemic light that grows dimmer the more light-drops float away from me. I watch them go. Tiny lanterns floating up, up, UP. They're almost gone when they smack into something solid. A hundred drops of light fan out against the barrier, giving me a vague sense of its shape.

A globe.

A golden globe stretches around me like a shield. It's small and getting smaller by the second, but at this moment, it's the only thing keeping me from being pulled apart. There is only one person who could have put it there.

Charlie.

The globe shimmers. More drops of light crash into it, awaiting their turn to escape. If I could figure out a way to slow them down, if I could just find a way to reach for them, maybe I could—

A handful of light-drops pass through the globe. The Black Nothing rips them away. Pain floods my nerve endings. The agony stops everything, even time. In that frozen moment, I see it. A single light floating right in front of me. A note of happiness in the gloom. A still shot of a memory. Charlie last Christmas. Grinning and wearing the hat I knitted for him. Happy. We were happy that day. The trailer smelled like cinnamon and Mom's perfume. We were sitting around the miniature tree decorated with her costume jewelry and eating French toast. She smiled as she moved around the kitchen, and for a second, things were the way they used to be.

The memory starts to float away with the others. Desperate to hold on to it, I focus on Charlie's face like it's the only thing that's real. The shape of his brows. The scar across his chin. I say his name in my head over and over. It becomes a song. One to drown out the dark noise all around me.

Slowly, almost shyly, the drop of light reverses course back to me.

I push myself to recall more details about that day. The tunes on the radio and the sweet lilt of Mom's voice as she hummed along.

I concentrate harder, and my whole being vibrates with a different type of music, one coming from inside of me. More light-drops drift back to me.

The furrow on Mom's brow as she sewed.

The sound of laughter through thin walls.

The smell of violets and sugar mixed with the taste of butterscotch, and the way Charlie's baby leg would jerk right before he fell asleep.

They are my memories. They are my Light. My Color. My Sound. All the beauty and the joy and the bittersweetness, and I refuse to give them up.

With the last of my strength, I pull in my memories. The drops of light fall around me like armor. A hundred pins and needles stab me as my nerve endings flare back to life. I home in on the pain because it's real. Because it means I am more than a spool of unraveling thoughts. I am skin and flesh and bones on fire. I let the fire fill me, and then I will those bones to move.

I rise to my feet.

Space is strange in the Black Nothing. I can't tell if I'm standing or floating. There is no ground and no sky. No up and no down. There is only blackness, and pain, and the light inside of me, fighting not to go out.

Charlie is here somewhere. He's using whatever power he has to shield me, just like he shielded all the others. But he can't keep it up forever. The globe is still shrinking, which means I have to find him. Before there's nothing of me left.

A spot of color pops to life in the distance. Brilliant gold against the dark. Siren song. It calls to me, and the tug inside of me—the one I've felt since I fell into the Fold, returns with a vengeance. Gritting my teeth, I move toward the distant light.

My muscles quiver with effort, but one step at a time, I push forward. The picture in front of me sharpens, and I see it isn't one big light up ahead. It's a thousand little lights shining like stars in the distance. And right in the middle of the cluster, the brightest light of all.

Charlie.

The Black Nothing beats down on me, sucking a little more of my light through Charlie's shield.

Pain brings me to my knees. Unable to get up, I crawl.

Charlie's globe shrinks until it is too small to hold me. More light-drops fly away into the void, and then I can't crawl. Can't move. Can't even breathe.

No.

Even as I think the word, I know it's useless. The word is just like me. Too small a thing to stand under the weight of this crushing darkness. My song stutters in the dark. My light gutters around me, a candle about to go out. And there's nothing I can do to stop it.

I'm sorry, Charlie. I'm so sorry.

The words shoot out from me in a blaze of gold. They shimmer through the darkness, down a winding line to the light ahead. The one that shines more brightly than all the others. My thoughts travel down the golden thread between us, and then something travels back.

Charlie's familiar song fills me. Warm and sweet and pure. It reaches inside of me like an electric prod, waking parts of my mind I didn't know were sleeping. And then I'm not looking at the Black Nothing through my eyes.

I am looking at it through his.

A network of delicate threads stretches out around me in more colors than I have words. They form an intricate tapestry that reaches out in every direction, weaving through folds of time and space stacked on top of one another like accordion rings. They sprout from my chest and my fingertips, strings of energy that connect me to the past, the present, and a million other realities I can't see but can somehow feel. The sheer number of threads makes my head hurt, so I focus in on the handful that spring out of my core in a blazing river of color. These threads are thicker than the others, and they glow with an intensity that puts the rest to shame.

I reach out and touch one in a dazzling pink.

There's a sensation of falling sideways as part of me is conducted down the thread like electricity through a wire. At the other end is Becca, huddled on the sandbar, her hand tightly gripping Blaine's. The picture is so clear. So real. I can smell the smoke mixed with the antiseptic Jeremy used to clean Blaine's wounds, feel Becca's worry and fear as if it were mine. But there's something else, too, something buried deep under the uncertainty and the pain of not knowing. Something warm and bright and ...

My breath catches when I recognize it.

Faith.

It sets the globe around me ablaze with rosy brightness. I let Becca's light fill me, and then I let go of that thread and reach for another. This one neon green.

I plummet straight down until I'm hovering over Blaine lying on a strip of burning sand. Flames dance in his eyes as he turns to his friends. He says the word that scares him most, but he doesn't regret it. *Go.* Because he can't run, but they can. Because what's right and what's easy aren't always the same, and because it's the *choice* that makes us.

Courage.

It travels up the thread and into me, and my light burns a little brighter.

The next thread, bright orange, sends me crashing sidelong into Jeremy. His lungs are raw, and his arms tremble, but he lifts Blaine to his chest. Because there are a million things that separate us, but none of them will ever be as strong as the ties that bind us together. And those ties don't allow us to leave one another behind.

Friendship.

The next thread glitters in the corner of my mind, a steady blue. My fingers brush it. The world shifts gently until I'm hovering over Ian. His hands are dirty and bleeding as he pulls himself over the ledge those last few yards toward me. His head bows as he cradles my limp body against his. The wormhole is a hundred yards away and closing fast. Next to it he looks impossibly small. His handsome face contorts with effort. It's taking every ounce of his control to fight off his own darkness, to keep from touching my hand and coming in here after me. But he's doing it.

Because I asked him to.

Emotions swell inside of me as I watch his lips move. Every word he speaks is a promise that sets the thread between us blazing. I let it touch me, and then I send it back.

Trust.

Reluctantly, I shift my focus to the last two threads.

I touch the one that glints of copper. A song weaves through me. One that brings tears to my eyes. It tastes like butterscotch and smells like sawdust. It sounds like laughter and feels like the weight of a callused hand as it cradles mine against the handle of a hammer.

Dad.

I want so badly to follow that thread to where it leads, but it's beyond me. Not even Charlie's eyes can help me see that far. But I can sense something at the end. A song of Light like the one inside of me, only a million times stronger. One that sends the shadows of the Black Nothing scuttling back to their corners.

I let go and move on to the last thread. Pure gold. It's the brightest of them all. The one that brought me into the Fold. The one that's been tugging at me all along. The one that's shielding me, even now. My hand lingers over it, and I know where it will take me long before I finally build up the courage to reach for it.

THIRTY-NINE

Golden fire burns my skin, scorching a path through my nerves all the way up into my brain.

The current carries me over the edge into the dark.

Falling. I think I'm going to fall forever when gravity hits me with a thousand pounds of pressure. It crushes me face-first into the ground.

I lie in the dirt. My lungs suck down hot, humid air that reeks of clay and diesel fuel.

Humidity rushes over me in a sticky wave as the picture in front of me sharpens. The last traces of daylight filter through the branches above my head. Woods. I'm in the woods. Only these are nothing like the ones I left behind. These trees aren't Douglas fir, but loblolly pine and oak, overrun by kudzu.

When my head finally stops spinning, my eyes open to a packed campground flanked by Oklahoma woods. Part of me was expecting it, and still, the sight of those two long rows of trailers has dread coiling in my stomach. My gaze cuts to the entrance, and beyond it, the highway. Dark is falling fast.

It won't be long now.

Bile burns the back of my throat. This is happening. It doesn't matter that I'm not ready for it. Charlie's hints. My shadow self—everything has been leading back to this.

A figure materializes out of the darkness. The girl walks slowly along the roadside toward the park, her back hunched. The last heat of the day shimmers against the pavement as she cuts through the clotheslines and rusted lawn furniture toward me.

Hurry! Please, hurry! I scream, but she doesn't hear me. I want to reach into her head and shake her until she pays attention. If I can warn her, if I can make her listen, maybe I can stop all this from happening.

The girl keeps walking. Helplessness builds inside of me until I'm drowning in it. My eyes scan the park, taking in details I never noticed before. Like how quiet the night is. Dozens of families live here, but the only sound comes from a dog barking somewhere nearby.

As if sensing the change, the girl pauses at the top of the longest row of trailers to wipe the sweat from her brow. Her body goes rigid when she spots the truck. It's parked in the shadow of an ancient RV. The familiar orange flames painted across the hood practically glow in the darkness. I know what she's thinking, feeling, dreading at this very moment, but even in the memory, it's like looking at a stranger. Shock crosses her face, followed swiftly by terror. Then she is running as fast as her legs will carry her.

OhGodOhGodOhGodPleaseGodPleaseGod. Every footfall is a plea as she races for the fifth trailer on the right. The door hangs on its hinges. The lock is busted in. Broken glass crunches under her feet as she climbs the step. The girl pauses on the threshold, her heart slamming against her ribs. How did he find them? She'd been so careful. Finding a job where she'd be paid under the table. Using fake names. She'd thought they could disappear. Didn't people do it all the time?

She crosses over the threshold. Everything is upside down. The couch. The coffee table. Mom's box of costume jewelry, smashed to pieces. Maps lie on the floor in tatters. A thousand fragments of three fragmented lives.

Something moves in the corner of my vision. A hand reaches for me.

Charlie.

I scream his name, but the word comes out of her mouth. We fall on our knees beside him. Blood drips from his temple, down his chin. Glass dusts his face, and cuts fan out over his skin.

No! Please. The words echo through my head as she reaches for him. That's when I feel it. The sweat dripping down her back. The glass cutting into her legs. The cracks on her lips straining as they move. I can feel it because it is my face. My legs. My lips saying prayers they don't believe in. And it doesn't matter. Right here and right now, it doesn't matter what I believe, or what I said, or what I think I know. Charlie. Charlie is the only thing that matters. He is my reason. My meaning. The answer to every question in my universe.

"Breathe, Charlie," says a voice. Mine. "Just keep breathing."

And I promise. I promise whoever is listening. If you get us out of this, I will stop running. I'll build someplace safe for us to hide. I will dedicate my life to protecting him. Please, Charlie. Just stay with me a little longer, and I swear I will never leave you.

Prayers tumble from my lips as my fingers crush the fabric of his shirt.

It happens so fast I almost miss it.

A tug in the center of my chest.

A glimmer of gold.

The flash of a gilded thread that runs from my chest to Charlie's.

I barely catch a glimpse of it before it disappears.

I blink and look around me for the girl who was here just a second ago. The one who is living this night for the first time. But like the thread, she's gone. It's just me and Charlie in this trailer torn to pieces. And then my brother is lying in my arms.

Every part of his exposed skin is covered in blood, and his left arm hangs limp at his side.

I reach for his pulse to find it quiet but steady. Same as it was the first time I lived through this.

I've lived through this. We've all lived through this.

Then Charlie moans, and every thought leaves my mind.

I grab one of the cushions and place it under his head. His eyes stay closed as he reaches for me with his good hand. Our fingers lock. Tears of gratitude burn my eyes. Because even though he's hurt, he's here. We both are. For however long this lasts.

"He took her." The words are all breath.

I nod. Mom isn't the same woman she was when my father was alive, but she never would've left Charlie like this. That monster had to drag her out of here.

"Where?" My mouth asks the question even though I already know the answer. My thoughts feel crowded and a little foreign. Almost as if I'm sharing headspace with the girl who should be here instead of me. Like this scene has already been written, and I have to say the lines.

"I didn't—" The words drain him. "I didn't hear him drive away."

I know where the monster took her. I know exactly what I'll find when I walk out of this trailer, but I grab a towel and press it to the gash in Charlie's head. When that's done, I lift his good arm and use it to apply pressure to the wound. The rag turns red within seconds.

"I'll be back soon." It takes all of my resolve to stand up. To leave my brother when I've only just found him, but whatever darkness I am here to face, it is waiting for me in those woods.

Charlie says nothing as I pull a quilt over him. Bits of glass clatter to the linoleum. When he's as comfortable as I can make him, I slip outside. My feet hit the dirt road at a run.

Too much time has passed. I can't change what has already happened. I can't fix the damage that's already been done, but if I can just get to a phone. If I can get a call out to the police, maybe I can stop what happens next.

"Help! Help!"

Not a single person is out. Not a single door is open. I pound on the nearest one.

"Please! Please, I need to use your phone!"

A scream rises from the woods. My gut clenches at the sound. It's already too late for Mom, but maybe, just maybe, it doesn't have to be too late for me.

I pick another door to pound on. Televisions blare behind it, but there's nobody home.

Footsteps sound behind me. I spin on my heels to see the weary woman from the neighboring trailer. She approaches, her tired eyes looking everywhere but at me.

"Can I use your phone?" When she doesn't answer, I step directly into her path. "Please. My mother. There's a man with her. He's hurt her before. We tried to get away but he's found us and now she's—"

The woman pushes past me. Desperation claws its way up my throat. *"Please."*

"We don't want any trouble." Her words are mumbled as she opens the door. The one I was pounding on less than thirty seconds ago. A thin man with a beard stands behind her in the opening. The smell of stale cigarettes curls my nose as she ducks under his arm. He starts to close the door right in my face, but I move faster than he does.

"Damn," the man hisses as the door collides with my shoulder. Pain shoots up my arm. The man doesn't move to help me, but he doesn't push me back, either. He just watches me with eyes that are already erasing this moment from his memory.

Just like all those people who walked past a broken woman on a park bench in that beautiful city park in Illinois.

I grind my teeth against the throbbing in my arm. Begging hasn't worked. It's time for a new strategy. "Call the police. Something terrible will happen if you don't."

I don't give them a chance to brush me off. I walk down the dirt lane toward the scrap heap.

I've lost precious time trying to find a phone. The moon hangs full and heavy over the trees. I've almost reached them when something moves at the edge of the woods.

"Mom!"

Dirt and blood stain her dress. The one my father loved, with soft folds of blue fabric that crashed around her ankles when she moved. Now it hangs off her frame in tatters. Her cheek is already turning black. Blood oozes out of an ugly gash in the side of her head. The monster usually avoided her face, but today, he was out to prove a point: This is what you get when you try to run away.

The neck of Mom's dress is torn straight down to her waist, revealing the plain white bra underneath. I've shared a bedroom with my mother for years, but I've never seen her look so naked, so *exposed*. Her humiliation is an open wound. There is no more hiding it.

Her gaze slides past me. Vacant. Unseeing. My proud mother. My mother who always walked like she mattered even when she was carrying other people's dirty plates. My mother who sang along to the radio, and who never let us leave the house without looking our best, even if our best was secondhand. She's already halfway gone. I can see it in her eyes, and I don't blame her for leaving. Because sometimes you have to leave to survive.

There is more to life than survival, Rosie.

I push the fabric back over her shoulder. It falls right back down again. Moaning, she crawls past me. Cuts fan out over her knuckles, and her nails are filthy half-moons. Rocks bite into her bruised knees as she drags herself down the thirty-yard stretch of dirt to our door.

"Mom, stop."

She keeps crawling, framed by the silhouette of homes on either side.

Hot tears flow down my cheeks as I approach my mother. She shrinks away. Like she can't stand to be touched. Like she doesn't even know me.

I kneel beside her. "Mom, look at me."

Blinking, she meets my gaze. Recognition rocks through her. Tears slide down her face. She grasps at her dress, trying to cover herself.

I rip off my shirt and throw it over her shoulders. The night is hot and clammy against my bare skin. Mom pushes me away,

342

but I'm stronger than she is. I've been stronger for a long time. I just never knew it until now.

Sweat drips down my back as I heave her to her feet. Together, we stumble for the trailer. A flash of movement in a window to my left. I lift my chin because if anyone is watching this, I want them to know. That this shame is theirs. Not hers. Not mine. Because doing nothing is the worst crime of all, and pretending not to see is like pretending not to be human.

I can't pretend anymore.

The police don't come. I didn't really expect them to. Even though the monster is still out there somewhere in those woods, the first thing I do when we're back inside is tend to Charlie. He'll need stitches, but the trip to a hospital in another town is going to have to wait just a little longer.

In the bathroom, I turn the water up as hot as it will go. Gently, I help Mom into the shower. There isn't room for her to sit, so she stands, huddled in the corner while steam fills the room. Sobs rack her body as I use a cloth to clean her cuts and bruises. All the while, the sadness inside of me solidifies into hate.

When Mom is finally sleeping in our bed, I pick up a shirt from the mess on the floor. Charlie's favorite green hoodie. I throw it on over my bra before I move to the back of the closet where we keep what's left of Dad's things. The box I'm looking for is there on the top shelf. I pull it out. When the monster comes back for his keys, I am waiting.

He walks in the door like he owns it. This monster that beat my brother. He walks in the door, and he studies me with eyes that are too dark and too dead of anything human. And I know that he isn't going to stop this time. This will never stop unless I end it.

I stand in front of him, my dad's gun clutched in my hand.

The monster laughs. He laughs, and he tells me that I won't shoot him. That I don't have the balls.

"Rosie, no." Charlie tries to grab me, but his hand won't work. It won't work because it's broken.

My brother, who would never touch anyone in anger. My brother who rescues fireflies from glass jars and dying rabbits on the side of the road. Broken.

Because of him.

Something awakens inside of me. A monster to meet the one standing there in this broken trailer. It screams at the sight of Charlie, injured on the floor. My vision goes black at the edges.

I squeeze the trigger.

The force of the blast rocks me back into the wall.

Blood splatters my face. It fills my mouth with coppery sweetness.

Dazed, I stare down at the gun in my hands. The red stain down the front of my hoodie. Charlie on the floor. Looking at me with our mother's eyes. A violet dulled by sadness that knows no words, and suddenly, I can't breathe. I can't breathe because I know.

I'm the one who put it there.

Charlie cries. Silent sobs that won't let up. I watch the tears fall down his cheeks, and I realize the thing I have broken, the thing that can never, ever be fixed isn't my brother.

It isn't even the man lying still in a growing pool of blood.

The world spins, and then I'm on the floor, rocking back and forth like I did the first time this night happened.

Just like then, the monster inside of me goes quiet, taking all the rage and violence with it. Another emotion rises up to fill the void they leave behind. It hits me with everything I've done to survive. All the things I've tried to become to get back to this one single moment. So much effort.

Wasted.

The feeling of failure is too big to hold. It's going to break me apart, and I don't care. I don't care about anything anymore. Because this was my chance. My one chance to fix things. To make a different choice. To chart a different path and I couldn't. I wasn't enough.

You never were.

The gun falls from my hands. I watch it clatter to the floor, and I try to clean the blood from my hands. It won't come off. No matter how hard I rub. Just like the first time this happened.

Then something happens that didn't happen before.

My skin. It ripples. The change starts at my fingertips. Black tendrils of shadow seep out from under my nails to wrap around my hands. They travel up my arms, around my chest, an oil slick spreading over every inch of me.

It makes me want to crawl out of my skin.

The shadows rise higher. Up my shoulders. My neck. I rear back, but they don't stop. I claw at them, leaving deep gouges in my flesh. The shadows just keep spreading.

I scramble backward into the wall, and then I keep going, right through it.

The trailer walls. The body on the floor. Charlie. Everything disappears until it's just me and my dad's gun alone in a darkness too loud for thoughts.

The shadows reach my face. They stain my cheeks. Cover my eyes with nightmares. They break for my mouth.

By the time the shadows reach my lips, nothing can get past them.

Not even my screams.

FORTY

Drowning.
I am drowning in
Black.
Not a color.
A place.
Roaring Ocean between worlds.

Don't, *says a voice low and rich as*
gravel.
Don't disappear without me.

Drowning
Drowning
                    Almost gone.

Sometimes there are no
good choices.
You made the only choice
you could live with.

Now let it go.
Let it go, Rose.
Another voice. Softer. So soft.
You promised.
Drowning.

I am drowning.

Remember your promise, Rosie.

Remember, *the second voice says.*

Over and over and over.

Drowning.

I am drowning

I am . . .

Someone. Somewhere. Once . . .

upon a time I read the words and the words were magic. They belonged to him and he was

Twilight eyes.

Wind-chime laugh.

Baby hair gliding through my fingers, falling

> *falling*
>
> *falling like feathers*

to the bathroom floor.

Lying side by side in the dark. Secret stars streak past the window.

Sand dollars and promises

Umbrellas on dashboards and eggs made of straw.

This, *says the voice.* THIS is important.

Why?

Why?

Why?

Because.

Not just a voice. HIS voice.

> *His eyes.*
>
> > *His laugh.*
> >
> > > *His hair.*
> > >
> > > > *CHARLIE.*

Once upon a time I read the words and the words were magic. They belonged to him and he belonged to me.

Because, Rosie, THIS is all there is.

The Noise stops.

The Roar goes quiet until there is just

THIS.

Charlie and I floating in the Black Nothing.

A golden thread between us.

My brother hangs behind a wall of darkness just like all those times before. His light fading. Almost gone.

The golden thread shimmers. I have to follow it to Charlie. I have to break through this wall and reach him. I have to

Remember

that without the dark there are no stars.

His voice winds through the darkness, and a light turns on somewhere in my head.

This wall. I recognize it.

I recognize it because it is mine.

I built this wall, and I know the secret it is hiding. There. At the base.

Shadow creature crying in the dark. I hear her sobs. I see her rocking with her arms wrapped around her knees. The gun clenched in her bloody hand.

Broken thing.

Shadow girl trapped behind a wall.

I feel what she feels. The sorrow. The anger. The guilt of not being there when it counted. For everything that happened after.

The thing I couldn't forgive her for. People would never understand it. They'd assume the worst. Hadn't they done it to my mother? Over and over again? They'd take me away from Charlie. I couldn't let that

*happen. I tried to push her out. To erase what she did, but I couldn't. So
instead, I made her small, and I tucked her away behind the wall to keep
her hidden.*

All that time, I never realized.

All this time, I didn't understand.

The shadow girl was not my darkness.

The choice she made was never my crime.

My crime was the wall I built to hide it.

The last wall now standing in my way.

*I crouch beside her. Sad, broken shadow. I pry her hand from the handle
of the gun.*

Don't cry, *I tell the shadow girl.* You don't have to hide. Not
anymore.

We made the only choice we could.

And we would do it again.

We would do it again.

I hold out my hand.

*The shadow girl's grip is weak, but mine is strong enough for both of us.
I pull her through the wall until, finally, we stand facing each other on
the same side.*

*The shadow girl stares at me, and I stare back. All the things I've done.
All the scars I've tried to hide are right there on her face. I look at them
all, and I don't flinch. I don't run away.*

Not this time.

I close my eyes and step into the last few inches of space between us.

*The darkness spins, sending us crashing into each other. Everything
goes still.*

When I open my eyes, they stare at the Black Nothing from her *face.*

When her heart beats, it beats in my *chest.*

Together, we smile with one mouth, and the wall of darkness falls like a curtain.

And then there he is.

Charlie.

I forget everything but THIS.

I reach for his hand.

FORTY-ONE

CHARLIE

Shooting star.

Her light burns through the Black Nothing.

She sings my name and she reaches through time and space and a thousand doors to reach me. Our hands brush, and our heartbeats join through our fingertips.

The Black Nothing screams. It pushes her out.

Four colored threads are there to catch her. Spools of light.

Pink.

    Green.

        Orange.

            Blue.

They pull her.

Away from the dark.

To the place between.

But first, I invite her into my head. I let her see the things I see.

Two thousand two hundred thirteen silver threads weaving between my fingers.

Two thousand two hundred thirteen stars resting in my hand.

So beautiful. So precious. What makes everything worth it. Even the ugly. Even the beauty and the terror and the pain.

Do you see it, Rosie?

Do you hear the song it's singing?

Always the same and forever changing.

Golden thread.

Reach for it.

Reach for it.

She hears me.

Her face lights up the dark.

She finds the golden thread between us.

She pulls and our song turns to fire.

It burns a hole through the Black Nothing.

The colored threads carry Rose, and she carries me.

Together, we carry the stars.

Two thousand lights in a silver net.

Silver net on a golden string.

It leads out of the dark

Back into the Light.

FORTY-TWO

jerk back to consciousness to the smell of rain and motor oil.

The world flies into focus.

I'm staring at a patch of green framed by the curve of a muscular arm. *Ian.* He's cradling me to his chest, rocking me gently back and forth. The wind blows through the clearing that lies at the top of the drop-off, bringing with it thick clouds of grayish smoke.

Fifty yards over Ian's shoulder, the wormhole lurks, trapping us in this clearing at the edge of a cliff. Every second eating up more ground.

"Rose?"

Starburst eyes scan my face. "I'm sorry. I had to pull you back. I couldn't wait any—"

When I smile, he crushes me to him. We sit like that for a moment before I feel it. A soft tug on my insides.

Balloon on a string.

Golden thread.

My heart skips in my chest as I glance around Ian's wide frame. There. In the grass. An egg lies on the ground beside me. An egg identical to the one I've been carrying. But I gave my egg to Becca, which means this one must belong to—

I look up. A person is walking toward me through the smoke. I know that walk. I'd know it anywhere.

A gust of wind cuts through the clouds of gray, and then Charlie is standing in front of me.

I scramble out of Ian's arms and face my little brother.

Black hair tumbles over his forehead and into his closed eyes. I trace the familiar lines of his face. The scar across his chin. The shape of his ears.

"Charlie." His name is a prayer. The only prayer I know.

"Hello, Rosie."

The wormhole. Ian's dazed expression. This patch of earth suddenly filled with the noises and movement of two thousand people. All of it falls away.

I throw my arms around Charlie's neck. We drop down to our knees in the grass, and the universe shifts like a kaleidoscope with us at its center.

It isn't until Ian clears his throat that I realize something's wrong. Charlie's hand hangs uselessly at his side. His legs give out even as I hold him in my arms. I lower him gently to the ground and search his face, but his eyes. His beautiful eyes don't open.

"The Black Nothing did this to you?" I force the words past the lump in my throat.

Charlie nods. "I gave it most of my light to keep the dark from drowning the stars. I . . . I don't know if I can walk, Rosie."

"I'll carry you." Just like I did when he was a baby and we were alone in an empty trailer. Or from that playground the day he fell from the slide. The way I've wanted to carry him so many times.

I'm reaching down to grab hold of him when a figure fights its way toward us through the sea of people groaning and stirring. A flash of pink and white.

"Mom!"

She launches herself into the island Charlie and I have made in the middle of the clearing. I return her hug with an unrestrained joy I haven't felt since I was a little kid. The kind of joy that sends roots shooting through you deeper than any foundation, because they're anchoring you to something more solid than earth and infinitely more precious.

"Mom, it's okay." I say the same words I've said to her a hundred times. Only this time, it's different. This time, I'm saying them without the walls between us. And I know it doesn't matter where we are, or what we have, or what problems we face.

My brother's heat, and my mother's arms.

More than a word.

More than a place.

More than four walls and a roof to keep out the rain.

Everything I need, right here in this shrinking clearing.

"Such . . . a good girl." Mom's voice is barely a whisper. "My Rosie." Her arms fall away from my waist as she slumps. Ian catches her at the last second. Together, we lower her to the ground.

"Mom!" I lean over her. Fear burns through my guts like acid.

"The Black Nothing took most of her light," Charlie says. "I gave her some of mine, but she'll need to find the rest on her own. You'll have to help her, Rosie."

Ian pulls me to my feet beside him. "We may have to shelve that for another time."

His comment brings my attention back to the commotion around us. A glade full of dazed, disoriented people, struggling to their feet. Some are crying. Most of them don't know what to do. There must be thousands of them—every single one tired, and scared, and barely holding on to their calm.

People call out the names of their loved ones. Families find each other in the chaos. *So many stars*, each with their own worries and loves written all over their faces.

We have to get them out of here.

"Everybody, listen." My voice barely makes a dent in the mayhem around me.

I wish I had some of Rowena's attitude. Some of Jeremy's magnetism or Ian's quiet strength. But I'm not Rowena or Jeremy or Ian. I'm just me. And it's going to have to be enough.

I whistle between my teeth. A shrill sound that cuts through the pandemonium. Every head turns toward me. A handful of men approach. I recognize a few of them from my shifts at the Dusty Rose. They all start speaking at once.

I look out over these people, all that is left of our town, and I know that I can't hide anymore. I can't be afraid to speak or be seen, because if I don't lead these people out of here, who will?

"If you want to get out of here, you need to follow me," I say, raising my voice above the din. "This drop-off is too steep. We'll have to find another place to climb down. There isn't much time. Some people will need help. If you can lend a hand, do it."

They all look from me to Charlie. My brother doesn't say a word. He just wraps his arms around my neck when I lift him to my chest. He's light. Much lighter than he should be. My stomach twists. It's as if the Black Nothing took more than his light.

It took some of his substance.

"The aftershocks caved in part of the wall," Ian tells me. "The incline isn't so bad there. It's how I was able to reach you. We should be able to make it down."

I nod and let Ian lead the way to a more gentle part of the wall. The men from earlier come forward to help. Charlie rests his head against my shoulder as strangers help us slowly work our way down and back toward the river.

The noise two thousand people make clomping through the brush blocks out even the roar of the rapids. There's no warning. One moment we are cutting through dense forest, and the next, the river is right there in front of us.

Ian carries my mom over the edge while I lay Charlie on the ground and help him slide down the ravine side and onto the beach.

"Rose!" Jeremy sprints across the sand toward us. His wide eyes move from Charlie to the dozens of people lining up on the beach. "You did it." A grin breaks across his face.

"We knew you would," Becca says, peeking around his shoulder, her smile an exact replica of her brother's.

"So, what's the plan?" Jeremy scans the crowd of people pouring into the ravine, probably searching for his parents.

I study the wildfire blazing across the river. The wormhole making its way through the trees. My mind scrambles to come up with a way out of this trap, but there's nothing but dead ends in every direction.

It hits me that I might've brought all these people here just to die, and the thought fills me with fury. At myself. At the universe for being so fundamentally unfair.

"I don't have one." I keep my voice low so that we aren't overheard. The last thing we need right now is a panicked stampede.

"Maybe we could get around the wormhole somehow," Jeremy offers weakly.

"We can jump into the river," Ian says. "Let it carry us out of the ravine and past the fire. Buy ourselves a few hours."

I study the ragtag crowd of people on the beach. Young. Old. Every stage between. All of them weak and terrified out of their minds.

"Most of them won't make it," I say.

"But some of them will. At least it gives them a fighting chance," Ian insists fiercely.

It isn't a perfect solution, but right now, it's the only solution we have.

I'm about to say so when I notice Charlie is no longer beside me.

For one agonizing moment, I'm back in that Illinois park, searching for my brother in a crowd of strangers. Panic claws its way up my throat until I see him, kneeling on the beach beside Blaine and another man. A man with long hair and sharp, kind eyes. A taller, older version of Blaine.

Arthur Jackson.

He and Blaine are both staring at Charlie with matching expressions of wonder.

Oblivious, Charlie keeps his head bent, his ears cocked as he listens to something the rest of us can't hear. Calm. Quiet. Unafraid.

My brother. The eye in the center of the storm.

I kneel beside him.

"Charlie?"

He turns toward the sound of my voice. "I feel it," he says.

"Feel what?"

"The door back to our world." Lashes fan out against his cheeks. "I can hold it open, but not for long."

"You can access the door between the Fold and our world?" Dr. Jackson's eyes go wide.

Charlie nods.

"How?" Blaine asks, without an ounce of his usual skepticism.

"There are lots of doors," Charlie says. "They live behind the curtain where eyes can't touch."

"In the extra dimensions? Like the threads?" Dr. Jackson asks. "The ones you showed me?"

Charlie smiles. "The in-between places. I can show you the door you need, but you'll have to walk through it."

Quiet descends over us. The only sounds now are the roar of the fire across the river and the occasional rumble of the ground under our feet.

What Charlie is suggesting is a leap into the unknown. There are no guarantees that we'll be able to see these doors or move through them the way that he can.

No guarantees but the word of a ten-year-old boy who can't even walk on his own.

"Show me." Blaine's voice is paper-thin. Tears of pain and something else shine in his eyes. "Show me the door, Charlie."

Blindly, my brother reaches for Blaine. His hand hangs suspended in the air between them.

A question. A leap of faith.

Blaine trembles as he clasps Charlie's fingers. As soon as their hands touch, a light shines across Blaine's face. Tears leak out of his eyes, and then the Light is all there is. A flash that is nearly blinding. When it goes, Blaine goes with it.

Jeremy swears. "Where'd he go?" He clutches Becca's hand, keeping her a safe distance away from Charlie and whatever miracle he just performed.

"Home," Charlie says. "Where all of you are going."

Every person on the beach stares at my brother. The light inside of him, the one that used to scare the hell out of me— that still does, even now—on full display for everyone to see. I expect them to run screaming. To assume to worst and tear down what they don't understand, but I don't give them enough credit.

Maybe you never did, says the young girl inside of me.

The one no longer trapped in the shadows.

Dr. Jackson moves first. He bends his mouth to Charlie's ear and says something too low for me to hear. Then he follows in his nephew's footsteps, taking Charlie's hand and passing through the door that Charlie shows him. A door like the one Dr. Jackson has spent his whole life searching for.

Right there. All along.

One by one, the people of Fort Glory move toward Charlie. Two thousand people who owe their lives to my brother. Two thousand little lights twinkling in the dark. They don't fight. They don't jostle. They stand in line as if the Fold isn't falling apart around them, because my brother asked them to.

One after another, the people of Fort Glory take my brother's hand. One after another, they pass behind the curtain and are gone.

It doesn't take long. A few seconds to show them the way only Charlie can see. A few more to let them pass through. Still, fewer than half of them have made it out when the strain on Charlie begins to show.

He starts to tremble. Sweat drips down his face onto the beach. Another hundred pass through him. A few hundred more. He drops to his side.

"Charlie!" I fall to my knees beside him.

"His strength is fading," Ian says. He helps me lift Charlie back up. Behind us, the wormhole has pushed to the top of the ravine. We have five minutes till it reaches us. If we're lucky. "We've got to move faster."

"Come on!" I wave at the small crowd of people still waiting. "Take his hand. A few at a time. Hurry!"

People pass through Charlie in groups. It cuts down on the amount of time, but it doesn't lessen the toll. When the last stranger walks through, my brother is pale and trembling, curled up on the beach.

Becca moves to stand in front of him. I think she's reaching for his hand, but instead, she places something on his palm. The egg I gave her. The one I've been saving since that day in the school parking lot. Charlie's fingers curl around it. He struggles to his knees.

"Take care of it for me, Bright Light. Can you do that?" With effort, Charlie places the egg back in Becca's hand.

Becca's cheeks glisten as she tucks the egg into her pocket, near her body where it will stay warm. She drops to her knees in front of Charlie. Carefully, slowly she presses her lips to the corner of his mouth. The moment is over and Becca is gone in an instant, but somehow, I know that I'll never forget it.

That none of us will.

Beside me, Jeremy takes a sharp breath. "Thank you, Charlie." His voice breaks as he takes my brother's hand and steps into the light.

Ian moves to stand beside us. He's still holding my mother in his arms. "I'll carry her through," he says.

I nod. "We'll meet you on the other side."

Ian's gaze drifts between me and Charlie. A sorrow I'm not ready to face is written in the lines around his eyes.

"You were right. About everything," Ian tells Charlie.

He reaches for Charlie's hand but pulls back at the last minute. Ian lays my mother down on the beach and kneels in the sand in front of Charlie. He pulls off Will's hat and pushes it down over Charlie's head, adjusting the sides so they tuck behind his ears. Ian studies him for a moment before he smiles. "Goodbye, Charlie." Tears shine in his eyes as he lifts my mom and takes my brother's hand.

And then it's just me and Charlie alone on this beach in a small bubble of space that is rapidly disappearing.

Charlie tips his face to mine. "It's time to go now, Rosie."

"Take my hand. We'll do it together." The way we always have and always will.

Me and Charlie against the world.

"No."

It's just a word. One small word.

"You have to walk through the door, Rosie, and I have to hold it open."

"Why?" The pressure in my chest makes it impossible to breathe.

"Because I'm the only one who can."

My hands tremble as they grip Charlie's arms. "I won't go." I squeeze him, hard. "Not without you."

"Everything has a proper place, Rosie."

"Your place is with me." My voice breaks. "*You* are my place, Charlie."

A single tear streaks down his cheek. His forehead rests against mine, featherlight. "The dark pulse is searching for a way out. I can't let it escape. I have to close the door from the inside. Do you understand?"

I do. We can't let the dark pulse through. We have to contain it in the Fold. No matter what it takes. Something shatters inside of me.

I force a smile for Charlie's sake. "It's all right," I lie. "I'll close it. Just show me what to do."

"You can't."

The answer guts me, even though I was expecting it. "Then I'm staying here with you."

"No. I don't need you, Rosie. Not anymore. But they do." Charlie nods in the direction of the door. The one only he can see, and for one second, I am back in the Black Nothing, looking at the world through his eyes. For one moment, I can see them. Shining threads in every color, tying me to Mom and Ian. To Blaine and Becca and Jeremy and hundreds of other people I haven't even met yet.

People who are waiting for me.

Charlie shows me their faces. And then he shows me a beautiful house on the ridge. A house like the one Dad designed. With a porch swing for Mom and a shed for all my tools. The smell of sunshine and the sound of laughter as two little girls with star-burst eyes chase each other through the yard. Charlie shows me all of this before he lets me go.

My eyes burn as they focus in on his face. Over his shoulder, the wormhole hits the beach.

He wipes the tears from my eyes with the back of his hand. The same way I used to do when he was little and hungry, and I had nothing else to give him. "You can't fix this, Rosie, but I can. You have to let me fix it. *Please.*"

Ten years of memories dance like leaves in the air between us. Charlie's skin burning like a candle. Mom's singing. Big hands dusted with calluses. They built us a swing and then pushed us so high, the ends of our hair touched the sun.

A small house near a cornfield. A missing step and a broken door. A truck packed with things that smelled of wet earth and goodbye. Our mother, her face turned toward the baby in her lap. Perfect triangle. Perfect moment. Perfect hands. I remember them wrapped around my mother's waist. Her laugh like bells only he could ring.

Charlie reaching for me through the bars of his cradle. Dogs with silly straw hats and sand dollars on the beach. Songs and stories. The two of us lying side by side on the pullout couch, not talking but saying everything. Spinning circles across the hot pavement until the night sky danced above our heads.

Kneeling over a broken nest. His hand in mine and the eggs held between us.

"I don't want you to be alone," I tell him through a rain of tears that may never stop.

"We are never alone." Charlie smiles his smile—the one that makes the world a wonderful place—and the light inside of him becomes almost too bright to look at. It transforms his whole face, until I see him. Not as the squirming bundle in my mother's arms fresh from the hospital. Not as the little boy with holes in his jeans, and cuts on his knees from being pushed down again and again. Not as someone who needs me to fight his battles for him.

For the first time in my life, I see Charlie for who he really is.

A boy who saved an entire town, two thousand two hundred eighteen people simply because he *could*.

The wormhole closes to within a foot as I wrap my arms around my little brother one last time. I press my lips to his ear, and I say all the words I should have said but never could. And it doesn't matter. None of it matters because Charlie already knows.

He has always known.

I take a step back, and I tell myself that this is just one more road. One more door Charlie has to walk through, and I have to let him.

I just wish it wasn't so hard.

Charlie places his hand over his heart, and I do the same, my fingers kneading over the spot where the golden thread runs between us.

I stand back, and I breathe through the pain, and when Charlie reaches for me, I take his hand. Because the best thing about my father is that I still remember him. Because when things disappear, that doesn't mean they are gone forever. Just misplaced for a time. Because there is beauty even in the deepest pain. You just have to know where to look.

I am looking at it now.

A light goes on somewhere deep in my head, and there it is.

A door at the end of a hallway I couldn't see until Charlie showed me. A tunnel of Light, Color, and Sound leading out of the Fold to a place just beyond. Charlie grips my hand and walks me toward it. Like I used to walk him to the bus on the first day of school.

I wait until the last second, and then I do the one thing I never thought I could.

I let him go.

The world shifts sideways as I fall. Into a forest filled with as many people as there are trees. Helicopters scream through the sky above us, their bright lights cutting through the forest canopy draped with night.

Arms close around me. Mom's. Ian stands behind her, a load-bearing wall in the life I suddenly see, stretching far into the future.

A life Charlie gave me.

So I reach down to my mother, and I tell her one more time that things are going to be okay even though I don't know how. Because there are things in this life you don't have to understand to believe, and these are the things that matter.

My brother taught me that. And he taught me that we are never alone. Never. Even in the darkest places, there is light. Always. Everywhere. We just have to look for it.

Once.
Once upon a time.
Once upon a time you read the words and the words were magic. They belonged to you and you belonged to me.
Our words.

Our story.

Forever.

And ever.

Not the end.

The beginning.

AUTHOR'S NOTE

This book is a work of science *fiction*. Particle accelerators, like the LHC in Switzerland, are amazing feats of human ingenuity that are not to be feared. The brilliant people who design, build, and work with them are revealing the mysteries of this beautiful universe. Their work is an inspiration.

ACKNOWLEDGMENTS

This book has been on a long journey, guided by many wonderful people along the way.

Heartfelt thanks to my agent, Caryn Wiseman, of the Andrea Brown Literary Agency. You believed in my words and helped find them the perfect home. I wouldn't be here without you.

My deepest gratitude to Kat Brzozowski, my brilliant editor. Your vision and passion for this book helped me take it to places I never imagined. Thank you for your insight and your unfailing kindness. Working with you has been a dream come true in every way.

Thank you to all the wonderful people at Feiwel and Friends/MacKids: Melinda Ackell, my production editor; Kim Waymer, my production manager; Shivani Annirood, my publicist; designer Katie Klimowicz and illustrator David Curtis, for creating my gorgeous cover; and Jean Feiwel. Also, thanks to Brenna Franzitta for copyediting.

I am lucky to belong to several amazing communities of writers. Special thanks to the Bookpod for being a source of positivity and knowledge. I am also deeply thankful to my fellow Novel19s for their kindness, generosity, and the gift of their beautiful stories.

Thank you to all the people who have read this book and

provided feedback: the groups at Big Sur Writing Workshop; Karen Chaplin, Kristin Ostby, Sara Sargent, and Eric J. Adams for their comments on my earliest chapters; thanks to Courtney Koschel for attending conferences with me; also, Lindsay Garlow, A.E. Marling, Elena Patel, Polly Miller, and Julie Cremin for reading this book during various stages of construction. Your notes and feedback helped make this story what it is. Also, thank you to Cheryl Barclay, marvelous CP and conference roommate; Prashant Patel for talking physics with me and checking my math; and my husband, Josh, and my brother David for their assistance with the climbing scenes. Any mistakes, of course, are my own.

Thanks to Carolyn Lee Adams, amazing writer and human. Also, thanks to the late Margaret Wise Brown for the treasure that is *Mister Dog: The Dog Who Belonged to Himself*—the book Rose reads to Charlie and one that is beloved by so many, including me. Your friendship is a blessing, and your notes on the first half of this book were instrumental. Because the difference is we "can."

Lisa Maxwell, you talked me back from the brink a million times, championed my work, and encouraged me at every turn. Not to mention your insightful comments helped me fix my ending. You inspire me with your words and bless me with your friendship. Also, thanks to Sara Raasch for reading and blurbing and reading and being generally amazing.

Olivia Hinebaugh, my dear friend, CP, and fellow Novel19, your belief in this story sustained me when my well ran dry. Thank you for every email, comment, phone call, and playlist, but most of all, for your friendship. I am so proud to share this debut year with you and your incredible book.

Thank you to Ashlee Cowles, my bosom friend and the other half of my brain. You read this story at its rawest and you helped me find its shine. You never once doubted what I could barely bring myself to dream. You are a brilliant writer and even more brilliant friend.

I couldn't have done this without my family: my parents and first readers, Mark and Loretta Cremin; my brothers, Kevin, David, and Thomas; and my sister-in-law, Krista Cremin; Frank and Brenda Stinson for their love and unwavering faith; also, John and Polly Miller for being part of my village. To all Cremins, Stinsons, Langtons, Kevanes, Bennets, D'Amores, O'Days, and Rizzos—you have shown me what it is to be part of a network of threads that can never be broken.

All my love and gratitude to Josh. You made my dreams yours and then you helped me reach them. Thank you for being at my side through this and every adventure.

Last but not least, thank you to my beautiful boys, Uriah, Isaac, Daniel, and Caleb. You are my reason and my meaning. The shining lights at the end of my golden thread. My love for you will outlive the stars.

Thank you for reading this Feiwel & Friends book.

The friends who made BEFORE I DISAPPEAR possible are:

JEAN FEIWEL
PUBLISHER

LIZ SZABLA
ASSOCIATE PUBLISHER

RICH DEAS
SENIOR CREATIVE DIRECTOR

HOLLY WEST
SENIOR EDITOR

ANNA ROBERTO
SENIOR EDITOR

KAT BRZOZOWSKI
SENIOR EDITOR

VAL OTAROD
ASSOCIATE EDITOR

ALEXEI ESIKOFF
SENIOR MANAGING EDITOR

KIM WAYMER
SENIOR PRODUCTION MANAGER

ANNA POON
ASSISTANT EDITOR

EMILY SETTLE
ASSOCIATE EDITOR

KATIE KLIMOWICZ
SENIOR DESIGNER

MELINDA ACKELL
COPY CHIEF

Follow us on Facebook or visit us online at mackids.com.

Our books are friends for life.